Praise for
Guy's Girl

"Emma Noyes's stunning adult debut is raw, real, and an emotional page-turner that will stay with you long after the last page. This love story is a must-read."

—*New York Times* bestselling authors Krista and Becca Ritchie

"Heartbreaking and romantic, *Guy's Girl* is a beautifully written and authentically raw story about the human journey through trauma, self-exploration, and self-love."

—*New York Times* and *USA Today* bestselling author
Samantha Young

"Emma Noyes completely captivated me with her spectacular debut! *Guy's Girl* is an honest, no-holds-barred look at life as a twenty-something struggling to find love and find herself. Noyes deftly handles incredibly tough topics with care and sincerity, culminating in a sparkling work of fiction that I could not stop thinking about. This one stuck with me long after I finished the final page!"

—Falon Ballard, author of *Just My Type*

"Noyes beautifully captures the joy and stress of becoming a newly minted adult. This sings of both restlessness and hope."

—*Publishers Weekly*

"Noyes captures moments of soul-searing drama in thi- ----ter-life-crisis love story."

list

Berkley Titles by Emma Noyes

Guy's Girl
How to Hide in Plain Sight

How to Hide in Plain Sight

Emma Noyes

Berkley Romance
New York

BERKLEY ROMANCE
Published by Berkley
An imprint of Penguin Random House LLC
penguinrandomhouse.com

Copyright © 2024 by Emma Virginia Rideout Noyes
Readers Guide copyright © 2024 by Penguin Random House LLC
Excerpt from *Guy's Girl* by Emma Noyes copyright © 2023 by Emma Virginia Rideout Noyes

Library of Congress Cataloging-in-Publication Data

Names: Noyes, Emma (Emma Virginia Rideout) author.
Title: How to hide in plain sight / Emma Noyes.
Description: First edition. | New York: Berkley Romance, 2024.
Identifiers: LCCN 2023054030 (print) | LCCN 2023054031 (ebook) |
ISBN 9780593639023 (trade paperback) | ISBN 9780593639030 (ebook)
Subjects: LCSH: Obsessive-compulsive disorder—Fiction. |
LCGFT: Romance fiction. | Novels.
Classification: LCC PS3614.O976 H69 2024 (print) |
LCC PS3614.O976 (ebook) | DDC 813/.6—dc23/eng/20231127
LC record available at https://lccn.loc.gov/2023054030
LC ebook record available at https://lccn.loc.gov/2023054031

First Edition: September 2024

Printed in the United States of America
1st Printing

Book design by Diahann Sturge-Campbell

To my brain—
You crazy motherfucker,
this one's for you.

Dear Reader,

What you have just opened is only partly a work of fiction. The story is entirely imagined, but the way Eliot's brain works ... is entirely not.

I have Obsessive-Compulsive Disorder. But the OCD I have is very different from society's "usual depiction" of the disease. It has nothing to do with fearing germs or touching doorknobs a certain number of times or stepping over cracks in the sidewalk. I'm not like Monk, the detective with eight different bars of soap on his bathroom sink. The OCD I have can only be described as inner torture.

I was twelve when my symptoms first showed up. At the time, of course, I didn't know that they *were* symptoms; I thought I had just lost my mind. My brain wouldn't stop looping over the same thoughts. Horrible thoughts. *Taboo* thoughts, things that cannot be spoken aloud in polite society. And no matter what I did, no matter how hard I tried, I couldn't make them go away.

Three years of torture later, my first therapist gave me my diagnosis. I didn't believe her. Not because I didn't want to, but because I so desperately *did*. The part of my brain that I once thought of as myself—the kind one, the compassionate one, the one that still knew she was a good person—wanted so badly for there to be a rational explanation for all of the horrible things happening in my mind, but the disordered part had taken over so completely that I was convinced I had no mental illness at all. I was just a bad person.

If this doesn't make sense to you right now, that's okay. It will once you start reading.

How to Hide in Plain Sight was scary to write. Even more scary to put out into the world. Still, I know that I must, because there are millions of people who suffer from this disease—and they do so in silence, with a false smile on their face, their disease hidden in perfectly plain sight.

I don't want to hide anymore. And one day, I hope they won't have to, either.

All my love,
Emma

Your presence is cordially requested
at the wedding of . . .

TARON BECK & HELENE MARCUS

Schedule

Day 1: The Welcome Dinner

Day 2: The Cradle Island Olympics

Day 3: The Bachelor Parties

Day 4: The Wedding

Beck Family Tree

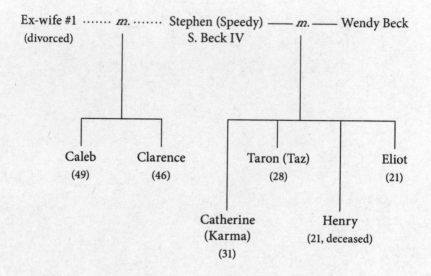

Ex-wife #1 ······· *m.* ······· Stephen (Speedy) —— *m.* —— Wendy Beck
(divorced)   S. Beck IV

Caleb   Clarence   Taron (Taz)   Eliot
(49)   (46)   (28)   (21)

Catherine   Henry
(Karma)   (21, deceased)
(31)

How to Hide in Plain Sight

Prologue

HERE'S WHAT YOU need to understand about my family: all of our money came from drugs.

Nothing illegal, of course. Not crack or quaaludes or even marijuana. All government sanctioned. The good stuff, you know? Prozac. Insulin. Cialis. (That's a PDE-5 inhibitor, a drug that helps men get it up—the alternative to Viagra. I know. The assholes at Pfizer ruined any chance we had at brand recognition. There's only so much brain space Americans are willing to commit to boner medication.)

Another thing you need to understand about my family: it's big. I couldn't tell you the number of times I've said those words. At parties, on the job. *Tell me about yourself,* says someone I've just met. *Well, I grew up in a big family.* It's a great opening line. People trust me right away, which makes no sense. As if being born into a big family says something about your character. As if there's a reproductive threshold above which none of your children become psychopaths or serial killers. As if Jeffrey Dahmer would have turned out okay if only he'd had a couple more brothers and sisters hanging around.

I was a happy kid. How could I not be? I was raised the way all parents dream of raising their children: in a big house in the suburbs of Chicago, right on the shore of Lake Michigan. Our town was just large enough for me to run free on the weekend, but just small enough to come home with nothing worse than a skinned knee. Our school district liberal enough to preach universal love, but so white that I didn't discover racism until we reached the chapter on slavery in our fifth grade history textbook.

I was given everything—including, but not limited to, that most elusive of gifts: the Happy Family. Undivorced parents. Siblings who can actually stand each other. Who vacation together and eat family dinner around a worn wooden table and only try to kill each other on special occasions. Who even—when the climate is right—*like* each other.

There were unhappy moments, too, of course. And chaos. Plenty of chaos. In a family of eight, if you want to be heard, you yell: at dinner, during card games, on long road trips, when the back two rows of the Suburban become louder and more political than the floor of Congress. Everyone talks over each other. Facts are not as important as volume.

As the youngest—and therefore least authoritative—member of the family, I was never going to be the loudest. So, instead, I watched. Listened. Took in the laughter and the chaos and the secrets and the broken parts. Because, yes, the Beck family is a Happy Family. But behind the curtain, we fight. We hurt each other. We even hate each other, for a time. But we forgive. We always forgive.

We have to.

We're family.

PART I

The Welcome Dinner

1

NOW

IN THE THIRTEEN hours it took me to drive from New York City to Port Windfall, Ontario, I drank three cups of coffee, started four podcasts, engaged in countless lively debates with drivers who couldn't hear me, and listened to every single one of my Spotify playlists. Twice.

When I ran out of background noise, I took reality and shaped it into copywriting templates. I do that sometimes.

HEADLINE: Disgraced Daughter Returns to Family's Private Island for Four-Day "Wedding of the Century"
OFFER: Ready to face your demons, relish lavish excess, and suffer through nightly political diatribes, all while wearing a smile that says you're having the time of your life?
CALL TO ACTION: Click for Free Trial!

When I tell people I'm a copywriter, most often they picture *Mad Men*: long rows of women in smart wool skirts pounding at typewriters, dodging the advances of male executives, locked out of the meetings where *real* decisions are made. You don't need talent to be a copywriter. You just need to be able to type.

Let me tell you a secret: copy is far more than words on an advertisement. It's everything. It's everywhere. We copywriters are the engine that moves society forward. Without us, progress grinds to a halt. Instruction manuals are blank. Street signs don't exist. Travel becomes impossible. No sentence comes from nothing, after all: from the saccharine Christmas message on the side of your soda to the *screw u bro* written on a bathroom stall; from the seat-back sign telling you LIFE VEST UNDER SEAT to the greeting that welcomes you to a website. Even the highway sign telling you that you're now leaving Ohio, bidding you farewell and asking that you come back soon. Do you ever think about who wrote those words? Of course not. Those words are not words to us, with authors and backstories and spellcheck. They're background. They're grass and trees, part of the landscape. EMERGENCY EXIT signs say EMERGENCY EXIT because that's how it is. Car mirrors tell us that OBJECTS IN THE MIRROR ARE CLOSER THAN THEY APPEAR because they do. Because they always have. These words, these pillars of society—they weren't *written*. They sprang into existence at the exact moment society needed them. Perhaps they were even created by God: *And on the third day, God created the sun and the moon and the instruction manual for how to set up your Google Edge TPU™ Application-Specific Integrated Circuit.*

Anyway.

My destination was Cradle Island: a mile-around private paradise purchased by my father during the coked-up height of his second marriage. He found it in a newspaper advertisement. ISLAND FOR SALE! I imagine the ad said. EXCELLENT VALUE! 100% SURROUNDED BY WATER!

The way Dad tells it, he almost flipped right past. But then he saw the bird's-eye shot of Cradle Island at the bottom of the advertisement. And the island looked like a cradle. An abstract cradle. A cradle on drugs. My father was also on drugs. He found this coincidence so funny that he laughed until he cried.

Then he bought it.

That was a different lifetime. By the time I got into the car borrowed from one of my coworkers to travel from Brooklyn to Ontario, Dad was almost thirty years sober.

As was I. Recovered from my addictions, I mean. Not to drugs or alcohol—to other things. Thoughts, food, people, places. Oh, yes—you can be addicted to a place. It happened to me as a kid. Every year, in the middle of February—deep in the bowels of the Chicago winter—I started to crave Cradle Island. The sound of sparrows in the afternoon. Its curving beaches, peppered with cattails. In the first light of morning, when the lake turns to glass. It was the strangest feeling. More potent than desire for food. Because when you want ice cream or crispy, hot buttered bread, the feeling pools right atop your tongue, but when you want a place, it calls to you with *every* sense, sight and smell and touch and sound and, yes, even taste.

When I moved to New York, I cut all cravings out of my life. All of them. I had to. "*No seas tonta*," Manuel would have said, waving a bottle of beer in my face. "Just have one."

I gripped the steering wheel. Squeezed my eyes closed and open. Blinked his face from my memory. *No. That was before.* Before I took control of my life. Before I worked my schedule down to an exacting science, to a well-oiled machine that left no room for darker thoughts. Before I learned to ignore the siren call of my memories, their taunts, daring me to jump down, down, down, into that all-too-familiar place—a hole into which at times I fell accidentally and at others I climbed willingly, allowing the rest of the soil to tumble in after me, shutting off all oxygen and blotting out the sun.

THE NERVES DIDN'T set in until just before I arrived at the marina. I was running late—Mom said to meet at the dock at five o'clock,

and it was almost half past. All those damn cups of coffee. I hadn't
accounted for the number of times I had to pull into a nowhere gas
station and sprint to the bathroom, buying a pack of gum on the
way out to stave off the cashier's cool glare. Plus, there'd been that
semi moving with hair-pulling sluggishness down the winding
one-lane highway . . .

All of that to say: I was late, and my siblings weren't going to let
me off easy. They never did. The pile of wisecracks was probably
growing higher by the minute.

My nerves probably should have set in long before then. Frankly,
they should have set in the minute I pulled the glossy RSVP card
from its envelope and laid it against the plug-in coffeepot in my
studio and left it there, untouched, its cheerful calligraphy mocking
me every time I walked in or out the apartment's front door. Even
then, in my hesitation, I wasn't nervous. I wasn't anything, really.

But I should have been.

See, the issue was this: on the day I arrived at the marina for
Taz's wedding, I hadn't seen my family in three years.

It wasn't that I'd been *avoiding* them. Not at first, anyway. I was
still there, still included in all the group chats and email threads
and family conference calls, during which Dad explained for the
fourth or fifth time *exactly* how capital gains or fixed-interest mort-
gages work. But I rarely contributed to these conversations. Instead,
I sat silently in my apartment in New York, a spectator to the continuing lives of my family in the Midwest.

I listened to what my parents told me growing up: Make your
own way. Live as if you will inherit nothing. Do not rely on anyone
else to save you—including us. So I did. After high school, I skipped
the pointless charade of college. Moved to Brooklyn. Lived on a
couch. Worked my ass off to find a job. Paid my own rent and taxes.
Never touched a dime of the Trust Fund, that grown-up allowance
that leaked tens of thousands of dollars into my bank account each

year. Doubtless they would prefer that I had a college degree, but such things are neither here nor there. I did it. I achieved financial independence. And at twenty-one years old, I'd done it well before anyone else had.

I imagined my solo arrival to this wedding as a moment of triumph. *Here she comes*, they would say. *Eliot Beck, Corporate Woman in the Big City!*

But when I crossed the bridge into Port Windfall, the town where we store our boats in the winter, I started to actually picture the scene that would be waiting for me. They'd be there, all of them, loading their bags into the *Silver Heron*, a fifty-four-foot Bertram yacht purchased by my father in 1975. Mom would be whirring around in one of her usual states. Dad would be up on the flybridge. Karma would be giving directions. Clarence and Caleb would be standing off to the side, arguing about God knows what—probably who would get the bigger bed in Tangled Blue, their favorite cabin on the island, that year. I never understood my half brothers' relationship; they hated each other, yet they insisted on staying in the same cabin every year. Both claimed it was their favorite and neither was the type to relent.

Every family reunion begins with a round of hugs and the promise you've missed one another. For me, that promise was always true. But that summer, after three years away, it was truer than ever.

And yet. And *yet*. I avoided everyone for a reason. For multiple reasons, actually, and it was only at the last minute—when I turned the steering wheel to pull into Kilwin Marina and heard the familiar crunch of gravel beneath the tires, smelled the algae and hull wax and molding rope—that I realized the full depth of what I was doing. Where I was going. I was driving toward not just a wedding but also a week spent trapped on a tiny island with no control over my diet. My routine. My exercise. No East River to run beside in the morning. No cabinet full of gluten-free, dairy-free, paleo-keto

Whole30 nutrition bars stolen from the pantry at work. Just me and my family. And suddenly, I felt nothing short of naked.

I parked the car. Unclipped my seat belt. Rolled down the car window.

The wind blew warm and lazy off Lake Huron, heavy with the smell of gasoline and fried fish. In the slip where the *Silver Heron* normally waited—tall, beast-like, built for function, the floating equivalent of a sensible boot—sat nothing. Just water.

I stared at the empty slip, dumbfounded.

They'd left without me.

HERE'S A RIDDLE for you: How do you form meaningful relationships with a family you didn't grow up with?

Sometimes, I think my entire life has been one long attempt to answer that question. When you grow up with gaps between you and your siblings as wide as the ones between me and mine (seven years at the smallest, twenty-eight years at the widest), you don't grow up with them, you grow up behind them. The rest of the family shares a wealth of memories that you'll never have access to. Those memories—the earliest, most formative moments—become the backbone of your family history. They're the stories you tell at dinners, at reunions, over beers at a bar your older siblings used to sneak into together, and seven years later, you snuck into with your best friend. Those memories become your origin story. An origin story you didn't get to write.

FOR A FEW minutes I sat in the driver's seat, unwilling to believe my eyes. How the hell was I supposed to get to Cradle now? Swim?

But then I spotted the *Periwinkle*, a twin-engine whaler used mostly for grocery runs. Next to the boat was a tall figure with dark hair—one of my brothers, probably. Left behind to pick up the spare.

I unloaded my luggage—one backpack and one gas station bag full of snack wrappers and coffee cups—and walked down the dock craning my neck to see which of my brothers it was.

But then the figure turned around and smiled. "Hey, Beck."

I froze.

No.

Only one person called me by my last name, and there was no way that person could be here, at this very moment, standing on the dock in front of me. I blinked hard. Tried to make his face go away, just as I had in the car. *Blink. Blink.* But he was still there.

No.

This cannot be happening.

I took a step back.

He looked different. He'd let his hair grow long and wild, the way my mom and I always told him he should. That was all I noticed, at first. His hair. How unfamiliar it was. And why shouldn't it be? Three years at college will do that. Will transform the lanky teenager you once knew into something resembling a man.

An old feeling, long forgotten—or, more accurately, long bound, gagged, and stuffed away in a corner of my mind from which I bade it to never return—yawned and stretched its wings inside my stomach.

No, no, no.

He stepped forward. "Surprise," he said, lips curving up shyly.

Saliva edged up the back of my tongue. *He's here. He's really here.* What was he doing here? The first few days of the wedding were *family only*—it said so in clear, shimmering letters on Taz and Helene's invitation. So, why was my former best friend standing two feet in front of me, soft chestnut eyes watching me warily beneath wild curls?

He reached out one hand. I froze, uncertain of what would happen next.

Then he grabbed my shoulder and pulled me into his chest.

Despite being skinny as a willow branch, Manuel Garcia Valdecasas gives hugs that feel like drowning. He sucks you into the void of his arms, drags you to the very deepest point of comfort.

"You're here," he said into my hair. That was it. Nothing else.

I thought I didn't miss him. Really, I did. For three years, I pushed him from my mind. Focused on my life in New York. That's what you do, that's what *everyone* does: you grow up, you fly the coop, you leave the other birds behind.

I knew I shouldn't let myself take comfort in his embrace. I'd been a bad friend. An awful friend, really. But I did. I let myself sink, just for a moment. And it felt good. God, it felt *so* good. It felt just the way they say it does—that clear, heady euphoria of death by drowning.

2

SUMMER BEFORE FIFTH GRADE

MY STORY BEGINS with the death of my brother.

I'm ten years old. I'm standing on the porch of Sunny Sunday, the main cabin on Cradle Island. The lake is the color of storm clouds. My mom has just come outside from talking on the telephone. She pulls me onto her lap and says something I don't understand.

"What do you mean, gone?" I ask. I study her expression. It's too close, her face. Old people look scary up close. I want to get down. I fear I might catch whatever it is that makes her old.

"He isn't here anymore."

"But he wasn't here in the first place," I say. "He stayed in Winnetka. You said he had summer school, so he stayed home."

She blinks. Her eyes are big and old.

"How can he be gone if he was never here in the first place?"

And then she starts to cry.

BEFORE THIS MOMENT, we numbered eight. Two parents, six kids.

Caleb, Clarence, Karma, Taz, Henry, Eliot. Caleb, Clarence, Karma, Taz, Henry, Eliot. A list I've given a thousand times—to every new teacher, new friend, anyone who cares to ask. I'm the youngest, and I love my siblings. When asked, I recite our names with near-religious pride. "CalebClarenceKarmaTazHenryEliot! CalebClarenceKarmaTazHenryEliot!" The list became a sort of spell. *Recite these names enough times and you'll finally belong to them!* Because that's all I wanted, really. To sit at the big kids' table.

When I reached the end of the list—when I got to say my own name, to attach it to those five fully formed humans, to claim my place among them, even as just the caboose, hitched to the train by nothing more than the fragile rope of familial obligation—I said it with shiny eyes and a plump-cheeked smile.

HENRY AND I were what you call Irish Twins—siblings born less than a year apart. From the start, we did everything together. We slept in the same crib, gnawed on the same toys, even ate from the same bowls. The first time Mom tried to acclimate me to real dishware, she dumped me onto the bench next to Hen and handed me a plastic bowl and spoon. The bowl was filled with my very own serving of mush. Henry, of course, had been eating mush for almost a year. The way Mom tells it, I looked at my bowl for only a few seconds before turning to the side and starting in on Henry's. He didn't say a word. Just pushed the bowl closer to my half of the table and kept eating. We took turns dipping into the mush. Then, when his bowl was scraped clean, we moved over to mine and kept right on going.

Henry learned to read first. Every night before bed, I'd burst through his door, and he would open whatever fantasy novel was on his nightstand and read aloud until my head started to nod. He created far-off planets for me. Gave each of the characters a different voice. Held dramatic pauses when appropriate. "Where are we going tonight?" I would say.

"The Sahara Desert," he would say. Or "Hogwarts." Or "To visit the dinosaurs."

And I cuddled in close, shut my eyes, and listened as we soared far, far away.

THE FUNERAL IS held at our church in Winnetka. All of our relatives fly in. Cousins and uncles and ex-wives and third cousins and third uncles and third ex-wives—people with whom I share blood but whose names I don't know. We fill every pew in the chapel. A big wooden box sits at the front, boy-sized, like a trick at a magic show. I understand that this is not a magic show. I understand that my brother is inside that box, and he won't come back out.

IN THE WEEK we spend at home before returning to Cradle, as I endure Henry's wake and funeral and hugs from relatives I don't know and paper plates sagging beneath cheese triangles and fruit salad, I cling to the fact that it's just a week. Just one. After that, we'll return to Cradle for the summer, and everything will be better. Mom calls the blue-green waters that surround the lake "healing." When I ask her why, she says human beings come from the water, that we're conceived in water, that we evolved from creatures who swam. So that's what I tell myself during that miserable week in Chicago. *We're going back*, I tell myself. *We're going back. And when we do, we'll heal.*

A WEEK LATER, we return to Cradle. We fly in on the jet. It has eight seats, just big enough for our family. We're one brother short, but every seat is full.

"What's that?" I ask, pointing at the oblong purple thing fastened into the seat next to Dad. It looks like a tulip vase, all curvy and long necked.

There's a long silence.

Finally, seventeen-year-old Karma says, "That's Henry."

I look back down at the object. That's Henry?

"No," I say. "That's a vase. Dead people don't go in vases."

"Sometimes they do."

"No," I say again. "Flowers go in vases. Dead people go in coffins."

Karma smiles sadly. "Sometimes. But sometimes, they go in one of those instead."

"It's not a vase, Gup," says Clarence from across the plane. "It's an *errrn*."

An *errrn*?

I turn the word over in my head. An *errrn*. Huh.

This is a surprise. There was a coffin at the funeral; I assumed my brother was inside. I assumed I wasn't allowed to see him, that seeing him was Big Kids Only. A lot of stuff in my life is Big Kids Only, especially since Henry died. But I know how funerals go. I've seen them in movies. And movies tell me that dead people go inside a coffin and then into the ground. So I assumed that, after the funeral, my family took him away and buried him in a graveyard with all the other dead people, the way they're supposed to.

I was wrong.

SHORTLY AFTER ARRIVING on the island, we gather on the porch of Sunny Sunday. The boys clear away the tables and lounge chairs. They lift them overhead and carry them down the rocks, leaving them scattered about like a poorly arranged living room. We cluster onto the empty patio, the whole family. Dad stands before us, his back to the lake. Clutched between two trembling hands is the *errrn*.

I glare at it. As it turns out, not only is Henry *not* safely underground, he's trapped inside a tiny tulip vase. What an abomination. How did they fit him in there, anyway? Did they shrink him to the size of a teacup? Did his body dissolve into a cloud and whoosh down the neck, like a genie?

Dad is talking. Cradle Island will be Henry's final resting place, he says. Dad will scatter Henry's ashes at the center of the island.

Ashes?

Ashes like after a fire?

"I'm going to scatter them alone," he continues, "so the rest of you won't see where."

Ashes like ugly grey powder, all thin and useless? A puddle of spent wood that used to be flame, and before that timber, and before that a tree, tall and sturdy, so tall it saw everything, saw clear across the island?

"Your mother and I . . ." He glances at Mom, who meets his gaze with watery eyes. "We don't want Henry to be just one rock or bush or tree." He smiles. "We want him to be the whole island."

I watch Dad's thumb. I think about burning trees. His thumb traces little absentminded circles along the bottom of the vase, slowly, affectionately, as if he believes the vase can feel it. As if it were made of skin, not ceramic.

And that's when I understand.

"What the hell did you do?" I blurt without thinking.

"Eliot!" says Mom, covering my mouth with her palm.

Dad looks down. Everyone does. I have their attention. They're waiting for me to go on, but I can't. A strange feeling bubbles at the base of my throat. It's hot. It's *boiling*.

Is it anger?

No. I know anger. I've seen anger. It makes you say things you regret, not lose your speech entirely.

"Eliot?" Dad asks.

Did you burn my brother alive?

"Eliot?"

Is that what you did? Was he so hurt that you tossed his body into a bonfire and let it burn, like nothing more than a fallen tree?

I look at Dad. I can't ask the questions. They're gone. They've turned to air in my throat. Instead, I ask, "When?"

"When what?"

"When are you going to do it?"

Dad pauses. "Later this summer."

Later this summer. Later this summer, Dad will dump my brother onto a bush and leave him there. Later this summer, the last traces of Henry will wash away in a heavy rain.

I can't breathe.

Every spring, Henry and I counted down the days until summer. Crossed them off the calendar on the fridge. A week before our flight, we packed books and sweatpants and every bathing suit in our closet. For Henry and me, summers on Cradle Island weren't just vacations; they were bliss. They were sunsets and swing chairs and writing musicals and forcing the Big Kids to watch. They were wild sun and roaring thunderstorms and white cheddar mac 'n' cheese and the wood-burning sauna we stoked until our faces melted.

And now, here on this porch, Clarence's hand on my shoulder, Karma clinging to Mom, my three living brothers standing straight-backed and flat-footed, just like at the first funeral, only now they're dressed in patterned swim trunks instead of black suits—even now, Cradle is still all the things Henry and I loved. It's just that now I have no one to share them with.

———

THE DAY AFTER Henry's second funeral, my family wakes to discover the island has been wiped clean of carbohydrates. Overnight, Mom cleared every last cracker, donut, noodle, and Lucky Charm out of the kitchen. Everyone is upset, but Karma, whose relationship with my mother is strained to begin with, is a living volcano.

"Are you shitting me?" she says, opening every single cabinet and slamming them closed when she finds they contain nothing but fruit and nuts. "What are we going to eat now?"

"Protein," Mom says. She's pan-frying scrambled eggs and cottage cheese. "And lots of it."

"Why?"

"Protein is medicine for your muscles and immune system," she says proudly. The line comes straight from *The Zone Diet*, which she read the night before.

"But I'm not sick."

"Yes, you are. You don't know it because simple sugars are all your body knows, but you are."

A plate appears before each of the kids. Karma scrunches her lips with disgust, says, "Absolutely not," slides off her stool, and storms out of the kitchen. For the rest of the week, she walks around Cradle with a sign taped to her shirt that reads, END CHILD HUNGER NOW.

THE FIRST PASTRIES Karma bakes are macarons—the French kind, perfect little sugary sandwiches that look nearly impossible to get right. She's never even made chocolate chip cookies before.

"Whoa," says Taz when he walks into Sunny Sunday. "This looks illegal."

Karma clucks. "Nothing illegal about a little bit of sugar."

"Where'd you even get that?" he says, eyeing the wrinkled bag of Domino Pure Cane on the counter.

"Let's just say that there are lots of cabins with lots of cabinets on this island."

Once Karma starts baking, she doesn't stop. She bakes aggressively. Vengefully. Blondies. Lemon bars. Cinnamon buns. Raspberry tortes. Peppermint bark. A week passes during which we see Karma only under the strawberry-orange light of the kitchen. Her recipes grow longer, more advanced, requiring two or three tries to get right. But she never gives up. Not until they're perfect.

Out of my sister's earshot, I hear Mom mutter, "This is, without a doubt, the strangest form of teenage rebellion I've ever seen."

"This isn't rebellion, Wendy," Dad whispers back. "It's mourning."

FOR AS LONG as I've known Taz—which is my whole life, actually—the only thing he's wanted to do is make animated movies. Everywhere he goes, his iPad comes with. When he walks, he folds it under his arm like a purse. When he sits, he flicks it open and loses himself in an unknowable universe of castles and aliens and fire-breathing math teachers. Pixelated smiles. Wide-brimmed eyes.

After Henry dies, Taz stops carrying around his iPad. Now, in the kitchen, he holds no electronics at all. He looks naked without them.

Instead he carries a sketch pad. He scratches at it throughout the day—simple drawings so faint they seem to have bled onto the paper from elsewhere. They aren't storyboards. In fact, there's no connection between them at all. I find them scattered about the island—decaying fruit, half-finished maps of the world, a face with no identifiable features. It seems he doesn't care what happens to them once he sets them down.

I start to collect them. When I find a drawing, I slip it into the pocket of my hiking backpack, just in case he needs them one day.

I THOUGHT CRADLE Island would fix us. I did. That the waters would heal us, just the way Mom said they could. But here we are, and everywhere I turn, I see grief. I see it in the strange actions of my siblings and the dead silence at the dinner table and the hushed voices of my parents in the hallway outside my bedroom door. Grief didn't leave; if anything, it burrowed even deeper in. Took the place of the one who left. Grief sits in Henry's chair at dinner, sleeps in his bed at night. The island, which once seemed ready to burst from all the life packed onto its shores, has become a colorless place.

As I lie in bed at night, I hear my mom whisper to my dad, "You really aren't worried? I swear, I haven't seen her cry once."

"Everyone grieves differently," says Dad. "She's so young."

I shake my head into the pillowcase. Mom is silly to think there's something wrong with me. I'm the only one who can say Henry's name without crying. I'm the only one who eats more than half of her dinner. I'm the only one who still goes out exploring. I'm the only one who hasn't lost her mind.

IT'S THE END of the summer. I'm hunched into a ball outside my parents' bedroom, ear pressed to the door. Dad is inside, rummaging about his suitcase. Mom is elsewhere. Tomorrow, we leave.

"This can't be happening," Dad says to no one. "They were in here two days ago." The rummaging increases in intensity. "I never took them out," he says. "I never even took them out!" Something hits the floor with a great crash.

Then I hear a new sound, an awful sound, like a tornado alarm or a bullhorn. I leap to my feet and throw open the door, forgetting I'm supposed to be hiding. What I find inside is not a siren. It's my dad, bent on all fours, wailing. That's the word that pops into my

head: *wailing.* I don't know where that word came from, but there it
is, and there's my father, hunched over himself. Wailing. The floor
is covered in what appears to be the contents of every drawer, closet,
and cranny in the bedroom. In the corner is a puddle of shattered
purple ceramic.

The *errrn.*

I stand frozen in the doorway. If Dad sees me, he doesn't say so.
In fact, after this is over—after Dad stops wailing, after I creep back
into the hallway, after he slowly picks up the destroyed bedroom
and turns on every light in the cabin and takes a thirty-minute-long
shower and crawls into bed for the night, even though it's only
7:30 p.m.—he'll never mention this scene, or the impossible disappearance that led to it, ever again. Not to me. Not to Mom. Not to
anyone, as far as I know. Why would he? Why be so cruel? Why tell
us that, when he was finally ready to scatter Henry's ashes, when he
grabbed the *errrn* and looked inside, there was nothing there? Why
tell us that he found only an empty ceramic hole, a dark pit almost
as deep as the one now yawning open within him? Why tell us he's
lost the ashes of our dead brother? Even at ten years old, I know he
won't. I watch him there on the floor, and I just know. He won't
make anyone else shoulder this burden. There would be no point.

His arms and legs quiver. His whole body shakes with the weight
of holding itself up.

A few months later, his legs will give out forever.

3

NOW

THE BOAT RIDE was excruciating. After taking my backpack off my hands and firing up the boat, steering us out toward the channel, Manuel offered no explanation for his appearance. Instead, he left me to fill the awkward silence with the only tactic I knew: incoherent babbling.

I talked almost nonstop from dock to dock. Filled the wind whipping past our heads with eight miles of banal nothingness. My legs shook. Out of nerves or too much caffeine, I wasn't sure.

"The drive was a nightmare. I haven't been behind the wheel of a car in almost three years. You just don't need one in New York, you know? Of course you know. You live in Boston. I mean, Cambridge. That's where Harvard is, right? Cambridge? Pretty funny that the best college in America is in a city named after the best college in England. Or would that be Oxford? I wouldn't know. Never been the smart one. That was always you, ha ha. Ha. Ha."

Et cetera.

Help.

WE ARRIVED, NATURALLY, to chaos.

"*Allergic to spice?* The hell does she mean, *allergic to spice?*"

We entered Sunny Sunday to find Karma and her wife, Shelly, huddled in the far corner of the kitchen, chopping fruit and whispering loudly. My half brothers, Clarence and Caleb, sat, wine in hand, in the cluster of plump linen sofas. Mom looked woefully lost as she fiddled with the stereo. Dad was nowhere to be seen.

"You can't be allergic to a taste," continued Karma as her tiny hands lined up a string of ripe strawberries. "You can be allergic to a food, like walnuts. You can be allergic to dairy or penicillin or grass or latex or bumblebees, but you can't be allergic to a goddamn *sensation*." The knife came down, severing the strawberries' green heads from their bodies.

People assume that because my sister is five foot one and owns the largest cupcake chain in Chicago, she's sweet as red velvet.

They are wrong.

Karma looked up and spotted us lingering awkwardly by the door. It was the first time we had made eye contact in three years, and she didn't even flinch. "Well," she said, pointing the knife right at my chest, "if it isn't our little workaholic, come home at last."

Before I could respond, a wave of fabric engulfed me. My vision went black. "Eliot, my *God*. I'm so happy to see you." Mom. Her words came out fast and practiced, like a monologue she'd rehearsed on the flight over. "You had me worried sick. When you weren't at the dock, I was sure your car crashed or a truck driver kidnapped you, I swear to God. This is why you shouldn't drive up here alone. I tried to tell you. I *tried* to tell you. Your father . . ."

When I managed to peel myself out of her embrace, she clutched my face between her hands, eyes aglow. Then she turned to Manuel, spread her arms as wide as they would go, said, "And *Manny*—thank you *so* much for bringing her," and ran him through the same punishment.

In the corner of my eye, I saw Karma roll her eyes at Shelly.

Next, I found myself face-to-face with Caleb, the firstborn. First of *all* of Dad's children.

Dad might've been our father, but Caleb was our patriarch. Stately and doctoral, nearly thirty years my senior, he had an almost inhuman talent for leadership. During long family discussions, he let everyone else speak first—and talk in long-winded circles—only to chime in at the very end. He'd take all the nonsense we'd spewed and sum it up concisely, wrapping our ideas and presenting them back to us with a tight little bow.

"Yes," we would say, nodding. "That's what we meant."

I didn't grow up in the same house as Caleb or Clarence. By the time I elbowed my way out into the world, they'd both grown up and settled into their own lives. While Clarence made a concerted effort to connect with his younger siblings—and to this day would probably volunteer to sit at the kids' table, even though there were no kids left—Caleb was as foreign and unknowable to me as a stone tablet. He had his own life, a family—a wife, two teenage kids—a medical practice, and he often passed on coming to Thanksgivings or Christmases. On the rare occasion he *did* join, he almost never brought his wife or kids along. It was as if he feared that, were his smaller family to meet his larger one, they might get swallowed up entirely.

I didn't exactly blame him. He married his wife, Addie, just after he finished medical school. Addie was tall, gorgeous, and had this carefree way of laughing, where she tipped her head back and let it all go at once. Though I hadn't gotten to see her much as a kid, on the few occasions that she *had* come around, I'd watched her with starry-eyed wonder, like a preteen seeing a pop star on the street. She was easygoing, fun, and had a sense of humor to rival Clarence's. She and Caleb were completely, utterly in love.

It was a life worth protecting.

Next came Taz; his fiancée, Helene; and Helene's parents. Second of Mom's children and fourth overall, Taron Beck was the leading candidate for Favorite Child™. He was brilliant, steady as a freight train, logical as a computer, and most notably, had never once yelled or caused a scene in public. He moved through life on his own schedule. Took his time, weighed all options. Chose his next move based on logic, not emotion—a trait which few can honestly claim.

Which is why, when he texted a picture of an enormous diamond ring on a delicate, manicured hand just six weeks after telling us he had a girlfriend, the family erupted.

Within seconds, Karma started a text thread with all the siblings except Taz. The message said, meaningfully, WTF?

Even I—hidden away in my shoebox in Bed-Stuy, a black hole of my own making—felt the shock waves. I had always known that, in order to bring someone successfully into the Beck family, you have to allow time for acclimation. I mean, Karma and Shelly dated for *eight years* before tying the knot. Eight years! If I were ever to get married, it would be after a long courtship, allowing plenty of time for my theoretical fiancé to pass a long series of approvals and, of course, to give him a fair chance to run.

That night, the first in four days of wedding celebrations, was also my first time meeting my future sister-in-law. At that point, the facts I knew about her were as follows: Helene Marcus (twenty-five) was a principal ballerina at the Joffrey Ballet in downtown Chicago. On the night her company wrapped performances of *Don Quixote*, they went out drinking at a bar in Streeterville. That's where she met Taz. They exchanged numbers, met for their first date shortly thereafter. According to my mother, in the six weeks that followed, Taz left work early every day to walk the twelve blocks from his office to the Joffrey, stopping each night at a different restaurant. When Helene emerged from rehearsal, there he'd be: Taron Beck, long limbed and shy, a bag of takeout dangling from his left hand.

Helene and I didn't shake hands. Instead, she placed a delicate palm on each of my shoulders and said, "We are *so* grateful you made it." Her big eyes melted with warm sincerity. "We know how busy you are."

Helene was followed by her parents, Pam and Tim, who wrapped me in excited hugs. Helene was their only child. They seemed pretty excited about the prospect of inheriting five more.

Poor saps, I thought. *No idea what they're marrying into.*

And then: Shelly. My sister's wife.

She stepped forward, dark curly hair swishing, and squinted her eyes playfully, wrinkling the dark skin around them. "You promised to tell me about every restaurant you tried in New York," she said, reaching out one hand and lightly squeezing my arm. "Three years, and I haven't heard about even one."

Food is what brought Karma and Shelly together. Karma's a baker, Shelly's a chef. Both women are Big Deals in their own rights, but when they met, they were nothing more than kitchen interns who frequented the same bars after work. The culinary scene in Chicago is small. The single, gay, early twenties scene is also small. The single, gay, early twenties, involved-in-the-culinary-world-in-Chicago scene is nearly microscopic.

I love my sister-in-law. When I was a kid, Karma teased me relentlessly—*Eliot and Manny sittin' in a tree, K-I-S-S-I-N-G*—but Shelly always had my back. A wink, a squeeze of the arm, a few words saying, "Ease up, Karm. Let Boose do her thing." Quiet comfort, the counterpoint to my sister's loud confidence. But don't mistake her kindness for weakness; I've seen what Shelly can do with a knife.

My siblings call me Boose. Or Gup, sometimes, as in Guppy. As in the youngest, the smallest, the tail end of the family. I used to love my nicknames. In many ways I still do, but since Henry's death . . . I don't know. It isn't the same. I'm still the caboose, but my link to the rest of the train vanished a long time ago. They're all chugging ahead, far ahead, years ahead, and I'm back here.

On my own, as ever.

"I haven't been out to eat . . . much," I said weakly to Shelly. An understatement if I had ever spoken one. "But I'll text you the next time I do."

"*The Boose*," came a voice from across the cabin, "*is in . . . the . . . building!*"

I turned to see Clarence charging at me like a loose bull. He scooped me up and swung my body in circles, an act that always made me dissolve into laughter as a kid. Big, genuine bellows, straight from the gut. I heard that same sound echo in the rafters of the cabin that afternoon and almost didn't recognize it as coming from me.

Clarence looked different than I remembered. Occasionally, he posted photos on his musician page—blurry concert shots that focused on his guitar, not his face—but they didn't give much away. You couldn't see the wrinkles of age that now blossomed at the corners of his eyes, the razor burn beneath his five-o'clock shadow. The sun spots and smile lines. The subtle wave in his once pin-straight hair.

Despite the twenty-five years that separated us, Clarence and I had been close. Not as close as him and Karma, but enough to matter. Enough that I knew it would have hurt him when I disappeared.

He set me down. "Jesus," he said, shaking his head. "Little Boose Beck. All grown up."

WHEN THE HUGS were over, I was released from the throng. Finally, a moment to breathe. To clear my head. I turned away from the group—

Only to find myself face-to-face with a roadblock.

A very tall, very handsome roadblock.

"Beck." Manuel's soft brown eyes smiled. He nodded his head at the side porch. "Can we talk for a minute?"

"Um."

All those words, that effortless stream of copy that flowed from my lips during the boat ride over, the same way it does at my job . . . all of it, gone. Poof.

"Um," I said again. "Actually—" *Think, Eliot. All you need is one excuse. Just one.* "Actually, I thought I saw my dad out back."

Manuel glanced over his shoulder. "You did?"

"Yeah. So. I'm just going to go look for him. To say hi."

"I'll come with," he said automatically. "I haven't seen Speedy yet, either."

"No," I said too quickly, too forcefully.

Manuel's eyes widened. Behind me, I could practically feel Karma's eyes flick up from watching strawberries to burn holes in the back of my head.

"I mean—" *Think, for fuck's sake.* "There's . . . something I need to discuss with him. In private."

Manuel may not truly be family—may have been born to different people in a different country and grown up in a different house—but he knew me better than anyone in that cabin. Better than anyone on Earth, if I was being honest. He knew my moods, my quirks, the twisted knots of my mind. Three years before, I could never have gotten away with that lie.

I could only hope that enough time had passed for him to forget just how intimately we knew each other.

His eyes narrowed.

No such luck, then.

"Anyway!" I said too brightly. I pushed past him and practically sprinted outside.

Out on the back porch, I gripped the railing and stared out at the waves, at the whole of the North Channel—wide and windy, the pulmonary artery of Lake Huron. I heaved in deep, calming breaths, the way Dr. Droopy taught me to do.

Cradle Island. I'd forgotten how beautiful it was. Really, I had. I hadn't been able to properly take it in on the ride in with Manuel. I was too busy groping the air for words, most of which didn't even emerge in full sentences—just unintelligible smoothies of speech and semi-hysterical laughter.

Cradle isn't a tropical island. Its outside—a thin, treeless shoreline—is not sand but rock. Rock that seems, impossibly, alive. It's orange and green and grey and turquoise. It moves without moving: up, then down, then up again. It grows and shrinks and piles up atop itself. Moss and feathery grass grow from its cracks. Here it's tall and reaching. There it breaks down into a beach made of ten thousand pebbles. Inside the harbor—a generous crescent protected on all sides by long, empty islands—are the cabins. They're connected by a boardwalk that blends into the rest of the island, as if the oak and white pine grew up around it, rather than the other way around.

My head throbbed. My fingers drummed the railing impatiently. Not even a day away from my job and my entire body ached for a keyboard, a monitor, a meeting to lead—something. Work. Work. All I thought about was work. I kept a strict schedule. Never turned off email or Slack notifications. Did tasks the moment they were assigned to me, truly unable to put them off. When I lay down to sleep at night, my to-do list for the next day played through my mind on an endless cycle.

It's not that I didn't understand the value of a vacation; it's more that when I wasn't working, I felt a constant gnawing at the back of my mind, as if I were forgetting something essential.

I tried to blink the nagging away, to bring the island back into focus. I made the decision to leave New York for this wedding; I should at least try to enjoy it. And hadn't Cradle Island once been my happy place? Wasn't it home to almost all of my best memories? Memories with my family, with Henry, with Manuel . . .

Oh God. Manuel was here. *Here.* Trapped with me on this island, nowhere to hide.

Footsteps and squeaking wheels sounded on the rocks beside the back porch, shaking me out of my trance. I looked over, and there he was: Stephen S. Beck IV (aka Speedy, aka Dad), flanked on either side by a pair of enormous women.

The women in question were the Nurses. Two of them. *One for each leg,* as Dad always said, usually followed by a bout of wheezing laughter. The Nurses changed almost every year, but they always looked the same: thick, muscular, wooden faced. Tree trunks of women. Nothing like the friendly ladies who used to take my blood pressure at the pediatrician. To be honest, my siblings and I weren't even sure they were RNs; they looked more like ex-Marines. Their names were punchy little things, like *Kim* or *Mack* or *Gena.* That year, as Speedy told us in a text message the week before, they were named June and Jane.

It might sound impossible that a man without the use of either of his legs would choose to spend three months of the year on an island in the Canadian wilderness, but back in his heyday, Speedy had been king of it all. He led the hikes. He taught us to swim. He danced around the kitchen to Eric Clapton and tossed his pint-sized children into the air like weightless balloons. He was the best slalom skier in the family, bar none. Back in the eighties, Speedy Beck could hit a dry start off the floating dock with a joint between his fingers, ski twice around the island, and land smoothly back at the dock—joint still burning, not a drop of water on his head or hash.

Those days are over for my father. They ended the minute his legs did.

For some, losing mobility would have been enough to give up the whole thing: sell the island, find a house in South Florida with a chauffeur and an elevator. Not Speedy. He'd lost too much already—all of it due, in one way or another, to the whims and weaknesses of the human body.

Five decades, three wives, and six children later, Stephen S. Beck IV is not the playboy heir he could have been. He sold off his stake and his board seat at Beck Pharma just a few years before I was born, and then, retired, confined to a wheelchair, all he wanted was to kayak and fish and drive big boats and eat dessert twice a day.

Most people would probably be shocked to learn that my energetic, ALL-CAPS, DO-IT-ALL-DO-IT-NOW mother is married to a man in a wheelchair. But back when they met, Dad was still walking. In fact, even though he was already forty, twice divorced, and had two teenage kids, he was as youthful and springy as a college student. He traveled. He played tennis. He water-skied like an Olympian. He hiked and swam and cooked extravagant meals and drank wine with abandon. And to top it all off, he loved no physical activity more than romping about with his children.

Marriage to a much older, twice-divorced man had never been part of my mother's life plan. Though she grew up in St. Louis, same as my father, they didn't meet until they were adults. She knew who he was, of course—given that he was born to the wealthiest, most infamous family in the city—but by the time they formally met, Mom was a newly licensed lawyer with a degree from Mizzou and a job offer at the most prestigious firm in Chicago. She was doing it. She was leaving. Oldest of her family, first to fly the nest, first to find success. When she walked into the party that night, the last she would attend before moving to Chicago (a chance to see inside the home of the infamous Beck family? What a send-off!), her future spread as wide and promising as the streets of the brand-new city she would soon call home.

And then . . . there he was. Speedy Beck. With his green eyes and swimmer's shoulders and floppy blond hair, passing out drinks, bustling about the kitchen with his two children. They were with him that weekend, Caleb and Clarence, though their mother never would have allowed it had she known he was throwing one of his "small dinner parties." They wouldn't tell, my brothers. They loved cooking with Dad. When Mom walked in the door, all three of them stood behind the kitchen counter, chopping and singing loudly to Derek and the Dominos. They had on matching aprons.

Though she wouldn't learn it until many years later, that man—the one taking such good care of his children it made her ovaries ache—was also high on 3.4 grams of the best dust money could buy.

When my father spotted me standing up on the patio, he stopped, braking his signature black Feather Chair®—*The World's Lightest Wheelchairs*, I had looked up their slogan long before—down on the rocks and straightening up. Unmoving, unsmiling. Face like a stone. He still cut an imposing figure, even at almost seventy years old.

"Father," I said.

"Daughter."

There was a long pause. Then his face broke into a grin. "Get over here, Guppy."

BACK INSIDE, THE family was setting the table and tidying up the kitchen. I passed Manuel on my way to the sink. He was carrying a stack of plates out to the screened-in porch. We made eye contact over the plates, then quickly looked away.

In the kitchen, I picked up a wet rag and started turning it in circles along the counter's edge. Everyone pitched in except Karma and Clarence, who popped one of Speedy's "Best of" CDs into the stereo and started to dance around the open living room.

"Planning to help?" Caleb asked, hands wrist-deep in the kitchen sink.

"We are helping," Karma said. "We're providing the entertainment."

Providing the entertainment. That was an excuse Clarence and Karma used a lot when I was little. They said it so much I thought it was a legitimate reason to get out of work. I tried it out one time, when Manuel and I got in trouble for being disruptive during History. Told Ms. Jacobs we were just providing the entertainment for everyone else.

Didn't go over well.

I watched Karma and Clarence groove about, heads swinging, bare feet twisting on the wood-paneled floor. Long-stemmed wineglasses sloshed about in their hands.

I envied them. I envied their inside jokes and knowing glances, their private party within the swirling vortex of our family. How nice it must be, to have a best friend built into your bloodline. I looked at them and saw what could have been had Henry lived.

My sister and half brother have a miracle bond, overcoming seventeen years' age difference, the awkwardness of being not-quite-siblings, and vastly different interests. While Karma worked in food, Clarence was a researcher at Beck Pharma's Chicago office. On weekends, he played backup guitar for the country acts that traveled through the city. "To keep me young," he once said, eyes twinkling with more youth at thirty-eight than mine held at thirteen—or perhaps had ever held, period.

Three years might have passed since I saw them, but Clarence and Karma were just the same. Still throwing themselves at life with unbridled, unapologetic energy. As if the only way they knew how to love something was to get so pissed off about it they could barely form a coherent sentence. It scared me sometimes, but it was an intoxicating kind of fear. One that drags you closer even as you know you should run away.

4

FIFTH GRADE

ON THE DAY we return from Cradle Island—exactly one day after I find Dad wailing on the floor surrounded by the broken pieces of Henry's *errrn*—Mom walks straight through the front door of our home and up to her bedroom without saying a word. Doesn't touch her suitcase. Leaves it in the trunk and carries only herself up the stairs, as if the weight of her body is the only thing she can handle.

Mom kept a strong chin during our time up north, throwing herself into "improving our diet" as a way of distracting from her grief. But now, back in Winnetka, in a huge house with an excruciatingly empty bedroom where her youngest son should have been, she shuts down. Shuts the door to her bedroom. Climbs into bed.

We won't see her for a month.

IN THE WEEKS following Mom's disappearance, my family deteriorates. Karma stops inviting friends over. Dad stops playing Bob Dylan records in his office. Taz stops drawing. Clarence and Caleb, who have their own apartments downtown, no longer come for family dinner on Sundays.

It's August. The days are long and hot and suffocatingly humid, a quintessential Chicago summer. Cicadas drone. Fireflies twinkle at night. Our house sits right on Lake Michigan, the back door looking out over the private beach that we share with our neighbors. I spend the mornings reading on a towel in the sand or in our backyard, a long grassy hill surrounded by towering oak trees. In the afternoon, I curl up with my laptop in our upstairs library and log into the online games that Taz taught me how to play. At night, I sometimes bike to the ice cream shop in downtown Winnetka, eating Moose Tracks alone on a bench just for an excuse to leave the house.

It's quiet at home. Far too quiet. The only real activity comes from the kitchen, where Karma bakes her feelings into more batches of pastries than our house can handle. She keeps every tray that comes out of the oven. Even the failed attempts. Cloud-dolloped vanilla cupcakes sparkle next to beige bricks topped with oozing grey puss. She swaddles each batch in Cling Wrap and stores them throughout the kitchen. Anywhere—the counter, the windowsill, the breakfast table, the cabinets—just as long as they remain in plain sight. One lumpy, Saran-wrapped bundle atop another. Stacks turn into mountains. The kitchen grows thick with new aromas: charred chocolate, melted butter, biting sweetness. And, as the days pass, the subtle, ominous hint of mold.

Taz says, "Mom might spontaneously combust when she sees this."

Karma says, "Mom would have to leave her bedroom for that to happen."

For a week Karma makes nothing but brioche. Each batch comes out lighter, puffier, floating with air and yeast. The kitchen overflows with them. The loaves grow so large she stores them in garbage bags, not Ziplocs. Black ones, the Hefty kind. She fills every cabinet and the countertop, too. With nowhere else to go, she drops

the bags onto the floor. They pile up in the corner. The kitchen becomes confusing; it looks like a landfill but smells like a bakery.

Nobody stops her. Not even Dad. It's not like we need the kitchen
for cooking; our fridge is stuffed with more sympathy food than we
can handle. Every night, we choose whatever Saran-wrapped casserole looks best and stick a slice in the microwave. Sometimes, we
skip dinner altogether, eating Karma's desserts instead.

Anyway, Speedy doesn't have the bandwidth to care about the fact
that it has become virtually impossible to move about the kitchen.
For the first time in twenty years of marriage, Dad has to manage
all four of us—sorry, all three of us—alone.

It's not that he can't do it. He can. It's just that it's completely foreign territory for him. The arrangement between my parents has
always been the same: Mom manages the kids, Dad manages everything else. You'd be surprised at how much admin it takes to be this
rich—the bills, the banks, the taxes, the travel. But they handle it,
they've always handled it. Until now. Until Wendy Beck disappeared into her bedroom, leaving her husband to deal with *all* of it:
every last bill, every last dinner, every last child.

"I BET IT'S payback," Karma says one afternoon. We're standing in
the kitchen. Karma is teaching me how to pound dough. I feel guilty
saying it, but part of me is glad she stopped bringing friends around;
she finally has time to pay attention to me.

"What is?" I ask.

"Mom staying in their room and making Dad do everything. I
bet it's some messed-up version of payback."

"Payback for what?"

Karma looks up. "You don't know about Dad?"

"Know what about Dad?"

"He's sober."

"What's *sober*?"

"It means he doesn't drink alcohol or anything."

I absentmindedly tear chunks of brioche from the warm loaf on the counter. Huh. Now that I think about it, Mom *does* get red wine when we go out to eat, while Dad gets Shirley Temples. But I didn't think that was because he couldn't drink; I thought it was because red wine is gross and Shirley Temples are delicious.

"Why not?" I ask.

"Because." Karma looks down at the ball of dough and presses the heel of her hand to its soft belly, kneading gently. "Dad was a drug addict."

I know about drug addiction. I saw a documentary about it on TV. Hideous women with stringy hair and sunken eye sockets stared out from the flatscreen and talked about how their families don't love them anymore.

"What drugs did he do?"

"Cocaine, mostly." Her hand speeds up. "But there were other things, too. Alcohol. Marijuana. Cigarettes. But cocaine was the main thing. Cocaine was the 'problem.'" She sighs. "It wasn't his fault, really. It was the way he grew up. Everything pushed Dad toward addiction—his friends, his parents, his money. Even his genetics, for God's sake."

I try to keep up with what my sister is saying. I recognize that the story she's telling me is important. Very important. But I can't make the pieces fit. I can't reconcile the images of needles and scars and hideous, disfigured faces with my harmless, well-kept father.

"He was able to keep it secret for a long time, but when Mom finally found out about it, they'd already had Taz and me. The way Dad tells it, when she caught him . . ." Karma trails off. She looks up from the ball of dough. Her face is horrified, as if she only just realized she's talking about drug addiction to a ten-year-old. I'm not sure what my face looks like. She finishes briskly, saying, "He told me about it a few years ago. I'm sure he'll do the same for you one day."

I leave the kitchen in shock. I believed I already knew our family tree, with all its many branches and blossoms and bark. I believed I saw the whole story. But in fact, I saw only a small portion. None of its roots. None of its rings.

I WAKE ON the last day of summer with strange red bumps on my legs.

"Geez, Boose," says Karma at breakfast. "You leave your legs out on a rotisserie last night? Those are some ghoulish bugbites."

In bed that night, I wait for sleep to take me, trying desperately not to scratch my legs. Out in the hallway, Taz and Speedy whisper to each other. I don't hear everything they say, but they seem to be discussing bees; I catch the word *hives*.

I think back to my parents' conversation on Cradle Island. *You really aren't worried? I swear, I haven't seen her cry once.*

Could Mom be right? Am I not grieving for my brother? Am I even sad he's gone?

Don't be ridiculous, I tell myself. *Of course you're sad your brother died.*

Then again, it's true that I hardly cried. But that's just me. I'm not a crier. And it's not like I haven't cried at all, right? Surely I cried at the funeral. Surely.

But . . . did I?

As I sat next to my second cousin on that sofa, did I?

As I sat under the weight of Karma's trembling arm while the minister gave his speech, did I?

I can't remember. How can I not remember?

I scratch my legs harder.

If I don't remember crying at Henry's funeral, then how can I be certain that I'm sad he's gone? What if I'm *not* sad? What if I'm secretly happy about it?

That's crazy, I think. *You're not happy your closest brother is dead. You miss him so much.*

But what if I don't?

That's it. That's all it takes.

My mind picks up speed, running in endless circles. I tell myself that it's crazy to think I'd be glad my brother is gone, then in the same breath, I circle back to the fact that I didn't cry at his funeral. Didn't cry. At my own brother's funeral. Crying is the way your body tells you you're sad. If I didn't cry, I must not have been sad.

Then, as soon as I finish that thought, I circle back. Tell myself not to be ridiculous.

But then, as soon as I finish *that* thought, I circle back *again*, even though I don't want to. Because I didn't cry. I can't ignore that fact. I'm not grieving. That means I'm not sad Henry is dead. And if I'm not, does that make me a bad person? It must, right? Only a bad person wouldn't cry after the death of their brother.

I curl my legs into my chest.

My mind runs in circles, circles, circles. I don't understand what's happening. Soon, it isn't even about whether I cried at Henry's funeral anymore. Soon, I'm just worrying about how much I'm worrying. Then I start worrying about the fact that I'm worrying about worrying. Then I start worrying about worrying about worrying about worrying, and suddenly my mind feels so crowded, as if my thoughts aren't filtering out in the way most thoughts do. As if something is blocking the exit. As if, rather than in and out of my mind in an orderly line, one thought replacing another, they linger. All of them. Half sound like me; they speak with the internal voice I've always recognized as my own. The other half do not. The other half—they have their own voice. They're loud. So loud. They're a living thing. They're hundreds of blind moths in search of a flame, flying chaotically about my mind, crashing into each other, knocking things over. I cringe as glass shatters in places I can't see.

I try every method I can think of to shut out the noise. I hum. I turn my head to the side and recite the Spanish alphabet, a list of strange and wonderful sounds we learned at school the year before. I recite the letters as loudly as I can, speaking into the fabric of my pillow. It doesn't help. The moths keep beating their wings, keep knocking into precious artifacts in my mind, keep smashing them to pieces. I pick up both pillows and squeeze them over either side of my head. One for each ear. I assume it will muffle the noise. It doesn't. How could it? This noise doesn't come from outside my head. It comes from within.

I BURST OUT of my bedroom door, sprint down to the kitchen. "Dad!" I yell. "Dad!"

He's there. Sitting at the kitchen counter, drinking black cherry soda. A normal activity. One I've seen him perform a thousand times. He jumps when the door slams open, jolted from his normalcy.

"What?" he asks, looking wildly about. "What? What?"

I stare at him, at the bewilderment on his face. I blink. Though the Worry isn't gone—though I can still feel it turning and turning, a wheel in a track of wet mud—I recognize then that I'm the only one who can hear it.

"Never mind," I say. Then I shut the kitchen door and run back upstairs.

I WAKE THE next day with a clear conscience. It lasts about twenty seconds. Then I remember what happened the night before, and I fall right back to pieces.

From: Memory & Other Executive Functions <memory@eliot-beck.org>

To: Conscious Mind <consciousness@eliot-beck.org>

Subject: A Beck family dinner (before Henry died)

Below is a brief press release detailing Past Beck Family Dinners, intended to provide you with a comparison for the Current State of Affairs. Read & syndicate as necessary.

I (5) go first, ladling lopsided scoops of whichever dish has the most sugar onto my plate. Henry (6) builds a mountain of spaghetti. Taz (12) quietly arranges a neat rainbow along the edge of his plate. Karma (16) claims she hates spaghetti or chicken or whatever we're serving, and pours herself a bowl of cereal. Clarence (30) and Caleb (33) stand off to the side, holding glasses of red wine and waiting for the kids to finish making a mess of the buffet.

We cart our plates out to the porch of Sunny Sunday and each sit in one of the sturdy wooden chairs surrounding it. Dad sits down last. By the time he claims his seat at the head, half of us are done eating and ready to go back to blowing shit up outside. But now that we're together, Mom insists that we say grace. Karma picks at dry Special K flakes. My legs swing like bungee cords, toes miles above ground.

Mom closes her eyes and tells us to hold hands. We pinch each other's fingers and make faces across the table. At the end of the prayer, just before Mom says, "Amen," Karma sticks her tongue out and blows a fart wet enough to make even God blush.

Then the stories start. My siblings—well, they aren't just good storytellers; they're brilliant. Their eyes sparkle. Their arms wave theatrically. Caleb tells the story of eight-year-old Karma beating up the unfortunate boy who tried to steal Taz's Fruit by the Foot, and the whole table—down to the candles—shakes with laughter. Tears leak out of Mom's eyes.

In my head, I'm eloquent, too. Insightful. Wise. I have a story to tell, the same way they do, but I exist in this strange in-between: too old for a high chair, too young to be taken seriously by the adults. A child perennially annoyed by her place in the world. Dinner conversation is an exclusive club to which I have not yet been granted access. Membership includes time with the talking stick, the right for your jokes to be laughed at, and consideration of your ideas as valid suggestions. I sit in my chair and gaze up as their words ping-pong across the table. I want desperately to join, but everything takes place just a few inches too high for me to reach.

Henry and I quickly become antsy. We ask to leave, but Mom says no, so we find other ways to pass the time: we do handstands against the wall, invent plays using forks and knives as actors, draw presentations on construction paper, then tape them to the wall and make the rest of the family listen.

Sometimes, we just run around and around and around the table until our parents tell us to settle the hell down. Henry always listens. Sometimes I do, too, but mostly I don't. Mostly I keep going, arms cranking, blowing steam through my lips like a train's horn.

"The Boose is loose!" the older kids yell. "The Boose is loose!"

5

NOW

DINNER WAS BURGERS, fries, and salad, served buffet style as usual. After filling my plate with food, I tried to sit next to Caleb.

Mom stopped me. "Oh, Eliot, honey, don't be so diplomatic." She grabbed my shoulders and steered them over to the other corner of the table. "It's fine to sit next to your best friend. I'm sure you two have a lot to catch up on." She pushed me into the chair next to Manuel.

I glanced over at him. He immediately looked down at the table and began to studiously unfold his paper napkin.

Right. Oodles to catch up on.

After everyone sat down, Mom told us to join hands for the prayer. None of the Beck children were particularly religious, but Mom liked to pretend we loved Jesus just as much as she did. Manuel accepted mine the way you might accept a limp sponge. Our palms rested together on the table in an awkward pile. As soon as the prayer was over, they fled.

A transcript of the conversation that followed:

MANUEL: So . . . how's New York?
ELIOT: Big.

M: What do you do there, again?

E: I'm a copywriter.

M: Oh. That's cool. Do you live close to the office?

E: Not really.

M: So . . . you take the train?

KARMA [already on her third whiskey highball]: What is this, Twenty Questions?

E: Sorry?

K: What's wrong with you two? You're acting like you barely know each other.

M + E [in unison]: No, we aren't.

Logically, it was then my turn to ask Manuel about his life. And there was *so much* I wanted to ask. So many questions that had built up inside me over the years. *How are your parents? How is Valentina? What are you studying? Do you still refuse to go to the movie theater unless you can sit in the very last row? Do you still think Tater Tots are just overweight versions of French fries?* But I couldn't ask a single one. Not without clueing every other person in the room in to the fact that I hadn't spoken to him in three full years.

Of course I wanted to ask Manuel about his life. Of course I wanted to tell him more about mine. He's my best friend. *Was* my best friend. He was my best friend, and I used to tell him every idiotic, mundane thing that popped into my head. So *of course* I wanted to tell him everything, starting with the moment my foot landed on the pavement of New York City. I wanted to tell him about being homeless for the first time in my life because I'm a stubborn Trust Fund Baby who wouldn't ask her parents for money. I wanted to tell him about living for a month with our family friend, a Scientologist named Carl. I wanted to tell him that Carl was a filmmaker, that he was completely normal, that I couldn't believe my good fortune. That his apartment had tall, gorgeous windows that overlooked the terra-cotta building across the street, painted the same cherry-lip pink as a home in the Italian countryside. That in the mornings, I bought cheap coffee and stood on the apartment's windowsill, back pressed to the wall, craning my neck to try and catch that small sliver of the Empire State Building poking up in the distance.

Manuel would understand. He would understand why the first thing I did after Carl left was to search the apartment top to bottom for evidence of Scientology—to open the cabinets, scour the closets, shake the cereal boxes, flip open every book in the library to see if the pages within had been hollowed out. Manuel would know why I had to do it. He would get that it wasn't snooping; it was my right— no, my *responsibility*—as an outsider invited into the home of a member of the most secretive religion in the country. I had to discover what I could. And, of course, he would laugh when I told him that all I found were expired peanuts, ten identical pairs of eyeglasses, and a fridge filled with stacks of unopened camera film.

I didn't tell Manuel any of that. I couldn't. To speak candidly with my best friend would open a door into that darker passage of my mind, the one walked by only those most terrifying of thoughts and desires. The ones Dr. Droopy once labeled "intrusive." I fought like hell to lock them out, and I could feel how easy it would be to let them back in. The door floated before me, clouding my vision, begging me to grab its handle and pull.

"YOU EXPECTING AN important email or something?"

I looked up, shaken from my reverie. Almost without realizing it, I had pulled out my phone and checked it for messages, having forgotten that I was in a different country and that every gigabyte of data cost more than I could afford.

"Nope," I said, pocketing my phone and spearing a mouthful of salad.

"So, Manny." Karma leaned over my dinner plate. "What's happening with that girl you met at the Spee?"

I nearly choked on the piece of lettuce in my mouth. My eyes snapped up to see Manuel's response.

He cleared his throat.

Karma went on. "Your last text said she was getting pretty clingy."

As Karma spoke, a fleck of spit flew from her mouth, landing on the left side of my burger. The spit droplet bubbled over and dripped down the side of the patty. I tore my eyes from my plate, reminding myself that it didn't matter, that I no longer concerned myself with those obsessions. But even in my peripheral vision, I remained aware of its presence.

"Yeah." Manuel shifted his pile of French fries around with his fork. "To be honest, she ended up being pretty fake. I think she just wanted to say she was dating a Mexican."

Karma snorted. "Of course she did. How many times did you have to explain that you're Colombian, not Mexican? That not all Hispanic people come from the same coun—"

"You guys text?" I blurted out, interrupting.

An awkward pause. Then Manuel asked, "Me and the girl?"

"Of course not," I snapped. Then I drew back. *Rein it in, Eliot.* With two fingers, I plucked off a chunk of meat from the clean end of the burger and popped it into my mouth. "I meant you and Karma."

They glanced at each other. My sister pulled her lips into a tight bundle, raising her eyebrows at Manuel. I was struck, as she did, by the pronounced concavity of her cheekbones, her smooth jaw, the lone freckle just above her lips. Her dark curly hair permanently styled into a chic pixie cut. I had forgotten how beautiful my sister was. How naturally thin, even when the primary ingredient in her diet was chocolate chip cookies.

As I admired my sister's face, I felt—to my utter horror—a sudden pulse. *Down there.*

Oh God, I thought. *No. No.*

Beneath the table, I clenched my fists and squeezed my toes, an action that would sometimes make the sensation, the *arousal*—my chest constricted at even the thought of the word—go away. As if the tightening of other muscles could distract from the one that terrified me most.

And then I heard it. That little voice. The one that was me but not me, the one I'd spent years learning to shut out.

You're attracted to her, it whispered. *You're attracted to your older sister.*

No, I thought as firmly as possible, as if I were a small child in need of scolding. *No, you're not. Those are the Worries talking. Don't listen to them. You know who you are.*

If Dr. Ahmed were here, I know exactly what she'd say. "Your body's response has nothing to do with sexual arousal," she'd recite, crossing her legs in her fancy heather-grey armchair. My eyes would flick up to the gigantic Jackson Pollock painting behind her that might very well be an original. "It's Pavlovian. You check your groin to see if you'll find a response, and you always do."

Checking. A classic internal compulsion. One that I'd been performing since I was ten without ever knowing that that's what I was doing.

Breathe, I thought. *Don't let it drag you back under.*

I closed my eyes, exhaling and forcing myself back into reality. When I opened them again, I glanced over at Manuel and Karma. The two of them seemed to be holding a conversation with their eyes. The sight made me nervous. Since when had they become so chummy? I mean, they had always been friendly, considering that Manuel was practically part of our family . . . but this? Texting? What did they even *talk* about?

When I think about what Manuel might have told her . . .

"*So.*" Clarence's head popped down between us, making me jump. His voice was low. "What do we think of the new girl?"

I knew exactly who he meant. Grateful for the distraction, I turned to look at Helene. She sat at the opposite end of the table, chatting easily with Mom. Beneath the table, her hand was laced with Taz's.

Helene had this structured glamour. A beauty in parts, each so distinct that it should have belonged to a different person: long lush hair curled into knots that swung along her spine with a kind of gentle violence; a thin jaw, pointed and delicate, like the elbow of a doll. She spoke in abrupt, tightly measured sentences that etched themselves from her mouth in halting swoops, like lines from a printing press. Her default reaction—to anything, shocking or otherwise—was to gasp. To widen her eyes just a little. Just enough to show you she was listening.

For his part, Taz seemed utterly transfixed with his bride-to-be. He doted upon her shamelessly. Opened doors. Rearranged furniture to suit her movements. Built his dinner plate to be an exact match of hers. Then added two or three scoops more to ensure he always had a heavier meal. And he did it all so subtly. Only those of us who knew him before could have spotted his behavior. He was loving her quietly. Logically.

Under her breath, Karma whispered to Shelly, "If I ever start copying your dinner plate, please divorce me."

I laughed at the same time Manuel did. Our eyes darted to each other, then looked quickly away.

I scanned the table for something—anything—to distract me. My eyes landed on Speedy and Caleb, who were engaged in quiet, conspiratorial conversation. Dad had one arm slung over the back of Mom's chair and was absentmindedly rubbing small circles on her back. He leaned in close to Caleb, nodding as he listened to his eldest son. It was a familiar sight; Dad had Caleb at only twenty years old, which makes him closer in age to our father than he is to me. They're as much friends as they are father and son.

I watched Caleb's mouth, trying to decipher what he was saying. I thought I saw him whisper *Clarence*, and maybe *believe that story*, but I couldn't be sure. What were they speaking about? Had Dad gone to Caleb for advice about Clarence?

I eyed them enviously. Dad would never come to me in that way. Never. To him, I was still just a child.

I tried to focus on their conversation, straining my ears for whatever I could pick up. I would take just a sentence. Just a *word*. Anything to distract me from the heat of the chestnut-brown gaze I still felt beating into me, even with my eyes turned firmly away.

THE WEEK BEFORE the wedding, Taz texted our family group chat and said, What's everyone's favorite food?

In New York, whenever I see a text arrive in our family chat, I click it right away and leave the chat open, phone propped up against my laptop or the mug that always rests just to the right. I like to watch the messages roll in, to see the conversation unfold in real time.

> **CALEB:** Fettuccini alfredo.

> **CLARENCE:** Deep dish with sausage & roni. Duh.

> **KARMA:** Pulled pork with Sweet Baby Ray's. Sue me.

> **CLARENCE:** SBR's is an abomination.

> **KARMA:** You're an abomination.

I hear each of my siblings in their texts, so clear it almost feels like they're right there, right next to me. As if we're all sitting around a table together.

> **MOM:** Does mint chocolate chip ice cream count as a food?

> **CLARENCE:** If it does, then I'm changing my food to dry martinis.

> **DAD:** New phone. Lost contacts. Who is this?

I watch them riff, but I never respond. I've tried. It doesn't work. I write and rewrite, read and reread, pick my words apart until they sound robotic, all capital letters and perfectly placed commas. *Little Boose Beck*, I imagine my siblings texting each other off to the side. *The Family Robot.*

But not then. As the wedding approached, I became more and more aware of just how cut off from my life in New York I would be. I was taking vacation for the first time since I started working. My schedule would be completely disrupted, tossed into Lake Huron and left to drown. I needed to know that I would at least still have access to email, for God's sake.

> **ELIOT:** will there be wifi on the island?

I didn't think about the repercussions of sending that text until it was already too late.

> **CLARENCE:** oh shit, gup is alive??

> **KARMA:** wow.

> **KARMA:** to what do we owe this honor?

Bubbles popped up one after another, building a grey tower up my screen.

TAZ: hey, Eliot!

CLARENCE: THE BOOSE IS BACK!!!!

MOM: Eliot. Y didn't u answer my call yesterday?

DAD: Boose? Who is this? Eliot?

MOM: Yes

DAD: Is this about food at the wedding?

MOM: Yes

DAD: Oh.

DAD: In that case, I like sweets.

KARMA: yes, dad. we know.

My family didn't understand why I did what I did. Why I disappeared to New York at just eighteen, never coming home for holidays and rarely answering their calls. And, what's more, I never planned to explain it to them.

Not in this lifetime, anyway.

6

FIFTH GRADE

I MEET MANUEL Garcia Valdecasas on the first day of fifth grade.

He arrives in the afternoon. In the morning, I spend most of my time sitting at my desk and trying to fix whatever has broken inside my head.

That morning, I woke up in my four-poster princess canopy bed and decided that I knew exactly how to solve this. How to make the moths flying about my mind stop beating their torturous wings: I will *think* about it. I will think *really hard* about it. I will apply all of my brainpower to the task, to this one problem, the only problem that matters anymore, because that technique has always worked in the past, right? Stuck on a test question? Think about it. Think about it *really hard*. Close your eyes and press your palms to your forehead and think think think *think* and then—there! The answer. It pops into your mind as suddenly as a file opening on your computer.

So, I do. After hopping out of Speedy's navy-blue Suburban, I sprint over the pavement and into the Skokie School, Winnetka's only public middle school and my home for the next two years. Inside, the hallway is packed with fifth and sixth graders shouting greetings or swapping stories about the summer or shyly shuffling forward with their eyes on the tiled floor. Their skin is tan and freckled. The popular girls are resplendent in their First Day Outfits. I ignore them all, making straight for my new classroom.

Once there, I find the desk with my name on it and sit down. Then I start to think.

And think.

And think.

The result of all of this thinking?

Chaos.

You loved your brother, I tell myself.

But did you? Did you *really*?

Of course I did. He was my best friend.

But don't forget that you didn't cry at his funeral. Don't forget that even your parents noticed, that they were concerned about you.

They were worried about me because they wanted to make sure I was grieving.

Maybe. Or maybe they're really worried that you're a bad person. A person who wants their older brother to die.

That's not true, I thought. *Please, stop. Please. It's not true.*

Thinking doesn't find me a solution to the Worries. It only makes them worse. It makes them circle tighter and faster, the moths beating their wings as hard as possible, everything a tangled, awful mess.

Class starts, but I can't pay attention to anything Ms. Collins is saying. I open the lid of my desk and pull out a notebook. It's massive, a lined eight-by-twelve spiral with over two hundred empty pages. And so, as Ms. Collins talks about multiplication charts, I write out my Worries. That's the name I've given them: Worries. On my bookshelf at home are other, more sensible journals—palm sized, featuring flowers or puppies on the front, but this is the only option on hand.

And so—it becomes my first Worry Journal.

I'll eventually fill dozens of Worry Journals. Hundreds, maybe. I'll see the entries as confessions, a safe way to seek forgiveness. To empty myself of the horrible things I've done. Each entry a little apology. To whom am I apologizing? The Universe? God? I don't know. I've never believed in such things. But I want desperately to rid myself of these thoughts, and this is the only way I know how.

I'll write every day. Obsessively record every shred of guilt that passes through my mind. Over time, the notebook will grow heavy with pencil markings and memory. Add a good six pounds to my backpack. But I'll carry it everywhere. I have to. I'll think of the book as a sidecar—a small but sturdy vessel that carries a portion of my thoughts. Relieves me of them. Just a small one, but a portion nonetheless.

WHEN THE NEW boy arrives, Ms. Collins steers him into the classroom like a grocery cart, one hand on each shoulder. She announces that this is Manuel, then pushes him into the empty chair to my right. He glares at her back as she walks away. "*Puta*," he mutters, the meaning of which I will discover later that day while flipping through the inappropriate section of *Advanced Spanish Translation*.

I like him immediately.

"Hi." I offer my hand, the way my father taught me to. "I'm Eliot."

Manuel's only response is to stare.

"So, where *is* Colombia?" I ask, having absolutely no idea what the answer is.

Manuel just stares at me with an open mouth and slightly squinted eyes.

I've never been a talker. *Quiet as a woman on trial*, Clarence always says. It was Henry who sparked our dinnertime productions and presentations, Henry who led us in games of make-believe. But maybe that's not me. Not deep down, I mean. I've always *wished* I were a talker, that I could tell stories as skillfully as the rest of my family. But I can't. I'm only ten, for God's sake. Who wants to hear a ten-year-old's stories?

With Manuel, it's different. He *feels* different, even if I can't say why. I'm instantly comfortable around him in a way I've never been with the rest of the kids at this school. So I talk. I whisper. I give my thoughts on Ms. Collins's lessons or make jokes about the posters on the wall. I don't care if my observations are funny or interesting or even intelligible. I give them anyway. His only response is to stare at me with those same squinted eyes. Eventually he stops looking at me altogether.

Still, the comfort does not dissipate. Over the course of the afternoon, it only grows, as if his presence has created a little bubble of safety around our two desks. As if he's popped a cork on the well of words within me, the ones that have circled around and around and around in my mind, torturing me, dragging me through hell. In this moment, I feel that I can say anything. And I do. I jabber at his left ear about schoolwork, my family, the irritating things Molly Parker says during story circle.

I even graze the subject of Henry; Manuel's ear twitches slightly at the sound of the phrase *car accident*—my first clue that he might actually be listening—but that's it. No response. And me, I feel instantly guilty that I brought up a brother I disrespected by not caring about his death.

I switch subjects.

I tell that ear more in two hours than I've told the rest of my classmates since I first met them. After a month spent in the silence of my own home, it's an incredible release. I feel myself rise from the depths of my mind. The Worries don't disappear, not by a long shot, but they quiet, just a little. Just while I talk.

The ear doesn't respond.

Still, I don't give up. I'm determined to make him my friend.

After school, I repeat what I hear him mutter: "Ess-tay chee-kah ess lo-kah," I whisper. The syllables crackle atop my tongue.

THAT AFTERNOON, I arrive home energized in a way I haven't felt since before Henry's death. I sprint into the kitchen, only to skid to a halt beside Karma and Taz.

"Guys!" I say. "Guess what? There was a new kid at school today. His name is—"

But my voice dies on my tongue when my mother walks into the room. She's dressed in real clothing this time, not a bathrobe. I glance at my siblings. We cluster closer together, watching our mother like rabbits eyeing an unfamiliar beast from a distance—breath held, wondering if this new creature is friend or foe. She doesn't attack. Doesn't yell. Just picks her way through the piles of sweets clogging up the kitchen—Karma's excessive baking, which continued after we came back from Cradle—and puts on a kettle of water.

Dad walks into the room. When he sees Mom standing at the stove in a pair of jeans, he pulls up short. My siblings and I go still. By now, the tension and resentment between our parents has grown nearly obese with thickness. We feel it through the walls of the house. We hear it in the way Dad stomps about in the morning, as he prepares us both breakfast and lunch for the day. Often, he sleeps in Henry's empty bedroom. More than once I hear Karma or Taz whisper the word *divorce*.

Dad clears his throat.

Mom looks up. "Oh, there you are, dear." She smiles and points at the cabinet above the stove. "Would you mind grabbing me a box of Earl Grey?"

"Would I mind . . . ?" He takes a step forward. His face is blank. "What?"

"Earl Grey. The tea?"

He takes another step forward. "I know . . ." His voice trails off. He shakes his head. "Are you . . . are you back, then?"

"Back from where, dear?" she asks, picking absentmindedly through bundles of sugar and Saran wrap. "I've been here this whole time."

Karma, Taz, and I glance at each other.

Speedy blinks. Something about his expression scares me. It's completely lifeless. He steps forward again, but this time it looks mechanical, as if there's no purpose behind the movement, as if he's being dragged. I want to stand up and yell at him to stop. To my right, Karma's fingers close around her butter knife.

The last step my father ever takes happens right there, right before our very eyes. He tries to lift his leg, but as he does, something short-circuits. His knees buckle. His ankles collapse. He screams, and Karma screams, and my mother screams, and his legs fold beneath him, and his body hits the floor.

7

"SO, BOOSE," SAID Caleb.

At the sound of my name, I jumped. A small wave of water splashed out of my cup.

"Tell us about your job."

I straightened. I was childish to be so excited by the prompt, but I couldn't help it. It was finally my chance. My turn to talk. *Why yes, ladies and gentlemen, I did land a job right out of high school. I am self-supporting at the age of twenty-one. And no—I didn't use a dime of our drug money to do so!*

"Well." I raised my voice. Tried not to think about the spit still clinging to the burger on my plate. "Blossom is pretty amazing. It's a startup that—"

"Wait," interrupted Karma. "What exactly is your job title, again?"

"Global Content Manager."

"Which means . . . ?"

"She's a copywriter," said my mother proudly, as if she had any idea what that meant.

Karma waved a hand. "Which *means* . . . ?"

"It means she writes the jingles that brainwash you into buying expensive toothpaste," said Clarence.

"No," I said. "What I do is—"

"And how did you get that job?" Karma asked. "Don't copywriting positions usually require a college degree?"

"They do." I nodded. "But I started at the bottom at Blossom. Assisting other writers or doing admin work for the executives. Getting coffee, answering emails. That sort of stuff. But I worked really hard, and after two and a half years—"

"Personally," interrupted Caleb. "I think what Boose is doing is awesome. I mean, just look at how packaged organic products are disrupting the food industry."

"Yes, well," Clarence responded. "It's hardly surprising that you would approve of Boose's job, seeing as you only ever think about pumping money out of patients and insurance companies."

"Oh, is that so?" Caleb asked. "And what do you say to yourself, Clarence, after looking in your bank account and seeing a pile of money you made thanks to buying up patents that you can then shield from the rest of the research community?"

Clarence sat back in his chair and smirked. "You mean, the same money that you'll inherit as soon as Dad dies?"

"That's different," said Caleb. "At least I make a real, everyday difference with my patients. All you do is peddle Prozac and Cialis, while perfectly viable cures for cancer sit on a shelf somewhere, gathering dust—"

Caleb kept talking. I sighed. There was no point. Nobody actually cared.

"I care," said a low voice to my left. A voice that rumbled straight through my body, sending sparks all the way down to my toes.

Drat. Of course I said that out loud. Of *course* Manuel heard.

My eyes darted over to his before looking quickly away. "Never mind," I said, voice breathy, fake. "Just joking."

Disappointment seeped off Manuel. He turned slowly back to his French fries.

For a moment, as I watched the eagerness leak from his face, I wanted to break. To tell him everything. To tell him that, in preparation for my job, I had studied hundreds of products—at supermarkets, online, in the spam filter of my email inbox—and in almost every case, I found the same thing: truly talented copywriters are literary chameleons. You have no idea they're there. They separate themselves from their words. Think as their medium would. They don't ask, *What would Eliot say about this packet of almond flour?* They ask, *What would this packet of almond flour say about this packet of almond flour?*

Yet again, I didn't. Yet again, I was too afraid.

It's only four days, I thought. *Keep things polite. Keep things on the surface. Don't listen to that dangerous little thrumming inside your chest. Don't give in. It's for his own good. For everyone's own good. Four days, and then you'll never have to see him again.*

You can do this.

Be a copywriter. Separate yourself from your words. Think as your medium would. Take on the voice assigned, leave no trace of your own. Because once the bones are assembled, once they're wrapped in shiny plastic skin and sent off into the abyss to become plastic wrappers or tin cans or email marketing or blog posts or whatever the fuck, that's it. They're gone. Your words no longer belong to you. In fact, they never did.

All the research I did added up to one conclusion: to become a copywriter, I didn't need to learn a new voice; I needed to get rid of my own.

And that?

That I could do.

AT THE END of the meal, after the sun sank behind the lake's horizon and the plates had been scraped clean (Karma) or picked at until only the spit-stained half of the burger remained (me), the conversation settled. At the head of the table, Mom had surpassed the number of champagne flutes required to believe you absolutely *must* give a toast—right now, right this very second. She tapped the edge of her fork against the glass, filling the air with three loud, clear *pings*.

Ping, ping, ping.

"Everyone!" called Caleb. "Listen up. Wendy wants to talk."

"Teacher's pet," Clarence muttered.

Mom stood. "Everyone stop and look around."

Everyone stopped. Everyone looked around. I studiously avoided looking to my left, though I could feel his eyes on me. At the opposite head of the table, Speedy nodded off over his dinner.

"When is the last time we were all together?"

"If memory serves," said Karma. "It was just after the annual sacrifice." She turned to Clarence and asked, "Who'd we go for that year? Aunt Kiki?"

"*These moments*," Mom continued loudly, as if no one had interrupted, "don't come often. Take it in." She closed her eyes. Took a deep breath. When she opened her eyes again, her features had settled into serene contentment. She raised her flute and said, "To having the whole family together."

No, I thought as we raised glasses and began the complicated dance of connecting with every flute around the table. Henry's smiling face flashed through my mind. *Not the whole family. Not quite.*

When we finished toasting, I took a long drain from my champagne glass. I was going to need it to get through the rest of this dinner.

"Frankly," Clarence said, putting his empty flute down, "I think it's quite dangerous when we all get together."

"Damn right." Karma nodded. "Too much collateral damage toward unsuspecting outsiders."

"Hotel managers, flight attendants, schoolteachers"—he winked at Helene's parents—"in-laws."

They looked at him with obvious alarm.

"Speaking of hotel managers"—a grin spread across Karma's face—"remember the Petri Dish?"

"Holy *hell*." Clarence slapped the table. "You mean the place we stayed at in Moscow during our biennial Trek of Chaos? How could I ever forget?"

Ah, yes. The Trek of Chaos. My siblings' fond nickname for the weeklong excursions we took every two years to an exotic locale selected by Wendy—Rome, London, Stockholm, Tokyo, Budapest, Seoul. In theory, the trips were a dream. In practice, they mostly amounted to the six of us trying to pull each other's hair out in the lobbies of various Four Seasons resorts.

As she so often did when telling stories that took place "before my time," Karma turned to me specifically, providing context to a story I couldn't possibly remember. "Speedy and Wendy crammed all six of us—you included—into this one room on the top floor of the tiny hotel where we were staying in Moscow. Which would have been fine, but all the AC units up there were broken. Place was hotter than the inside of the devil's ass crack."

"Except for that one floor fan," Clarence corrected.

"Which you spent every night hogging."

"Until *you*, my loving little sister, tried to smother me in my sleep."

"And Boose howled so loudly that we covered her crib with a wool blanket we found in the closet, remember? The one with Rasputin's face on it?"

"Oh yeah. She kept shaking the crib, making it look like Rasputin was having a seizure."

"And every five minutes," Karma added, "we heard the *pshhh* of a bottle being opened, and we'd look over and find Taz holding yet another Coca-Cola he'd taken from the mini fridge—"

"—which he would only drink two sips of before he'd put it down, forget about it, and open another one five minutes later."

Karma grinned wryly. "Remember the KGB pocket watch?"

"Ho-*ly* hell." Clarence grinned. "You mean the one that Taz begged Wendy to buy him at the first stall we visited in the street market? The one about which he said, 'This is it, Mom. I need this pocket watch. It's the only thing I'll ask for this entire trip.'"

"And then"—Karma was starting to hiccup with laughter—"and then as soon as we got to the next stall and he saw all the vintage coins—"

"—he said, 'Mom'"—Clarence screwed his face up into an exaggerated pout—"'did I ever tell you I'm starting a coin collection?'"

Karma and Shelly howled with laughter.

And they were off. I already knew what the rest of dinner would entail: Karma, Clarence, Taz, and Caleb splitting the talking stick, telling stories of their childhoods. Stories of hijinks and hilarity, pranks and mischief. Stories I desperately wished I could remember.

But such is not the lot of the youngest.

To my left, a low, familiar voice spoke up, startling me. "You never answered my question."

All my muscles seized up at once. That voice. It was like a warning, like a memory. It rattled straight to my bones, shaking loose long-buried sensations that were once as familiar as the beating of my own heart.

I half turned to Manuel and cleared my throat. "Which question?"

"What's life like in the big city?"

"Oh." I mushed the prongs of my fork into the dirty end of my burger, the one that Karma's spit had landed on, leaving little imprints behind. "I mean . . . I've been there for three years now. There's a lot to tell."

"Well," he said, "why don't you just start from the beginning?"

The beginning?

Where begins the beginning?

Is it the first moment my feet hit Seventh Avenue? When Penn Station spat me out onto a yawning city block at five p.m. eastern time, the very peak of rush hour? Or does it begin even earlier, with a string of rejection letters from every college I want to attend? With watching my best friend get into Harvard? With it—the incident that happened the night before he left? With lying flat on my back in the sweaty box of my childhood bedroom every day for a week afterward, refusing to eat, refusing to pack, refusing, even, to turn on the air conditioner?

Any of those moments would have been a suitable place to start. But in the time I had spent trying to craft an answer, my siblings' conversation had died out. They were now looking at me. All of them. Waiting to hear my answer. And I found I could not begin anywhere.

Family isn't about telling the truth. It's not about starting from the real beginning. To your family, you tell the story they need to hear. And I knew that my family didn't actually care about the crowd of humanity that had swept me and my two suitcases down Seventh Avenue, about bobbing up and down in their current, gasping for air, praying I was moving in the right direction, whatever that direction might be. They didn't want to know that all I saw in my first few moments in New York City were a sea of legs and a sky bathed in concrete.

What they wanted to know was: Is it working out?

At my job, have I been promoted?

Have I been fired?

Do I regret it yet? My little indulgence? My little experiment in adulthood?

(cont'd) Birthdays are my favorite. On birthdays, everyone gets a chance to tell a story about the birthday boy or girl. The same ones resurface every year, but it doesn't matter that we've heard them all before. We still laugh just as hard.

The stories move clockwise, and eventually the entire room will turn their focus to me. My body still shakes, this time as much from nerves as delight. I want desperately to make this opportunity count. These stories . . . they aren't idle chatter. We aren't reciting the same boring details year after year. We're building an oral history. What is told will be remembered, what is not may never have happened at all. Each time we tell the story of Karma and the Great Wet Willy, we chisel it deeper into the family stone. To not participate is to have no say over the history we leave behind.

I want to come forth with something riotous, something that proves I'm as much a member of this family as anyone. But I'm just a child. I've had far fewer years and far fewer opportunities to gather stories worth telling.

And there's so much I've missed as the youngest. So many fights. So many tears and secrets and lies. Moments that form the backbone of our family history but can't be shared at a birthday. Moments that can't be shared with the youngest at all. Instead, they choose moments of laughter or moments of horror upon which we now hang our laughter like lights on a Christmas tree.

These stories create my reality. The family I think I know. I think, *This is how we were, and this is how we are.* We are a good family. We are a happy family. We are an open family. We have no secrets. Not us, with our raucous, bare-it-all family dinners. Not us, with our private island and our pile of money and our separate bedrooms. Not us.

The circle complete, everyone turns to look at me.

Silence around the table. Seven pairs of eyes.

I take a deep breath, and finally, *finally*, I tell my story.

8

FIFTH GRADE

NOBODY EXPLAINS DAD'S illness to me. Much like after Henry's death, there are whispered conversations and furtive glances in my direction when my family thinks I'm not looking. But I am. I'm looking and I'm listening. The last thing I want is for this to be a repeat of the week following the first funeral, a time in which I had to become a low-grade detective, leafing through hospital bills on Speedy's desk and searching the internet for news stories on the accident. *Not this time,* I think. This time I'll just ask.

I go to Mom first. She smiles sadly and says, "The doctors don't know, sweetie. They think it has to do with his brain."

His brain? I think. But that doesn't make any sense. His *legs* are what gave out, not his brain.

Unsatisfied, I seek another opinion, this time from the least intimidating member of the family. Taz furrows his eyebrows and asks, "Have you ever heard the term *psychosomatic*?"—an answer that makes even less sense than my mother's.

Out of options, I go to my sister. Karma stares at me for a long moment after I ask, eyes thin, as if my face were a billboard in the distance. She reaches out with one hand. "Some things just can't be explained by science, Boose." In a rare display of affection, she smooths my hair onto the side of my head. Tenderly, she says, "Some things are just a sick joke."

DESPITE MY BEST efforts, the bugbites on my legs only get worse. Each morning, I hose my body down with Off! spray. It makes me self-conscious; I'm keenly aware of the fact that I arrive to school smelling of aerosol and DEET, whatever that is.

Normally, I wouldn't care. I have no use for the opinions of my classmates—the ones I grew up with—who have seen my house and my basement and my sprawling backyard, with its private access to the beach. Whose siblings know my siblings, whose mothers know my mother. Who might like me not for who I am but what I have.

When Dad first sat Karma, Taz, Henry, and me down to talk about money, he said, "Be careful who you let into your life. There will always be those who want to take advantage of you. Don't run around making friends willy-nilly."

At the time, Karma was fourteen. I was six.

We nodded emphatically.

But now—here is a boy who knows nothing of my house or my inheritance. A wonderful, mysterious boy who mumbles wonderful, mysterious words. Close enough to hear but too far to understand. Someone to whom I can speak freely, even if he doesn't want to hear what I have to say. And I find that, for the first time ever, I care. I care about my appearance and the fact that I probably smell like mosquito repellant.

Every day after the last bell rings, I follow Manuel outside. I prattle away, continuing whatever story I left off at the end of class. He walks studiously forward, never telling me to shut up or go away, but never acknowledging my existence, either.

I follow him all the way to the carpool lane. A sleek black sedan waits for him. The windows are tinted. I can't see who's driving. He climbs in the back door and slams it shut, but the back window is open, so I keep talking. He rolls it up slowly. I keep talking, keep telling my story, right up until the glass meets the ceiling.

The next morning, I pick up right where I left off.

FOR ANY OTHER marriage, this would probably be the end. Losing your son to the Great Beyond and your husband to a wheelchair in just a few months? Nail in coffin; signatures on stiff legal paper. But not Wendy Beck.

Not only does Dad's illness not push him and Mom to divorce—it saves them.

Mom quits all her side hustles: resigns from boards, tastefully turns down invitations, pulls her name from the ballot for the Board of Education. Nobody faults her; they see us around town, our strange, grieving clan—three children, one beautiful wife, one aging husband. A man whose face, upon further inspection, isn't actually old but whose skin bears early wrinkles, as if sagging beneath the weight of something immense—a man on the cusp of age, drawing closer every day. We move through life together, our clan, and the community watches. At Christmas Eve service. In line at the grocery store. In the aisles of Barnes & Noble. At every theater performance and soccer game and orchestra concert I'm forced to attend. The adult worlds in which I pass my youth. At every one, Mom tends to Dad. Pushes his wheelchair. Marches right into the public bathrooms with him. Absorbs his pain, letting it make her stronger. Once, a condescending soccer dad remarks on how "noble" it is of my mother to stay married to "a cripple."

She punches him in the nose.

Caring for Dad gives her strength. Eventually, she doesn't just push his wheelchair through the grocery store parking lot; she runs behind it like a child, Speedy clutching a six-pack of black cherry soda in his lap, hollering, "Faster!" The rest of us pant close behind. Everyone on the sidewalk—mothers carrying plastic bags, crotchety old men instructing boys in blue aprons on how to carry plastic bags—stares like they're watching a clutch of chickens flapping across the lot.

You wouldn't know it from his gruff exterior, but Speedy is fiercely devoted to my mom. Fiercely. As if she's his first love, not his third. As if she's the only thing keeping him alive.

And maybe she is.

The illness *does* take its toll on my parents' marriage, as all illnesses do. It's not as if they're so deeply, deeply in love that divorce is unthinkable. No—they stay together for the Family, that strange concept created as much by the collective belief in a thing's existence as by the thing itself.

MY MOMENT ARRIVES a month after Manuel does. It's recess. He is doing what he always does: roaming around the edge of the field, muttering to himself, and hitting things with a stick. I'm doing what I always do, monopolizing the swing set and spying on Manuel.

Some of the kids nearby must hear him. As I watch, the boys— three of them, large, round like overripe pears—approach Manuel and start to circle.

"Hoe-la, Juan."

"Whatcha doin' this far away from Mexico?"

Manuel ignores them.

"Where're your tacos? Mama didn't pack none?"

Nothing scares a bully more than something they don't understand.

"Not gonna say hi back?"

"What's the matter, no speak-o English?"

"Nah. Look at his face. Juan here doesn't understand a goddamn word."

As they speak, my temperature rises. It doesn't feel like anger; it feels like foresight. The more they say to Manuel—the more abusive and hateful their words become—the more clearly I see my future. I see why I spent the last month browsing Spanish slang websites, why I listened so carefully to the things Manuel whispered during class. I see the things I have gathered, and I see what to do with them.

At the height of the swing's arc, I leap. I soar through the air and land with both feet in the woodchips, a wild splash of shaved earth. I don't even use my hands to steady myself. I straighten up and march toward the bullies. They're still circling Manuel, drawing closer, growling with their juvenile ignorance. I bend low as I approach the edge of the field. Just before the woodchips turn to grass, I scoop two handfuls into my fists. Don't even pause in my strides, just dig both hands into the ground midstep and keep walking, the movement smooth as an outfielder.

"*¡Oye!*" I yell, winding up both fists. "*¡Hijos de puta!*"

All three boys turn. As they do, I release my fists and launch two jets of wood straight into their faces.

"*¡Cabrones! ¡Hijos de puta!*" I yell every phrase I remember reading online. "*¡Ándate a la mierda! ¡Cago en tu leche!*"

They turn and flee, all of them, three overripe pears waddling in terror across the field.

I keep hollering, recycling phrases I already used and sprinkling in a few more. "*¡Chúpame la peña! ¡Béisbol! ¡Mariposa!*" I don't really know what I'm saying. I don't care. It feels so good to yell.

When they retreat far enough, I turn to Manuel.

I'm not sure what I expect to see on his face. Gratitude? Anger? I find neither. Instead, I see the same thing I always do: that blank wall. That portrait of incomprehension. The one I've seen every day for a month. Eyes squinted, lips slightly ajar. A face of mahogany concrete.

Then it cracks, all of it, and his face spreads into a grin wide enough to hold every drop of water in Lake Michigan.

ONCE THE SEAL of our friendship breaks, we become inseparable. At recess, rather than partake in the twisted *Lord of the Flies*–style politics of the rest of the kids, we walk. We carve massive circles around the playground, and as we walk, we talk. It's no longer just me talking. Manuel joins, too. And once he does, he has a lot to say—both in English and in his native language.

Our voices run at a dead sprint. He calls me Beck, and I call him Valde. We make jokes, tell stories. The stories never reach their conclusions, because some detail in them reminds us of another story and another and another, until we veer so far off track we can barely see the place we began. But we circle back, always saying, *Now, what were we talking about?* And we laugh at ourselves—breathless, mystified chuckles—baffled by our inability to stay on subject, awed by the great distance we traveled in doing so.

We have so much to tell each other. Two childhoods spent on different continents. Ten years of stories and details. We speak with this frantic energy, as if we're both keenly aware of the finite nature of new friendship. As if desperate to cram as much of ourselves into each other's ears as possible. *This is who I am!* we seem to say. *Can you see me? Can you see?*

WE START RIDING the bus together. It picks me up first. When I get on, I run straight to the last seat. At Manuel's stop, I stand. I catch his eye the minute he gets on. It isn't necessary, of course; he knows where to find me. But I do it anyway. I like the way his eyes expand

and brighten when he sees me, just a little, just around the edges. It's the best part of my morning.

He runs to the back, and I step out to let him scoot in. The bus rumbles toward school, its wheels catching every bump, every crevice. With each bounce, our stomachs plummet in that terrifying way that tells us we're alive.

9

AFTER DINNER, I took my usual place washing dishes at the left-hand kitchen sink. (We had two of them, of course, because what wealthy family can get by with only one sink?) My feet carried me automatically there, as if three days had passed since I last visited the island, not three years.

Unfortunately, I didn't consider the fact that the same could be said for Manuel.

Twenty seconds after I arrived at the sink to wash, he appeared at my side, rag in hand, ready to dry.

"Hi," he said, one side of his mouth curving up into a tentative smile.

"Uh," I said eloquently back.

He held up the rag. "Shall we?"

"I should . . ." I glanced around the kitchen, searching for a way out. It appeared to me in the form of two unopened cans of baked beans. I snatched them off the counter and waved them in Manny's face. "Put these away!"

Then I turned around and sprinted toward the pantry before I could hear his response.

The pantry was a huge L-shaped room lined floor-to-ceiling with shelves of canned and dried goods. Sacks of flour sat in one corner. Crates of wine in another. Around the bend and just out of sight were not one but *three* freezers, in which we kept all manner of frozen meats and vegetables and ice cream. The giant room was just another reminder of how excessive my family could be.

I slipped quietly inside and darted over to the left-hand wall, sliding the cans onto a free shelf. Exhaling softly, I stepped forward and laid my forehead on a cushion of cereal spines. It was only then, half-ready to fall asleep upright with nothing but a box of Rice Chex for a pillow, that I heard my sister's voice.

". . . that you have to tell her eventually," Karma was saying, her voice hushed. From the sound of it, she was just around the bend, standing in front of the freezers. "She has a right to know."

"Oh, honey, I don't know," came the response. It was my mother's voice, speaking at full volume—though she probably thought she was whispering. "We only just got her back."

I stiffened, my eyes flying open. *Are they talking about me?*

Karma snorted. "We're on an *island*, Mom. What's she going to do, swim back to New York?"

Yep. Definitely me.

"That's not the point," Mom insisted. "I've worked so hard to make this a perfect week for Taron and Helene. Why do you want to spoil that with meaningless drama?"

"Meaningless drama," Karma repeated flatly. I could just picture her face: eyebrows raised, lips pursed, staring at Wendy with the bemused disdain she reserved only for incompetent bakery interns and our mother. "I think Caleb would take serious offense to that."

Caleb? What the hell were they talking about?

"This isn't about Caleb. It's about making sure that everyone has a nice time up here. And we can't go telling Eliot something like this right after she got here."

"But everyone *else* knows," Karma said. "How do you think she'll feel when she finds out that she was the last one to know?"

Wendy sniffed. "She's the one who chose to disconnect from our family."

"I know, but—"

"Catherine," said Mom, and I didn't have to see Karma to know she was wincing. She *hated* her real name. "Please. Let's just keep things nice this week, okay? I don't want to spoil Eliot's time here with bad news. You know how she is."

"What the hell does *that* mean?"

"Oh, don't give me that look, Catherine. I'm just stating a fact: Eliot isn't like you and the others. You're all so strong and hard-headed. But Eliot is quieter. More emotional. She's . . ."

"Weak," said Karma. "That's what you were going to say. She's weak."

"You don't have to be so *crass* about it," said our mom. "I'm just being honest, since you won't. We need to protect her. We only just got her back, and I don't want . . ."

But I didn't stick around to hear the rest of their discussion. I'd heard enough. I'd heard *more* than enough. I turned around and slipped quietly out the pantry door before either of them even knew I was there.

HAVE YOU HEARD of an *Irish exit*? That's what it's called when someone slips out the back door without saying goodbye. That's what Henry did. That's how he exited life. So that's what I do, too. In stressful situations or at events where I'm no longer enjoying myself, I say I have to go to the bathroom and slip out the door when no one is watching. It saves me from those painful conversations, the ones no one wants to have—where the host has to pretend they care that you, one guest in a dozen, are leaving, and the drunkest ones in the group try to convince you to stay, and you have to think of thirty different polite ways to say no. Nobody has thirty different polite ways to say no. It's torture. So I avoid the whole thing. It's brilliant. The technique has saved me countless times in New York—from dull conversations, from two a.m. tequila shots, from coworkers' drunk college roommates. It's my move.

Irish twins, Irish exits.

While everyone else set up for a game of poker, I made my Irish exit. Just as I placed my hand on the back doorknob, however, I made the mistake of peering over my shoulder.

Which is how I came to lock eyes with Manuel.

He was seated at the card table, staring right at me. I froze. His eyes were narrowed dangerously. He knew exactly what I was doing, and I saw the entire ACCA pass across his face. I swear to God, I did.

ACCA is another copywriting template. It stands for Awareness—Comprehension—Conviction—Action. I learned the template after *it, that* night, during the month of feverish copywriting research that followed. In the most basic sense, ACCA is a way to get a new customer from "What is this thing?" to "I need this Self-Mixing Pocket Margarita® more badly than I've ever needed anything in my life."

The technique works as follows:

1. AWARENESS of product/service
2. COMPREHENSION of said product/service (This is key: lots of advertisers assume you can drop something brand-new in front of a consumer without explanation and the consumer will want it. Then they wonder why sales in their Shopify account hover just above zero.)
3. CONVICTION that the consumer needs *this particular* product/service

4. ACTION—Open your wallet and give us your money.
    Please.

Now. Let's pretend for a second that Manuel is a new product/
service. Better yet—Manuel is an *old* product/service that recently
released an updated edition. Now let's perform an ACCA.

AWARENESS:	Introducing: the fully upgraded Manuel® 2.0!
COMPREHENSION:	The Manuel® 2.0 is the very latest in cosmic justice technology. Built with all the features you love about the original Manuel®, the 2.0 also includes souped-up anger and the ability to hold a grudge.
CONVICTION:	You are not forgiven. You are not forgiven, and your best friend is not here to celebrate your brother. He's here to give you the punishment you deserve.
ACTION:	The only way to make it through this week alive is to turn away. Turn away and walk out the door.

Tearing my burning cheeks away from his gaze, I slipped out the
back door and darted across the patio. I was making for the stairs
that led from the patio down to the rocks below. The whole way
there, words from the conversation between Karma and my mom
echoed through my mind:

She's weak. That's what you were going to say.

I'm just being honest.

The words bounced like sharp-edged rocks about the corners of my mind, ricocheting off its soft, fleshy interior, leaving behind little gashes and trickling blood.

I'd been so foolish. So unbelievably stupid and naive. It didn't matter that I'd moved to New York by myself, that I'd gotten a job, that I'd never once asked for help. To them, I would always be sensitive, emotional Eliot. The baby.

She's weak.

Just as I reached the top of the stairs, a small, shadowy figure stepped in front of me, blocking the way down.

I jerked backward. "What the—"

"What the hell is going on with you and Manuel?" Karma asked. She was tiny but terrifying in the shifting shadows cast by the lights inside the cabin.

"Nothing is—"

She advanced, pointing a finger in my face. "Don't *nothing* me, Eliot Beck. He's your best friend, and the two of you are acting like estranged cousins."

I rubbed at my forehead, wondering if the cereal boxes left a crease. "I mean . . . it's been a long time since we've seen each other. Things are—"

"Is that so?" Karma crossed her hands in front of her chest. "How long, exactly? Tell me—have you visited him in Boston even once?"

I shuffled backward. "That's none of your business."

"*Bullshit* it's not my business."

"It's not," I snapped. I could feel my temper slipping away—the first time it had done so in almost three years. "This is *my* friendship, not yours. Maybe try butting out, for once."

Karma's dark eyes narrowed. "Manny might be your friend, but he's like a brother to me. He's part of this family, and I reserve every right to ask what the hell is going on with my family." She paused. "And, yes, by the way. To answer your earlier question. We do text."

I blinked. "What?"

"The first time was just a few months into his freshman year. He wanted to know if I'd heard from you since you got to U of M. Imagine my surprise to learn that your best friend didn't even know *where you lived.*"

My temper strained at its ever-fraying leash. "I'm not having this conversation with you." I pushed past my sister and started down the stairs.

"Have you found a therapist in New York, Eliot?"

I paused halfway to the bottom. "What does that have to do with anything?"

"Just answer the question."

I turned all the way around. "Yes. I have a therapist in New York."

"Good."

"Yeah. *Good.*" I crossed my arms over my chest. "Because God forbid batshit-crazy Boose goes off the rails again."

"That's not what I'm saying, and you know it."

"Do I? Then, what *are* you saying?"

"I'm saying . . ." She trailed off, looking out at the lake. To my surprise, all the aggression was gone from her face. "It's just . . . you're so far away now, Eliot. I don't know how to make sure you're okay."

"I'm fine."

She looked back at me. "You're my little sister."

"I'm *fine.*"

"Okay. I'm sorry. It's just . . ." She scratched behind one ear. "It was scary, you know?"

"When I moved to New York?"

"No, no. I meant . . . when Mom and Dad first told us about your OCD. It was scary."

I raised my eyebrows. "It was?"

"Yes. Not because we were scared *of* you," she said quickly. I understood what she meant. My siblings did this often: switch to *we* without saying what they really meant, which was *everyone in the family but you.* "It was scary because we had no clue. Truly. None. You were always the calm child. Serious. Mature. Never yelled, never got your feathers ruffled. After . . . you know . . ." She swallowed. "After Henry died, you didn't even cry."

My fingernails dug into my palms.

"And to find out that, all that time, you were suffering so badly on the inside. It . . . it nearly broke Mom and Dad. God . . . it nearly broke *me.*"

"Yeah, well," I said flatly. "Good thing that's all over now."

"Is it, though?" Karma asked, taking a step forward. Her face was oddly pleading. "Because you can tell me, you know. If you aren't as okay as you're pretending to be. You can tell me."

"Can I? Or would that just make me look *weak*?" I snapped before I could stop myself. "Oh, wait." I laughed harshly. "I forgot. I already do."

Shock flashed over my sister's face.

Before she could respond, I spun around and jogged the rest of the way down to the rolling waves of granite.

"Eliot, wait—"

I ignored her, jogging sideways down the hill. The rocks sloped down a good thirty feet, flattening out to a long pebble beach. When I reached the bottom, the pebbles wobbled and crunched beneath my shoes. At the end of the beach was a secluded entrance to the boardwalk. If I made it there, I'd be home free.

But halfway across the beach, a hand hooked around on my elbow and jerked my body backward.

"Hey!" I said, spinning around. "I told you I—"

I swallowed the rest of the sentence. It wasn't Karma behind me.

A black hole of a face towered above me, unspeakably handsome features blotted out by the glare of the light shining from Sunny Sunday's windows.

"Stop avoiding me," Manuel said. The words floated up from the black pit, flat and steady like a metronome. Light wrapped around his head like a halo.

"I'm not avoiding you." I tried to yank my arm back, but he held on. "I'm just tired."

"Right. I'd be tired, too, if I had spent the last three years running away from everyone who loves me."

"I didn't *run*." (Running was exactly what I did.)

"What did you do, then?"

"I grew up," I said. "Got a job and an apartment. I made a new life, all by myself. Maturity. Adulthood. Independence."

"You mean solitude."

"I like being alone."

"Bullshit."

"Excuse me?"

"Bull. Shit." He leaned in close. "I know you, Eliot. You hate being alone."

"You haven't seen me in three years. You don't know what I hate."

"Don't know what you hate." He laughed. His breath was warm and sweet. Red wine and summer air. "Eliot Beck. My best friend for a decade. I don't know what she hates. Right." He leaned even closer. That empty hole where his face should be. "Eliot Beck hates being alone. Eliot Beck called me every day after school for eight years because she had too much to say, too much that couldn't wait until tomorrow morning. Eliot Beck begged me to sneak onto the roof at sleepovers, even when I didn't want to. Eliot Beck talked my ear off, sunup to sundown, and a little after that, too. Right up until she passed out. Said she was afraid of the dark. But I knew the truth. She wasn't afraid of the dark; she was afraid of the emptiness that comes with it."

I stepped back, his words so accurate they felt like a slap across the face. "I don't even know why you're here."

"You know exactly why I'm here."

"Right," I said. "For revenge. Because I disappeared, and you hate me for it."

"Is that really what you think?"

"Yes. I'm not stupid. And I don't even blame you, okay? I've been a bad friend. A horrible friend. But . . . there are things you don't understand, Manuel. Reasons I had to leave. I couldn't . . ." I inhaled. I couldn't say more. Not without telling him everything. "It's okay if you hate me. Really."

For a small eternity, Manuel was silent. Then, quietly: "I don't hate you, Eliot."

I paused. "You don't?"

"No."

"Well, you should."

"Should I." He said it flatly. No question mark.

"Yes. *You have no idea how much you should hate me.*

I am not a good person.

I looked out at the waves. I wished suddenly that I were out there in the chop, not swimming, not skiing, not floating in a tube—just bobbing, letting the waves toss me about like a buoy. Hollow, light as air, no effort needed to stay afloat.

"You know," said Manuel. "You can be really self-centered sometimes."

I turned back to him. "Excuse me?"

"I'm not criticizing you. I'm just stating a fact. You spend a lot of time in your own head."

"You more than anyone should know that . . ."

"I know, I know. The OCD. It traps you up there. I know. But Karma and I both agree—"

"That's the other thing." I kicked a loose rock. "Since when are you and Karma so close? Since when does she know about your exams and girl problems and parties at the Spree?"

"The Spee."

"Whatever."

"Right. Whatever. *Whatever* that you don't know the name of the place I spend every weekend. *Whatever* that you don't know anything about my life whatsoever." Manuel bent over. Swiped up a handful of pebbles, sifted through them. Let the round ones trickle back through his fingers, leaving only the flattest. "Did you know," he said, "that you haven't even asked me about my parents yet?"

The stones lie belly-up on his palm, thick and dark, like tattoos.

"Yes, I . . ." But then I stopped, because he was right. I hadn't. "Oh."

As I stared at the rocks, I remembered a different moment on this beach. A moment from when Henry was still alive. Dad showed us how to check skipping stones for bumps and ridges, then spin them just so. His flew like frisbees and bounced once, twice, three, four, five, six, *seven* times before tumbling gracefully into the water. Henry and I copied his form. With a few tries, my brother managed two or three skips. I couldn't get even one.

I said, "How are they, then?"

"Busy."

I waited for more.

When he said nothing else, I asked, "Have you ever considered that the reason I don't ask you about your parents is that when I do, you give me cryptic answers like that? Answers that make it seem like you have no interest in talking about them?"

He ignored me. He'd found the rock he wanted and was turning it over in his fingers. "Is it really that hard to believe that I'm close with Karma?" he asked. "I mean—God. I didn't *ask* to be adopted into this family. You basically forced it onto me. So sue me for wanting to stay in touch."

"But you *have* a family."

"Don't make me laugh."

"I'm serious. You have parents. You have Valentina." I almost sounded like I was pleading. "You have ten thousand aunts and uncles and *primos* in Colombia. That's your family. That's your *real family*. Not us."

I was lying. Flagrantly. Violently. Manuel's parents are best friends. Their lives are each other; their son is a mildly entertaining afterthought. I know this fact better than anyone. He *knows* I know.

"And what about you, huh?" Manuel asked. "Independent Eliot, all alone in her apartment. How does that feel, really? Does it feel good? Or does it feel like nothing at all?"

"You have no idea what you're talking about."

"Don't I? You used to be *fun*, Eliot. You used to drag me to parties and football games and all that other American bullshit I had no interest in doing. That was *your* idea. And now what? What do you do in New York? Anything? Do you even have friends?"

"Of course I have friends."

"Oh, really? Name one."

His words cut dangerously close to truth. In New York, the only people I go out with are my coworkers, and only when dragged.

They're a different breed, my coworkers—the type of pseudo adults who snorted Xanax off their parents' coffee tables in high school. They grew up in New York or Connecticut. They eat sixteen-dollar bowls of rice for lunch and their principal interest is which bar they went to the weekend before. They're named Matt, Matt, or Matt. I tried eating with them my first two weeks on the job, but I learned quickly to steer clear. Their conversations, their competitions, the judgment and insecurity—the breakroom fogs up with it. It gathers in sweaty droplets at the lip of my water bottle. It chokes me. Leaves me with nothing to say. In high school, I ate lunch with the same person every single day. We said everything to each other, or we said nothing. It didn't matter. But not in New York. In New

York, nothing that came out of my mouth sounded like me. My voice was too loud, my words too juvenile. Better not to risk it. Better to stare wordlessly at the neon light of the vending machine and never open my mouth, not once.

So, no. I didn't have many friends in New York. But I wasn't going to tell Manuel that.

I hardened my voice, tried to keep it from shaking. "I hurt you, Manuel. I hurt you as hard as I possibly could. I ignored your calls. I ignored your texts. I pretended you didn't exist for three whole years. Yet here you are. And you can pretend all you want not to be angry with me, but you are. I know you are."

His eyes turned to almond flames.

"What do you want me to say, Eliot?" He stepped closer. "Do you really want to know how much it broke me when you cut me out of your life? Do you want me to tell you how I was depressed for months? How I had to hide from my roommates, to put on flip-flops and a bathrobe and walk down the hall to the communal bathroom just so I could sob my stupid, foolish, pathetic eyes out? How I ran to your sister for comfort because she was the closest thing I had to you?"

No. I didn't want to hear it.

"Or maybe you'd rather hear about how *fun* college is. All the friends I've made. The parties I've been to, the girls I've fucked. Maybe that's what you want to hear." He stepped back. His large frame wobbled. "You know what? So what if I'm here for revenge, huh? Shouldn't I be? Don't I deserve it, after all this time?"

"You're drunk."

"Maybe I am. But am I wrong?"

I said nothing.

"That's what I thought," he said. "You can avoid me for now, Eliot, but not forever."

"You're right," I said, the words equal parts anger and slippery desperation. "You *should* hate me. Okay? In fact you shouldn't even *trust* me. I've given you no reason to. So just stop. Stop talking to me. Stop trusting me. Trust me, it's better that way."

Manuel turned and walked away, an upright ship sailing slowly into the night.

I stumbled up onto the boardwalk. Rounded the oak tree and started down the other side of the hill. By then, we'd been in Sunny Sunday for hours, leaving the boardwalk wide open and available for spi˙˙rs to build their webs.

This island is covered in spiders. They swing from tree trunks, dangle below branches, perch in wait on webs as thick as wool. Orb weavers. Sheet weavers. Wolf spiders. Cellar spiders. Long bellied, star bellied. Hammock, garden, grass, hacklemesh, and—of course—the ever-present daddy longlegs. They build cobwebs and hide little yellow sacs filled with thousands of unhatched babies in places you don't expect to find them—inside wakeboard gloves or between the folds of a wet towel. They coat this island, every inch of it. There's no nook into which they cannot creep.

The winding path of the boardwalk, which zigs between boulders and zags around bushy trees, is the perfect place for spiders to build cobwebs. While the island sleeps, the spiders weave—just a strand at a time, thin as fishing line, pulled tight across the boardwalk. Sticky, silky, invisible to the naked eye. A thousand trip wires waiting for the unlucky first to rise.

They truly outdid themselves, that night. Didn't settle for a few isolated embellishments. They decorated the whole damn thing. Door-to-door security. I kept running—down the narrow boardwalk, through the tunnels of trees, around the edge of the lake, gathering cobwebs the whole way.

Was Manuel right? Was keeping a secret impossible when you were keeping it from a person who knows you better than you know yourself? Was it all going to come spilling out, dragged by the sheer gravity of closeness, despite my best efforts, despite the fact that telling him would almost certainly sever him from my life forever? Would earn me nothing but his disgust, his revulsion. Would perhaps even end with him reporting me to the police.

That was why I did what I did. Why I cut myself off from my family and best friend. Because seeing them brought me back to my old life, to the self-torture and self-loathing I worked so hard to eliminate. To the person I finally *stopped* being when I moved to New York.

Work was my saving grace. Goals and schedules and assignments turned in far too early—those were the branches to which I clung, white-knuckled, until at last they dragged me free of the river in which I had for so long been drowning.

I knew what I had to do this week: I had to plaster a smile on my face, to show my family just how *A-okay* I really was. Not only to prove that adulthood was going *just swell* for me—that I'd earned my spot with the grown-ups—but to protect myself, too. To shield me from my Worries. Because they might have been silent for now, but their memory remained; they lingered at the edges of my consciousness, like the little flare-up of obsession over a piece of spit at dinner, a silent reminder of the power they once held over me. A voice that could, at any moment, come roaring back to life.

And I was afraid that if it did, this time it would be for good. That if my family discovered just how broken I was, there would be no putting me back together.

Henry always told me not to keep secrets. "You can hide it from everyone else," he'd said, "but not me. We're practically twins, remember? We're connected. Anything that passes through your mind passes through mine, too."

But wait, I realized. That quote—that *couldn't* have been Henry. An eleven-year-old would never say something like that. Even a brilliant eleven-year-old. Or would he? Was he truly that exceptional? Or did Manuel say that to me much later on?

No. *No, no, no.* It was happening again. The confusion. That infuriating, torturous defect of mind. The one that only happened with Manuel and Henry.

It had been a problem as long as I could remember, but in the past three years, it had gotten worse. Sometimes, my memory replaced one boy with the other. Sometimes they appeared together, one being, a messed-up mixture of body parts, blended until I couldn't tell if the boy in my memory was my best friend or a ghost of the brother who once was the same. I shook my head, a dog trying to dry its fur of rain.

My cabin for the week was Little Lies. (If you can't tell, Speedy is a big folk music fan. All the cabins are named after songs by his favorites—"Sunny Sunday" by Joni Mitchell, "Little Lies" by Fleetwood Mac, "Tangled up in Blue" by Bob Dylan, etc. The soundtrack to his drug-fueled past life.) With just one bedroom, one bathroom, and a small screened-in porch facing out toward the water, it's the smallest cabin on the island.

Outside Little Lies, I stopped and bent to gather my breath. It was only then, stooped over my body, staring at nothing, that I heard the paradox in what I'd said to Manuel.

Stop trusting me. Trust me.

I sighed.

When I straightened up, I spread my arms to the trees. "Ladies and gentlemen," I said, "I give you: the Copywriter."

10

FIFTH GRADE

I MIGHT HAVE a new best friend. Mom might be out of her bedroom. But the Worries don't leave. Not by a long shot.

I *need* evidence that I'm not actually a bad person. During class or at the dinner table or in moments of quiet, I root through my past. Look for lies and crimes and rules broken. Where one dead body is buried, there's sure to be more.

As soon as I start digging, I find them everywhere. *Everywhere.* When I cheated off Hailey Richman's spelling test in second grade. When I stole a Twix bar from the grocery checkout aisle. When I skipped soccer practice to eat Snickers bars in the rec center lobby until my stomach hurt. They're all there, waiting to be found.

It's hard to believe, actually. Hard to believe I spent ten years beneath the weight of these crimes and felt no guilt. None at all. What's wrong with me? How did I live with myself? How did I wake every day and roll out of bed and brush my teeth and smile at myself in the mirror and think I wasn't a monster?

In the end, it's too much. I need relief. I need someone to absolve me of my guilt. So I do the only thing I can think to do: I confess.

"Dad," I say during my first confession. We're out on Lake Michigan in the boat we keep in Chicago. He's teaching me to drive. But since I'm only ten, it's mostly an excuse for him to buzz around in big circles for no reason. "I did something bad."

"What?" he yells. The boat is a Boston Whaler. Its engines are thunderous, and it has no roof.

"I DID SOMETHING BAD."

He eases back the throttle. The boat slows and its wake builds, thickening into long hills that lift the water we leave behind. When we come to a stop, the waves overtake us. The boat rolls about in the chop.

Speedy lifts me from his lap and places me on the spotter's bench. He looks me squarely in the face. His eyes are withdrawn, as if expecting pain. "What are you talking about, Eliot?"

I swallow. Try not to look away. "Two years ago . . . um . . ." Admitting to past wrongdoing is humiliating, but for some reason, admitting to *long*-past wrongdoing, the likes of which you already got away with, is worse. "Two years ago, you dropped me off at soccer practice."

He blinks. "Yes . . . which time? I did that three times a week."

"I don't remember. Just . . . one time. One time, you dropped me off at soccer practice, and then you picked me up afterward."

"Okay . . ."

"And I acted like it was just any other day, like I'd gone out to the field and practiced and come back and met you in the parking lot. And then we went home and had dinner and I never said anything—to you or to Mom. When you asked me how practice was, I said good, or something. But that wasn't the truth." I'm speaking too much. Babbling, really. But they're comforting, the extra words. Like a cushion for the coming fall. I stuff my sentences with as many as I can—a technique I'll use thousands of times in the future. "The truth is that I never went to practice at all. I skipped. You know the lounge in the rec center, the one with the TV and the couches and the vending machines? Well, I sat in that lounge, and I bought myself a bunch of Snickers bars, and I ate Snickers bars and watched *Johnny Bravo* for two hours. Then I went out to the parking lot and got in your car and pretended I went to practice."

I catch my breath. Dad stares at me, his mouth slightly agape.

I've never gotten in serious trouble with my parents. There were little things, of course. White lies and childish mistakes. But nothing close to the drop-everything-and-scream fights I'd witnessed between them and my other siblings. I saw it when Karma came home three hours past curfew. I saw it when Clarence drank too much at Thanksgiving and called Mom an *ignorant child*. Even Taz—perfect Taz—I saw it when he threw a baseball into the family portrait that hangs over the fireplace, sending it to the floor in a great spray of glass and metal. I saw all of it, and let me tell you—an angry Speedy is a terrifying Speedy. And I have officially thrown myself before the fire.

I look down. I wait. The flames, when they come, will be painful. I can only pray their heat will be strong enough to burn my guilt away.

Then, from the driver's seat, my father starts to laugh.

SPEEDY BECOMES MY judge and jury. In the course of just a few weeks, I confess no less than twenty or thirty crimes to him. Each time, he ruffles my hair awkwardly and tells me not to worry. "You're a good kid, Eliot. A good kid."

A good kid? I want to scream. *Haven't you been listening?*

AS HARD AS it is to believe, although I've gone to pieces on the inside, on the outside, life continues as normal. I eat eggs in the breakfast nook. I watch *Hannah Montana* on the Big Blue Couch. I puzzle out the nuances of algebra with Manuel, who has turned out to be almost embarrassingly brilliant. Every day, I crane my neck to catch a glimpse of his worksheets and find he's five or six problems ahead of me.

"*Oye*," I whisper. "How the hell do you do that?"

ONCE I EXHAUST the list of past lies to apologize for, you'd think the Worries would go away. But they don't. They just change shape.

It's Mile Day in gym class, a weekly event in which the entire fifth grade class is forced to run four times around cones spaced eight hundred meters in circumference. I'm behind Caroline Whittler, a girl I've known since kindergarten who once told me that a blow job is when a boy sticks his penis into an air duct. But I'm not thinking about that story as I follow her around the cones. I'm just spacing out, staring at her back. Staring at her butt. It's a nice butt, I think. All bouncy and round.

Then I stop.

Not running—I stop my train of thought.

Oh my God, I realize. *You just admired Caroline Whittler's butt. Are you a lesbian?*

No, I tell myself. I don't *think* so . . . I mean—no. Of course not.

But are you sure?

No. Look. I'll prove it. I'll just check a few parts of my body to make sure I don't feel any attraction to her. I'll check my gut . . . feels a little tight, like it does when I have a crush, but it's not the same kind of tight. It's not all deep and fuzzy. Now I'll check down *there*, the naughty place, the one that *truly* dictates to whom you are attracted, and surely I'll find nothing, only emptiness, only calm . . .

But then . . .

Oh God.

What was that?

Was that a . . . pulse? An unbidden clench of the muscles, like the kind that happens inside me when I rub my pelvis against a pillow in just the right way for just the right amount of time?

Yes. Yes, it was. That was a pulse.

But is it the *same* kind of pulse, or is it something different? Is it . . . *Shit*. There's another one.

No. Eliot. Stop. Stop thinking about that region.

But I can't, because there's another. And another. Why aren't they stopping?

That's it, my mind whispers. *That pulse? That's arousal. That's all the proof you need.*

But I'm not gay.

Are you sure about that?

Well . . . I've only ever had crushes on boys.

But how can you argue with your body?

Well . . .

Listen to that pulse. It's telling you something.

It's too late. I know it's too late. The possibility of me being a lesbian has entered my mind, and once that happens, it's over. I'll never be able to unthink it. It's just like remembering a past lie; I'll return to this moment, this pulse, over and over. It doesn't matter that I've never felt even remotely attracted to a woman before. It doesn't matter that being gay is fine, that my sister is gay, that she would be thrilled if I came out, too. In truth, *I* have no problem with the idea of being gay. What bothers me—what I come back to over and over and over again—is that I know I'm *not* gay. I know that, one day, I want to marry a man. But that pulse—that one, insignificant yet somehow more significant than anything else in the world, pulse—it has planted a seed of doubt in my mind. And that seed will grow. It will grow lips and teeth and a jawline. It will argue with me. It will send me in circles. Awful, torturous circles. I will never know the truth. I will never know my own sexuality. What matters is that pulse. I can tell myself I'm straight, but my body says otherwise.

FOR SEVERAL WEEKS, I argue with myself over whether or not I'm a lesbian. Every time I see an attractive girl, I check for that pulse, for that sign of arousal. And every time, I find it.

AT THIS POINT, the words *mental illness* do not exist in my vocabulary. Illness is there, certainly, but only in the context of strep throat or the flu or the horrifying wrinkled paper bag of a woman they wheeled into the school auditorium to talk to our health class about cancer. To me, thoughts can't be an illness. Illness implies that the change within you is not your fault. That it's foreign. Invasive. That an army of cells broke in and started messing with your insides. That—and this is key, this is the most important part of all—with the right drugs, it will go away.

But this isn't an illness. This can't be cured with a few hugs and a capful of pink goo. This is me. Every thought, no matter how bizarre, no matter how disturbing—I create it. It comes from me. It's made of me. Your thoughts are the mental manifestation of what you look like inside. Rotten thoughts? Rotten insides.

AT THIS POINT, I stop confessing to Speedy. How can I? *Dad, is it okay that I might be a lesbian, even though I don't want to be, even though I don't think I am, really, but still I might be because I felt this thing downstairs, and . . .* No. Not happening. And the relief a confession brings is temporary, anyway. There will always be something new. I see that now. Better to just write it down in my journal. To confess to the nonjudgmental silence of an empty page.

Dad watches me from a distance for a long time, waiting to see whether I'll approach him with a new confession. When I don't, I can't tell if he's disappointed or relieved.

I MEET MANUEL'S parents for the first time early one Sunday evening, a few weeks into our friendship. They aren't home often, but that night is an exception.

Cena at the Valdecasases' is nothing like dinner at the Becks'. Rather than laying everything out in a buffet and letting us serve ourselves, Manuel's nanny, Valentina, arranges a feast right in the center of the table—*buñuelos* and arepas and plantains and pitchers filled with fresh-squeezed juice, beautiful tangles of color I've never seen before—and then we sit down together, all of us, me and Manuel and Valentina and Señor and Señora, but "Oh, no, Eliot, *por favor*, call me Che, and me Juli, *sí sí, por favor*, we insist." Then we fold our hands and our heads, and Che says a prayer in Spanish, and even though I can't understand his words, I understand that this, too, is different than the hollow demonstrations of Christianity my siblings and I giggle through after we've already finished eating. This is what faith sounds like. Real faith. Then the prayer is over, and the Valdecasas family returns to the realm of the living and passes me the first dish.

And the food—well. There's no way to describe eating home-made Colombian food for the very first time. Especially after a decade of Wendy Beck's home cooking. How do you describe the first time you get drunk? The first time you fall in love? And I am in love. I'm in love with the newness of it all. I've never eaten a tostada or drank coffee after dinner or called adults by their first name. It's all so new, so wonderful.

So wonderful, in fact, that it quiets the endless spiral, the ever-present flap of moths' wings wreaking havoc inside my mind. Just for a moment, but I'll take every moment I can get.

Che and Juli dominate the conversation. They're best friends, a fact that becomes clear almost instantly. This, too, is new to me. I'm a child with parents who rarely display affection, who tell their children they love them but never seem to tell each other. I never found that fact strange. Not until I met Che and Juli.

Conversation runs at a dead sprint. Che and Juli tell all the stories, and they tell them together. Complete each other's sentences rather than interrupt them. Never run out of things to say. They speak mostly in Spanish. I don't ask them to switch. I don't want to. The words—they're mesmerizing. All long *r*'s and short *d*'s. Ten thousand *b*'s in the span of twenty seconds. *S*'s that disappear. Rapid-fire syllables that tumble from their mouths like rolling pebbles. The stories are intended for the whole table, but the couple seems to speak only to each other.

Manuel whispers translations into my ear from the side, but I tell him not to worry, I can keep up. A blatant lie—which he knows. I don't care. It's the most beautiful thing I've ever heard, even if I understand almost none of it. I let the rocks roll past, all of them, clicking and clacking and creating a soundtrack of countless stories whose plots I can only imagine. I listen to it, all of it, and I think, *This is a language.*

This is the moment I fall in love with words.

I look over at Manuel, hoping to share my joy with someone else. He isn't looking at me. He's watching his parents. And while he smiles at all the right moments and nods along with details he remembers, there's something else behind his eyes. Something distant, like a friend excluded or the smallest boy on the baseball field. Standing before the chain-link fence, fists clenched. Waiting. Knowing he will always be chosen last.

WHEN MOM ASKS me about dinner at the Valdecasas house, I don't say, *It was good*, and go to my room as I might have done in the past. I can't. Not anymore.

She's been better lately, my mom. Gets in bed at night and out in the morning, rather than staying all day. But if there's one thing the last few months have taught me, it's that nothing is permanent. Nothing. Not moods or legs or minds or lives. And I want to do whatever I can to keep Mom's mood on the right side of her bedroom door. To keep her from disappearing again.

I describe the entire evening. I talk about the food and the house and the Spanish and the *café con leche* we drank after the meal. I talk about Che and Juli, their mysterious and fascinating careers in diplomacy. I talk about Valentina. I talk and talk, just the way I did to Manuel that first month of school. I figure it will make her happy, all these details, this evidence that her daughter does, in fact, have a real friend.

Instead of reacting with excitement, Mom is horrified.

I've just explained the way Valentina hides candy throughout the pockets of Manuel's backpack on the days his parents are away. Mom puts down the wet rag in her hand. She says, very slowly, "You mean to tell me that this boy is being raised by a housekeeper?"

"No, no," I say. "Not a housekeeper. She's more like a second mom. And it's only for, like, half of each month. Just while Che and Juli are in Colombia."

Mom stares at me. Then she turns around and walks across the kitchen to the cordless phone, muttering something along the lines of ". . . and an only child, no less." She picks up the phone and calls the Valdecasases and thanks them for hosting me and asks to speak to Valentina.

I start to sweat. I have no idea what she's going to say.

"Valentina?" she asks. "Yes, hi, this is Eliot's mom . . . Nice to meet you, too. Listen, next time Julie and Jay"—I cringe at her pronunciation—"go out of town, I'd love to host Manuel for dinner. Return the favor, you know? . . . Absolutely. One night, two nights, every night until they're back . . . No, no, it would be no trouble at all. Whatever Manuel prefers. And while we're at it, he'd be welcome to sleep over. Of course."

She hangs up. "That's all sorted, then."

Then she ruffles my hair and walks away.

I stare after her. What just happened? Family dinner? Sleepovers? On *school* nights? It's unprecedented. Wendy has always been an open-door mother—the kind who volunteers to host every swim banquet and cast party and graduation brunch from September to June—but she draws a hard line when it comes to weeknight dinner. "This is our time," she always says. "Our time together as a family." But not anymore, I guess. Something changed her mind. Something about Manuel.

PART II

The Cradle Island Olympics

11

NOW

LAST NIGHT, MY eyes flew open to a darkness so black I could barely make out the ceiling fan. I was sweating; the sheets stuck to my body like wet bandages. I rolled over and reached for my phone to check the time. Nothing. Dead.

If I had been at my apartment in New York, I would have simply rolled to the dry side of the bed and prayed for sleep to take me. But that night, I couldn't count on prayers alone. My brother was getting married in three days, and our schedule until then was packed. I needed to sleep.

I decided to try something new. I wrapped the comforter around my shoulders, dragged it across the room, and opened the door to the porch. A gust of dark summer wind met my face. I waddled over to the twin bed pressed against the porch wall and collapsed onto it. My body went limp. Birds called in the trees outside. I shut my eyes and didn't open them again until the sun rose over the harbor.

EVERY DAY UP here starts with coffee. That's our ritual: eight a.m., everyone in pajamas, lounging about Sunny Sunday's many sofas and armchairs. Mugs in hands or atop makeshift coasters—discarded novels with covers decorated by dark overlapping rings. The buzz and drip of our plug-in pot in the corner. It had been the case for as long as I could remember, but in the past three years, coffee took on an enhanced role in my life.

Coffee was my lifeline. Coffee was my fuel. Coffee kept me awake, alive. Pure, dark cold brew was my favorite. No milk. No sugar. No ice. Nothing to taint the jet fuel guzzling into my system. My legs might jiggle ceaselessly, my fingers might drum on the plastic surface of my desk, but I didn't care. Not if it helped me write.

That morning, I was the first on the island to rise. I took my coffee out onto the porch and set it on the railing. Watched the waves toss about in the lake. Though it was still early, Manuel would be up soon—in the old days, he had always beat me to the morning. Yet another aspect of his effortless diligence. Then the rest of the family would rise. There would be eggs scrambled and bacon fried and endless chatter about the coming nuptials, and Karma would force the eggs and the bacon onto me, and Wendy would have fourteen different things she wanted me to do to help decorate.

Mom had said that, back in Chicago, in the weeks leading up to the wedding, she collected everything we needed to properly celebrate. Some of it was already in storage on the island—foldable chairs, craft supplies, fancy linens and dishware saved for special occasions—but most needed to be brought on the jet. I didn't see the haul in person, but I could imagine it: crates of champagne, bins full of flowers, long crisp garment bags around suits and dresses. Customs must have had a few questions.

My muscles vibrated with nerves and anticipation. I wanted to run. I wanted to do *something*.

In New York, everyone has a routine. It's a necessity. The sheer density of choice packed into that city—of options, of plans, of things to eat or events to attend—is nothing short of eyeball melting. If you try to live without structure, you'll lose your god-damn mind. For me, I ran the East River every morning to expel the black thoughts that accumulated overnight.

Happiness, to me, isn't a presence. It's an absence. The absence of Worry. Of fear. Of sadness. Of the thoughts and compulsions that directed my life for so long. I'd worked hard to get to where I was now. I'd pulled myself out of the chaos of my own mind, and routine was the rope that got me there. Run, work, dinner, TV, bed. Run, work, dinner, TV, bed. That was it. Those were the rituals that checked all the boxes and kept me sane.

When I went back inside to make a second batch of coffee, I heard the door open behind me. I detached the boiling-hot pot and poured a careful mugful. Footsteps approached from behind. I didn't turn around. I didn't need to. I would know his long, steady gait anywhere. Hide it inside a chorus of footsteps and I could still pick it out.

"Good morning," Manuel said.

My back stiffened. In my mind I traveled back to the last day of three summers before, the morning I woke to find my best friend's arm around me—our first and only spent tucked together in that way. I saw the fluffy white comforter, his tangle of dark curls. Felt our cheeks pressed into bare sheets, the pillows fallen to the floor. Heard him say, soft as the summer breeze, "Good morning."

I turned around and nearly collided with his chest. My heart seized—probably because I was already sipping my fourth coffee for the day. At that point, I'd surpassed the state in which caffeine gives you energy. I'd transcended it, moving instead to that place *beyond* caffeination, that cliff's edge from which you stare down into a never-ending well of panic.

"Um," I said eloquently. "Hi."

"May I get a cup of coffee?"

"Coffee. Yes." My heart was pounding. I stepped out of the way. "Go ahead."

"So," he said too casually, pouring his own cup of muddy hot liquid. "Should we talk about what happened last night?"

I shimmied down the cabinets, coffee sloshing back and forth in my mug. "I said everything I needed to."

"Did you?" Mug filled, Manuel turned around, leaning against the divot in the countertop. "Because I detected many, many holes in that half-assed explanation for why you shut me out of your life."

"I told you." I squeezed the counter behind me, its chipped wood digging painfully into my palm. "There are—"

"*Things I don't understand.* I know." Manuel shook his head. "Fuck if I didn't stay up all night replaying that conversation until it drove me half-mad."

My heart stilled within my chest. "You—"

"And after peeling it apart nineteen different ways, I could only reach one conclusion." He stepped closer. "You're afraid."

I swallowed. "Afraid of what?"

"Of me." He stepped closer again, far too close. *Not close enough.* "Of *us.* That's why you ran three years ago. I got too close, and you panicked, and you ran."

"I—"

"Tell me I'm wrong."

"You don't—"

"*Tell me I'm wrong.*"

By then, Manuel had wrecked the carefully laid distance between us. He crowded me up against the cabinets, just an inch between us, almondine eyes blazing with heated focus. I sucked in a breath—and instantly regretted it, because there it was: coffee and fabric softener, toothpaste and something deep, earthy, inexplicable. The smell of Manuel in the morning.

"You're wrong," I whispered.

He cupped his ear. "What was that?"

Louder, I said, "You're wrong, Manuel." And then, because it was the truth, and because I owed him at least a slice of the truth, I added, "I was afraid. But not of you."

He straightened. "You . . ." All anger slipped from his face, replaced by blank confusion. "What?" He shook his head. "But then . . . what were you afraid of?"

Me, I thought without hesitation. *I was afraid of myself.*

But I couldn't tell him that. Of course not. To tell him that would lead to all variety of questions that I was ill prepared to answer.

"It doesn't matter," I said.

"Doesn't *matter*?" Manuel stared at me incredulously. "How could you say that? If someone scared you enough to run off to New York . . ."

All at once, realization seemed to settle in his mind. A dark realization. One that made Manuel—my best friend, my quiet, brilliant, even-keeled, snaps-at-no-one best friend—twist his face into a look of such blind, murderous rage that I took a shocked step back.

"Who was he?" Manuel asked, voice deathly quiet.

"Wh-who was who?"

His teeth ground together as tight white fists balled up at his sides. "*Who. Was. He?*"

"I don't—"

"The guy, the guy," he said, hand gesturing jerkily, as if he wanted to hit something. "The guy who hurt you. Who was he?" He grabbed my shoulders, looking deep into my eyes. "Who did this to you?"

And that's when I understood.

"Oh," I said softly. "Oh, Manny—no. It wasn't like that. It wasn't . . ."

Sweet Jesus. This was exactly why I went to New York in the first place. Why I cut Manuel out of my life and my family and anyone else who might care to ask me these sorts of questions. I couldn't answer them. Not without revealing the ugly truth of myself. All I could do was lie and lie and lie, until the lies wound around my throat, dipped into my mouth, curled around my tongue, gagged me, choked me, left me unable to speak, to eat, to breathe.

"Then what was it?" He shook my shoulders. "Tell me, Beck, *please*. Why did you run?"

"I . . ." I swallowed thickly, glancing around the room. "I, um . . ."

I saw the exact moment that Manuel shut down. Saw his mouth go slack, his eyes close up, his entire being draw protectively around itself, like storm shutters drawn for the winter.

"I see," he said, dropping his hands from my shoulders. He stepped back. "I see."

"Manuel—"

"No." He stepped back again. "Don't bother. I can tell you don't feel you owe me an explanation. And it figures, doesn't it? You were always like that. Always thought you belonged to no one but yourself."

Then, before I could say anything back, he turned around and walked toward the back porch. I inhaled raggedly. Ducked my head and made for the front door. Pulled it open and slammed it behind me, vanishing into that vast, familiar abyss of questions left unasked.

No, I thought as I emerged into the morning sunlight, tears stinging at my eyes. *No, Manuel. I've never belonged to myself. I've always been yours.*

OUTSIDE, THE AIR was still and hot. Muggy. Standard summer weather for New York City, but not for the North Woods. I hopped off the boardwalk. Crunched my way over twigs and peat grass, crossing the short distance to the entrance to the forest.

Once you cross that boundary, leaving the island's shoreline, you're swallowed up by its untamed center. Cicadas call. Leftover raindrops drip from pine needles. Thriving colonies of moss stretch from rock to rock in a blanket of vibrant green.

"Never step on moss," Henry once told me. "That's where the Moss People live."

Here's the thing about losing a brother at age ten: you wobble atop that precarious point, the threshold of lasting memory, when every moment could fall to either side—into the slim collection of images that will one day make up your past, or into the far more extensive chasm of the forgotten, of moments too ordinary or too shameful or too terrifying to keep forever. You might live every moment, but they don't stay. Not all of them. Most disappear, sucked into that yawning abyss of memory. And those that *do* remain will be nothing but snippets. Hazy photographs. Paper memories to which you'll return over and over, running your fingers along their edges until they crinkle.

I walked. Deeper and deeper into the island, farther from civilization, from the boy I most wanted to talk to. The boy I could not, under any circumstance, talk to right now.

Instead, I thought of Henry.

When I thought of my dead brother, a long history of memory didn't play before my eyes. I wished it did. I saw his face, but was it *really* his face, or was it the face supplied to me by photographs— the ones Mom had arranged in chronological order, then dropped into a beige storage box? A box she labeled *HENRY* and shoved onto the highest shelf in the attic.

Sometimes I would dig out one of those old photos and just stare at him. Study him. Separate his face into individual components, working meticulously, as if with tweezers, until each feature floated before me, alone in its own purpose, its own importance. Then I put it all back together. It was the same technique I used when learning how to spell. First understand the letters, then understand the word.

I did it over and over, trying to decide whether the boy in my hands matched the boy in my mind.

INSIDE THE ISLAND, no matter how deliberately you steer, fallen trees block your path—trees ripped up by their roots, trees with branches dangling pathetically at their sides, trees cracked right in half by a bolt of lightning, split down the center in a jagged fault line, the top a crown of splintered wood. After a storm, Henry and I used to explore all of that beautiful destruction, in search of whatever we could find. In search, perhaps, of magic.

The year before he died, we found that magic.

The Fort was birthed by wind and lightning. When a big tree falls and drags its entire trunk out of the ground—and I mean *really* out of the ground, roots and all—it becomes something new. The roots rip from the earth, pulling a mess of mud and moss with them. A few remain burrowed in the soil, but the rest now form a jagged arch around the base of the trunk. Sometimes, if everything bends just so, that arch becomes a cave.

We found our cave towering above a wide clearing. A sturdy wooden wall, roots curved into rafters, mud collapsed into a soft pile on the ground: the perfect hideaway. The skeleton of something wonderful.

It took us three days. Henry stole a thick roll of sandpaper from the boathouse and used it to sand down the inside of the tree, which turned from a muddy, gnarled mess into a smooth ceiling. We dug up the juniper bushes and weeds that clogged the clearing. Once we stripped that circle of forest to be as clear and flat as nature can be, the job became as simple as making the Fort feel like home. We laid tarps atop the mud. Lined the inside with thick blankets and pillows wrapped in flannel. Hung an electric lamp from the ceiling. Stole battery-operated Christmas lights from the craft closet and looped them around the remaining twigs and knobs; when turned on, the lights made a lopsided constellation. As a final touch, we punched ten holes into one side of a tarp and hung it from the wild crown of roots at the top. A front door.

This was it. This was our fortress. Here, we wouldn't be just the youngest ones on the island. Here, we would have our own voice. Our own life. It was gorgeous. It was hideous. It was a pile of wood and mud and moss and tarp, and it looked like something you could cover in gasoline and set on fire.

I could find the Fort in my sleep. That's how many times I've walked that unmarked trail through the forest. So when I left Sunny Sunday that morning and started walking, I didn't even choose to head toward the Fort; my legs carried me in that direction automatically. I was almost there—just a few more trees to pass, a few more rock faces to skirt—when I hit a patch of juniper. I could see the entrance to the clearing; it was right there, right on the other side. Rather than double back or skirt around the prickly bushes, I plowed right through.

Three steps in, my legs were already clawed raw. "Damn." I looked down. Thin red lines blossomed along the pale skin of my shins.

I turned around. As I did, I heard the four ascending trills of a white-throated sparrow. My ears perked up. White-throated sparrows were my favorite bird. Henry's too. And Dad's. Speedy was the one who taught my brother and me to identify their call. "They call them the Whistlers of the North," he said. "If you listen close, you hear them in Chicago, too, but just for a few days. Just as they're passing through. The North Woods are their true home."

So we did. Every year, we listened.

Once we started listening, we heard them everywhere. While walking the boardwalk. Winding through the trees to reach the Laundry House. Belly-up in a swing chair on the porch of Chelsea

Morning, feet against the wall, toes pressing smooth planks of cedar to push the chair back and forth, back and forth, back and forth. We swung. We listened. We whistled back. We whistled to the Whistlers, mimicking their white throats' perfect four-note ascension.

In the woods that afternoon, the sparrow called again. Another joined in. I closed my eyes to listen.

A shiver passed across my chest. My eyes popped back open. The treetops were still. No wind. No chill. Flesh raised on my arms. I shivered again. I spun around. Why was I cold? Where was that breeze coming from?

And then I felt it.

The presence. The familiar illusion.

Henry.

I spun around and started to run.

A blind sprint, no destination. Pine needles clawed at my arms and legs. It didn't matter where I was going; all I wanted was to leave that forest, to find open air. A few minutes later, I pushed through a wall of leaves and burst out into the morning sun. I sprinted down the flowing rock, headed for a long slice of granite that stuck out into the lake, a natural jetty. At its very edge, I stopped. Stripped to nothing and stood naked on the smooth stone. Shivered in the warm summer air.

This had happened periodically, growing up. A tingle at the base of my spine, on the bottoms of my feet. The sense that my dead brother was there, *right there*. And I don't mean in a foggy, ethereal way—I mean *there*. Literally. His ashes. Right where I stood. That, after they were lost, of every place on the island, they ended up below my feet.

I thought I'd grown out of this illusion, the same way I grew out of my Worries.

Apparently not.

My feet ached. I listened to my breath drag in and out of my chest. Just beyond my toes, the rock dropped in a flat wall straight into the water. Straight to the bottom.

I've always been yours.

I took one last breath and dove in.

IN WINTER, THE North Channel freezes. Not just a partial freeze; the water hits complete subzero, creating one unbroken crust of ice, five or ten feet deep, that stretches over the entire channel like an extra layer of skin. In all of the 162 kilometers that make up Manitoulin Island—the massive stretch of land where Port Windfall is located—there is only one bridge that connects to mainland Canada. In the summer, locals drive fifty miles out of their way just to get off Manitoulin. But in the deepest weeks of winter, when the lake turns to stone, they drive wherever they please. Their pickup trucks plow straight across the water. That's how strong the lake becomes. That's how deep its freeze. In spring, the ice melts, and by the time summer begins, the lake is a lake once more. But the ice's whisper remains.

My body plunged into the water. In seconds I traveled from July to January—down, down, down, right to where the last breaths of winter remained. The cold was worse than I remembered; it stiffened my bare limbs. Sunk straight through skin and muscle, straight to the bone. I recognized the shock but felt no pain. My body reacted instinctively—half somersault, legs down, arms up, kick and kick and kick, eyes squeezed tight, no need to look, could find the surface anywhere. I knew this water. I learned to swim in this water. It couldn't hurt me if it tried.

I surfaced and gasped in the morning air. Paddled over to the rocks. Pressed my palms to their slick surface and hoisted myself up. I turned over into a seated position and pulled my knees up to my face. Took a few deep breaths. Water lapped at my ankles.

The feeling—the presence of my dead brother—passed. It always does. But the *memory* of the feeling stayed, and does that really count as relief? Memory of pain is often worse than the pain itself. It drives us. What we do or don't do, embrace or fear, repeat or avoid at all costs—all of that is dictated by our memory of pain.

I cast my eyes across the lake. As they moved, they spotted a white speck on the horizon, the first sign of an approaching boat. I nearly jumped out of my goose-pimpled skin, grabbing my clothes as I scrambled to cover my naked body. But when I blinked, the speck disappeared or else moved or else had been nothing more than a bird flying low.

12

FIFTH GRADE

THE NEXT TIME Che and Juli travel, my new friend arrives on our front step with a small roller suitcase. I throw open the front door with a grin wider than my face. For any self-respecting ten-year-old, to have your best friend move in for two straight weeks—essentially an eternity—is nothing short of a fantasy on par with climbing into an alternate reality via a wardrobe or building a time machine.

His parents are at a two-week-long conference in Argentina. The business of *diplomáticos*. Something secretive and important and, most likely, uninteresting. We've spent enough hours rifling through the papers in Che and Juli's locked file cabinets—opened with a stolen key—to know.

"Sleepover!" I yell, bouncing about the doorframe.

Manuel rolls his eyes. "Calm down, loser."

I've long since accepted that my best friend doesn't express emotions the way most human beings do. He buzzes at a low frequency. It's all there—sadness, joy, excitement, frustration—but you won't find it on his face. It's in the air. Seriously. I don't believe in auras or energies or any of that hippie stuff, but I swear to God, the kid emits something. To sit next to him is to pick up on it. Sometimes I think that's why I was drawn to him in the first place—his frequency. It's never fast, never chaotic. When he's happy, it hums. When he's angry, it flattens out or disappears altogether. And I'm left alone with my own frequency, the swarm of moths inside my mind—an incessant beating of wings so loud, so terrifying, that at every moment I'm afraid someone will hear.

AFTER MY PARENTS go to sleep, I slide out of bed and pad silently down the hall. When I reach Taz's door, I crack it open, slip inside, and dive-bomb the bed, whisper yelling, "Cannonball!"

"Hey!" Manuel wiggles out of the covers. "What are you doing?"

"Follow me."

We unhook the latch from the bedroom window and shimmy out onto the roof. The shingles rattle as we flip onto our backs. We stay up late, talking into the dark, counting the number of satellites drifting across the sky. I walk him through the complex political dynamics of the American middle school and he teaches me curse words specific to Colombia. The rough asphalt leaves imprints on the backs of our legs. We do this every night. Amazingly, my parents never figure it out. Not when we laugh so loudly the whole block can hear. Not when we start nodding off over our eggs in the morning. Not even when we break a cluster of shingles off the roof. "Damn pigeons," says Speedy, rolling about the garden and glaring at the treetops.

Two weeks is a long time. You might think we'd start to hate each other. And, listen—it's not like we don't fight. We do. Some nights our giggles devolve into angry whispers, which end with both parties flipped onto their sides, faces pointed toward opposite ends of the roof. But the next morning I tumble into his bedroom and wake him by blowing a raspberry into his ear, and the friendship moves on. We fight like siblings: cruelly, carelessly, operating under the principle that the person on the other end of your anger will have to forgive you.

I start to understand Clarence and Caleb a little better.

Even at the deepest point of a fight—lying plank-straight on my side, steaming with rage at whatever great wrong my best friend committed against me—I don't kick him off the roof. And if he tries to crawl back into the window, I say, "Don't *gooooo*, Valde. There are scary monsters in the woods!"

And he rolls his eyes. "Eliot Beck, the Permanent Baby."

If only he knew how accurate that is. How my heart seizes at the thought of walking back to my empty bedroom. How silence pulls thoughts from my mind that I work hard, so hard, to keep down. To shove beneath the floorboard of my mind. How a warm, familiar body is the only thing that keeps them there.

We watch the stars together and drive to school together and eat lunch together and come home together and suffer through Wendy's cooking together. "What is this?" he asks on his first night at our house, in reference to the hamburger casserole on the buffet.

"That," I say, "is the You-nited States of America."

At night we climb out onto the roof with a grainy map of constellations we printed earlier that day in the library. We struggle to connect the hazy pixels on the page to the twinkling lights in space. Quickly we lose steam. Stare up at the bright Midwestern sky. My head nods to the side, drifting onto his shoulder. By the time I find sleep, Worry has become nothing but a distant memory.

"This is bullshit," says Karma one morning. Manuel is upstairs, in the shower. From the kitchen, I can hear the pipes running. "Eliot's little boyfriend getting to sleep over for weeks on end? None of us ever got to do that."

"Catherine." Mom doesn't even look up from her crossword. "Watch your language."

"No. This is just another instance of Eliot getting away with whatever the hell she wants, all because she's the youngest. You never let Jack sleep over, and I don't even *want* to fuck dudes."

Mom flinches. My sister only recently came out, and although my mother's words profess that Love is Love, that she supports Karma no matter what, her face sometimes says otherwise.

While I would never say so, Karma is right: Mom *does* treat Manuel differently. Yes, she's always been an open-door mother, but never like this. Eventually, there will be birthdays and road trips, spring breaks and winter vacations, long summers in Canada. I will ask, and Mom will never say no. In fact, she'll invite him herself, throwing open her door and her heart to a boy she barely knows. Almost as if he's her best friend, not mine. Almost as if she needs him as badly as I do.

ON THE LAST night of our two-week-long sleepover, Manuel and I change into pajamas in our separate rooms—we wear almost the same thing, boxers and a T-shirt—and, as usual, crawl out onto the roof. We're quiet for a moment. Then, I ask, "Are you excited to see your parents?"

Silence.

"No?"

Grunt.

"Haven't you missed them at all?"

He turns away. "Just drop it, okay?"

THE FIRST TIME I tell Manuel I love him, it's an accident.

It's the next morning. We're waiting outside for him to get picked up by his parents' driver. After a few minutes, a shiny black car with tinted windows that look like they could take multiple rounds of bullets before breaking turns the corner and starts up our block. As soon as I spot its headlights, I tackle Manuel, pulling him into a bone-crunching hug. I don't let go until I hear the tires pull into the driveway.

"Bye!" I say as I release him. "Love you!"

It's an accident. A reflex. An instinct built by ten years of tacking those two words onto the end of every phone call with my parents, every holiday, every goodbye after a long summer on Cradle Island. *Love* slips out just as naturally as adding *how are you* to the end of *hello.*

The surprise on Manuel's face is obvious. His eyebrows climb higher than I've ever seen them go before.

"Oh. Uh." I realize what I've done almost immediately. I keep my face completely neutral, watching him without expectation or acknowledgment, as if love is something we toss around on a daily basis. *Don't panic*, I think loudly, hoping the words will reach him. *Please don't panic.*

"I . . . love you . . . too!" He turns and runs down the stairs. The car door opens and shuts. I can't be sure, but from behind the windshield, I think I see a smile.

AT THE END of those two weeks together, I feel the best I've felt in months. The Worries? Gone. Silent.

That's it, I think as I watch the black car drive away. *That's my cure. He's my cure.*

I close my eyes. I imagine a grey shower plug at the base of my skull, the same kind I have in my bathtub. I imagine reaching around my head and pulling the plug. A gaping hole opens at the bottom of my skull. I watch as all the Worries—the noise and pollution and terror that have clogged my brain for the last several months—drain out. All of them. Every last drop. They drain away. They drain away and my head is empty, and I've never been so happy to be empty-headed in my life.

I exhale.

But then again . . .

The exhale stops.

But then again, there was that first night, when Manuel asked you about Henry.

No. Shut up. You're supposed to be gone.

Manuel saw Henry's empty bedroom and all the pictures and flowers. He asked you about Henry, and you lied.

I didn't lie. I told him what happened. Go away.

Right. You told Manuel your brother was hit by a car. But you left out a few key details, didn't you?

Did I?

You left out what happened after the funeral. You left out how easy it's been for you, how you've barely cried, how for a long time you thought you weren't even sad. You left out all the parts that make you look bad. And if you only tell the parts of the story that make you look good, isn't that just as bad as lying?

Is it?

Doesn't Ms. Collins say that "lies of omission" are just as bad as regular lies?

I guess so.

Leaving things out is just another kind of lie. You have to tell Manuel. If you don't, that makes you a liar.

But if I tell him, he'll think I'm a bad person. He'll think I'm crazy. He won't want to be my friend anymore.

But if you don't tell him, you'll feel guilty about lying.

I turn around and open the front door. I run through the hallway, up the stairs, into my bedroom. Slam the door.

Guilt stays with you. Forever. Next time you see your best friend, you'll know you lied. You'll carry that guilt everywhere you go. Homeroom. Sleepovers. Lunch tables. Laps around the field. If you stay friends forever, you'll still carry that guilt with you. You'll be ninety years old and laughing with your best friend at the nursing home and trying to be happy, but at the back of your mind, you'll always remember that you lied to him, that you're a liar, that you don't deserve his friendship.

Shut up, I say to the now familiar voice in my head, the one that isn't me but is inside me and so must be me—who else could it be?

How are you supposed to live with yourself now, hmm? How?

That's when I understand, I think. Lying on the floor of my bedroom, hands pressed to my ears. That's when I get it. This voice, these thoughts. These Worries. They aren't temporary. This is my new reality.

13

I ARRIVED BACK from my brush with Henry's ghost—overcaffein-ated, towelless, clothes damp—to find my entire family awake and gathered on the rocks behind Sunny Sunday.

Caleb was stretching his calves. Taz was helping Helene fasten the Velcro straps of her waterproof Tevas. Pam and Tim were point-ing excitedly at the rock bass swimming around the floating dock. Clarence was following Karma around, poking her with a piece of kindling. And Karma was pointedly ignoring Clarence while snoop-ing around Mom's shoulder, trying to get an early peek at the event list. Everyone was dressed in bathing suits, loose T-shirts, and run-ning shoes.

And that's when I remembered.

The Olympics. The Olympics were today.

"Do we have to do the Opening Ceremony?" Karma asked loudly, holding out a foot to try and trip Clarence during his next attack. "I thought that was just for little kids. None of us are little anymore."

"Speak for yourself, princess," said Clarence, giving up on both-ering Karma to begin his search for a branch large enough to serve as the Opening Ceremony torch. "Adulthood is for alcoholics and suckers."

"Or," said Caleb dryly, raising an eyebrow at his little brother, "anyone who regularly remembers to check their mailbox for parking tickets."

"Hey." Clarence frowned over his shoulder. "That was one time." He paused, chewing his lower lip. "Or maybe four. I don't know."

Caleb rolled his eyes.

As I watched the two of them go back and forth, I thought about what I'd overheard the night before:

How do you think she'll feel when she finds out that she was the last one to know?

The last to know *what?* It was something to do with Caleb, that much I'd gathered. Perfect, mature, wise, put-together Caleb. Whatever it was, it couldn't be that bad. Still, I couldn't help but be curious. Something was going on in our family, and as usual, I was the last to know.

I could have just gone over to him and asked directly. Treated the situation as I would if it were Karma or Taz or even Clarence. But then . . . who was I kidding? I'd never have the guts to do that. He might have been my brother, but the truth was, he wasn't *just* a brother. He was my *oldest* brother, the gap between us almost thirty years wide. He'd been married for longer than I'd been alive. He spoke to Speedy not as a father but as a close, confiding friend. I could never measure up to someone like that. Not a chance. When you're stuck at the bottom of the family tree, the distance to the top feels unscalable, like clawing your way to the top of a redwood using nothing but your fingernails.

Caleb intimidated me. Always had and probably always would.

Up by the cabin, the screen door slammed shut. I turned around to find a towering head of dark, curly hair step out onto the back porch. His eyes found mine right away, as if they'd been looking for me.

We both looked quickly away.

"What exactly *are* the Cradle Island Olympics?" asked Pam, Helene's mother.

"Excellent question," said Mom. "The Olympics—"

"—are one of the oldest Beck family traditions," interrupted Clarence. "Started decades ago, back when we spent months up here at a time. There were water balloon fights and scavenger hunts and capture the flag and Greased Pig, this truly psychotic version of water polo we play using a watermelon slathered end-to-end in Vaseline." He smiled wickedly. "Things get vicious pretty quickly."

Pam shifted awkwardly from foot to foot.

"Ostensibly it's a fun day for the kids," said Clarence, who had finally located a branch of the proper size, height, and heft. He picked up the toilet paper roll on the deck and stuffed it onto the end of the stick. "But really it's more of a safe outlet for all the grudges and frustrations that pile up when eight white people with too much time and too much money share one island for an entire summer."

Helene laughed openly—a loud, appreciative sound. Mom looked like she wanted to murder her stepson. Clarence laid the unlit toilet paper torch against the patio railing and grinned cheekily.

I admire all of my siblings, but if I'm being honest, I probably admire Clarence the most. He possesses this magnetic self-certainty. Plays three instruments, speaks intelligently but never seriously, adopts conspiracy theories for the fun of it, and defends them with greater confidence than most display when naming what they had for lunch the day before. At every moment, he wears the same expression—glittering eyes and a bemused smile, as if someone has just said something childish and amusing. As if he's always on the cusp of sharing some hilarious inside joke, then thinks better of it.

"You know what?" Mom said, eager to change the subject. "Let's run through the whole schedule for the week."

"*Schedule?*" Karma sighed. "So much for vacation."

Mom ran inside and fetched a stack of sturdy four-by-six cardstock. The same kind we used at Blossom for mail-in promotions. She circled the group, handing them out.

Taron & Helene

A WEEKEND OF LOVE . . .

Day 1: Welcome Dinner

Day 2: Cradle Island Olympics

Day 3: Bachelor Parties

Day 4: Wedding

I ran over the schedule three or four times. Tried not to cringe openly at the copy she'd written. The dramatic ellipses. The Hallmark subheader. Karma elbowed me in the side. When I looked up, her jaw hung open in a display of feigned astonishment. I covered my mouth to keep from laughing.

"We're not here for vacation, Karma," Mom was saying. "We're here for Taz and Helene's wedding. In case you forgot."

"Well," my sister replied, fanning herself with cardstock. "I certainly won't forget now."

"Each member of the family is responsible for one part of the weekend," Mom said. "Caleb and Clarence are running the Olympics today. Karma and Shelly have generously volunteered to cook the wedding dinner—"

"*Volunteered* is a nice way to put *blatantly forced*," muttered Karma.

"—Speedy, Helene's parents, and I will handle the rehearsal dinner. Eliot—" She turned to me. "You're in charge of organizing the bachelorette party."

I stared at her. "Sorry?"

"The bachelorette?" Karma spoke slowly, a mother to a slow child. "A heteronormative tradition where a group of drunk sorority sisters wear tiaras and scream at each other outside dingy nightclubs? Surely you've heard of it."

"Right," I said. "Except we're not sorority sisters, and we're on an island miles away from anything even resembling a bar. How the hell am I supposed to plan a bachelorette party?"

"You're a writer," said Mom, patting my shoulder. "You're creative. You'll figure it out."

A copywriter, I wanted to say. *Not a bard spinning fairy tales.*

"And if you come up empty, you can always speak to Manuel." Mom pivoted to look at my best friend, beaming proudly. "From what I understand, he's already put together *quite* the schedule for the boys."

"Uh-uh." Clarence shook his head adamantly. "No girls allowed."

"I was only suggesting that they share ideas," Mom said.

"Sorry, Wendy." Manuel flashed his disarmingly beautiful smile at my mother. "Clarence is right. The bachelor party is strictly top secret."

My mom smiled back at Manuel. She wasn't mad. She could never be mad at her precious Manny. How could she, when he faced her with a smile like that?

Against all my better judgment, I found myself wishing that he would look at me that way, too. A smile from Manuel Garcia Valdecasas is a rare, achingly beautiful thing.

We began splitting off into teams of two. As adults, one might assume us capable of choosing our own partners. Unfortunately, that wasn't the case. The process quickly became so heated Mom had to shut the whole thing down and assign them herself.

Surprise, surprise! The partner she gave me?

I'd always known that Mom wanted Manuel and me to end up together. Not right away, obviously—fall in love too young and the jig's up, the relationship explodes before we've even had the chance to figure out who we are. But eventually. Eventually, Wendy wanted her unofficial son as an official member of the family. To do that, we'd have to pull back the veil of friendship and discover we were made for each other.

Ha.

We shuffled awkwardly toward each other on the rocks. I kept my eyes on the soles of his well-worn running shoes as they drew nearer. *Fuck.* Less than an hour ago, Manuel and I were fighting in the kitchen. Now we were supposed to spend the entire day together?

Damn my mother.

Caleb, who was walking around the group passing out sunscreen, placed a brown bottle of Sun Bum at our feet. We both stared at it. Glanced at each other. Looked quickly away. Manuel's throat bobbed. Then he grabbed the hem of his shirt and pulled it over his head.

I froze.

Manuel was shirtless. Shirtless and standing less than a foot away from me.

I shouldn't have been so shocked. Of course Manuel was shirtless; we were on an island. The primary activities here all involved the lake: swimming, tubing, waterskiing, wakeboarding, paddle boarding, rope swinging . . . the list goes on.

But the last time I saw Manuel shirtless . . . it had nothing to do with family-friendly fun.

He bent over and picked up the tube.

While I did my best not to stare at Manuel rubbing shiny orange sunscreen all over his tan skin, Karma's loud voice drifted over to us. "Got enough SPF over there, kiddo?" She was talking to Caleb, who had slathered his body in so much Neutrogena he resembled a ghost.

Caleb is almost twenty years older than Karma, but she speaks to him as if it were the other way around. She's the only one in the family—parents included—who does so.

"We'll see who's laughing when you're getting melanoma scraped off your body at forty-five," he said, stretching out on the rocks with a satisfied sigh.

"What would you know about melanoma? Aren't you an ass doctor?"

"Even ass doctors go to four years of med school, *Catherine*."

"Oooooh." Shelly grinned and ruffled her wife's hair. "Careful, Caleb. You know how this one feels about her real name."

"Your real name is Catherine?" asked Pam. "Then where does Karma come from?"

"No one knows," said Karma, deadpan. "That's what makes it such a bitch."

ONCE PARTNERS HAD been assigned, Clarence dumped a quart of gasoline onto the roll of toilet paper, flicked open his lighter, and sent the torch up in flames.

"All righty then," he hollered. "Line up, kids."

"No way," said Caleb. He snagged the branch and handed it to Taz. "The groom carries the torch."

Taz pushed it away. "I'm good, really. Clarence can do it."

Caleb pivoted. "What about Helene?"

"I'll stick back here with Taron," she said.

"Well, in that case"—Caleb turned to me—"I believe the torch should be carried by the youngest, as is tradition."

I'm not used to being addressed directly by my oldest brother. The experience is always somewhat unsettling. "Um," I said.

"Or is Manuel slightly younger?" Caleb swiveled to the left.

"Oh, for the love of *God*." The voice came from up on the porch. It was Speedy, who had just rolled out of Sunny Sunday, the Nurses in hot pursuit. "June, get me out of this chair." Nurse June hunched her hulking figure over and scooped Dad into her arms. Once comfortably secured, Speedy yelled, "Music!"

The first crashing cymbals of the Olympic fanfare sounded from on high. We turned around. Mom stood at the wide back window of Sunny Sunday. On the sill before her: a massive set of speakers. She beamed and waved at the crowd.

"Let's show the children how it's done," said Speedy.

June marched down the porch steps, Dad dangling from the basket of her grip. She breezed past Caleb, and as she did, Speedy grabbed the torch out of his son's hands. "Onward!" he yelled.

Normally, we line up in a neat, single-file line organized by team and proceed down to the water. Not that year. That year, it was less of a parade and more of a mob. Pam and Tim slipped as they dashed down the rocks. Karma and Manuel caught them before they fell. When we reached the shoreline, June turned around so the sturdy rag doll of my father could face the crowd. By then, the fire had consumed nearly all of the toilet paper, leaving behind just a charred cardboard cylinder and a few pitiful flames.

"We are gathered here today," Speedy began, "to revive a—" But at that moment, the fire burned all the way through the cardboard and consumed the stick itself, crumbling the torch in a shower of glowing embers—several of which landed in June's hair.

"Christ!" she screamed.

"Shit, shit, shit!" Dad frantically brushed smoldering cardboard from her hair with his free hand. The other gripped a branch that was now on fire.

Caleb ran forward. "Give him to me!"

June, whose hair was now burning in earnest, tossed my father into Caleb's arms. She turned and dove straight into the lake. Caleb stumbled and fell ass-first onto the rock, catching Dad in his lap with a gentle thump.

The crowd surged forward.

"Oh God," said Pam.

"Dad!"

"Are you all right?"

"Give me your hand!"

Dad and Caleb flapped their hands. They didn't want assistance. Offshore, June resurfaced and spat out a stream of water. She swam back to the rocks and hoisted herself out. Her hair appeared intact.

"June?" called my dad.

"I'm alive, you big asshole." She shook the water from her shorts and T-shirt.

Speedy nodded approvingly. Then he shut his eyes and slumped sideways in Caleb's lap.

"Is he okay?" whispered Helene.

"Honey?" asked Mom.

"Dad?"

"Hospital," Speedy mumbled without sitting up.

"Oh God," said Pam again.

"Is he having a heart attack?"

"Someone call 911!"

"Can we get a helicopter out here?"

"Oh, quit scaring them." June reached down and pulled Dad back up into a seated position. "He does this shit every day."

Dad's head peeked mischievously back up. He started to laugh. He laughed so hard it looked like he might fall out of Caleb's lap.

Out of habit, I glanced over at Manuel. He was already looking at me, wearing the smirk he used to wear back when we would sit side by side and admire my family's insanity.

Before I could stop myself, I flashed it back.

14

SUMMER BEFORE SIXTH GRADE

THE QUESTION OF whether or not Manuel will join us at Cradle Island this year isn't a question at all. When I ask, Wendy practically rolls her eyes.

She's greedy for his love, my mother. Eager to absorb him into our family, to erase any hint of his unhappy past. He even appears on our Christmas card this year—and will every year hereafter—a fact she dubs "sheer coincidence."

"Is it my fault that you bring him everywhere we go?" she asks, whistling as she stuffs envelopes. "We don't have a single photo without him."

In the grocery store, I even hear one of her friends ask if we've adopted a new son, an "adorable little Mexican." I whip around when I hear her words, elbow knocking into a pyramid of cantaloupe. The falling melons drown out my mother's response.

THIS SUMMER, WHEN we pull up to the boathouse—a perfect landing by Speedy, who had an accessible lift installed on the *Silver Heron* this spring to help him reach the flybridge; he is *not* going to lose the childish joy of driving a boat—my siblings mobilize, throwing suitcases over the gunwale and yelling about who's staying where. Caleb and Clarence argue over beds in Tangled Blue. Taz quietly loads bags into the carts that we wheel down the boardwalk. I pay little attention to them. Instead, I focus on Manuel's face. On his expression. I watch as he takes it all in.

I'll never forget this moment. The roundness of his eyes. The parting of his lips. I'm immensely self-conscious, as if we've just crossed a barrier in our friendship from which there's no returning. I look up, take it in myself. And I see, for the first time, that this is not just a vacation home.

It's an island.

"You know," Manuel says finally, "in Colombia, my family was considered rich."

He doesn't say anything after that. He doesn't have to.

OUR FIRST NIGHT on the island, a massive thunderstorm rolls in. It's a quintessential summertime display of whipping wind and crashing, crackling electricity. The entire family gathers on the porch of my parents' cabin to watch. We spread blankets and sleeping bags along the cushioned benches, then hunker together beneath them. Under our wool blanket, Manuel grips my hand. His palm is sweaty. I wonder if they don't have thunderstorms in Colombia.

In the morning, the storm leaves behind its usual destruction. I look over the cracked branches and fallen trees. It gives me an idea.

"Come on," I say to Manuel, "I want to show you something."

When I tell him we're going into the woods, he looks unsure. He peers up at the sky, as if nervous that at any minute it will open up again.

"Trust me," I say. "This will be worth it."

All his fear disappears as soon as we enter the forest. The middle of Cradle Island, a jungle even on the driest of days, has come alive. Leftover raindrops drip from pine needles. Damp leaves stick to our shoes as we walk. I hop from rock to rock, careful to avoid thriving clusters of Moss People. Rock cress and wormwood blossom in tight clusters. Bristleleaf and wild rye wave in the breeze. Manuel reaches out and runs his fingers through it all.

I haven't visited the Fort since before Henry's death. I had no desire to sit in the middle of the forest alone last year. The idea depressed me. But something tells me the time has come.

I'm right.

Manuel falls in love with the Fort right away. It becomes our headquarters for the summer. Every morning, we shovel Lucky Charms down our throats and clear out of Sunny Sunday as quickly as possible. We nap in the Fort. Play cards in the Fort. Manuel reads. I write. When I finish a piece, Manuel reads it aloud so I can hear how it sounds. I stop him periodically to make notes. Sometimes, if I ask nicely, he translates the story into Spanish, painting an entirely new canvas of words onto the back of the page. I crawl up onto the top of the Fort and—stance wide, face tilted to the sky—perform a dramatic reading of the translation. I don't know most of the words on the page, but I take my best guess. The higher my confidence, the louder my volume. The louder my volume, the worse my pronunciation. Manuel rolls around the clearing with laughter.

"You're a regular Don Quixote," he tells me, tears leaking from the corners of his eyes. I have no idea what that means. I grin anyway.

"Where do you two go all day?" Mom asks one morning.

"To the office," we say in unison.

Karma snorts. "They're definitely sneaking off to make out in the woods."

We look at each other and make identical gagging faces. Then we fill two Ziploc bags with Oreos and race out the back door.

MY DAYS ON Cradle with Manuel are the closest I come to real contentment. We read dystopian thrillers on lounge chairs while our bodies bake under the sun. We beg Clarence to take us tubing because he drives the fastest. We chug cans of root beer while the adults sip wine. After dinner, Taz appears with kindling and matchsticks and volunteers to fire up the sauna. In half an hour the tiny wooden hut is hot enough to burn itself down. We strip to swimsuits and pile in, all of us, eight half-naked bodies packed into one eight-by-eight room. Pale, perspiring sardines. We lock ourselves inside as long as possible. Toss cup after cup of water onto the blazing-hot rocks. Grit our teeth when it hisses back into the air as clouds of steam—the most delicious form of torture. Then, just when the steam becomes so thick it feels like you're drowning in a pot of boiling water, someone throws open the door and we all rush into the night and sprint down the dock and dive into the moon-bright lake.

Then we run back to the sauna and do it all over again.

And again.

And again.

By the end of the night, we're exhausted. When we fall into bed, we pass out in seconds.

EVEN WITH MANUEL, the person who makes me happiest, in the place that makes me happiest, the Worries don't leave. At every moment, I live half in this world and half in another. One world is physical, the other invisible. I'm perfectly capable of remaining engaged in the physical one—the "real" world, the one with action and dialogue and the ever-present passage of time—while silently running through my standard list of Worries, one leading right into the next, like the endless all-caps ticker that sprints across the bottom of a newscast.

The ticker contextualizes the physical world. Provides the set of rules by which I must live. The Worries might have nothing to do with what's actually happening at the moment—in fact, most often they don't; most often they're leftovers, past wrongdoings or passing thoughts onto which I graft meaning. And although I might look happy on the outside—I might smile with my teeth and laugh with my belly and dance with my feet—at every moment, inside my mind, the ticker runs on.

OUR LAST MORNING on the island, Manuel and I wake before sunrise. We gather everything we need for the day into one backpack, and as soon as the first glimpse of sunlight peeks over the horizon, we're out the door. The air is cool and brisk, the first sign of fall.

One year has passed since I first lost my mind.

When we reach the Fort, we drop our bags at the edge of the clearing and remove books, papers, pens. We take only what we need, nothing more. Manuel lifts the tarp and crawls inside. Before following, I pause to admire our little home. For the last four weeks, we've spent almost every waking hour inside this place. I miss it already.

Manuel pokes his head out of the tarp. "Coming?"

And there they are. Those eyes. The ones that pull words from my mouth.

One year.

One year of internal chaos. Of false beliefs and self-loathing and intrusive thoughts, though I don't yet have the words to name them as such.

In the end, I don't do it on purpose. It isn't some sweeping act of courage, some terrifying admission toward which I built all summer long. I don't wake up and think, *Today is the day I reveal my biggest secret.* I stare into those eyes, those unblinking almonds that pull words from my mouth I never intend to share, and it just happens.

"I have to tell you something," I say.

He tilts his head. "Yes?"

"I'm . . ." Suddenly his eyes are too much. I can't talk to them. I look down at my feet. "I'm . . . there's something wrong with me."

"What do you mean?"

I kneel down. The juniper buds in the soil are tiny, still soft. Too young for thorns.

"I have these . . . thoughts. Thoughts I don't think are true, but I also can't convince myself are not true."

"I don't understand. What kind of thoughts?"

"Um. They're like . . . like worries."

Dry grass crunches as Manuel crawls all the way out of the Fort. "Everyone worries, Eliot. That's nothing to worry about." He pauses, realizes the contradiction in his words. "I mean, uh . . . you know what I mean."

"These aren't regular worries." Still I don't look up. "These are worse. They're like . . . it's like . . ." I have no idea how to explain them. "Lemme just give you an example."

I glance up. Manuel nods.

"So, it's Mile Day in gym class, and we're all running around those stupid orange cones, and I'm right behind Caroline Whittler. You know her, right? The one who looks like she's drowning in her own hair?"

Manuel snorts.

"Yeah. Anyway. So we're going around the cones, and I'm spacing out, like I always do when I run, you know. Thinking about the math test or what to have for lunch or how much time I can spend on *Club Penguin* after school before Mom notices."

I'm doing it again—stuffing my confession with as many irrelevant details as I can. Padding the cushion I hope will soften the fall when I finally jump.

"So, yeah. I'm spacing out, thinking about whatever, and then I sort of come back to the present, and when I do, I realize that, the whole time, the whole time I was spacing out, I was staring at Caroline Whittler's butt."

I pause. Manuel says nothing.

"And I think to myself, 'Wow, she has a great butt.' And then, immediately after, I'm like, 'Oh my God, you're staring at Caroline Whittler's butt. You're a lesbian.'"

I glance up again. Manuel grins, then covers his mouth when he sees I'm not laughing.

"And I know it's crazy, 'cause I tell you about my crushes all the time and they're all boys and whatever, but like . . . once I thought the thought, I couldn't unthink it, you know?" Now I'm really off, really talking. Now that the confession has started, I can't stop. "It's out of my control. No matter how many times I tell myself I'm not a lesbian, I always go back to that one instance, to the time I stared at Caroline Whittler's butt. Because that's evidence, and you can't just erase evidence, you know?"

"Eliot."

I stop. I look up at Manuel.

His face is serious now. "You're not a lesbian."

I nod.

"You're not a lesbian. You know that."

I nod.

"You spent a month analyzing the fourteen words Robbie Siegler said to you on Field Day. You made me draw a Venn diagram."

I nod a third time.

"And even if you were, who cares? It's not 1908. There's nothing wrong with being gay."

"I know. I know, I know. Obviously I know. That's not the point."

"What is the point, then?"

"Maybe this is a bad example. There's other stuff. Worse stuff. But it's not really about that. It's . . . it's . . . it's these thoughts. They won't leave me alone. No matter how many times I tell them to. And they feel, like, weirdly separate from me, you know? Like . . . they don't sound like me. Or, at least, they didn't when they first started. Now . . . Now, I . . . I can't really tell the difference."

The confession is over. I fall silent.

I wait for the rush of relief. The fake, fleeting relief that sticks around for an hour or two whenever I confess a crime to my father. I wait for Manuel to forgive me, the same way Dad did. Here I am. I am giving you this bizarre part of myself, these thoughts that dog me, that won't leave me alone. Take them. Drain me of them. Wring me of their poison and tell me what to do with it. Purify me. Please.

I hear nothing. I look up. And this time, when I do, I find a familiar sight: Manuel, eyes squinted, lips parted, wrinkle in the middle of his brow. His face of incomprehension, the one he wore for a month after we first met.

I begin to sweat. I'm naked and raw before the eyes of my best friend. I wish I could take it back, all of it. I've done something disastrous. Something irreversible. I see that now. On the day we met, I drew a clear line between Worries and Non-Worries. Only the latter could be shared. No matter how heavily they weighed upon me, no matter how much mental space they occupied, the Worries were still confined to the four inches between my left and right eardrums. The inside of my head might not feel safe, but at least the rest of the world did. Why did I let all those words, that whole psychotic monologue, leak out of my mouth as casually as any other collection of noises? Now the thoughts are out there. They're free. By speaking my fears aloud, I thrust them out into the cool, bright light of day.

I can't bear to watch his face any longer. I look down again. I want to run away. I bet he does, too. I wonder if it's more polite to let him go first.

Then my vision blacks. My face smushes into a blindfold of dark fleece. I inhale in surprise. Take in a familiar scent. One that calls me not just to a certain place but to a specific time of day, too. Linen and cedar and the mysterious, distinctive scent of boy. The first thing I smell every day. Manuel in the morning.

"It's okay, Eliot." The words sound out of place in his voice. They're adult words, and we're still just kids. "You're going to be okay."

15

FOR THE FIRST event—the Tug-of-War—we divided into two teams, two pairs of partners per team: Clarence and Caleb plus Karma and Shelly on one team, Helene and Taz plus Manuel and me on the other. My parents, along with Pam and Tim, stayed ashore as judges.

The Cradle Island Tug-of-War is no rinky-dink middle school Field Day contest between a bunch of screaming eight-year-olds. It's vicious. Just offshore, two water trampolines are anchored fifteen feet apart. They're held in place by long chains wrapped around heavy cinder blocks at the bottom of the lake. The trampolines don't particularly like staying in place; they wiggle and wobble beneath your feet, tipping at the mercy of tides. For the Tug-of-War, each team stands on one of the trampolines with a rope pulled taut over the open water. You tug until one of the teams falls into the drink.

As I swam out to my team's trampoline, I thought about the Olympics we held back when I was still just a kid. For my siblings, they were the highlight of every summer. For me, the only thing they highlighted was how painfully young and small I was. I participated, but only in ways that emphasized my own inadequacy, my certainty that I didn't belong. I filled water balloons and handed out towels. I designed prizes for the award ceremony, misshapen slices of construction paper smeared with glitter glue. I sat on Speedy's lap during the Diving Contest and waved scorecards as high as I could. I never joined Greased Pig. At seven years younger than almost everyone else—except Henry—I was more suited to being the watermelon than to being a player.

I had every intention of winning the Tug-of-War this year. In fact, I had every intention of winning the entire Olympics. I was an adult now, just as qualified to win as any of my older siblings. Not to mention I was in the best shape of my life, thanks to all my early morning runs next to the East River.

This was Manuel's first Olympics, too. By the time he started coming to Canada, we'd retired them; everyone else was too old. They'd found other outlets for pent-up emotion. Healthier, more mature outlets, like sarcasm or alcohol or grudges buried so deeply they never see the light of day.

Up on the water trampoline, I ended up positioned between Manuel and Taz. Manny's back was so close to me that I could smell the cedar and sunscreen leaking from his pores. It was a traitor-ously nice smell. Just as I caught myself leaning a little too close, hands loose, nose hovering just a millimeter from his skin, Speedy blew his whistle and the contest started. I jerked forward, grasped for the rope, missed entirely, and tipped headfirst into the lake.

THE SECOND EVENT was a long-distance relay swim. One partner swims from one end of the harbor to the other, and the second swims back. First team to finish wins.

No sweat, I thought. *I'm a runner; cardio is my thing.*

Unfortunately, running didn't seem to translate to swimming. I hardly made it fifty meters before my arms and legs and lungs were screaming at me to stop. I lifted my head out of the water, and when I saw how far the beach still was, I groaned. In doing so, I accidentally inhaled a mouthful of lake water. I coughed it up. My arms flailed wildly. I pounded at the water and wondered if this was what it felt like to drown.

When I finally made it back to shore, I dragged myself through the knee-high water on all fours. I squinted up at the sky only to find a hand waving in front of me, blocking the bright sunlight. I grabbed it without thinking. As soon as it wrapped around my palm, I knew who it belonged to—the warm palm, the rough skin, the long, nimble fingers . . . My hand had been in that hand before. More times than I could count.

Manuel hoisted me out of the water, helping me up onto the sand. I sprawled out on the beach, breathing heavily. When I turned my neck to look for him, to say thank you, he was already gone. Off swimming the second leg of a race we'd already lost.

I let my head flop back onto the sand. My eyelids were about to flutter shut, but before they closed all the way, a pixie-haired face popped into view: Karma, captain of her high school swim team.

She grinned victoriously down at me. "Glug glug, Guppy!"

"DON'T SWEAT IT," Manuel said as we toweled off back up on the rocks by Sunny Sunday. "It's only the first two events. We can still win."

"Right," I said dryly. "Things are really looking up."

He nudged my side. "A little positivity wouldn't kill you."

That one touch—it did something to me. Something unexpected. Something dangerous. Ever since *that night*, I'd done everything I could to repress sexual impulses within myself—even the ones I didn't see as problematic. Warm pelvis, tight belly, flutters in the stomach . . . I shut it off. *All* of it. I had to, because letting it in risked letting in everything else, everything that goes along with arousal. Better to tamp it down. Better to feel nothing at all. And it worked.

Until then.

Until that very moment, when one elbow against one side sent a thousand volts of electricity dancing through my body. Switching on lights. Dusting off corners. Pulling levers that should never be pulled. Awakening every part of me that I tried so desperately to put to sleep.

No.

No, no, no.

My breath became very shallow. I cast about for something to do, a distraction, a roadblock to grind whatever was happening within me to a halt. I wished I could reach for my phone. Check Instagram or TikTok, even though there was only one person whose updates I actually cared to stalk, and he was standing right beside me. At least holding my phone in my hand would provide me with a repository for my attention. But there's no Wi-Fi and hardly any signal on Cradle Island. Most summers, I just leave my phone in my cabin and let it die.

Thankfully, my mother chose that moment to yell down at us from the porch: "Manny! Eliot!" We craned our necks to find her waving a bottle of Neutrogena at us. "Don't forget to reapply!"

I exhaled sharply. "Mom, it's been a half hour since we put sunscreen on," I said, doing my best to keep my voice light. "We're fine."

"Nonsense." She clopped down the stairs, flip-flops slapping the smooth wooden boards, to head for where we were seated. "Didn't you hear what your brother said about melanoma? I won't have either of you catching cancer on my watch."

"I wasn't aware that cancer was something you caught," I said flatly.

My mother set the bottle of sunscreen in my hand. "You never know with these things." She straightened up and turned around to flip-flop away. Before making it all the way back to the porch, she paused and looked over her shoulder. "Oh, and Manuel, dear—do help Eliot with her back and shoulders. She's too modest to ask for it herself and always ends up with splotchy burns." Then, with a pleased nod, Wendy Beck turned around and marched up the steps.

The bottoms of my feet broke out in a cold sweat.

Slowly, as slowly as possible without staying frozen in place, I pivoted my head to look at Manuel. To my surprise, when my eyes finally landed on him, he appeared to be holding back laughter.

It was a reflex; seeing his smile, I couldn't quite hold back my own. "What?" I asked.

His lips twitched. "She could be a little less obvious about it, couldn't she?"

I smirked back. "You know as well as anyone that Wendy has been plotting to marry me off to you since the first moment you set foot in our house."

His mouth stretched into a full-on grin. "Do I ever."

We stayed like that for a small eternity, best friend grinning at best friend. And for those few seconds, I forgot that I wasn't supposed to be enjoying myself. I forgot that I wasn't allowed to fall back into him. That we weren't allowed to just be Eliot and Manny anymore. I lost that privilege three years ago on the night before he left for Harvard.

We kept staring for far too long.

I don't know who looked away first.

NEXT CAME THE Diving Contest. I knew we'd fail that event spectacularly. Manuel stands a full head taller than most of my brothers. Watching him try to swan dive is like watching a tree trunk fall off a cliff.

By the time Greased Pig rolled around, the heady, electrifying buzz of competition had taken hold of me. We'd lost the first three, but there were four more events to go. Taken together, they were worth more points than all of the previous ones combined.

I might have been the youngest, but I was still determined to win.

We switched up the teams from Tug-of-War, Clarence and Caleb joining Manuel and me, then put heads together to discuss strategy. On our side, Manuel and Clarence dominated the conversation, speaking in hushed, scheming tones. I watched their connection with mild confusion.

Throughout that morning, it felt like every time I looked over at Manuel, he was goofing off with a member of my immediate family—teasing my mother, bumping fists with Taz, making Karma laugh so hard she spit her gum out. He even appeared to be the resident favorite of Pam and Tim, who peppered him with so many questions about Colombia and Harvard that I feared he might run out of responses. But he never did. He took them in stride, all of them—just as he always had.

It takes a certain kind of fearlessness to let yourself be absorbed into a family as massive and chaotic as my own. Luckily, Manuel was nothing if not fearless. He moved to the US at ten years old— that awful age, when most children go from innocent to something short of evil—and even though he talked about missing parts of his life in Colombia, I never saw him cry. Not once. He embraced his bizarre new American family. He embraced all of us, from Taz's long silences to Clarence and Karma's aggressive hijinks. At the time, it was perfect. To have your best friend so seamlessly absorbed into every aspect of your life? It's every child's dream.

But as I watched him laugh and plot and generally take center stage among the family whose acceptance I had so desperately craved as a child, the same family who clearly hadn't forgiven me for my yearslong absence, I felt this creeping dread, this pit in my stomach that felt like recognition: Had I been so easily replaced?

Speedy, who was in charge of kicking off Greased Pig, was positioned up on the porch in his Feather Chair. The Pig—a watermelon covered in a thick layer of slippery Vaseline—sat in his lap. On Wendy's whistle, he tossed the Pig into the lake. It was a fall of over fifteen feet. It hit the water and rocketed halfway to the bottom before it boomeranged back upward. By the time it broke the surface and leapt into the air, sending up two great flourishes of water, the other players had already dived after it. Caleb snatched the watermelon first. The game was off.

My siblings had no problem playing dirty; that much became clear within the first few seconds of the game. Karma attacked Caleb from behind, pushing his shoulders down until his head submerged and grabbing the Pig. Clarence splashed water in Karma's face. Momentarily blinded, she let the Pig slip through her fingers and into Clarence's arms. Clarence kicked as hard as he could, drawing near the other team's inner tube. Taz was waiting, playing goalkeeper. He dove for Clarence, but at the last minute, my half brother passed the ball to Manuel, who slam-dunked it into the tube.

Clarence let out a victorious whoop, rubbing Manuel's hair affectionately. "That's our guy."

One point to our team.

We could do this. We could win. I wasn't just going to sit back and watch; I was going to swoop right in and bring us to victory.

Once again, Speedy tossed the Pig off the balcony, and the second round began. Karma snagged it right away, kicking water into Clarence's face as he advanced on her. Thankfully, her attention was all on my half brother; she wasn't even looking at me. Probably didn't even consider me a threat—youngest child and all. I capitalized on her negligence and pounced.

What resulted was a kicking and scratching match between Karma and me. It was like we were little girls again, fighting over a favorite toy. We kept our kicks light, not wanting to actually injure each other, but our faces were screwed up into twin expressions of gritted teeth and wild eyes, fingers scrabbling for purchase on the greased watermelon.

"A-*ha*!" hollered Karma, ripping the Pig from my hands and tossing it into the air. Taz was waiting behind her. He snatched it, then tossed it to Helene, who floated closer to our goal. Helene shot, and the Pig went into the tube.

It went on like this, back and forth between the teams, them scoring once, us scoring twice, them scoring three times. I did my best to participate, but it quickly became clear that I wasn't built for this sport. I was built for long runs along the Hudson and even longer days sitting at my desk.

Yet again, I was the weakest one of the group. Yet again, I wasn't enough.

Eventually, I decided I needed a break. I paddled away from the game, over to the rock we used to climb out of the water—an enormous box of a thing with a perfectly smooth top, like a swim raft. When the water is low, the rock sticks a full foot out of the water. I wriggled up, not bothering to push with my arms, just flapping my legs until enough of my torso slid up and over the rock's flat top. I rolled over onto my back. Then I went limp. My legs dangled into the water. A cloud shaped like a light bulb drifted past. Hungry smallmouth bass could have nibbled at my toes.

Somewhere in the distance, Karma yelled, "Eat grease, asshole!"

As I lay on that rock, I couldn't help but come back to a question

I had pondered a thousand times in my life: How *do* you form meaningful relationships with a family you didn't grow up with?

The answer, I had come to see at last, was this: you can't. You might think that as you grow up, it gets easier. To make friends with your siblings, I mean. You age. You mature. You harden from that adorable, irritating little bag they have to carry around into something resembling a human adult. When that happens, you get to take your seat at that proverbial table. Right?

Wrong.

That gap might shrink, but it will never close altogether.

You're left with one option: Build your own family. Choose your own identity.

But here's the problem: the older kids get to the rest of the world first—to the parents, the teachers, the local law enforcement—which means they define what it means to be a Beck. And they're human, right? They have no idea how to grow up properly. They make mistakes. They fight. They self-destruct. Sometimes, they self-destruct rather *publicly*. In that way they stumble into adulthood, drunken explorers weaving through the jungle of life and hacking shit down as they go. By the time you, the youngest, come along, you stand at the jungle's entrance with a machete in your hand and envision carving your own path, but shortly after you start, you realize it's impossible. The damage is done. The jungle is razed flat. If your oldest brother was a goat fucker, it doesn't matter if you commit your entire life to saving the planet. It doesn't matter if you're hotter than a supermodel or faster than Usain Bolt or ordained by God as the second coming of Jesus Christ himself. You'll always just be the sister of a goat fucker.

But the craziest part, the most baffling, ridiculous part of all, is that these people—the ones who cut the paths you must follow, who standardize familial traditions, who leak personality traits and isms that you absorb without meaning to, an accidental human sponge—you don't know them. Not really. You're so young that by the time you're old enough to make your own decisions, they're gone. Off to college, to jobs, to that slow process of disentangling who they are from who they were raised to be. They're well out of the jungle, but you're lost in the thick of it, no map, no guide, clutching at your side what you thought was a machete but you see now is nothing more than a pen.

THE FIFTH EVENT—the final round before lunch—was the Sauna-Off.

All morning, the Nurses had been stoking the fire, juicing the sauna up to skin-melting temperatures. The rules for the contest were simple: Whoever stayed in the longest won the most points. Five points for first place, three for second, and one for third.

"This will be a walk in the park for us both," Manuel said as we followed the group into the small wooden hut. "We grew up spending almost every summer night in here."

"As did the rest of us," Karma said over her shoulder. She leapt up onto the lower wooden bench—one of two that lined the walls of the sauna, interrupted only by the vintage metal chimney and hot rocks in the corner—and sat down, crossing her freckled legs. "I wouldn't get too cocky, Valde."

I stiffened. A bizarrely possessive feeling rushed through me at the sound of someone else using my nickname for Manuel.

How ridiculous, I thought. *It's just a shortened version of his last name. Of course other people are going to call him that. In fact, I bet his entire club—what did he call it, the Spree?—knows him as Valde.*

It happened all at once, like a boat filling with water so fast it was sure to sink: I was furious. Not at Manuel. Not even at the Spree.

No, I was furious at myself. For not knowing the name of the place he spends the most time. For not knowing the names of any of his friends that are in that club with him. For not knowing *anything*— not one significant thing—about the life my former best friend led in Cambridge.

"Eliot?"

The sound of his voice shook me out of my spiral of self-loathing. I came to only to realize that I was standing in the open sauna door while every member of my family was already seated inside staring at me, waiting.

"You coming in?" Karma asked. "Or are you just going to stand there in your own world and keep letting all the hot air out?"

"I—" I shook my head, shutting the door behind me. I hurried forward and took the only open seat left, muttering, "Sorry."

As soon as I was seated, Clarence stood up from his place on the upper wooden bench. "Right." He clapped once. "The Sauna-Off. You all know the rules: the longer you make it, the more points you get. No breaks. No splashing water onto your body." He pointed at the buckets of water on the floor, all of which had wooden ladles sticking up from their insides. "Tossing water on the rocks and steaming the place up is fair game. Understood? Good. May the best man win." With that, he sat.

And we were off.

HELENE LEFT FIRST. Taz left approximately fifteen seconds later, even though he wasn't even sweating yet. Ten minutes passed. Fifteen. Caleb left. Shelly left. Karma yelled after her wife, calling her a "disgrace upon the gay community." Shelly mooned her through the glass door.

"And then there were four," said Clarence, wiping his forehead with the back of his hand.

He, Karma, Manuel, and I glanced around at each other inside the tiny, sweltering wooden box. Sunlight streamed in the window that looked out over the back porch and the lake. On the porch, the family was gathered, chatting with each other or watching us with keen interest. Mom waved when she caught my eye.

"How bad do you think Wendy wants to join right now?" Clarence asked.

"Given that she has worse FOMO than anyone I know," Karma said, "I would say pretty bad."

Clarence grinned. "Unless it would mess up her clothing."

"Oh my God." Karma leaned her head back, and her short hair, matted with sweat, dangled back, too. "Wendy loves to pretend she's low-key, but she's really the highest maintenance of us all. Remember on that one Trek of Chaos, when she ripped her favorite Loro Piana shirt?"

Clarence groaned. "I'll never forget it. Speedy was trying to calm her down by telling her that we could mend it, and she said, 'No, it's over—'"

"'—just like my life,'" they finished in unison.

Manuel burst out laughing.

I tried to listen, to laugh along, but the task proved difficult. My mind was drifting. Away from the conversation. Away from sound and toward sensation. Specifically—the sensation of Manuel's sweating body sitting not five inches away from mine.

All morning, I'd done my best not to notice the hard lines of his chest muscles, the tanned, freckled skin of his arms and shoulders. I pretended not to see the water dripping from his matted curls or the tan lines around his thighs or the little V of muscle sloping down into his swimming trunks. But here, inside a sweltering cedar hut, that same tanned skin dripping with salty-sweet beads of sweat . . .

I was trying not to breathe.

Because when I did—when I let the smell of him seep even a tiny bit into my nostrils—it sent my entire body into a spiral. A heated, sweaty spiral of sparks in the stomach and a tight, aching pelvis. Breath that barely made it in before I had to push it back out again.

When the others had dropped out, he could have moved. Could have scooted away, giving me even one or two extra inches of space to breathe. But he didn't.

And I think he did it on purpose.

Help.

Thankfully, Karma chose that moment to stand. "Well," she said, jumping off the bench, "I'm officially out."

"You're *leaving*?" Clarence looked aghast. "So much for all that big talk."

"Talk is fine, but it's hot as the devil's left tit in here. I'm gonna go hang out with my hot wife instead."

"Loser," Clarence called.

"Asshole," Karma yelled over her shoulder as the door swung shut.

And then there were three.

To be honest, I was starting to feel the heat. I might have grown up sitting in the sauna all summer, but three long years had passed since I had even set foot in one. Perhaps I overestimated my perseverance. Perhaps it was my earlier overconfidence during Greased Pig at work again.

"Fuck." Clarence bent his head. Sweat dripped from his forehead to the cedar floor. "How are you two not dying?"

"I am." Manuel flashed his vivid white teeth. "But I want to win more than I want to cool down."

"Touché, brother." Clarence pushed himself off the bench. "Well, then, kids. It is with a heavy heart"—he bowed low, leaking more sweat onto the floor, then straightened again—"that I concede to the victors. See you in the lake."

And with that, it was just Manuel and me.

We did it. Our team won. Still, he didn't move and neither did I. I wanted to—wanted to scoot an inch to the left, creating just a smidgeon of breathing room between us, but I was smushed up against the wall, Manuel's body blocking the rest of the bench. Why didn't he move? There was a whole sauna we could fill. Why did he have to stay so damn close?

And then he looked at me.

And like an age-old reflex that would never leave my body, I looked back.

Which was a mistake, because his head—while a foot taller than mine when we were standing up—was tilted down such that his lips were a bare breath away.

Fuck.

I needed to turn, to look away. But I was trapped in his gaze, his eyes like almonds swirled with caramel, his lips dark and lush beneath them. Breath climbed high and shallow in my chest. In my stomach it felt as if a tower of rocks were teetering back and forth, just seconds from crashing and shattering every inch of my insides. It must have been the heat. The heat was making me lightheaded, making me feel as if I wasn't actually the one inhabiting my own body.

"So," Manuel said.

I swallowed. "So."

"Technically, it doesn't matter which of us stays in here the longest."

"I know."

"We're on the same team. Either way, we win."

"I know."

What is happening to me? Why can't I move?

"Then why don't you leave?"

My fingers dug into the bench. I whispered, "Why don't you?"

Manuel leaned down. His breath whisked hot and sweet along the bridge of my nose. "I think you know why."

His lips were so close I could lick them if I wanted to.

And, God, did I want to.

No. Panic spiked through me. *No. Shut up, Eliot. You can't think things like that.*

"I think you know exactly why I'm still here," he murmured. "And I think you're here for the same reason."

"I—" I swallowed again. "I don't—"

Manuel leaned away. "Because you're a competitive psycho, and you want to see which one of us can last the longest."

Oh.

Right. That. Of course.

"Right," I said aloud. "For sure. I'm here to kick your ass."

Manuel grinned. "I know. You like to pretend not to care about competition, but you're secretly a killer."

I scoffed. "I don't pretend anything. I'm open about my murderous side."

"You should be." He lifted a hand and brushed the back of his fingers down my cheek. "Your darkness is my favorite part of you."

Everything in my body went still at once. Manuel didn't withdraw his hand. He left it there, his eyes burning deep into mine. He said nothing more, and neither did I. I couldn't move. Couldn't think. The heat, the vertigo, the lack of food, his words, his fingers on the side of my face . . . it was too much. A windstorm of sensation, of emptiness, of desire.

I want him.

The words erupted into my consciousness like storm shutters flying open.

I still want him.

I pushed myself off the bench so abruptly my sweat-slick feet slipped on the floor. I nearly tipped backward.

"Eliot?" Manuel said, alarmed. "Eliot, are you—"

But before he could reach *okay*, I was out the door and sprinting for the lake.

16

SIXTH GRADE

MANUEL SAYS I should tell my parents. I say no. "They'll be able to help," he says. I shudder to think of admitting to my parents that I have voices in my head that tell me things I know—or at least I think I know, or at least I'm *sort of* certain I know—aren't real. "Don't tell them the specifics, then. Just say you need to talk to somebody."

To say my parents are surprised when I tell them I want to see a therapist would be a massive understatement. The way they look at each other . . . you'd think I said I want to move to Switzerland. *Eliot?* their eyes say. *Quiet, steady, uncrying Eliot?* "If you really think you need it," Mom says doubtfully.

Dr. Drier works out of a strip mall in Northfield. Speedy drives me to my appointment in our new car, a Ford that has been retrofitted for disabled drivers. He pulls up outside a sterile building with the words CHILD PSYCHOLOGY on the window. Thick white blinds block my view into the office.

What follows is the longest conversation my father and I will ever have about my mental health.

"Well, are you going in?" he asks.

I shrug. Don't unbuckle my seat belt.

"What's up?"

I shrug again.

"Are you nervous?"

Nod.

"Listen," Dad says, swiveling in his seat. I ready myself for a speech, but a few moments pass and I hear nothing. I look up. Dad's head is turned away, staring out the windshield. He hesitates. Then he turns back to me. "You're going to spend a helluva lot of time up there," he says, reaching up one finger to tap my forehead. "Your entire life, in fact. You better get used to the shit cluttering up the floor."

I TALK FOR forty-five minutes straight. I don't know what not to say, so I decide to play it safe and tell him everything. He isn't silent like the therapists on TV. He speaks, just not much. Mostly he blinks. And not just regular blinks—long, hefty ones. The kind that linger so long at the bottom it seems he may never open his eyes again. I wonder if I'm boring him.

"You made a very wise decision in bringing her in to see me," Dr. Droopy Eyes says to Dad after the appointment. They're speaking inside the room where my session took place. The door is closed. I'm supposed to wait in the lobby. Instead, I squat in the hallway with my ear to the smooth acrylic paint on the door. "I tend not to diagnose after just one session, but your daughter exhibits many, many of the symptoms of anxiety and Obsessive-Compulsive Disorder. If I had to guess, I'd say there are things she's still holding back, which is natural. But based solely on the things she shared—"

"What exactly is that, the Obsessive-Whatsit?" interrupts Speedy's voice. "That's the handwashing disease, right? The one in *Monk*, where he's scared of germs and needs everything to be organized in groups of five, or whatever?"

"That's one form of OCD, yes. But the disorder manifests itself in many different ways. It's less about being afraid of germs and more about the way the patient reasons and rationalizes."

"You're saying my daughter isn't rational?"

"No, that's not what I'm saying." The shrink's voice never dips or wavers. Just chugs forward with the same patience it used when asking me questions during our session. "Let me explain it a different way. Thoughts are disposable, yes? The brain spits out garbage all day long. Strange impulses. Bizarre fantasies. Gross images you don't go looking for but pop into your mind anyway. Yes?"

Speedy chuckles.

"Right. It's completely normal. People with healthy brains just brush the thoughts away. OCD is, essentially, a rupture in that sweeping mechanism. If you suffer from OCD, you can't brush them away. Your mind gets stuck on them. It obsesses over them."

"I thought little kids didn't get mental illnesses. I thought it only happens later, to really messed-up adults."

"It is unusual for OCD to crop up at such a young age. But it's not unheard of. There are plenty of cases in which symptoms arise in children even younger than Eliot. Early onset is often triggered by a traumatic event, such as the death of a loved one."

"Oh."

Long pause.

"I see," says my dad.

"I recommend you bring her in twice a week. Talk therapy can be very beneficial for children with OCD. You may also want to bring her to a psychiatrist to be evaluated for medication if—"

"No drugs," Speedy says, cutting off the doctor.

"Studies have shown that early intervention can be very—"

"No drugs," he repeats. "She's eleven. No psychiatrists, no drugs." Pause. "Whatever makes you comfortable."

You're wrong! I want to scream at both of them. *This isn't a disease. I'm just a bad person. I wasn't traumatized by the death of my brother. I didn't even cry.*

But I don't yell. I don't say anything. They're almost done talking. I stand and slip silently down the hall.

"YOU AREN'T A lesbian," says Dr. Droopy.

"How do you know?" I ask.

"Several of my patients are gay, Eliot. Being in the closet is a difficult, often traumatic experience. But a mind that *worries* over being gay is different than a mind that actually *is* gay."

"I know. But your sexuality is an inherent thing, right? You don't choose it. So what if I'm gay and just not willing to admit it to myself? Because of the stigma or whatever? I mean, I found this girl's butt attractive, right?"

"There's a difference between finding someone attractive and being sexually attracted to them. Do you feel a desire to kiss Caroline?"

I consider. I picture what it would be like. Imagine my mouth on hers, my fingers in her abundant hair. I check my body for a reaction and, of course, I find one. I find that stubborn, insistent pulse. While the logical part of my brain tells me that I'm not a lesbian, that I've never felt attracted to a woman before, my Worries insist that I might be. That a pulse is enough evidence to throw the whole equation into chaos.

But I can't say that to Dr. Droopy, can I? Tell an old man about something happening in my vagina? No way.

Bodies don't lie. And I think my body knows something I don't.

"DO YOU JOURNAL?" asks Dr. Droopy the next week. "Do you write about these thoughts? These Worries, as you call them?"

I nod.

"Does it help?"

"I mean." I pick at my lower lip. It's chapped. It's always chapped. "I'm here, aren't I?"

He doesn't laugh. "Journaling can be a great way to get out all the thoughts and feelings stirring around in your head. But"—he shifts in his chair, the way he does every time he's about to say something he believes meaningful—"for someone like you, it can also be dangerous."

"Dangerous?"

"Yes." He shifts again. "The entries where you write about your Worries—how long are they, usually?"

"Long. Like, multiple pages, usually."

"And at the end of all that writing, do you feel better?"

I consider the question. As I think, I tug at a thread of skin on the corner of my lip. It pops off. "Not really."

He nods. "That's common for someone of your temperament. As I said, sometimes journaling is a release. Sometimes it's exactly what you need. But sometimes"—shift—"all that writing, those pages and pages of careful examination . . . they send you further down the spiral."

The spiral. Huh. I suppose my thoughts *do* look like spirals. They don't feel like it, though. If anything, they feel more like tunnels. Like digging deeper and deeper into a place you never wanted to go in the first place.

17

NOW

WE BROKE FOR lunch.

As the rest of my family filed into the cabin to grab the sandwiches Wendy and the Nurses had set out, I stood on the floating dock and toweled off the lake water, gazing at the horizon and longing for my laptop. I'd been on Cradle Island for almost twenty-four hours now, and I hadn't opened my computer even once. We only had Wi-Fi in my parents' cabin, which meant I'd need to sit in their living room if I wanted to check my email. I wasn't particularly keen on all of the prying questions that Mom would ask if she cornered me down there.

Still, being away from my job was starting to take its toll.

I could feel it. I could feel it in the direction my thoughts had taken in the sauna, in the little flare-up of spit obsession I'd experienced the night before. At some point that day, I needed to make an escape to my computer. My boss had told me to take this week entirely off, that I deserved it, that I'd worked *so hard* on Blossom's behalf for the last three years. There would be no immediate tasks for me to complete. But that didn't mean I couldn't get ahead on future work, right?

"You coming inside?"

I startled, turning around to find Manuel standing on the porch, staring down at me. His swim trunks were damp with water. His curls were messy, freshly rubbed with a towel. He wore a strange expression that I couldn't quite decipher.

"Yeah," I said. "Just a minute."

He nodded, then turned and walked into the cabin.

Taking a few deep breaths—and pinching my arms for good measure—I crossed the floating dock and started up the rocks, following him.

Inside, bags and chips and sandwich makings awaited. I put together a quick ham and cheese, topped it with a handful of Ruffles, and walked out to the dinner table, where everyone else was already seated. The closest open seat—of course—was right next to Manuel. I could walk all the way around the table and take the chair next to Karma, but the move would be pretty obvious.

I gritted my teeth and walked over to the chair beside Manuel.

"So. Eliot," said my mom before I even sat down, "I meant to tell you, just the other day, I was watching this *60 Minutes* episode on Obsessive-Compulsive Disorder."

My fingers slipped, dropping the paper plate awkwardly onto the table. I said nothing, did not even react to my mother's words. I lowered myself into my chair and carefully picked up the chips that had scattered over the checkered tablecloth.

"And I must say," Wendy continued, "the victim in question . . ."

"Victim?" Clarence interrupted. "Does having OCD also make you the target of a serial killer?"

Karma snorted.

"No." Mom spoke crisply, the word its own punctuation mark. "I meant . . . the *person* in question—the OCD patient—she wasn't anything like you."

"Hey, Mom." Karma nodded at Helene and her parents. "Maybe don't talk about mental health in front of the new folks, hmm? They might not want in on all the family secrets just yet."

I glanced at Helene. She smiled kindly.

"I'm sorry," said Mom. "I thought, since it's all in the past now . . ."

I glanced sideways at Manuel. His face was resolutely neutral, betraying nothing. I took a deep breath.

"No, no," I said. "Mom's right. It's in the past. It's fine."

Mom looked pleased. "Right. As I was saying. This woman—she was hyperneurotic."

"Right," I said. "And I've told you before: the type of OCD I had wasn't about germs."

"I know, I know. I just . . . it got me thinking." She spun her cup with two hands. "You never really explained it to me. If it wasn't about germs, then what *was* it about?"

I felt a pulse. A throb. *Down there.* Quick as a heartbeat but still clear. Distinct.

Shit.

I shifted to the side. Tucked one leg over the other. Hoped the extra pressure on my crotch would keep it from happening again. "It's hard to explain."

"Can you try?"

I could feel Manuel's eyes on me. "Well"—I dug one fingernail absentmindedly into the cushion of my chair—"I didn't *seem* neurotic on the outside because my disorder was happening all on the inside."

"What does that mean?"

"My compulsions—for the most part, they were internal. Like checking, for example, or seeking reassurance, whether from someone else, like Dr. Droo—like Dr. Drier, or from myself, from what I found in my body."

"What's checking?"

"It's a pretty common compulsion with people who have the type of OCD that I do. You check and recheck certain parts of your body, wanting to see if you'll find a . . . response there." God, why the hell was I talking about this?

"I still don't understand. What kind of a 'response' were you looking for? What were you so afraid of?"

My stomach clenched. For the first time in years, I ran intentionally through the list of Worries that plagued me, on and off, for almost a decade: lying, confusion of sexuality, cheating, incest . . . and *it*. The worst one of all.

The one I could tell no one, not ever.

I decided to start with the easiest. The least terrifying. "Well." My vagina throbbed again. More acutely, this time. I shifted. "For example, I went through a phase where I was really obsessed with the possibility that I might be a lesbian."

"Hey!" Karma clapped. "I didn't know that! That's great news!" She patted the chair next to her. "Come on over to the Dark Side, Boosie. There's plenty of room."

I laughed. "No. Not like . . . I didn't actually think I was gay. I was just worried that I *might* be."

Karma blinked. "So . . . you were questioning your sexuality?"

"No, it's not that, either. It's different. It's more to do with *worry* than reality."

Everyone stared blankly.

I couldn't believe I was saying this out loud. I felt especially aware of Helene's poor parents, who were surely feeling in over their heads. "What I mean to say is"—I cleared my throat—"I didn't hyperclean my room or count to twelve over and over or refuse to touch doorknobs or any of those other compulsions you see on TV. Those are germ-based compulsions. Mine was more of . . . well . . . the way my therapist described it was that OCD is a bad medical patient."

"What does that mean?" asked Mom.

"Imagine this: Your head hurts. But instead of thinking, 'Oh, my head hurts—I have a headache,' you think, 'Oh my God, my head hurts—I have brain cancer.'"

"Ha!" said Clarence. "Sounds like my WebMD search history."

"Right," I said. "But this goes beyond that. You go to a neurologist. They scan your head. They say, 'Nope, nothing there. Take two Advil and drink lots of water.' But instead of listening, you think, 'No, no, that can't be right,' and you seek a second opinion. Another doctor. And this one says, 'You definitely don't have brain cancer. Take two Advil and drink lots of water,' and now you have *two* medical professionals telling you that you don't have brain cancer. That's an overwhelming amount of evidence, right?" I paused. "Wrong. To OCD, no amount of evidence is enough. OCD says, 'Nope. I know more than either of these board-certified experts, and I'm telling you that there's still a chance that you might have brain cancer.'"

"But I thought you said you didn't have illness OCD?" said Mom.

Frustrated, I shook my head. "I didn't. That's just a metaphor." I couldn't believe I was delivering a monologue about OCD to my family. When had I ever delivered a monologue about *anything* to my family? "The point is this: OCD doesn't listen to reason. It didn't matter how many boys I dated or how many Disney Channel celebrities I had a crush on or how many times my therapist just flat-out told me I was straight. My OCD always found some reason to doubt my heterosexuality."

I stopped. Heaved in a deep breath. When I glanced at Karma, her mouth hung open, as if she was appalled by what she'd just heard.

Shit, I thought, averting my gaze.

For a moment, I was scared. Scared she would yell. Call me ignorant and selfish, a straight woman co-opting the trauma of the gay experience.

To my right, I felt something wrap around my hand. I glanced over. Manuel's eyes were warm on mine. I inhaled sharply. *It's okay,* he mouthed. He squeezed my hand again, sending little tremors dancing up my arm and across my chest. I glanced down at our folded hands. Back up at Manuel. He smiled encouragingly.

After a few moments, I was finally able to bring myself to look back up at Karma. When I did, I saw in her eyes—to my surprise—not anger . . . but pain.

"And you didn't just worry about being a lesbian?" Karma asked.

I shook my head. "There was more. Plenty more."

Karma's face crumpled slightly. She opened her mouth—to say what, I'm not sure, because my mother chose that moment to cut in.

"Well, that's just silly," said Wendy. "Of course you aren't a lesbian. You don't even *look* like one."

Karma's eyes snapped away from mine. "Mom. Jesus. How many times do I have to tell you? That's not how it works."

"You know what I meant."

"No, actually, I don't."

"I meant . . . you know." Wendy waved her hands aimlessly. "She doesn't look all . . ."

"Butch?" Karma pronounced the word as if it had two syllables: Bu-*tch*.

"I don't know. I'm sorry, okay? So sue me for not knowing how to identify a lesbian."

Karma rolled her eyes so far back I thought they might fall out of her head. "We aren't woodland creatures, Wendy. You don't *identify* us."

I peeked over at Shelly, curious to see what her reaction to all of this would be.

She was barely holding back her laughter.

18

FRESHMAN YEAR

ON THE LAST day before high school, everything changes.

I'm sitting on the front steps of our house. My foot taps out an anxious rhythm on the step below: *tap-tap-tap, tap-tap-tap, tap-tap-tap*. My eyes are glued to the street beyond, the same intersection upon which our house has always sat. A paved cross surrounded by streetlights, varyingly green lawns, and an electrical box atop which I used to sit while waiting for the school bus. I'm waiting for a black car with tinted windows to appear in that intersection. I'm waiting for it to make the left turn that means it's going to pull into our half circle of a driveway.

I haven't seen Manuel in almost a month. He came up to Cradle for a bit, as always, but he had to leave early for a two-week-long track-and-field camp, followed by another two weeks in Colombia, visiting family. Naturally, we've kept up over text and FaceTime, but it isn't the same as having him here, in person, sitting side by side as I've always known we were meant to be.

After a small eternity, the Escalade finally appears. I jump to my feet, grinning as it rounds the intersection and pulls into our driveway. The driver has barely brought the car to a halt before the back door swings open and Manuel slides out.

The moment he lands on the pavement, I freeze.

My best friend is nearly unrecognizable. Gone are his round cheeks and the tuft of hair between his eyebrows. Gone is the acne that flooded both of our faces in seventh and eighth grade. Gone are his gangly, awkward arms and legs, the ones that used to be far too long for his small torso. Gone is the curly hair that he never quite knew how to tame.

In their place?

"Beck!" hollers the devastatingly handsome stranger bounding up the front steps. He sweeps me into his arms with impossible ease and swings me in huge circles. When he sets me back down on the top step, he grins and places two strong hands on my shoulders, squeezing them affectionately. His smile is dazzling. "I missed you."

Oh no.

That's my first thought after finally seeing my best friend again.

Oh no. Oh shit. Oh fuck.

His thick dark eyebrows pull together, creating lines in his smooth tan skin. His skin is *always* slightly bronzed, but after two weeks under the Cartagena sun? God. And has his jaw *always* looked like that? Strong and stately, two perfectly carved lines meeting at that round, dimpled chin?

"Beck?" he asks, frowning his heart-shaped lips. "Are you all right?"

"Stop talking," I blurt before I can stop myself.

Those strong eyebrows shoot up toward his hairline. "What?"

"I mean . . ."

I mean, stop talking, because when you do, I have to look at your lips. Those round, cherry-pink lips. And I've never noticed how soft they look before, two plump, juicy fruits that I'd love nothing more than to take a big—

I inhale sharply. Where the hell did *that* thought come from?

Manuel is still staring at me, his expression growing more nervous by the second.

Pull yourself together, Eliot, I think desperately. *He's still Manny. He's still the boy you said goodbye to a month ago, even if he's grown, like, six inches, and also gained a disturbing amount of muscle. And probably a six-pack. None of that matters, because he's your best friend. The only person at school you've ever been able to stand. The only person who makes your Worries go quiet, even if it's just for a few minutes at a time.*

He is your best. Fucking. Friend.

And I would never jeopardize that friendship for something as trivial as him becoming insanely hot overnight.

Never.

So I don't. I push my observations about his looks down, *deep* down, just as I do with my Worries. I push them down, and I lock them away in a box that I will never, ever allow myself to open. Not for anything. Because nothing could possibly be worth ruining what he and I have.

I curve my mouth into the most convincing sarcastic smile that I can manage. "I mean, stop talking, Valde, because we have a fresh box of Fruit Roll-Ups to eat inside."

His expression falters. It's barely a half second of change, but in that moment, I think I see something bizarre.

I think I see disappointment.

It's gone just as soon as it appeared. He matches my smile, throwing a muscled arm over my shoulders and tugging me toward the front door. "Well, we wouldn't want those to go to waste, now, would we?"

THAT YEAR, WE start dating. Both of us—Manuel first, then me, like dominoes collapsing toward romance. For him, it's inevitable.

And at the sight of his newfound height and lean, muscular runner's body, girls practically flock to him. He has his first girlfriend by the end of the first week of school, they've broken up by the end of the second, and he has another by the third.

Me, I've never had a boyfriend before. Not even one of those preschool boyfriends, the ones you hold hands with one week and break up with the next. But something must have changed about me over the summer, too, because I catch guys checking me out in the hallways on multiple occasions. They never approach me, though. Not the way girls do with Manuel. In class, a few guys start flirting with me, but it always ends after a week or two. I never know why. One day they're friendly, and the next they give me the cold shoulder when I say hello.

More than once, I check to see if my deodorant is still working.

It's not surprising that Manuel finds love well before I do. I mean, I'm not *ugly*. I have clear skin, high cheekbones, and a mostly symmetrical face. A mouth that, when it laughs, could swallow a small school bus. I wear my dirty-blond hair long and straight. I almost never put on any makeup but mascara and the occasional zit-covering foundation. To be honest, I haven't thought much about my looks until this year.

"You look like that folk singer," Manuel once told me.

"Which one?"

"The one with the long hair and the middle part."

"That's, like . . . every folk singer ever."

"No, no, no. I'm thinking of just one. She married Johnny Cash."

"June Carter?"

"Yes. June Carter. You look like June Carter."

I tried to picture Carter, but all I remembered was Reese Witherspoon playing her in *Walk the Line*. All I remembered was Carter holding Cash as he shivered and screamed, a decade's worth of addiction bleeding out onto his bedsheets.

———————

THREE YEARS HAVE passed since I first went to see Dr. Droopy. Since then, we've kept a regular appointment schedule—every week, twice a week. I don't know if I'm getting better or worse. I still worry about being a lesbian almost every day, even though I know I'm not. Or, at least, I'm pretty sure I'm not. Or, at least . . .

Ack.

Some days, the thoughts are bad. Torturous. Some days, I can turn them into background noise, a steady hum of worry. Every day is different. Every hour, really. Every minute.

They're quietest when I'm with my best friend.

ON THE DAY I turn fifteen, Manuel and I carry a backpack full of Busch Light down to the beach. It's October, and the air is still warm, but we dig a small hole in the sand, just deep enough to reach the layer that holds the lake's freeze. We press a few beers into the hole and wiggle them down. We push until only the tops stick out, tabs and locked lids gasping for air. Manuel covers the hole with his backpack.

He sighs, and I glance over to see him staring at his phone.

"What?" I ask.

"Is this what all American relationships are like?"

I peer over his shoulder. He's texting Sara, the latest in his line of women. I see little grey bubbles popping up in quick, angry succession. Some contain entire paragraphs.

I shrug. "You're asking the wrong girl."

"Man, dating was so much simpler in Colombia."

"You mean . . . back when you were nine?"

"Yeah."

"Ah, yes. I forgot you were *Señor Popular*." I drain the last sip of beer and toss the can over a rotting driftwood log. "Manuel Garcia Valdecasas: first-grade lady-killer."

He sighs. "You have no idea."

Honestly, I probably shouldn't be drinking. Alcohol lowers your inhibitions, right? If I had to guess, that also means that it loosens the locks that we keep on the boxes within ourselves. Very *important* boxes, in my case, such as the one that I chained up on the day my best friend returned from Colombia. And as I sit here, snuggled deep in the sand, I can feel that box rattling. I can feel it as my eyes slide sideways, drinking in Manuel's profile as he squints down at his phone screen. His smooth skin. The sharp pitch of his jaw. The—

Stop. I tear my eyes away, forcing myself to look out at Lake Michigan instead. *You can't let yourself go down that road.*

But I can't let ridiculous, unattainable fantasies keep me from enjoying myself and being young, either. I only turn fifteen once. I'm going to enjoy it.

I grab another Busch Light and crack it open.

"Something weird is happening at school," I say as I lift the can to my lips and take a sip. The beer is watery and too warm.

"Oh?" Manuel doesn't look up from his phone. "What's that?"

"I don't even know how to describe it." I scratch the back of my head with my free hand. "It almost feels like I'm wearing a Do Not Disturb sign on my back and don't even know it."

He snorts. "What do you mean?"

"I mean that . . . well, there have been a couple of times in the last few months where I genuinely thought that a guy might be interested in me . . ."

Manny's head jerks back suddenly, eyes snapping up from his phone to my face. He looks shocked. Alarmed even.

"But every time," I continue, ignoring his expression, "just when

I think they might ask me out, they suddenly lose interest. Like *that*." I snap my fingers. "They stop texting me, stop talking to me in class . . ." I shake my head. "It's bizarre."

His face relaxes. "I'm sure it's nothing, Beck. They're probably just cowards."

"But what could they possibly have to be afraid of?"

His lips twitch, as if he finds my question funny.

"I'm serious, Valde. It's borderline offensive. I mean, you have a new girlfriend every week, and I can't even get one guy to ask me out?" I smile wryly. "I get that you and I are in completely different leagues, but am I really *that* hideous?"

I meant it as a joke. A little self-deprecation that I thought would make him laugh.

Instead, his face ignites with fury. Eyes narrow, nostrils flare. I startle, twitching backward. I've never seen my best friend look at me like this before, and—to be perfectly honest—it's *terrifying*.

"Don't you *ever* say that about yourself again," he says, voice low and dangerous. "*Escúchame*, Eliot. Don't call yourself ugly. *¿Me entiendes?*"

I can only stare back, mouth hanging open.

Manuel leans forward, grabbing my shoulders as he repeats himself in English. "Do. You. Understand?"

"Yes. *Yes*, Jesus." I shake off his hands. "I was just kidding."

He turns back to the lake, a muscle pulsing in his jaw. "Well, I didn't find it funny."

"Clearly," I mutter. What the hell has gotten *into* him?

After a few minutes of tense silence, Manny exhales. "And," he says, rubbing the back of his neck, "there's something else I should tell you." Pause. "It's probably my fault that you're getting the cold shoulder from so many guys."

I blink. "What?"

"I may have, um . . ." Is that a slight pink I see creeping into his cheeks? "Insinuated a few things to the guys on the track team. About you. And what I would do if they tried to pursue you."

My heart stumbles. I try desperately to push it back into line as I ask, "What kind of . . . things?"

"Oh, you know." He still doesn't look at me, but I *swear* his blush deepens. "Nothing much. Physical violence. Bodily harm. Secret Colombian assassins that my parents are in contact with." He shrugs. "The usual."

Is he . . . ?

I shut off that question before I can finish it. *Don't get carried away, Eliot.* He's just being overprotective, the same way that Caleb or Clarence or Taz would be. Nothing more.

Then, as if he could read my thoughts and wanted to confirm them, he quickly added, "But I may have taken it too far. You clearly want to be able to date these guys, and you should be able to. I'm sorry for my interference."

"That's not . . ." I search helplessly for the right words. *That's not true. Those aren't the guys I want to date. There's only one guy I want to date, and he's sitting right next to—*

Nope. Stop. None of that. You don't think about your best friend that way.

I do the only thing I can. I smile and say, "Thanks, Valde."

I MEET HIM later that year, during my first day at the *Trevian*, our school newspaper. I already know who he is, of course. I've seen him everywhere. On Facebook. In the lunch room. From afar. From behind, as Manuel and I bring up the rear of a group wandering down a street called Elm or Oak or Pine. In the McDonald's parking lot, where on certain Saturday nights a crowd gathers. Not to eat cheeseburgers or smoke weed or drink stolen alcohol—just to show their faces. Just to show that they know where to loiter.

Manuel forces me to join the paper. "You quit soccer ages ago," he says. "You need a new thing."

"A *thing*?" I ask.

"Yes. A thing. Colleges want you to have a thing."

We're freshmen, but college is already top of mind for Manuel.

"Okay, Mom," I say. "Why the newspaper?"

"Come on, Beck. You've been in love with words since the day I met you."

"Have I?"

"Of course you have. Remember all those stories you wrote in the Fort?"

"Absolutely not," I groan. "And I'd appreciate it if you didn't remind me."

"*And* you have an entire shelf full of journals in your room."

"Fine," I say. "Fine, fine, fine."

It starts innocently enough, as all dangerous relationships do. On my first day at the *Trevian*, I choose a section. I already know I can't do News. Every comment on my English and history papers reads the same—*Good argument, voice too informal.* I don't get it. To me, writing is just transferring the words in my head onto paper. I don't write with a certain "voice"—I just write.

A history paper written like an anxious fifteen-year-old girl?

Yeah. Doesn't play well.

So I join Op-Ed, instead. Which is how I meet Leo.

Leo is popular. Not the normal kind, the kind that comes from good looks and a mean spirit. He's different. Weird. Loud and unselfconscious. He has opinions about everything. He interviews teachers and spies on the AV Club and gives presentations on the time his little brother put the cat in the freezer. He tries, really *tries*, in a way no cool kid is ever supposed to. But it works. For him, it works. He figured out, long before anyone else, that laughter is the way to get someone to like you. Give it freely. Reek with irony. Apologize for nothing. Live your life as one long inside joke.

And he's cool. *Cool* cool, a block of ice in a warm room, dripping at the corners, and everyone else is thirsty. They gather around him and lap at the puddles, and their tongues sound like laughter, and for some reason, for whatever reason, out of all those people, he chooses me.

HE KISSES ME at a party. To be more specific, he pulls me onto his lap on a couch in the middle of a party and sticks his tongue down my throat. A dog marking his territory. Manuel sees it from across the room. The next day, everyone knows, which I suppose makes me his girlfriend.

TO SAY MANUEL is skeptical would be an outrageous understatement.

"What's this guy's deal?" he asks grouchily. "Doesn't he sit at the jock table?"

"You're a jock," I say.

"I'm a *runner*. It's not the same."

"Isn't it? Because I'm pretty sure rowing and cross-country are actually the same sport. Both are just dudes with long legs wearing tiny shorts."

"Good one. I'm just saying. What do we even know about him?"

"What do *you* even know about the eighty-seven girls you've dated since setting foot in America?"

"That's different."

"Sure it is."

He sticks out his tongue. So do I.

———————

DESPITE MANUEL'S SKEPTICISM, Leo turns out to be the perfect boyfriend. He writes me love notes on wrinkled paper and shoves them through the slits of my locker. He brings flowers to the *Trevian* on our one-month anniversary. He waits for me after second-period math just to walk me to my next class. Just the way you're supposed to.

Despite all of that, being in a relationship doesn't feel the way I thought it would. Looking at Leo doesn't create that cloud at the base of my gut, the one you hear about in romance novels, that feels at once both tight and loose, both heavy and light as a feather. But maybe none of that matters. Maybe love has many narratives, and that's one, and this is another.

THE FIRST FEW weeks of my relationship with Leo are, for the most part, sunshine and rainbows. And then—*surprise, surprise!*—who walks in? The Worries.

It's another day at the *Trevian*. I'm in my usual position—back corner, fingers laced with Leo's—when I hear my name called from out in the hallway. I crane my head around and find, out in the hallway, Manuel.

"Hey!" I spring out of my chair, bounding out into the hall and throwing my arms around Manny's neck—my typical greeting. I feel Leo's eyes drilling into my back, so I pull quickly away, smiling up at my best friend. "What's up?"

He smiles back. "Nothing urgent. Just wanted to see if you're down for a Tarantino night after you're done at the paper."

"Obviously."

"*Qué chimba.*" He nudges my shoulder with his fist. "See you at seven."

On the s in *seven*, a spit droplet soars out of Manuel's mouth and lands on my chin. Just below my bottom lip. We both see it happen, but in the name of sparing his embarrassment, I pretend like it didn't.

Wipe the spit off your face, say my Worries.

I can't, I say back.

You have to. That spit came from his mouth. If it goes into yours, that's as good as kissing him.

No, it's not. That's ridiculous.

It's not ridiculous. Do you want to feel guilty about cheating on Leo?

I plaster a smile onto my face and bump Manny with my hip. "See you at seven."

When I get back to my usual corner, Leo takes my hand. "What did Handsome Manny want?" There's a strange bite to his voice when he says Manuel's name, but I don't have the mental capacity to analyze it. All I can think about is that spit droplet.

Wipe the spit off your face.

Normally, I *would* just wipe it, right? Use the back of my arm. Not think twice about it. But I can tell that this droplet has taken on increased significance. If I wipe it away, I'll be giving in to the Worries.

So I do the opposite. I lick it. I lick the spit right into my mouth.

Take that, I think proudly.

THE PRIDE LASTS roughly twelve seconds. That's how long it takes for doubt to creep in. *You just licked the spit of another boy. On purpose. Do you think Leo would like that?*

No, I realize. I don't.

After class, I dig out my phone and google is it cheating to lick someone else's spit while you have a boyfriend. I click through each of the top links, scrolling through listicles and blog posts that, one day, I will understand have been written by a copywriter or a PR firm or a bored sixteen-year-old with no college degree but, at the time, are the closest I can come to moral guidance.

I keep searching. I press on a page called "Does This Count as Infidelity?" That's how I first learn the terms *precheating* and *emotional affair*—which, as the experts agree, is in some cases even worse than sleeping with someone. I scroll frantically through headlines and subheads and four-line blocks of text. The more I read, the less certain I become.

19

NOW

THERE WERE ONLY two events scheduled for the afternoon: Orienteering and the Fishing Contest.

Orienteering is a navigational sport that, at its core, amounts to an hour of walking through the woods in various straight lines. Each team starts at a given point on the edge of the island armed with nothing more than a compass and a number. The number—ranging from 1° to 360°—indicates the direction in which the team should walk. Earlier that day, Wendy and the in-laws trekked through the middle of the island and set up navigational "checkpoints"—ribbons tied to trees or rocks or jumbled-up cairns that marked the end of each leg of our journey.

Manuel and I started out the contest in silence. Personally, my mind was on the conversation we'd had at lunch around OCD. Had I really admitted—in front of my *entire* family—that I used to worry about being a lesbian? Three years ago, I wouldn't have dared. Wouldn't have admitted to a single fucked-up thought in my woefully fucked-up brain, fearful of the reaction that the words would receive. But now that it was all in the past, I thought it would be okay to talk about. That maybe we could even laugh.

But what had that expression on Karma's face been?

After a few minutes, I came out of my mind enough to notice the silence blooming thick between Manuel and me. As usual, it made me almost instantly nervous. Normally, I would grasp about for the first possible subject, launching into some embarrassing monologue. But Manuel's words from the night before echoed in my head: *self-centered*, he had called me. And look—he was right! Look how I'd spent the entire walk so far living inside my own mind, my own body, not even wondering what might be going through his.

"So," I said, the word startling us both, like the burst of an unexpected balloon, "what's your major?"

Manuel glanced at me, as if amused by my humiliatingly obvious attempt at selflessness. "We don't have majors, actually."

"You don't?"

"Nope. Apparently, *major* is a term far too pedestrian for the great institution that is Harvard University. We have *concentrations.*"

"I see. Well. What's your *concentration*, then?" I asked, wrapping the word in the same biting sarcasm that he had.

He smiled. "Biomedical engineering."

"Oh." As usual, I felt somewhat helpless before his brilliance.

"Yep."

Just then, we rounded a tree trunk and found ourselves face-to-face with the first ribbon. This ribbon was bright green and tied to a thick branch of an oak tree. Below it was taped an envelope.

"We made it," I said.

"Try not to sound so surprised." Manuel reached into the envelope and pulled out a little blue note card. Scrawled on the front in Wendy's familiar handwriting was: *217°*. "That's that, then," he said, sliding the note card back into the envelope. Then he reached out one hand, palm flat to the sky.

For a moment, I wasn't sure what he was doing. Was he offering to hold my hand?

But then he said, "I'll take this round," and thankfully, just in time, I remembered the compass in my hand. I scrambled to pass it over to him. He readjusted the needle, and away we marched, leaves and sticks and daddy longlegs crunching beneath our feet.

"So," I said again. I saw the corners of his mouth tug up into a faint smile. "What does a biomedical engineer do for fun at Harvard?"

"Well," said Manuel, lifting a pine branch to let me pass underneath. "I think you remember Karma referencing the Spree, as you called it?" His tone was teasing.

My face reddened. "Yes."

"Well, the *Spee* is my Final Club."

"Oh. I remember those."

I did, actually. I remembered the week after Manuel received his acceptance, when we sat on the couch in his basement and binge-watched every piece of content we could find that took place at Harvard. I remembered learning strange new words—*Widener* and *Annenberg* and *Hasty Pudding* and *Wigglesworth*—most of which felt, to me, as foreign and inaccessible as a dinner menu written in Mandarin. "You'll have to learn a whole new language," I'd said as the end credits rolled for *The Social Network*. "You'll be *tri-lingual*, now."

Final Clubs, I remembered, were Harvard's equivalent of fraternities. "What does one do at the Spee?" I asked.

"Oh, you know," Manuel said. "All the usual Final Club things. Drinking Keystone and beheading sacrificial lambs and snorting lines of flaked gold."

I burst out laughing. The sound echoed against the tree trunks and fluttering leaves, as loud and genuine as the laughter that came out of me the day before when Clarence scooped me up and spun me around in Sunny Sunday.

After passing beneath a thick cluster of tree branches—again held up for me by Manuel's long arm—we found ourselves staring at a tall face of rock. I glanced down at the compass in his hand. Its needle pointed directly into the rock.

"Well," I said. I looked up at Manuel. "Guess we're climbing, then."

He laughed. Its sound pleased me more than I wanted to admit. When I lifted one leg to step up onto the first ledge of rock, he didn't argue or suggest we go around. Instead, he offered his hand. This time, I knew it was to hold mine.

When our palms touched—mine draped over his like a snug blanket—warmth flooded my hand, passing my wrist, traveling all the way up my arm. His other arm wrapped around my lower back, hand grabbing the bottom of my elbow to help push me up onto the wall. I shuddered slightly, an involuntary response that I tried to still before he noticed.

There it was again. The bodily reaction I needed so desperately to avoid.

With every minute I passed in his presence, it was getting more and more difficult to do so.

We scaled the rock, a short climb that spat us out atop a ledge with a view out to the lake. I straightened, catching my breath at the sight.

"Damn, Beck," said Manuel, and at the sound of that nickname, my stomach did a stupid little flip. "Do you recognize this place?"

I blinked and looked around, taking in the smooth rock and juniper bushes that covered most of the island. "Sort of?"

Manuel crouched next to a long patch of juniper. He dipped both hands into the bushes and pushed them aside. A mischievous grin curled up the sides of his mouth. "Check this out."

I walked over and peered inside. There, among the tangle of prickly armed bramble, was a pile of bottles, beer cans, and handles of liquor, all worn and wilted by years of snow and rain.

I looked at Manuel, who was still grinning. "No way."

"Yes way."

Our compass led us right to our old dumping ground—the place we hid an adolescence's worth of alcohol. We made eye contact over the empty booze. For a long moment, we held each other's gaze. Then, in perfect unison, we dissolved into laughter.

WE GAVE UP on orienteering in favor of sitting on the hilltop and staring out at the lake.

"If we're near our old stash," I said. "You know what else that means we're nearby?"

"Of course." Out of my peripheral vision, I saw Manuel smile. "The Fort."

We fell into a warm, comfortable silence. As I listened to his steady breathing, I became aware of the closeness of his hand to mine. I felt a strong urge to reach over and take it. Instead, I asked, "What does a biomedical engineer do for his summer job?"

"Well"—Manuel looked down at his hands, which were playing with loose pebbles—"I've spent the last three summers interning for the pharmaceutical empire known as none other than . . ."

My jaw fell open. "Beck Pharma? Are you serious?"

"Your mom and dad's influence helped out a lot with that one, no doubt. Though Wendy would be aghast if I ever so much as insinuated I didn't get the job on my own."

I laughed, but it sounded more like a shocked cough.

"This summer, I did my time at Beck Pharma in St. Louis, drove up to Chicago, spent a week with Che and Juli, and hitched a ride up here."

"Who . . . ?" I trailed off, recognizing the question's rudeness as I spoke it aloud.

"Invited me?" Manuel guessed.

I nodded.

"Take a wild guess."

"Let's see . . . could it be . . . my mother?"

"Ding, ding, ding!"

I rolled my eyes. "Shocker."

He pushed my shoulder lightly, just a second of contact that sent sparks rippling all the way across my chest.

"You know," I said, trying—and failing—to ignore the sparks altogether. "I wonder if, in any of the many books Wendy Beck has read on How to Mother Someone Else's Child, she ever reached the chapter on White Savior Complex."

Manuel laughed. I felt a spit droplet flash wet on the back of my hand.

Shit.

It might not have been real. It might have been a phantom droplet, like so many before it. But the movement came to me instinctually— I raised my hand up to my mouth and blew on it. To dry the droplets. To chase them away.

When I lowered my hand, Manuel caught it, long fingers wrapping around my wrist. "What did you just do?"

"Nothing," I said quickly, tugging.

"*No me mientas*, Eliot. You just blew on your hand."

"No, I didn't."

"Yes, you did."

"No, I *didn't*. I don't do that anymore."

His eyes flared. "How dare you!" he said. "How fucking dare you!"

I flinched. "How dare I what?"

"You know *exactly* what," he said.

I tugged my wrist again. He tightened his grip.

"You know what, Eliot? I get why you hide your compulsions. I get that they scare you. I get that there are thoughts you have that you never shared, even with me." He leaned in close, so close our noses almost brushed. "But after everything you put me through.

After *everything* I did for you in high school, all the lies I saw right through, all the ways your Worries tried to get in the way of our friendship, how hard I worked to make sure they couldn't. After *all* of that—how *dare* you lie to my fucking face! Me. Of *all* people."

I scrunched inward, eyes down, trying desperately to fold so far into myself that Manuel wouldn't be able to see the shame blossoming up from within me.

"I . . ." I started, then trailed off.

Manuel didn't fill the ensuing silence. He wouldn't give me that mercy.

"I'm . . ."

I didn't know what to say. A decade of friendship, of always having something to say, of allowing his warm brown eyes to tug words from me without ever questioning how they would land, and I was speechless. I didn't know how to deny his accusations. I didn't even know if they were true.

Manuel finally released my wrist. "Hey," he said, voice gentler. "Look at me."

I did.

"Are you okay, Eliot?"

My breath curled up into my chest, building, congealing, pushing into the walls of my lungs until it felt as if they might burst. How could I answer him? How could I possibly respond when I didn't know the truth myself?

20

FRESHMAN YEAR

THE WEEK BEFORE Thanksgiving, Karma marries her girlfriend of eight years, Shelly, on the roof of their condo in Lincoln Park. Almost a hundred people show up for the ceremony, standing room only, friends and cousins and teachers packed together between four precariously low railings. Caleb officiates. Every single one of my siblings is a bridesmaid, men included. Manny sits up front with my parents, right next to the aisle. He pelts grains of rice at my face when I walk past.

After Shelly and Karma kiss—to thunderous applause and an unseasonal snowfall of rice—the reception begins. A metal staircase connects the rooftop and their top-floor condo. The party spreads itself between the two levels, with the roof acting as the dance floor and the inside as the lounge. Guests flow freely between the two. Manuel and I spend the whole night on the roof. We dance beneath dangling lights until our feet hurt, stopping only to steal sips of champagne from other guests' abandoned flutes. At midnight, the new couple smashes cupcakes into each other's faces.

Manuel and I don't keep track of how much we steal from the other guests' glasses, and eventually, the sips add up. By two a.m., we're tipsy. I find, to my utter joy and fascination, that the more I drink, the less I worry. When I find one of the female guests attractive or remember some lie I told the month before, it's a quiet kind of reminder. Not as relentless as before.

By the time the party ends, Manuel and I are wheeling about the roof like unleashed puppies. The guests clear out. Soon, only the core family remains. We stumble down the metal steps and into the condo to inhale what's left of the buffet. Everyone fills plates and collapses onto the couches that were pushed up against the wall. Manuel and I grab three pieces of pizza each. I glance around at my family. They seem to be falling into a pit made of melted cheese and seat cushions. To Manny, I say, "Let's go back outside."

We carry our pizza back up. The roof, now littered with cups, napkins, and a light frost of rice hulls, is otherwise empty. We drain the last few abandoned champagne flutes, then climb up onto the wide brick-lined perimeter. Our legs dangle over the other side. The street twelve stories below contains nothing more than a few midnight drivers.

I take a bite of pizza. "I'm drunk," I announce.

"I'm also drunk," says Manuel.

We giggle.

We're freshmen. The beginning of the end. But I can't know that, of course. The night doesn't feel like the beginning or end of anything. It's just my best friend and me on the roof of a building filled with my entire family, the way it's always been. There's no future, no past. No graduation. No college. Just starlight and cold mozzarella. My bare feet—shoes came off immediately following the ceremony—bounce off the building's brick exterior.

"How's Leo on this good evening?"

"Beats me." I throw a pinch of crust off the roof.

"You aren't texting?"

"I mean"—I pick up a new slice of pizza—"he's texting me a bit. But it's my sister's wedding. I'm trying to be present, you know?"

"Makes sense to me."

I eye him over the cheese. "You don't like him."

"When did I say that?"

"You didn't. But I can tell anyway."

Manuel sighs, rubbing a hand through his short dark curls. "It's not that I don't *like* him, Beck. It's just . . ."

"Just what?" I prompt.

He opens his mouth. Closes it. Shakes his head. "Never mind."

"Nuh-uh." I wave my pizza slice at him. "No way. You don't get to do that."

"I just . . ." He sighs again, eyes on the buildings across the street. Then, all at once, he turns and looks directly at me. His face is serious, almost grave. "Are you happy with him?"

"What?" I ask. "Of course I am."

"Your honest answer," he says. "No stock bullshit."

"That *is* my honest answer."

"Is it, though?" He leans closer. "Is it?"

I shake my head, taken aback. "Where is this coming from, Manuel?"

"I just . . . Maybe it sounds ridiculous, but I just get this . . . bad feeling whenever the two of you are together."

I bunch my eyebrows. "A bad feeling?"

"Yes. It's . . . it's something in my chest. This . . . tightness. Like the way I feel whenever you do something foolish and dangerous. When you jump off a cliff into Lake Huron or climb out onto the roof at your house. It's like . . . like fear, almost."

"Fear," I repeat.

He shakes his head, frustrated. "Not quite that. But similar."

"So, you're . . . afraid when I'm with Leo? But of what?"

Manuel blinks at me once, long and slow. Then, he turns away. Looks back at the buildings. "Just forget it."

"Manuel—"

"Drop it, okay? I don't even know why I said anything in the first place."

I look down at my slice. Go quiet. I hate moments like this. When Manuel is angry, he doesn't shout. I wish he would. I always prefer his words to his silence, even when those words carry the weight of fury.

For several minutes, I stay silent, too. Then: "Do you think," I say, peeling off a pepperoni with two fingers, "that in life, you need true love to be happy?"

Manuel looks back at me. "What do you mean?"

"I mean . . . do you need romantic love?" I place the pepperoni inside my mouth. Salty pork tingles atop my tongue. "Or do you think you just need a Person?"

"A person? Like . . . a body?"

"No, no. A Person. A go-to. For example: You, Manuel, are my Person. For better or for worse. If I need advice, I go to you. If I'm sad, I call you and cry like a little baby. I tell you everything. You know all my secrets."

His lips twitch. "Yeah. That's definitely for worse."

I elbow his arm, but not forcefully enough to tip him off-balance. "You know what I mean. You're my Person. I could spend a thousand hours with you and never get bored. And I flatter myself to think I'm the same, that I'm your Person, too."

"Eh." Manuel tosses a crust off the building. It lands on the hood of Clarence's car. "You're a contender. But Wendy might be my Person, too. Depends on the day."

I elbow him again. A bit harder this time. Too hard. He grabs the stone ledge to keep balance. "Jesus, Eliot!" He scoots away from me. "Be careful."

"Sorry." I look down. "I didn't mean to push that hard."

He grunts, then looks away, far away.

I did it again.

In these moments, I become suddenly, painfully aware of the gap between us. The mental one, not physical. I recognize the fact that I don't know what he'll do next. That it could be anything. *Anything.*

We often make the mistake of believing humans are predictable. That they live by patterns. Especially if it's someone you trust. But when Manuel stops speaking, I'm reminded that I don't know his brain, not really, and it terrifies me. It terrifies me to lose the only bridge I have to his mind. To feel deprived of his words, the ones he chooses so carefully—the ones that float to my ears like small vivid rings of smoke.

EVERY THANKSGIVING MORNING, the family descends upon our home. Taz from his job in Connecticut, Karma from the construction site where her first bakery will go up, Clarence and Caleb from Real Middle-Aged Adult Life, unless they're spending the holiday with their own mother. Our doors and hallways, normally deserted, fill to their usual state of chaos. I love that chaos. I lie in bed and listen to the sound of it, the laughter and slamming doors and socks on the spiral staircase.

My room sits right at the top of those stairs. All my life, I've listened to my family go up and down, around and around. Each carries their body with a unique rhythm—Caleb with purpose, Clarence two at a time, Taz near silent, Karma with such force you'd think the stairs had wronged her. I know them all.

Taz is working at Blue Sky Studios. When he comes home, he brings a suitcase full of cords and tablets and clunky laptops that whir when you plug them in. He sets up an editing studio in one of Dad's old offices and spends most afternoons there, buried in Photoshop.

Occasionally, I poke my head in the door and watch him work. I see pixelated planets. Talking sheep. Pirates and robots. I watch them dance or run or just hold perfectly still as my brother edges them to perfection with a stylus.

One morning he catches me spying. I start to duck out the door, but he smiles and says, "Want to watch?"

I stand over his shoulder. He talks as he works, long sentences filled with words I only sort of understand, like *skins* and *masks* and *layers* and *vectors* and *integration*. As he speaks, I peek at his face. I'm struck for the first time by how old he looks; he's only been working for two years now, but already his face is stubbled and sun wiped, as if the winds of Connecticut blow stronger than they do here. He doesn't look like my brother anymore; he looks like a handsome man.

Ew. You think your brother is handsome?

Yes, I say back to the Worries. You're allowed to find your brother handsome, right?

You can find him handsome, sure. But you can't be attracted *to him. Are you attracted to him?*

No. Yuck. That's impossible.

Is it, though?

Why don't you check down there? Just to be sure. Just to make sure there's no reaction.

Okay, fine. But you're wasting your time. There's no way I . . .

Oh.

There it is. There it is again. That pulse. That sign of arousal, right in the groin.

No, no, no, no, no . . .

Blind panic rises in my chest. I'm still there, still standing beside Taz, but I no longer hear a word he's saying. All I can think about is that pulse, that throb.

I feel an immediate sense of loss. Of grief for every moment that led up to this one. Fifteen years spent free from the knowledge that I was attracted to my brother. Sixteen years. I watch that old life slip away. Oh, how lucky she was, Eliot of Thirty Seconds Ago. How good she had it. How simple her life. And she didn't even know.

I love you, Leo texts me while we're in the middle of dinner.

"Oh," I say out loud.

"What?" asks Manuel, who is with us for Thanksgiving as always.

Karma glances down the table.

I hide my phone.

"What is it?" Manuel leans over to look at my screen. "Oh. Yikes."

The tiny screen glows in my hands. I try to type, but my thumbs won't move.

"Well, do you?" he asks.

My fingers hover over the keyboard—planes above water, searching for a life raft.

I WANT TO love Leo. Really, I do. I doodle his name at the top of my biology notes. Write love notes in return. Let no sentiment go unmirrored. I wonder why, as my pencil sprints over lined paper, as I echo back all the things Leo says, none of the words sound like they were written by me.

I even attempt to fantasize about him before bed. Halfway into the fantasy, unfortunately, I remember Thanksgiving, remember that I found Taz handsome, which meant I'm sexually attracted to my brother, which meant if I'm not careful, Taz's face will appear in my fantasy instead of Leo's, and then it does appear, because of course it does, because I told it not to, so now I'm no longer making out with Leo, I'm making out with my brother, and maybe it's because I willed it into existence, but maybe it's because I was never attracted to Leo in the first place, maybe it was all a cover, a socially acceptable outlet for my deeper, darker, truer impulses. And even if

I wipe the image away as soon as it appears, that doesn't change the fact that it was there. It entered my head. I pictured my brother while sexually aroused—and if I didn't already have enough evidence to put myself away for life, that would be it.

So.

Better to avoid sexual fantasies altogether.

CHRISTMAS. WITH MY sister in the throes of opening her first bakery and my half brothers long grown up, it's our first meal together in a while. Karma tells us about blowing up a pot full of chocolate. Caleb does a spot-on impersonation of Speedy telling one of his long, rambling stories. Clarence rags on his coworkers at Beck Pharma, telling stories that make me laugh so hard I almost spit up my barbecued chicken.

And me—well, I never have much to say at family dinner. It's because of Henry, I think. He was my life vest, the buoy that gave me the confidence to entertain our family with self-produced musicals and long, rambling monologues. But ever since he died, I've spent most of these meals in silence, legs folded beneath me, elbows on the table. I have stuff to say, too. But at a table full of the people I admire most—and with Manuel at his own house for Christmas—I forget what it is.

"Karma, did you have a good session with Dr. Scherman yesterday?" asks Mom.

"Mom." The word comes out round and heavy, Karma's humiliation obvious.

"You're seeing Dr. Scherman?" asks Clarence.

She shrugs.

"Oh, don't be embarrassed, Karma." Clarence claps her on the shoulder. "A little mental illness ain't nothin' to be afraid of. Myself, I got the Big D."

Karma's eyes light up. "Depression? Really?"

"Full-on, kid."

"No shit. Me too."

I watch Karma's face change. I watch it open, slowly, like a flower in the sun.

FROM THAT MOMENT on, Clarence and Karma are inseparable. A bubble of cheerful nihilism, inaccessible to the rest of the family. Filled with inside jokes and antidepressants. I'm not invited to the mental illness party. Too young, I guess. Or maybe I have the wrong disease. Maybe they won't invite what they can't understand.

Between the two of them, Karma and Clarence are on every antidepressant on the shelf. "Wait," I say to Speedy. "I thought we weren't allowed to take drugs."

Karma laughs. "Clarence and I are adults. We can take whatever we want."

They compare notes on dosage, side effects. Swap stories about weight gain and vertigo. Their mental illnesses become a sort of game. Before breakfast, they toss pills into each other's mouths like little grapes, cheering when they catch them, laughing when they don't. More often than not, they miss, and the meds fly over their heads, falling to the ground somewhere they'll never be found. Disguised by bugs and dust.

I come across the stray pills from time to time. Between cracks in the floorboard, nestled among couch cushions. Innocent and unsuspecting. Like loose change. I bend over. Pick them up. Study them. Wonder how they work. Wonder if it's just like Advil, just one tiny circle to make the pain go away.

From: Memory & Other Executive Functions <memory@eliot-beck.org>
To: Conscious Mind <consciousness@eliot-beck.org>
Subject: OCD Question & Answer Form [ACTION REQUIRED]

What does OCD do?

OCD ruins things. Parties. Conversations. Relationships. Dinners. Plane rides. Walks down the street. It can ruin anything. It *will*, if you give it the power to do so.

Why is OCD hard to identify?

It's not a regular illness. There's no well-known path forward. You don't know what you're fighting against. You throw flames on a piece of you that looks like it needs burning only to find that it was the wrong piece, that you're not actually in love with your brother, that the problem is elsewhere, is elsewhat, is tens of thousands of things.

Society says, "If you come down with the sniffles, go to the doctor." Society says, "If you think you're in love with your brother, you should be in jail."

Imagine knowing that jail is the only logical future for you. Imagine knowing that since you were fifteen.

What does OCD feel like?

Well, that's the trick. After a certain point, OCD isn't a feeling; it's just your life.

21

NOW

KARMA GAVE UP on the last event, the Fishing Contest, before it even started. As soon as the *Silver Heron* was anchored in our lucky spot, she cracked open two beers—one for herself, one for Shelly—and planted herself on the lid of the cooler meant to hold our catch.

"Hey, asshole," Karma said to Clarence. "Want a beer?"

"I'm concentrating." He stood off to the side, silently threading and baiting a series of fishing rods. His fingers worked deftly, as graceful as spiders' legs. When he finished a rod, he laid it against the rail. They formed a tall, regal lineup—knights at attention.

"Your loss," said Karma. She clinked bottles with Shelly and took a swig.

Normally, it would strike me as odd to hear Clarence turn down alcohol, but the only thing my half brother likes more than having a good time is catching a big fish. When I was a kid, he went every morning. Seriously. Every day, crack of dawn, Clarence was out trawling for early risers. Sometimes, Caleb, Taz, Henry, or, eventually, Manuel went with him. For them, it was a novelty, a fun activity to do once or twice a summer. Not for Clarence. For him, it was an obsession.

Unlike the boys, I never accompanied him. Sit on a boat and stare at the water in silence for three hours? Try to think of something interesting to say to my coolest brother? No, thank you.

Manuel carried our rods over to the starboard corner of the stern, placing them inside the little holes meant to hold fishing poles. I pulled over two folding chairs and set them up on the ground while he peeled the lid off a Styrofoam cup filled with soft dirt and wiggling worms. I watched in semi-disgust as he used a fishing hook to saw one of the worms in half, then skewer each half in turn. He handed one of the baited rods to me.

"Yummy," I said before sitting down.

"The worms aren't for you," he said, settling into his own chair. "They're for the pike."

"Is that what we're fishing for?" I asked. "What about rainbow trout?"

"It's more likely that we'll catch a pike. Rainbows do happen, but not often. They prefer rivers and creeks."

I cast my line, then peered suspiciously over at him. "Since when did you become an expert in Southern Ontario fish patterns?"

Manuel shrugged. "Clarence and I did a fair bit of fishing last year, and I—"

He shut abruptly off, realizing his mistake.

I almost dropped my rod. "Last year?"

"Uh . . ." Manuel glanced over his shoulder.

I leaned closer to him. "Did you say 'last year'?"

He glanced nervously about. Looking for an escape, maybe. Then, as if making a decision, he looked back at me, rolled his shoulders, and lifted his chin. A challenge. "Yes," he said firmly, "I did."

"You were here last year," I said, "without me?"

"I was." He paused. "And the year before."

"You . . ." I was dumbfounded. "But . . ."

"I'm a part of this family, too, Eliot." His chin lifted higher. "Just because you chose to disappear, to cut us all out . . . that doesn't mean I had to do the same."

I opened my mouth. Closed it again. I wanted to say something back, to argue with him, but the thing is . . . he was right. He *was* part of our family.

Maybe even more than I was.

Before I could find the words to reply, Manuel turned away, adjusted his rod, and focused on the water, on the fish, on anything but me.

AN HOUR INTO the tournament, people started to get nervous. Dinner that night was supposed to be a fresh fish fry—emphasis on *fresh*.

"It's just not the same when it comes from the store." Mom always pouts.

But so far, all we'd hauled in was a big, juicy twenty-inch nothing.

"Everyone else has had a bite but me," Dad called out from the bow, where his wheelchair was tied to the railing with two lengths of rope. He looked suspiciously over at Clarence. "You give me faulty bait, son?"

"Everyone gets the same bait, Dad."

"Well, something's wrong with mine."

By that point, Karma was drunk enough to actually be enjoying herself. She teetered about the boat, making lewd comments about rods. She spent extra time over in Clarence's corner, poking him and dangling worms before his nose and knocking his hat down over his eyes.

Manuel and I hadn't said much to each other in the previous hour. We'd mostly stared out at the lake or the unmoving rods in our hands. Eventually, he mumbled something about needing the bathroom and slipped inside the *Silver Heron*'s cabin.

As soon as he was gone, another body plopped down into his chair.

I turned to the side, expecting to find Karma. Instead, I was shocked to see Caleb pick up Manuel's rod and cast it into the water.

"Had to get away from Karma and Clarence," my oldest brother said, winking. "I think they're about to get into an actual fistfight."

I snorted. "Sounds about right."

"So, what's new, Boose?" He leaned back in the folding chair. "I feel like we haven't had much of a chance to chat this trip."

His question probably shouldn't have taken me as far aback as it did. Shouldn't have made me curl into myself, made my cheeks burn with the spotlight of attention I wasn't used to getting. But I couldn't help it; Caleb was still the oldest, wisest, and most mature of the family, and I was still the baby.

I cleared my throat, trying to think of a witty response. "Oh, you know." I cracked a smile. Already my voice sounded weak, uncertain of whether it actually wanted to be leaving my mouth or not. "Staying out of the cross fire."

"Smart girl." He nodded sagely. "But I meant, what's new *outside* of the inevitable shitstorm that is family reunions? How do you like living in New York? I know I sort of asked last night, but there were some rather"—he raised his eyebrows and tilted his head in the direction of Karma and Clarence—"*insistent* voices fighting for the mic then, and I'd really like to hear."

My heart lifted. Here was Caleb, the brother I'd always felt impossibly distant from, taking a real interest in my life. Asking me questions about the life I'd built for myself, as if I were a proper adult, like him.

It was the first time all trip that I truly felt like I wasn't sitting at the kids' table anymore.

"You know, I actually love it," I said, launching into the monologue that I'd prepared on the car ride from Manhattan. The one I'd wanted to tell the whole family at dinner. "The corporate world really suits me. I know that probably sounds crazy coming from a twenty-one-year-old, but it's true. Sure, the two years I spent as an assistant weren't exactly thrilling, but now that I've made copywriter, I really feel like I've found my place in the world. Like I'm where I'm supposed to be."

When I practiced this speech during the drive over, I'd thought it sounded great. Not too gushy, not too vague. I'd been channeling my skills as a copywriter, carefully choosing my words, adopting what I thought was the appropriate tone. But now, after twenty-four hours on the island . . . after arriving to a former best friend and running from my dead brother's ghost and fighting off the return of compulsions I'd thought long gone . . .

Now the words didn't feel so true anymore.

"That's great." Caleb smiled, and cheerful lines crinkled beside his eyes.

"What about you?" I asked, suddenly desperate to turn the conversation away from myself. "How's Addie?"

"Oh." Caleb's smile disappeared. "You . . . don't know?"

My heart picked up speed. *Is this it? The thing that Karma and Mom were whispering about in the pantry? Did something happen to Addie? Are they divorced? Separated? No, that can't be right. His ring is still on his left hand.*

"Don't know what?" I asked, pulse racing.

"Addie is . . ." He looked down, Adam's apple bobbing as he swallowed. "She's sick."

The words landed at the bottom of my stomach like a crate full of bricks.

Addie.

Sick.

What?

It wasn't possible. Not her. Not the beautiful, brilliant, fun-loving woman I'd always looked up to. *Addie?*

"Well"—Caleb laughed hollowly—"if the look on your face is any indication, you *didn't* know." He shook his head. "No one told you? Really? Not even Karma?"

"I . . ."

What was I supposed to say? *No, sorry. I feel awful that you had to be the one to tell me when it's clearly so painful for you, but actually, neither Karma nor my mother thought I was strong enough to handle the news of your wife's illness. They thought my fragile, mentally ill mind might fall to pieces and ruin Taz's wedding.*

"No," I said finally, "they didn't tell me."

Caleb nodded, looking back out at the lake. "Well. She is. Breast cancer. We caught it early, but . . ." He shook his head. "I wanted to stay home with her this weekend. I tried to stay, hadn't even packed my bags two hours before the flight took off, but she put her foot down. 'Stop acting like I'm bedridden,' she said. 'I'm perfectly fine. This is your brother's wedding we're talking about. These days with your family are precious, and I can take care of myself. You're getting on that plane. End of story.'" He laughed, the sound heavy but genuine. "So, here I am. Worried sick but doing exactly what she wanted me to do."

As a copywriter, I think of myself as having words for any situation. Marketing campaign? No problem. Instruction manual? You got it. Apology email because our holiday gift boxes went out without any gifts inside them? I'm your girl. I can always find the right words, the right tone, the right cadence to suit Blossom's needs.

But when your older brother tells you his wife has breast cancer?

Well, on that, I drew a blank.

"It's okay to be speechless," he said, glancing sympathetically at me. "When we got the news, I was, too."

I'd never seen my oldest brother look like this before. Bruised. Breakable. And, for the first time in my life, I realized that he *was* both of those things. That he wasn't just Caleb Beck, Acting Patriarch of the Beck Family. He was also Caleb, a person with flaws and troubles that he hid well from the world around him.

Just like me.

For a moment, I thought about opening up to him. I thought about telling the truth, the *real* truth, about my life in New York.

But before I could even open my mouth, Manuel returned, claiming his seat. And Caleb was gone as quickly as he'd arrived.

TEN MINUTES LATER, my fishing rod leapt from my hands with such force I almost dropped it into the water. "Shit!" I grabbed for the handle, leaping up out of my folding chair.

"She's got something!" called Helene.

Manuel appeared beside me. I looked at him helplessly. He nodded once, then took the rod. "I'll get you started, but this guy is yours."

All pretense of competition quickly dissolved when it became clear that our team had something big on the line. My family gathered around and started yelling cheerful obscenities at the fish:

"Let's go, big guy!"

"Get your ass up here!"

"Papa wants pike for dinner!"

For the previous hour, every glance I'd made in Manuel's direction had felt like a violation. Like a failure on my part to keep a promise he didn't know I'd made. But with everyone else's attention squarely upon him, I was free to look. To ogle. I watched him shout and shift and reel. He cranked aggressively, angrily, as if he hated the fish even before laying eyes upon it. Sweat built on his brow until he had to remove his hat altogether. When he did, frenzied curls sprung outward, falling into his eyes or sticking to his glistening forehead. Inchworm-sized things, damp and dark as soil.

Unfortunately, because I was busy studying my best friend, I missed the entire tutorial on how to reel in a fish. So when Manny turned to me and shoved the rod back into my hands, I realized that my entire family was counting on me to land this fish and I had no idea how to do it.

I started to reel.

"Not like *that*, *jueputa*!" Manuel grabbed my wrists and pulled them upward. His big palms wrapped around my slender arms. This did not help my ability to pay attention to what he was saying. "Reel and yank! Reel and yank!" He let go of my wrists but stayed close to my side.

Tugging my attention away from the memory of his calluses on my skin, I homed in on those three words: *Reel and yank! Reel and yank!*

Yes. I could do that.

I reeled and yanked for several minutes. Whatever was on the other end of the line had no interest in joining us. Just as I started to worry the rod would snap, it disappeared from my hands.

"I'll finish this off," growled Clarence.

Manuel opened his mouth to protest, but I shook my head. My half brother clearly needed this.

Clarence's fishing didn't look like fighting. It looked like dancing. It took only a few minutes of reeling and yanking before he hollered, "Net!"

I spun around and snagged the tall metal pole.

"Get down in there and scoop him up," he said.

I leaned over the gunwale and plunged the mesh into the water. The surface bubbled with angry white foam. Inside the chop, I made out a thrashing tail. I slid the net's wide mouth over the tail until I felt the fish's full weight under my arms. Then I tugged upward and nearly fell headfirst into Lake Huron.

"*Christ.*" My knees caught the gunwale, saving me from splashing into the drink.

"Pull, Eliot!" Clarence's teeth were bared with the gleeful insanity of expectation. "Pull!"

I pulled. Nothing happened.

Something wrapped around my back—something soft and supportive. I glanced down and saw a pair of long sandy arms wrap around my own. Their hands grabbed the pole just above mine.

"We'll pull it in together," said Manuel. His voice was low. It came from just behind my ear.

He placed both feet against the gunwale, mirroring my stance. Manny's thick frame held me upright as we inched steadily backward. Grunt by grunt, the pole made its way into the stern. Two dozen torturous seconds later, we heard a gleeful, "*MINE,*" and opened our eyes to see Clarence hauling in the single largest fish I'd ever seen emerge from the North Channel. For one moment, he cradled it with greedy tenderness, like a mother clutching a newborn child. Then the net tipped, dropping the fish—a forty-inch rainbow trout—onto the beveled white floor. It slid sideways, flopping and thrashing, leaving behind an erratic trail of slime.

Thus the scene came to rest: Manuel and me sprawled on the floor, my body tucked into his; next to our waists, a slimy being forced unwillingly into sunlight from the safety of its dark, wet home; and the rest of the family above it all, gazing proudly at the creature we'd pulled out of oblivion.

"THREE CHEERS FOR the least likely fishermen on Earth," said Clarence, grabbing our wrists and waving them about in the air. "Little Boose Beck and our Resident Harvard Genius!"

The family erupted into applause. My cheeks burned with pleasure as Clarence released our wrists so Caleb could pass us the official Fisherman's Trophy. Manuel grabbed one side of the trophy. I
grabbed the other. Together, we hoisted it into the air.

We did it, I thought as Karma and Shelly whooped and whistled.
We won.

Granted, we didn't win the entire Olympics; that honor went to
Karma and Shelly. But we won the most important event—the one
that would feed the entire island.

When the Closing Ceremony ended, everyone else dispersed to
change out of their wet bathing suits, but Manuel and I stayed. In
exchange for saving the day, we had the honor of cutting our prize
open and yanking out its insides.

"Eugh," said Manuel when I made the first incision in the trout's
neck.

"Scared of blood?"

"You know this."

I ran my knife down the trout's shiny back, tracing a slit down its
lateral line as cleanly as in a pat of butter. "Not me."

"No?"

"Nope." I flipped the fish over and lined the knife up just above
the pectoral fin again.

"How do you know how to fillet a fish like such an expert?"

"You don't remember?" I asked, looking up at Manuel, genuinely
surprised.

"Remember what?"

"Dad put a knife in my hand when I was like four years old. Said
it would teach me 'safety.'"

Manuel burst out laughing. "He *what*?"

"Oh yeah. I always filleted what the boys brought back. In middle school, you sat beside me while I did it."

"I did?"

"Definitely. You didn't want to touch the fish yourself, but you liked watching me pull it apart."

Manuel tilted his head. "I don't think so." He frowned. "In fact, I *know* I didn't. I remember now. I remember you liked filleting. And I remember you inviting me to come watch, that first summer I was up here. But the idea of looking at fish guts grossed me out. I thought you were sort of insane for enjoying it."

"That's so odd. I swear to God, I have this memory of you sitting right here, right next to me, same as you are now, watching me do exactly this. Your eyes were as wide as saucers."

He shrugged.

I closed my eyes, running a thumb along the knife's handle. *Was* that Manny in my memory? Or was it Henry? The boy in my memory has tan skin, like Manuel's, or like Henry's after a long summer under the sun. His eyes are brown. No—hazel. No—brown.

Agh. It's happening again.

I pressed my fingers to my temples, forgetting about the knife. The blade nicked my forehead. "*Ouch.*"

"Whoa, whoa, whoa," said Manuel. He grabbed my wrist. A thrill of sparks shot up my arm, completely distracting me from the pain of the cut. "What the hell was that?" He took the knife from my fingers and laid it next to the half-carved fish carcass. "I knew you were crazy, Beck, but I didn't think you were suicidal."

"I'm not," I said too quickly. "I'm just . . . that was stupid."

"No kidding." Manuel reached out a hand and brushed his thumb below the scratch. He touched my skin gently, tenderly. The gesture sent little shivers down my body. When he pulled his thumb away, red pooled on its surface.

For a long moment, we just stared at the sight of my blood— which came from within my veins, which pumped through my heart, which represented the most private, hidden part of me— resting on his finger.

I averted my eyes. Picked up the knife and started filleting again.

"You're okay," Manuel said as he wiped off his finger, even though I hadn't asked. "I'll get you a Band-Aid." He stood up and disappeared through the back door of Sunny Sunday.

I didn't touch the fish the whole time he was gone. I couldn't. I was stilled by nerves, knowing what would happen next.

When Manuel returned, he said nothing, just crouched by my side and dabbed at my forehead with an alcohol wipe. He tossed the wipe aside and peeled the Band-Aid from its wrapper. His fingers worked quietly, deftly. I watched them dance along the paper and cardboard, feeling oddly jealous of inanimate objects. When the Band-Aid was extracted, he raised it high and pressed it gently to my forehead. I stayed perfectly still throughout the whole process. It was a regular, everyday act—a friend putting a bandage on another friend's cut—but it felt oddly intimate. Every shift of his body brought him closer. Every dart of his eyes was a secret glance. Every touch a caress.

I had to still my very skin to keep the shivers from showing.

When he was finished, he left his fingers on my skin a beat too long. They lingered. Luxuriated. Then—slowly, so slowly, as if waiting for me to stop him—he brought them up to my hairline and drew them down my cheek, tucking one long strand of hair behind my ear.

I was no longer breathing.

"Eliot," he whispered.

No. That look in his eyes—God, I desperately wanted to tell him not to stop. To keep touching me, even if it was only right there, at the base of my ear, where my jaw met my neck. Anywhere would suffice. But I couldn't. I couldn't let this go on. It wasn't fair to Manuel.

So I did the only thing I could.

I pulled away and picked the knife back up.

Manuel looked down. Cleared his throat.

I did the same.

"So," he said, eyes searching the dock below us, "tell me more about being a copywriter."

I exhaled. Held back a laugh. "Are we . . . making small talk?"

A small smile pulled at his lips as his eyes darted up to mine. "I guess we are."

Huh. Never thought I'd see the day.

"Why?" I asked. "You considering switching careers?"

"No," he said. "It's just . . . well, it seems like your schedule is pretty grueling, what with you never being able to come home for any holidays."

Little alarm bells sounded in my head. *No. This is not a good direction for the conversation, either.* Lightly, I said, "You know how it is. The busiest times for e-commerce companies are during the times when everyone else is resting. Christmas and Black Friday, especially. But we have sales on all the other holidays, too. President's Day, July Fourth, Memorial Day . . . all of that."

"But that doesn't explain why you never came to Cradle over the summer," he said, and I knew that he was pushing for the information he really wanted. "Surely you had vacation days. Personal days. *Sick* days, for God's sake. You never took any of them?"

"I wanted to establish myself," I lied smoothly. "To show that I'm committed to the job. You know, most investment bankers don't take *any* holiday their first year on the job."

"But you're not an investment banker. You work a cushy tech job, and it's no secret that those jobs come with plenty of benefits and a relaxed work environment."

"You don't know anything about my job," I snapped. It came out too harsh, too defensive, even to my own ears. "You're still in college. You've never worked full-time."

Manuel's voice softened. "I know. And that's not really what I'm trying to say. What I'm trying to say is . . . well, I know how work culture is in New York. And I know that OCD and work obsession, they . . . they go hand in hand, two passengers on one bus. That's how my psych professor described it, anyway, and he—"

"Would you relax?" I slipped the blade back into the first incision on the trout's back, edging it to one side of its spine. I kept my voice as light as humanly possible. "Just because Dr. Phil gave you a nice bus metaphor doesn't mean everyone you know is riding it." I sliced and, with one stroke, took nearly half the fillet with me.

"I just—"

"So I work a lot. I love my job, and it makes me happy. End of story."

"I just want to make sure someone is keeping an eye out, you know, since you're living alone and . . ."

"I'm *fine*, Manuel," I said. "Okay? I don't need another lecture. I've had enough to last a lifetime, thank you very much. Especially from my sister."

"Right." He looked down at the fish he was supposed to be filleting, a small perch caught by Clarence just after we landed the trout. It sat untouched. "I'm sorry. I just worry, you know? I worry about you being alone in the big city."

"Yeah, well. Get in line. Queue starts behind my mom."

"Well"—he picked up the knife by his knee—"let's talk about something else."

Finally. "Sure. Tell me about the food at Harvard."

"Oh God." He cut into the perch. Skewed left, missing the lateral line by a full half inch. "It's complete shit."

I half smiled. "And the rest of it?"

He shrugged. "You know. It's college. It's the Ivy League."

"No." I folded open the loose fillet and repositioned the knife. One long stroke and the entire fillet came free. "I really don't know."

"It's an incredibly expensive way to get a high-paying job."

"So, you don't like it?"

"I didn't say that."

"So, you *do* like it?"

He sighed. Scraped the point of his knife absentmindedly into the soft, weathered wood of the dock in a way that made me wince. First rule of filleting: keep your knife sharp as hell.

"Yes. No. Yes, I do like it." He nestled his knife back into the perch, copying the way I hugged the spine, and started to drag it down. "I love it, actually. The people there . . . they listen to me, you know? They listen to my thoughts and opinions in a way high school kids never did."

"In a way I never did, you mean?"

"Yeah, well. At least none of these kids blocked my phone number."

"Hey"—I pointed my knife at him—"I didn't block you *literally*. Just metaphorically."

He laughed. A real laugh, too—not forced, not withheld.

Did that just happen? Did I reference our separation, and did he *laugh*?

Could it really be this easy?

As casually as possible, I asked, "Any girlfriends?"

He looked up at me, raising his eyebrows. "Seriously? That's your next question?"

"Yes."

He rolled his eyes. "Well, then. Absolutely. I've got girlfriends. I've got all the girlfriends. Girlfriends for miles. Girlfriends coming out the eyeballs."

"Makes sense. You always were a lady-killer. Especially back when you had a unibrow on your forehead the size and shape of downtown Manhattan."

He picked up a stray fish gut and chucked it at my head. I laughed. Then he started scraping the knife against the dock again. "Can I tell you something?"

"No," I said, "I prefer we sit here and gut these fish in silence."

"I'm serious."

"I know you're serious, Manuel. You frown, like, eighty percent of the time. It must be a requirement for getting into the Ivy League."

"I just . . ." Scrape, scrape, scrape. "I miss you, Eliot."

Silence.

By then, I was almost finished filleting the back half of the trout. I felt Manuel's gaze, but I didn't look up. I couldn't. I focused entirely on the raw muscle beneath my knife. I sliced off two more chunks, clean and quick, and then it was over. The whole operation. I set my knife next to the severed head and reached for the dirty rag on the ground. As I massaged my palms into its grimy cotton, wiping away as much gore as I could, I said, quietly, "I miss you, too."

"Do you?"

I looked up. I didn't find anger in Manny's eyes. It would have been easier if I did. Instead, I found hope.

My chest constricted.

"Of course I do." I swallowed. "I haven't seen you in three years."

"That's not what I mean." He reached out and placed his hand over mine. "You know that's not what I mean."

I looked down at the fish skeleton at my feet. There wasn't a single thread of meat left on it. It was perfectly empty. I glanced over at Manny's fish, which was a hacked-up mess, an amateur operation that left juicy pieces of flesh dangling loosely up and down the spine. Little clusters of translucent white muscle and fat. I sighed, pulled my hand gently from his, and pushed my pristine skeleton aside, then picked up Manny's and started working its flesh with my knife.

"This is a mess," I said. "Let's see if there's anything left for me to save."

22

FRESHMAN YEAR

IN AN ATTEMPT to ensure I remain as faithful to Leo and guilt free as possible, I start tracking spit droplets. Not just spit that flies from the mouths of attractive young men—spit from anyone. Because I might be a lesbian, right? And I might be attracted to my family members, right? And if either of those are true—which Dr. Droopy says is impossible, but of course my brain doesn't listen—then it isn't just non–family member boys who pose a risk. It's anyone.

I didn't realize how prolific human saliva was until I started to track it. Every time someone speaks, there's a chance a fleck of spit might fly from their mouth and land on some part of my body—hands, arms, legs, whatever. Sometimes, I don't even see it happen; I just feel a sprinkle on my skin. Those moments are the worst, because I can't be sure whether the droplet is real or a figment of my imagination.

Each time I see—or feel—someone else's fluid make contact with my body, I enter into an internal debate: to wash or not to wash. I always end up saying yes. I make up an excuse to run to the bathroom or the kitchen sink, scrub my hands and any other body part the spit might have touched—an elbow, the edge of my collarbone. Then I blot my skin dry and return to the conversation, refreshed.

The list of people I can't be around grows longer and longer. I start avoiding family gatherings. Impossible, really, when you're the youngest of such a large group. But I do the best I can.

I feel droplets everywhere, all the time. Even when no one is talking.

What happens is this: I feel a wetness, a chill. Like a single raindrop. Laser-pointer tight, focused on one area of my body. It's phantom saliva, I think, but what if it isn't? What if it's spit from the mouth of Manuel or my mildly attractive female history teacher, and that spit lands on the back of my hand, and I don't wipe it off, and later, when I'm eating lunch, that spit goes from my hand to my sandwich to my mouth? What then?

"It's not cheating for someone else's spit to land on your body," says Manuel for the fortieth time that week. He's the only person I've told about this Worry besides Dr. Droopy. We're sitting at our usual lunch table, just us two in the back corner.

"I know," I say, sitting on my hands to keep them safe.

"It's just your OCD," he adds, also for the fortieth time. "It's trying to trick you into thinking you're a bad person again."

Poor Manny. I'm ten years old again, confessing to Speedy every bad thing I've ever done. Only this time, my best friend is the stand-in for my father. I feel awful. I don't know why I keep going to him when the Worries get bad. I don't want to burden him. But he always claims that it's no burden at all, that he loves being here for me. He even did a bunch of research on *Relationship OCD*— which is what Dr. Droopy says this is—and often uses what he learned to help calm me down.

Still, I can't help but worry that he's lying. That I *am* a burden. That my stress is bringing him down, too.

It's exhausting. I wash my hands every chance I get. I have to. If I don't, there might be residue leftover from someone else's body that might then touch my mouth or—worse—my *vagina*. I shudder at the thought. I wash even more. I wash so often that the skin of my wrists cracks open and bleeds.

KARMA WAS RIGHT: Dad does give me the Talk eventually. He tells all of us, individually, once he deems us mature enough.

His Talk isn't about how babies are made; it's about his life as a drug addict. That's how it goes, right? Sex and drugs. Drugs and sex. One always follows the other. All of life's Harsh Truths! Let's have 'em!

I already know many of the details, obviously, but I pretend not to. It's his story; he should be the one to tell it.

At the beginning of his marriage to Mom, it was easy for Speedy to hide his addiction. They settled in Chicago, which is a full 298 miles from the connections he'd accumulated over the course of his life in St. Louis. He began a new life there—a clean life, with a clean house and a clean wife and two clean children. In Chicago, he didn't use. He didn't even want to use. In fact, if he'd never returned to St. Louis, Mom might never have discovered his secret. The problem might have resolved itself.

But he did return. Because guess what? Speedy had two other kids. Two sons, both of whom still lived with his ex-wife in St. Louis. And even if he was terrified to leave his clean house and his clean wife and his clean babies, he was more terrified not to leave. He knew how precious those years were. He couldn't miss them. Every month, twice a month, he returned to his old home, a city that housed his friends and connections and phantoms and opportunities. Every month. Over and over. And every time he drove south on I-55, he told himself he was just going for the boys. This time, he'd stay clean. This time, after spending the day at the park or the hockey rink, he'd drop the boys back off at his ex-wife's home in Lafayette Square and drive straight to his hotel room.

And every time after dropping them off, night closed in, bringing with it bottomless craving and a room empty of every person who could make it go away. He didn't drive straight to his hotel. First, he made a stop.

He never came home sober.

"Your mother saved me," he tells me. "Without her, I would be dead."

When Mom found out about what he was doing every time he went to St. Louis, she didn't yell. Didn't even raise her voice. She just looked at him and said, "Clean yourself up or I'm taking them. Both of them."

So he did. Just like that. No counseling, no rehab, nothing. Just Dad and his will to live.

Getting clean isn't a question of doing, Dad says; it's a question of *not* doing. Of not going back. Of not getting high again. Of not calling the wrong people. During the day, he distracted himself however he could. He asked Mom to hide his wallet and car keys. Once, he even tied his wrists together to keep himself from picking up the phone.

Nights were worse than days. Much worse. At night there was nothing to distract him, nothing but the fleshy darkness of the backs of his eyelids. He stared into that darkness with gritted teeth, projecting onto it the image of his two babies and a wife who would leave him. He sweat his addiction out into the Egyptian cotton of their bed. In the morning, he says, his body's imprint looked like a shallow river.

"NOT YET," I say every time Leo asks if I'm ready.

"Why not? Don't you love me?"

"Of course I do," I say. "I'm just . . . not ready for *that* yet."

"Whatever you want," he always says. But each time he does, I see his eyes harden just a little bit more, as if patience is a softener and I'm watching it drain away.

23

NOW

AFTER PRYING AS much clean flesh from Manuel's mangled skeleton as I could, I wiped all the soft webbed fillets down until the meat shone clean and white. He offered to help, but I just laughed at the green tint in his cheeks and told him to go wash up.

I dumped the blood and guts and bones, brittle like pine needles, back into the lake. Back where they came from. Then I sealed the meat into a plastic bag, wiped down both knives, and carried it all back up the steps onto the porch.

When I reached the top, I found my father parked before the railing, staring out at the choppy water. The Nurses were nowhere in sight. I walked over and stood next to him. We stared out at the water for a few quiet moments. Then, before thinking about what I was going to say, I asked, "Dad, do you ever think about drugs anymore?"

He looked over at me in surprise. I was about to apologize, to take back the question, but then he started to laugh. Big, rattling cackles, the kind that make you gasp for air.

"I'm sorry. I shouldn't laugh," he said, still laughing.

"I don't . . ."

"I forget you've never been a drug addict before."

I smiled awkwardly. "I don't understand."

"Asking an addict if he ever thinks about drugs is like . . ." He cast around for a suitable comparison. "Is like asking a priest if he ever thinks about God."

"Oh. So . . ." I laid one hand on the railing. A sliver of wood pressed into my palm, not quite piercing the skin. "The answer is yes."

"The answer is yes."

"And . . ." I picked at the sliver with one finger. "It never goes away?"

He sighed and looked back out at the lake. "There's a reason addicts are only called *recovering*, never *recovered*."

"Oh. I didn't know that."

We became quiet again. The lake was now well stirred up into its evening churn. I watched the wind make wrinkles across its surface.

Finally, Dad cleared his throat. "How have the, uh . . ." He drummed two fingers on his padded armrests. "You know . . . how've they been?"

"How have who been?"

"Not who, not who." He waved one hand. "The thoughts, the Worries. The *stuff*, you know. Has all of that . . . has it been okay?"

Now it was my turn to look over in surprise. Dad never asked me about my mental health. Not since the first time he drove me to therapy.

"They're . . ." I wasn't sure what to say. "Yeah, they've been okay."

It wasn't a lie. Not really. The Worries *had* been okay for almost three years. Just as I'd hoped, the move to New York—a city where I knew no one, and more importantly, no one knew *me*—let me start fresh. Stuff that portion of my life into a little box. Wrap it in cinder and chain, sink it to the bottom of the East River.

It was only now, away from the safety of the city, that I felt them starting to creep back in.

He nodded. "Good. Your mother . . . she worries about you living all alone in New York."

I almost laughed. *Oh, does she? Does she worry?*

"I'm fine, Dad. Really."

"You know . . . you've always impressed me with your independence, Eliot," he said. "It's remarkable. You never ask anyone for anything. Never. Not even when you were little."

"That's not true."

"But it is. You never *needed* us, any of us. That's why your mother and I were so shocked when you told us about the . . . the thoughts. You never gave us any reason to think you were suffering. You always seemed . . . I don't know . . . content. Happy, even." He sighed. "Shows you how much I know about being a father."

"Don't say that, Dad. How could you have known?"

He looked at me head-on. His wispy blond hair blew across his forehead. But I could see his eyes, the same eyes staring out from my own face. They looked helpless in a way I'd never seen before.

"No, Eliot." The words rolled out in a tight knot. "How could I *not* have known?"

"TAKE OFF YOUR shirt," I instructed.

"Excuse me?"

Manuel and I had decided to go for a sunset swim. After our moment while filleting fish . . . I don't know. Something had shifted between us.

We stood on the floating dock, which held two days' worth of vacation debris: goggles, flippers, frisbees, water skis, inner tubes, sunscreen. Off in the far corner, there were two concrete blocks and a long coiled chain—supplies to make a new anchor for one of the water trampolines. Next to all the brightly colored fun-time gadgets, the concrete looked oddly menacing.

"You heard me," I said.

"Okay, then," said Manuel, and he obliged.

"Where's your phone?"

"On the kitchen counter," he said through folds of cotton. "Why? Do you want to take a picture of my hot—"

"Spectacular," I said, then shoved him into the water.

He reemerged with a splash and a sputtered, "What was that for?" I scooped up two masks and tossed one to him. He caught it before it could sink. Still standing on the dock, I pulled back the plastic strap on mine and snapped it onto my head.

"You look like the fish we caught today," he said.

"Shut up."

We spent a full hour in the lake that evening. Once we were in, I wondered why I hadn't spent the entire vacation there. The water was so clear you could see twenty feet in every direction. A school of smallmouth bass lingered under the dock. Manuel swam beneath it and they all scattered, darting away in one terrified mass. We swam to the bottom and looked for bright pops of color that indicated lost frisbees and tennis balls. Manuel took my hand underwater and pulled me over to the rocks, where we inspected vast swaths of zebra mussels—the prolific, invasive clam shells with razor-sharp mouths that coat every inch of rock deep enough to be protected from waves and ice. We held out our hands to the zebra mussels, then pulled them back, then forward, then back, and watched the shells open and close their tiny mouths as we did.

After snorkeling I hauled two inner tubes into the water. We floated atop the surface, letting the warm evening wind roll across our bodies. I leaned my head back and closed my eyes. Only a few moments later, I heard a splash off to the side. "Hey!" I yelled, opening my eyes just in time to see Manuel leap from his tube and tackle the side of mine, sending us both back into the drink.

Finally, pumped full of energy and a long-forgotten giddiness, we swam out to one of the water trampolines, where we bounced for a few minutes, then did synchronized backflips off the side. Our bodies sliced into the waves, plummeting as one toward the bottom—just like they used to. When we tired of flips, we collapsed onto the trampoline. Its webbed mat was older than we were; it sagged beneath our bodies. In the air above, a cormorant traced wide circles with its wings.

We didn't talk. It had been a long time since I'd lain out on the water with Manuel, nothing else pulling at our time.

As kids, my siblings and I played King of the Hill out here, a game that involved shoving each other off the trampoline as hard as possible, bodies flopping into the water, until only the victor remained. As the youngest, I never won, but Henry, lithe and nimble, knew how to use his small size to his advantage. He bobbed and weaved beneath the long legs of his brothers, tripping them at the knees rather than using brute force.

The cormorant gave up flying. It landed in the lake with a great splash. The waves swallowed all its body but the head. They have these gorgeous, whip-thin necks, cormorants. Long but muscular. It bobbed gently on the waves.

Manuel's fingertips brushed the back of my hand. He turned his head to face me. "What are you looking at?"

I felt daring that evening. Maybe even a bit crazy. I was so confused by the competing emotions within me, the urges in different directions, but that evening in the water . . . it had been so nice. It felt just like our friendship used to feel.

Rather than answer, I turned onto my side, rolling until my nose was just millimeters from Manuel's. He stared back at me. The trampoline undulated beneath our bodies. If I wanted to kiss him, all I'd have to do is close the gap, to move forward just a breath. I felt him suck the air between us and hold it inside.

That was the first time I thought it. The first time I really allowed myself to think: *Maybe I've been a fool. Maybe this is where I was supposed to be all along.*

"What are you doing?" he whispered. His words smelled like freshly cut cedar.

"This," I whispered, leaning in.

Then I pushed him over the edge and he splashed back into the lake.

24

FRESHMAN YEAR

IT'S FRIDAY NIGHT, the end of our freshman year. Manuel's parents are out, as usual. We take two Razor scooters and push ourselves to Jewel-Osco through the springtime slush, where we buy Red Vines and Busch Light with IDs made in China. The sky outside glows pink and grey. We stuff the beer cans into Manuel's backpack and scooter home.

Waiting just down the block are Leo and Lisa, Manuel's current fling. When Leo spots us scootering together, his face twists into a sour expression. I smile as wide as I can.

We usher them in the side door and down the steps to the basement. Once inside, I turn on just one lamp, as if the half darkness can protect us from being found out by Valentina. We make a loose circle on the ground. The nylon inhales our legs in a way that only basement carpets can.

Someone hands out the beer. We each crack one open.

One beer is enough for Manuel to stop worrying about Valentina's presence upstairs.

"Lisa and I are going to my bedroom," he announces. "Don't wait up." Then he sticks his tongue out and closes the door. I laugh louder than intended, an attempt to cover up the crack that widens in my heart every time I see him leave with another girl.

Without Manuel, the room feels too quiet.

There's a beat of silence. Then Leo says, "It's him, isn't it?"

I look up. "What's him?"

"The reason you won't sleep with me." He nods at the door. "It's Manuel."

"What?" I try to laugh.

Leo shakes his head. Slowly, at first, then with increasing intensity. "I knew it. I fucking knew it." He stands up and throws his empty can in the garbage. "All my friends told me this would happen. 'Never date a chick whose best friend is a dude.' They all said it."

"Leo, what are . . . ?"

"No, Eliot. Just . . . no."

"Leo." I stand. I've only had one beer, but on an empty stomach, one is enough. The room tilts. "Leo, I don't know what you're talking about, but if I've done something wrong, I—"

"You haven't done anything wrong. Not yet." He shakes his head. "But I know how this ends."

I try to collect my spinning head. *Is this really happening?* "Leo, you don't—"

"I see the way you look at him."

My jaw snaps shut. *I see the way you look at him.* I grasp for words. For excuses and explanations. But in the space where I normally find them, the soothing sentences that coax my boyfriend back from the ledge, there's nothing. Just a whisper I'm not quite ready to hear.

Leo collects his backpack. "This is done. Okay? We're done." Then he turns and walks out the way we snuck him in.

———

WHEN MANUEL AND Lisa return, hanging on to each other and giggling quietly, I'm seated in exactly the same place I was when Leo left, staring at exactly the same doorway.

"Where's the Almighty Lion Man?" asks Manuel. Lisa giggles again.

"He left."

"Like . . . for the night?"

"No." I fondle a loose thread of carpet. "Like forever."

"Oh." Manuel and I make eye contact. He seems, for the first time, to absorb my deflation. I see him start to move away from Lisa, as if to comfort me, then pause. Second-guess himself. A hazy confusion clouds his face.

Then he straightens up, moving farther from Lisa as he does so. "Well, to hell with him. It's not like you really loved him."

YOU'D THINK MY Worries would end once my relationship did. That without someone to cheat on, spit droplets would become irrelevant.

You would be wrong.

Every ounce of guilt dedicated to the possibility of cheating transfers, almost instantaneously, to guilt over my possible sexual deviancies. When (I imagine that) a drop of spit from someone's mouth lands on my hand, I no longer feel compelled to wipe it away because I think I'm cheating on my boyfriend; I feel compelled to wipe it away because I think that to leave it on my hand is akin to admitting that I am, in fact, a lesbian. Or sexually attracted to one of my family members.

In fact, the Worry expands. It grows to encompass almost all bodily fluids: spit, period blood, pee, anything. If I don't wipe away *every last drop* after using the bathroom, the pee will be on my pants, and if I sit down on a chair in class, the pee will now be there, and then someone else will eventually sit in that chair, and it will get on *them*. And it came from my vulva, and my vulva is the source of my sexuality, and only someone to whom you're attracted is supposed to go near that. And if I just *let* that happen, if I just leave the pee there without wiping it away completely, does that mean I wanted that to happen? That I wanted someone else to touch my pee?

By bedtime, I've collected so many hot spots—tiny circles of skin upon which a droplet might have landed, a constellation of wrongdoing—that my body feels like it has an invisible case of chicken pox. An illness that only I can see. So I wash it away. All of it. I develop a highly specific end-of-day shower routine. I start at the top, always the top, and work my way down. Hair, neck, shoulders, chest, torso, legs. Don't start with your pelvis. Don't break the routine. Ensure every last drop funnels down the drain.

ON MONDAY, LEO doesn't show up at the *Trevian*. Not on Wednesday, either, or the next week or the following. On the fourth, the editor in chief tells us Leo resigned. All eyes glance at me.

I wait for the sadness. For grief over our back corner, his hand around mine.

Instead, all I feel is relief.

FOR THE REST of the year, the Worries stay steady. Awful but steady. By the time summer rolls around, I need Cradle like a man in the desert needs water.

"Any regrets?" Manuel asks on our first afternoon out on the lake. We're lying on a paddleboard, floating off the empty western side of the island.

Today, the lake is glass. We've arranged ourselves in a comfortable yin and yang: face up, heads next to each other in the center, torsos pointed in opposite directions. Legs dangling into the water off either side of the board. On our bellies, we balance two cans of Labatt Blue.

"Regrets about what?"

"I dunno. Freshman year. Things you wish you did."

"You mean, like . . . care about homework?"

Manuel snorts. "No, no. You were doomed in that regard from the start—except maybe in English." He traces a circle in the water. "I mean serious stuff."

"Such as . . ."

He takes a sip of Labatt. "Well, what about Leo?"

"What about him?"

"Were you upset? About the breakup?"

"Not really."

Another circle. "What happened, at the end?"

"Diverging interests."

"What the hell does that mean?"

"It means"—I flick my Labatt can, leaving small dents in the side—"he wanted things that I wasn't willing to give him."

"Wait." Manuel rolls his head over on the board to face me. "Are you telling me . . . after all that time . . ."

I shrug.

He laughs. "Why the hell not? Are you secretly a God-fearing Christian and I didn't know?"

"Absolutely not."

"Then what?"

I sigh. "It's like you said."

"What?"

"It's not like I loved him."

OUR LAST FULL day on the island, Manuel and I wake up earlier than we usually do. Earlier than *anyone* wakes up, except maybe the loons. We slip out of bed and scamper up to Sunny Sunday. We turn the cabin over. Mom drinks only beer and wine, and Dad hasn't touched booze in almost thirty years, so finding hard alcohol isn't easy. But finally, in the back of a cabinet otherwise filled with canned beans and maraschino cherries, we locate a yellowing bottle of brandy. A milky crust leaks out from under the cap, nearly sealing the bottle shut. If anyone ever cared about this bottle, that time has long passed.

"Jackpot." I wiggle my tongue at Manuel.

We secret the bottle back to our room and slip it under the bed.

That night, after the sun sets and the dishes are done and the old adults head for bed and the young adults settle in for wine and card games, we fetch the bottle and sit with it on the end of my bed. I claw at the cap, trying to pry it from its thick crust.

As I do, Manuel asks, "Have you ever been drunk before?"

"You know the answer to that question."

"No, I mean like . . . *drunk* drunk. Not buzzed, like at Karma's wedding."

The cap breaks free. "Oh. Well, in that case—yeah, all the time. Speedy and I split a six-pack before bed every night."

"I'm serious."

I put the bottle right to my mouth and take a big gulp. "Jesus." I shove it into his hands and gasp for air. "People drink this shit for fun?"

We pass the handle back and forth. One shot. Two shots. Three shots, all straight to the face. When I hand over the bottle, I do it gingerly, like a new mother afraid to drop her firstborn. Before the fourth, I hesitate. Do I feel anything yet? I don't think so. One more, then, just for good measure.

"All right," says Manuel after the brandy burns a fourth hole in my esophagus. "I think that's enough."

"Eughhh." I rake my fingernails down my tongue. "Does every hard alcohol taste like this?"

"Pretty much."

"How the hell am I supposed to make it through college?" I glance out the window; a bright orange harvest moon peeks through the treetops. "You know what? Let's go run around."

Outside, the moon casts a hazy orange glow over the rippling waves of the lake. Manuel and I weave carelessly about the boardwalk. We stick close to the harbor, away from the trees. I come to a halt at a place that feels like standing atop water. I hear waves. The sky is wide and open. The Earth sways. I look down and see that we're standing on the floating dock. How did we get here?

A voice says, "Tell me the real reason you broke up."

I startle. I turn to the left and there's Manuel, standing right next to me atop the swaying earth, peering down into my eyes.

"Hi," I say.

He smiles. "*Oye, gringa*."

God, he's tall. Has he always been this tall? "I already told you," I say. "Diverging interests."

"But were you *really* not interested in that?" Manuel asks. "Or were you just not interested in it with *him*?"

The waves are gentle. They rock the floor beneath us; I wonder if this is what it would feel like to live inside an actual cradle. My eyelids are heavy, but I'm not tired. In fact, I feel better than I have in a long time. What is this feeling? What's happening to my body? Hazy, slippery thoughts. Numb skin and a racing heart. Desire to do absolutely everything, all at once. Realization—brand-new and wonderful—that I can. That I can do anything I want, because nothing matters—not now, not ever.

"I don't know," I say honestly.

"Come on." Manuel inches closer. When did he get so close? "You've really never thought about it?"

"I—" I try to process his words, but my mind can't hold on to them. *Have* I thought about sex? I must have, right? Somewhere along the way, I must have wanted to. But my mind has been so occupied for so long with sex-related Worries, with *remember that time you didn't mourn your brother, remember that time you flirted with a boy who already had a girlfriend, remember that you're disgusting, you're a pervert, and remember that the only way to atone for these perversions is to remind yourself of them, over and over and over*, that I shut my sexuality off altogether.

And right now, they're still there. I can still look for reasons to hate myself, the trails of thought I've walked so many times I could find them blindfolded. It's not that they're gone. I see them all, feel them, sink my foot into the groove in the dirt where their paths begin.

The difference is that I no longer care.

I swallow. It turns things off, doesn't it? The alcohol. The drunk.

I see now, with surprising clarity, exactly how my father became an addict.

"Eliot?" Manuel knocks on the side of my head. "Are you in there?"

I blink several times. Come back to the present. "Yes," I say. "Yes, of course, sorry."

"Where'd you just go?"

"I just . . ." I trail off.

Manuel eyes me knowingly. "You're worrying."

"Nope." I plaster a fake smile on my face and take a step back.

Another. "Nothing to worry about here! Just booze and a good time and—"

I step back yet again, but there's no floor, nothing, I've stepped right off the edge of the dock, and suddenly I'm falling, and what's below must be cold, wet darkness into which my body will plunge, plummeting down three or five or uncountable feet, and the orange moonlight above will grow ever smaller, shrinking until it disappears altogether.

But that doesn't happen—not this time, anyway—because Manuel catches my shoulders before I even hit the water. He pulls my face right up close to his, closer than I ever could have reached on just the tips of my toes, and whispers, "Do not"—his breath is warm in the cool night air—"lie to me about your OCD again."

"I—"

"¿Me entiendes?"

I nod.

"Good." He sets me down, but his hands linger on my shoulders, his eyes on my neck. The harvest moon casts a warm orange glow on his face, illuminating his short curls and high cheekbones from behind. He looks like a statue. Like Adonis carved in moonlight.

I swallow thickly.

What the hell is happening to me? I feel something strange in my pelvis—the same place I check every time my Worries tell me that I'm sexually attracted to a woman or a family member or a dog or any other being to whom I'm not supposed to be attracted. A place I've tried for years to freeze, to keep from feeling anything at all. It never listens. It isn't listening now.

This feeling, though . . . it's different. It isn't tight and throbbing and painful, like it is when I worry. It's warm. It's a growing, glowing warmth, right at the base of my gut.

Manuel releases my shoulders, but I find that I don't want him to. I want him to hold on a little longer.

25

NOW

THE FRENCH FRIES went in first. Dad forced Taz to sit in the rocky throne next to the firepit, then nearly cried from laughter at how uncomfortable he looked. Glasses drained quickly. Once the fries started coming off the fire, they looked too good to resist. Karma was the first to sneak one from inside their nest of greasy paper towels. Its skin crackled between her teeth. She groaned. Her eyes rolled back in her head. Caleb dug in and took a handful. So did Taz. He arranged them on a small paper plate and passed them to Helene. Mom fed one to Speedy and giggled.

Clarence fried. He seemed to be having fun—real fun, I mean. Relaxed, effortless. Not the aggressive happiness he normally put on. When he finished all the potatoes, he switched to fish. His cheeks glowed pink in the firelight as he dunked fillet after fillet into a bowl of batter—once, twice, three times, a generous coating— then transferred them into the vat of bubbling oil. He moved from bowl to boil as quickly as he could, but batter still drizzled from the bottom, dripping first onto the ground and then into the hot oil, droplets crisping almost instantly into free-floating flakes that bubbled up and gathered to one side like a school of fish.

Karma fetched another bottle of champagne from the coolers

and refilled everyone's glasses. "Who wants to give the first toast?" she asked. "Clare?"

"Mine is too good," Clarence said. "Nobody will be able to follow."

"How noble of you. Dad?"

"Oldest never goes first."

She sighed. "Fine. Youngest first, then. Boose?"

The fillets bobbed about in the oil.

"Um."

Caleb stepped in, as usual. Always the leader. "I'll go first."

The circle shifted.

"Taron Beck," began our patriarch. "Taron Samuel Augustus Caesar Tasmanian Devil Beck."

"Whoop, *whoop!*" cheered Wendy.

"He hasn't even said anything yet," said Karma.

I hadn't considered the possibility that I might need to give a toast. I thought back to Karma's wedding, tried to remember the rehearsal dinner, whether I'd spoken. Mostly I remembered sending ugly selfies to Manuel under the table. If I *had* spoken, surely it was no big deal. Surely I'd gone in with a memory or two on hand, gassed up, needy as always for the approval of everyone at the table.

Not this year. This year I had nothing.

"You okay?" whispered Manuel, laying one hand on my knee to keep it from bouncing. I looked down. I hadn't noticed it start.

"Yeah," I said, unable to take my eyes off his hand resting on my leg. "Yeah, fine." I stood abruptly. "Gonna get some more champagne."

I walked over to the cooler and fished out an unopened bottle. Propped it up on my hip and tried to twist off the cork. In the fryer, the trout crisped to a perfect gold. Clarence dipped in his slotted spoon and scooped out a few strips. Hot oil dripped to the ground. I started to refill my glass but stopped. Thought for a moment. Decided to take the entire bottle.

Caleb finished his toast, and Mom went next. Or tried to—before speaking even a word, she burst into tears.

Karma looked at me and rolled her eyes.

As we listened, freshly fried fish made its way around the circle. We each took a fillet. Mine was small and chubby, like a chicken nugget. Manuel's looked like a lopsided map of Florida. We clinked them together like goblets. Our prizes. Deep-fried evidence of something wonderful. We both took hearty bites.

The toasts moved clockwise, just like the stories at birthday dinners. I knew I should think of what to say, but instead, Manuel and I pretended to make our fish fight like swords. It was ridiculous how wonderful it felt. How completely natural.

"So," Karma asked Helene after she'd had enough champagne, "have we scared you off yet?"

Helene glanced at Taz and smiled. "Not at all."

"Tell us," Mom said, leaning forward. "What's one thing we don't know about you?"

"Oh. That's easy," she replied. "I can see spirits."

The way she said it—there was no showmanship or embarrassment. No theatrics of revelation. She spoke as if she were reciting a trait as obvious and uninteresting as the color of her hair.

I perked up. "You do?"

"Sure," she said.

Something fluttered in my stomach. "How long have you been able to see them?"

"For as long as I've had eyes, I guess."

"What do they look like? Do they talk to you?"

"No, no. It's not like that."

I leaned closer. I didn't mean to ask so many questions, but they kept coming, as if I had no control over my own voice. "Are they dangerous? Or nice?"

"Neither," said Helene. "They're not interested in us. They only hang around certain places because they have unfinished business there."

Shelly said, "The theaters where you dance must be *crawling* with them."

Helene nodded sagely. "That's true. Lots of unresolved grudges in the dance business."

I was still going. "Have you seen any here? On the island?"

"Geez, Boose." Karma snorted. "Chill out. Let someone else have a turn interrogating the new girl. Besides"—she twirled her champagne flute—"since when did you become so interested in the spirit world?"

I looked down. Felt my face heat up. "Sorry. I didn't mean to be rude."

"It's okay," said Helene.

When I looked back up, she was watching me. The edges of her mouth turned up in a soft smile, but behind her eyes was something else. An unspoken recognition. A confirmation of what I'd known all along.

I waited for him, for the familiar sensation that Henry's ashes were right there, right below the rock where I sat. But before he could arrive, Karma's voice pulled me away.

"So, Eliot," she said, "tell us about the dating scene in New York." *Oh God.*

"Yes, yes," said my mother, clapping excitedly. "You haven't said a *thing* about boys since you got here."

I could feel Manuel breathing next to me. "That's because there's nothing to tell."

"Nothing?" Mom pretended to pout, but I saw her eyes dart hopefully to the boy next to me.

"Nope."

"No boyfriend? Nobody special? Never?"

I tried to grin. "Ouch, Mom."

Not only had I not dated a single person since leaving Chicago, I hadn't even tried. Hadn't downloaded any dating apps. Hadn't drunkenly made out with someone at a bar. And I only thought about sex—like, the physical act of sex, which I'd never actually experienced—approximately once every three months.

Things weren't looking good for me in the romance department.

"You know what's funny?" said Caleb through a mouthful of fish. "I always thought you and Manny would end up together."

Manuel and I stiffened at exactly the same moment.

"So did I!" Clarence raised his glass so quickly a bit of champagne sloshed over the side.

"I mean," said Karma, raising one eyebrow suggestively, "you two *did* always disappear into the woods for hours at a time."

Everyone laughed.

Including Manuel and me. We forced our laughter so hard we almost choked.

The group went back to general chatter. An uncomfortable silence settled over my best friend and me. I looked out at the water, pretending to care about the slight ripples along its surface.

After a moment, I felt something on my cheek. I jumped. Looked over. Manuel had reached up and plucked a flake of crisp gold from the corner of my mouth. He held it out to me on the tip of his finger like a stray eyelash.

"Make a wish," he said.

AFTER DINNER, THE group migrated to the couches in Sunny Sunday, telling misty-eyed stories over glasses of red wine. Rather than join in, Manuel turned to me and said, "Speedy told me we're due for a meteor shower tonight."

"Oh, I bet he did." I snorted loudly. "How long did he spend describing the exact degree at which the rocks will be entering the atmosphere?"

"Not long. Just the better part of an hour."

I laughed.

"Should we go check it out?"

The sun had set decisively, taking every cloud over Southern Ontario along with it. I peered up. The night sky shone bright and clear.

"Yeah, okay."

Neither of us asked which direction we were headed. As kids, we always stargazed from the floating dock. It stuck straight out into the lake, affording the most sweeping view of the sky. We carried our champagne glasses out to the end and set them carefully on the slatted wood. Then we stretched out onto our backs.

The sky over Cradle Island is not the sky over Brooklyn. It's not the sky over Chicago. It's not even the sky over rural Illinois, far from the pollution of city lights. It's something else. It's a sky untouched by industry—no automobiles or cell towers or tractors or grids filled with a town's worth of electricity.

"So," Manuel asked, "are we finally going to talk about it?"

"Talk about what?"

He turned to face me. "You know what."

I didn't meet his eyes. I kept mine locked on the sky.

Unfortunately, there's something about stargazing that loosens one's tongue. I think it's that talking to the stars is easier than talking to someone's face. Flat on your back, sending words into that vast, empty blackness—it's easy to feel that those words are of no consequence. They go nowhere. Sucked straight into the vacuum. So you speak freely, and always—*always*—you reveal more than you intended.

"Aren't you . . ." I began, then stopped. Took a breath. "Aren't you angry with me?"

"Angry with you? Why on Earth would I be angry with you? Just because you avoided every single one of my calls and text messages for the last three calendar years?"

"Yeah."

"Nah."

I turned to look at him. "What?"

He looked back up at the sky. "I mean, I was at first. At least, I think I was. I don't know. It was right when freshman year started. I was completely overwhelmed." He exhaled. Even though the night was hot and muggy, for some reason I expected Manuel's breath to curl before him in a milky-white cloud. "Was I angry? I mean, I felt a lot of things. Maybe anger was one of them. I don't know. But there was also this overwhelming excitement. Like . . . pure, bizarre, manic energy. Seriously. I mean, you know me. You know I'm not the most excitable person ever."

I laughed before I could stop myself.

He smiled. "Right. But those first few months of college . . . I threw myself into it. All of it. I joined clubs. I went to dorm parties. I raised my hand in lecture, did every single one of my assigned readings— even *after* I learned no one actually does those. I thought I was having fun. I thought I was having more fun than I'd ever had in my life."

I didn't speak. Like a flag popping out of the ground, I thought, for the first time all evening, *I need to check my email.*

"But then, in October, Che and Juli came to Boston for Parents' Weekend. They sat in on my classes and met my roommates and did all the shit I'd been doing for so long. The shit that made me 'happy.' But what's the first thing they ask, before even asking how I like my classes or what concentration I'm considering?" He paused. "They ask about you. What you were up to, whether you liked U of

M. And I lied. I lied straight to their faces. Told them you were crushing it, that you got a job at the school paper, that we talked every day, that you had a roommate named Alexandra and a pet fish the two of you bought together and killed within a week." He laughed and shook his head. "I made up a whole life for you. All because I couldn't just tell my parents that you and I weren't speaking." He flicked unconsciously at a loose splinter on the dock.

My hand twitched, as if it itched to grab my phone. I knew that there would be nothing important in my inbox—I *knew* it—but I had suddenly become overwhelmed by the sensation that there was something pressing I was supposed to be doing. Some meeting I needed to join, some slogan I needed to craft, some marketing campaign I forgot to create before I left.

"But obviously, none of it was true," Manuel was saying. "I didn't know anything about your life. The only reason I even knew you'd moved to New York instead of Michigan was because I texted Karma on her birthday and she said, 'Thanks. X-O-X-O. Have you visited Boose in the Big Apple yet?' or something like that. Imagine my shock to learn you'd skipped college without telling me."

The splinter broke off, leaving nothing for him to pick at.

A beat of silence. Then he said, "I came to New York, you know."

"You . . ." I exhaled. "What?"

"Yeah. Right after Parents' Weekend."

"Why didn't you . . ." I stopped myself. Swallowed. I was really starting to panic now. Breath labored in and out of my lungs. It was as if the distance from my job was giving me a panic attack. Or maybe it was this conversation with Manuel. Or maybe it was this entire wedding week, I didn't know, I couldn't know.

"You have no idea, do you?" Manuel said.

No idea about what? I wanted to ask, but I couldn't. I needed to stand up. I needed to go down to my parents' cabin and check my email.

I sat up.

"Eliot?"

"It's my friend's birthday," I blurted out. "My friend in New York. I completely forgot. I need to call her."

Then, before he could protest, I struggled to my feet and slipped away.

26

SENIOR YEAR

SENIOR YEAR, AT Manuel's urging, I apply to be editor in chief of the *Trevian*. It's not a position I particularly want, but my best friend has been oddly pushy about extracurriculars throughout high school. Whenever there's a charity event, we volunteer. Whenever clubs are looking for more members, he urges me to apply. It's bizarre; he seems to care about my résumé more than my own mother does.

Two years have passed since Leo ended our relationship, but he never showed back up to the *Trevian*. Manuel surmises that it was, and I quote, "too painful to see me three times a week, every week," an idea that, to this day, I find preposterous. Our relationship only lasted a few months, and I'm nowhere near beautiful enough to warrant that level of heartbreak. Manuel—who has known no beauty *but* the heartbreaking kind, with his own devastating looks—just doesn't understand what it's like to be average.

Besides, Leo never *acts* heartbroken around me. When we pass in the hallway, he nods stiffly at me, as if he feels nothing at all.

All of that is just to say that by the time I apply to be editor in chief of the *Trevian*, Leo is long gone, along with most of the other more qualified candidates. Which is how I land the position.

At first, I do my work as editor begrudgingly, spending long nights in the newsroom staring glumly out the window, only half listening to the assistant editors. But when the real work begins—when pieces from writers and editors start to come in—I find myself strangely enchanted by the work. By reading stories written in a dozen different voices, with a dozen different purposes—sports news is not academic news, which is not entertainment news, which is certainly not Op-Ed. As I edit, I ensure my changes don't interrupt the flow of the piece, which means I need to speak with another person's voice. It's fascinating, like slipping into someone else's shoes for an hour.

It doesn't take long for fascination to turn to obsession. I started reading about writing with voice online. Checked out *On Writing* by Stephen King from the library. Spent every free period editing articles. Kept a running list of things that needed to be done, both in my head and on paper. Became addicted to the feeling of finishing a task, whether that be editing or formatting or leading a successful meeting—to that little burst of endorphins that came from ticking a little box. It felt *wonderful*, like for the first time in a long time, I was working toward something, even if I wasn't quite sure what that something was yet.

I thought about my duties as editor in chief so much that, almost without my even noticing, I thought less and less about the other things. The Worries.

"That's excellent progress!" says Dr. Droopy when I tell him about this new fixation. It's not what I expect him to say. I wait for him to go on. He blinks lengthily, then continues, "Achievement is a very normal thing to think about at your age. It's grounded in reality, not fantasy. Do you see the difference?"

I think for a moment. And then I do.

I see it.

WHEN THE FIRST round of ACT scores release, I call Manuel right away. "Twenty-seven!" I yell as soon as he picks up. "I knew math and science would be a wash, but I got near-perfect scores on the Reading and English sections. How'd you do?"

"Fine."

"No, but how'd you *do*? What was your score?"

"I'm gonna retake it," he says.

"Okay, sketchball." I hang up.

I can't stop thinking about the test. Wondering which questions I missed, how my English skills could be improved. And man, let me tell you: Dr. Droopy was right. The more I think about what I can achieve, the less I obsess over the other things. The scarier things. So, what do I do?

I lean in.

If I want to be a talented editor, I decide, I need to understand language from every possible angle. To feel adjectives and metaphors in my soul. To take language and mold it like clay, bend it to my will. I reread my favorite books, trying to parse apart what makes them so wonderful. I pick up cereal boxes and frozen peas, analyzing the words that were chosen to entice someone into buying them. I pause to puzzle over the advertisements blown up at the local mall, assigning adjectives to their voices, like *formal* or *peppy*. I sit next to Speedy every morning, coffee in hand, and open the newspaper, intending to read it front-to-back for the first time in my life; despite being the editor of a high school newspaper, I've never been much for the real thing. At first, Speedy looks at me sideways, like he thinks I'm teasing him. When he realizes I'm serious, he tries to hide his smile behind the *Wall Street Journal*.

Reading quickly becomes not enough. I want to write, too.

Stephen King says that the best way to start writing is to just *start*; I open a blank Word document on my computer and record the first thing that comes to mind. *Medium* tells me that the best way to improve is to put pen to paper every day for at least fifteen minutes; each morning, I set a timer on my phone and sit down at my desk. I dig out my old journal, that behemoth already half-filled with psychotic OCD scribble, and decide that I will give it a new ending. A better ending. I start to detail the things around me. Incidents at the *Trevian*, conversations with Manuel, lists of homework assignments, stupid fights between Karma and my mom. I stick to reality, the way we would at the paper, and it feels good.

No, it feels *better* than good. It's the ultimate distraction.

And, of course, I make a plan for the future.

I spend hours trolling through websites with titles like "So, You Want to Write for a Living" or "12 Word-Minded Careers That Will Take You to the Top." Through this research, I learn that writing is far from a dying career; in fact, most major companies are in dire need of those talented with words. They're flush with programmers, spreadsheet makers, and business degree–wielding graduates. What they need—what they *always* need—is someone to put ideas into words.

They need copywriters.

It's the first time I've heard this word outside the context of *Mad Men*. The first time I ever considered it as a possible life choice. But the more I think about it—playing with the word in my head, whispering it aloud to see how it sounds coming out of my mouth—the more right it feels. It's a goal. A concrete directive toward which I can work.

The result is remarkable; the more I plan my future, the less time I have to worry. The less time I have to obsess over other things, scarier things, things less grounded in reality. It's even more effective than alcohol—and less problematic. I flip through the pages of my journal, damp and heavy with black pen, and wonder: Is this what it feels like to find a passion?

WHEN THE SECOND round of scores come out, I run to Manuel's house and open the front door. Che and Juli told me long before that I never needed to knock. I take the stairs to his room two at a time and throw open the door.

Manuel is in the middle of putting on his pants. He jumps and nearly trips over his own waistband. "Jesus, Eliot!"

"How'd you do, how'd you do, how'd you do?" I run around the room in search of the envelope. "Where is it?"

Manuel lifts a stack of papers and holds them to his chest. "I did fine."

"Fine like . . . better than last time fine?"

"Just fine."

I try to snatch the papers. He holds them out of my reach. "Jesus, Manuel, why are you being such a freak?"

"I'm not. It's weird to talk about your test scores."

"Not with your best friend. When's the last time I didn't tell you something?"

Manuel shrugs.

"I told you about accidentally ramming my nose into Jared Marshall's face under the gym bleachers. I told you about all my psycho-crazy-OCD shit. You know when I'm on my period, for God's sake."

He rolls his eyes. "Do I ever."

"Yeah, well. That's not my point. My point is that it doesn't matter if you botched your score. We both know you're smarter than me. Hell, we both know how messed up the education system is. That test is probably biased toward native English speakers. But you're still you. You're still psychotically brilliant."

His shoulders slacken. His arms unclench. He's thinking, I can tell. Going into one of his signature trances. I capitalize on the moment to reach around and grab a fistful of ACT results.

"Hey!"

My eyes fall on the box at the top of the page.

Thirty-six.

AT DINNER THAT night, I shovel food numbly into my mouth and quickly excuse myself.

"Where are you going?" asks Mom.

"To write," I say. But no matter how many other lines I put to paper, I cannot shake the one running through my head: *You're going to lose him. You're going to lose him. You're going to . . .*

THAT FRIDAY, WHEN Manuel calls and asks if I want to steal some Aguilas from his parents' fridge and go sit by the lake, I tell him I can't.

"You can't?" He sounds baffled. "Do you have another best friend you aren't telling me about?"

"Of course not," I say. "But I signed up for this writing group that responds to prompts via email, and I have to get this out by Sunday—"

"*No seas tonta*, psycho," he interrupts. "That can wait until tomorrow."

"Nope. No can do. I'm a Saturday-night-only girl now. And only if all my work is done."

You see, if I skip out on one night of work, what's to stop me from skipping tomorrow, too? What's to stop me from disregarding the assignment entirely? And all that free time—it can only have one conclusion. A return of the Worries. Of my *addiction* to worrying.

I didn't understand that before, but I do now.

See, there are two kinds of cravings: safe and not safe. For a normal human, that distinction is easy. Chocolate cupcake craving? Safe. Heroin craving? Not safe. But when you come from a family of addicts, the line blurs. Craving a chocolate cupcake or a vial of heroin or the horrible familiarity of immediately jumping to the worst-case scenario . . . they're the same. They're all the same. They come from the same place—a hidden place you cannot see or name—and they do the same thing to your mind. They gum up the inside. Clog the pathways through which other thoughts normally pass. And it doesn't end with sobriety. It lingers in the blood. Festers. Weaves invisibly up the branches of your children, and your children's children, and so on and so forth, like heartrot up a hardwood trunk.

Because of this, for addicts, for true addicts, the type who wear addiction in their very blood, there is no middle ground. It's all or nothing. You lean into the craving or you cut it out, all of it, even the things just tangentially related to the craving, things you might not have meant to cut. There is no middle ground. Just ask Speedy. If he could have cut cocaine and kept wine, he would have.

So, yes—I used to take Fridays off. But not anymore. I can't. I might not be an addict, but addiction is in my blood. It's in all of our blood—me, Karma, Caleb . . . everyone. It's curdling, rotting us from the inside out.

And of every way I want to be tied to my family, that's the very last.

FOR SO LONG, I lived like this: Chase the thoughts. Feed them. Water them. Let them grow, fester, snake around your mind in a white-grey tumor that will eventually cover it all, every last inch of healthy pink tissue.

But I'm different now. I've learned. Don't chase, Eliot. Let the thoughts float through your head. They aren't real. They're just thoughts, and they can't hurt you. Dig your fingers into the cracks of the crusty grey tumor. Wiggle them apart. Make room. Pull off entire chunks of the cancer that has for so long controlled a life that should be your own. Expose the raw pink tissue beneath. Let it breathe. Let it produce thoughts long unthunk. Pulsing, tender, squishy.

IN APRIL, MANUEL gets a letter from Harvard. We gather around the counter at the Valdecasas house—me, Manuel, Valentina, Che, and Juli, one of the rare nights his parents are actually home—and he opens the envelope, fingers trembling. We all lean over his shoulder. Straining to see his future.

Juli bursts into tears.

"I *told* you so," I try to say, but my words are drowned out by his mom's sobs.

Manuel looks up in shock. "*Dios mío*, Mom. Are you okay?"

"It was worth it." Her face presses to the fabric of her husband's shoulder. "*Dios mío*, Che. It was all worth it."

I GET INTO none of my top choices, all of which are within spitting distance of Boston. I feel a pit open in the base of my stomach. During my morning writing sessions, I push my pen so hard that it tears the paper.

AT THE VERY last minute, I gain a spot at the University of Michigan, selected from their long waitlist. And by the time high school graduation rolls around, my OCD is . . . not *gone* . . . but under tight control. The most terrifying thoughts have faded to background noise. Dr. Droopy was wrong; my disease *can* be cured. All I have to do is turn my mind to healthier things, like goal setting and ambition. To lean in. I can't believe I spent almost a decade obsessing over whether or not I was a liar or a cheater or in love with my brother. All those concerns feel far away. So far away.

"See?" says Speedy on the day of my last appointment with Dr. Droopy. "What did I tell you? No drugs necessary."

AFTER GRADUATION, WE head up to Canada with the rest of my family. We only have a month on the island before we have to come home and pack our lives into the smallest number of boxes possible. We'll be apart for the first time since Manuel moved to Chicago, and we're desperately aware of our own expiration date.

We aren't *worried*, though. Of course not. We're Manny and Eliot. The package deal. We've got it all figured out: we'll visit every month, and after four years, we'll get our degrees and move to a new city together—it doesn't matter where, as long as we have each other. Manuel will get a job as an investment banker or rocket scientist or whatever the hell you do after going to Harvard, and I'll live on his couch.

But before then, we have a month. One month in our favorite place on Earth. That's it.

We're going to make the most of it—which includes me putting away my notebook.

We do everything we can. We're up at eight and done with breakfast by eight thirty. We ski. We hike. We tube. We take out the *Periwinkle* and buzz out to explore the many deserted islands around us, picking blueberries and talking about nothing. We haul three cans of paint out to the largest rock on Cradle and paint a mural on its bumpy surface. We unroll a pair of paper-thin air mattresses on the beach by Chelsea Morning and spend the night under the stars.

The next day, our backs hurt so badly we do nothing but lie on the couch and read old *Archie* comics.

"Am I having déjà vu?" Mom asks as she cleans our dirty breakfast bowls one morning. "Are you kids twelve years old again?"

"Nah," I say. "That's wishful thinking, Grandma. You're exactly as old as you think you are."

"And *you're* grounded."

"Excellent choice, Wendy. Ground the daughter in a place she can't leave anyway."

"Fine. You're grounded forever, then. No college." She shakes the excess water from both bowls and lays them on the drying rack. "But seriously, where do you two go all day?"

Without missing a beat, we say, "To the office."

Karma, reading the newspaper next to Shelly, snorts. "Oh yeah," she says, "this time they're *definitely* making out in the woods."

Manuel and I look at each other. Our eyes glitter mischievously. Then, in unison, we open our mouths and pretend to gag. Then we fill two Ziploc bags with Oreos (for Manuel) and trail mix (for me) and run out the back door.

OUR LAST NIGHT on the island, Mom cooks a special dinner, rosemary potatoes with Speedy's barbecued chicken. She pours two deep glasses of red wine and hands them to Manuel and me. She winks conspiratorially and says, "Better to have your first drink in the safety of home, right?"

We eat by the flickering light of driftwood candelabra. After we scrape our plates clean, Mom proposes a toast to our bright futures. She takes unwarranted pride in Manuel's Harvard acceptance, as if a decade of being his best friend's mother lays claim to his brilliance.

After that toast, we're released from duty. Manuel and I jump up from the table. When we pass my mom, we pause to plant kisses on her head. Then we dump our plates in the sink and hurry out the door. We have plans for the evening: one old bottle of brandy, three-fourths empty, lying in wait on our bedroom floor. The same place it's been since we left it there three years ago.

Down in Chelsea Morning, I reach one hand under the bed and push the bottle with my fingertips. It rolls out the other side, where Manuel is waiting to grab it. My head pops up on my side. Manny's pops up on the other. He lifts the bottle. We grin at each other across the bed.

"I have an idea," he says as we push ourselves up off the floor.

"What?"

"Let's go to the Fort."

It's been years since we last visited our old stronghold. The structure looms ominously at the other edge of the clearing. A series of deep Canadian winters and summers free from regular romp and maintenance allowed a thick coat of spores and moss to sprout from the trunk. The tarp we draped over the entrance lies in a puddle on the ground. The roots, which once stuck proudly into the sky, seem to droop at the edges. The clearing is no longer clear; juniper bushes run wild, mushrooming up in deceptively fluffy patches. We pick our way around them. At the entrance, we stare down into a dark, tiny cave.

"Well," I say, "this is an absolute shithole."

"It's not so bad." Manuel stoops to shine the flashlight around inside. "Maybe a bit smaller than I remember."

I snort.

He looks up. "Do you want to go back to the cabin?"

I glance around the unclear clearing. I take in the twigs, the weeds, the juniper bushes waving beneath the bright white moon. I rip them up with my mind—pull them from the earth and toss them into the forest, emptying the space of all its obstacles. I place eleven-year-old Manuel inside it. He's holding the battery-powered boom box we stole from Sunny Sunday. He pushes a Simon & Garfunkel cassette into its mouth and presses play. Now I'm there in the clearing flailing my arms, dancing in the shameless way only an empty forest enables. And Manuel stands off to the side, head tipped back, bursting at the seams with laughter—the only audience who feels, to me, just as safe as no one at all.

Back in the present, I bend down and pick up the tarp.

"Nah," I say. "Let's get this place back into action."

Manuel grabs a fistful of the fraying rope that dangles from the tarp. Together, we tease loose the knots from its spine. Then we tie both ends of the rope onto the crown of roots and let the bottom of the tarp fall to the ground in one wrinkled curtain, and the Fort disappears from the island once again.

WE'RE DRUNK. PROPERLY drunk.

I'm cross-legged. The neck of the brandy handle rests against my thigh like a small child. Manuel kneels before me, waist-deep in an impersonation of my mother so spot-on it hurts my side.

"They're wonderful people, Jay and Julie, truly wonderful, but I just feel like they don't understand my . . . sorry, I meant *their* son . . . the way I do," he says. "I just feel like . . . I mean, look at the journey he's taken. Talk about the American Dream. It's enough to make you cry. I might start crying right now. Not that you would understand, Catherine. Not everyone is born into a family like ours. Not everyone has the luxury of growing up with so much money they can just skip college and decide to become a happy-go-lucky cupcake-making lesbian. That's called privilege. *Privilege.* Something you children seem to know absolutely nothing about."

I'm still laughing. The brandy bottle sloshes about in my lap. "Oh my God," I say, gasping for air. "Karma would lose her shit if she

heard the phrase 'happy-go-lucky cupcake-making lesbian' come
out of your mouth."

We laugh until the hysterics die down, slow to a soft trickle, then
flatten completely. We sigh. Then we look at each other. Manuel's
lips twitch up at the edges. So do mine. Our eyes widen. We try to
push down the giggles bubbling up in our throats. Nobody makes
another joke, but it doesn't matter.

We lose it anyway.

The laughter that follows is the kind of laughter that makes a
standing man weak at the knees. It rolls straight up the spine, tipping you over. I collapse onto my side. So does Manuel. My hip
knocks into the brandy handle, sending it rolling out of the tarp
and into the night. We writhe about, bumping into the tarp and the
dirt-lined walls and each other. We've reached that delicious point
at which your body is no longer your own, when you have no choice
but to surrender it to the mercy of the joy forcing itself out from
your insides. You can't think. You can't worry. You can't stop to
wonder if you look like an idiot. You wouldn't even know if your
body disappeared entirely. For all you know, your arms, your
thighs, your skin, your hair—it could all be gone. Vanished. It feels
so good. All of it. I can't remember the last time we fell victim to an
attack of this magnitude. As kids, it happened every other day—
random moments in which we happily came apart at the seams, in
which we became nothing before the power of total hysteria.

We give in. We give in and it feels so good, and now we're riding
those good feelings as far as we can. Because laughter is finite. Even
at peak hilarity, when you lose control of your body and your anxi-
eties and all those other horrible details that make you human, in
the back of your mind you know that it cannot last. None of it. This
beautiful terror will end, same as a heartbreaking movie or an
outburst of anger or a particularly delicious bowl of ice cream.

Everything ends. So our laughter shrinks within our bellies, turning from great cascading waves to nothing more than a ripple.

Released from hysteria, our bodies go limp. We lie face up on the floor. We sigh. This time, it's a sigh of finality. A period instead of a semicolon. I lift one hand and slap Manny's stomach, hard. He grabs it before it has a chance to escape. Our chests rise and fall. Then, like silk-lined cotton, stillness settles over our bodies.

Stillness and silence. By this point, we've weathered thousands of silences together. It isn't stiff and awkward, the way silence feels with other people; it's warm. I snuggle into its warmth.

"I had a thought the other day," Manuel says.

"Oh?" I turn my neck to look at him.

"An answer. To the question you asked me at Karma's wedding."

Present Drunk Brain struggles to remember a conversation logged by Past Drunk Brain. "Which question? That was, like . . . four years ago."

"You asked whether you need true love for happiness, or if all you need is a go-to. A Person."

"Ohhhh." I push myself up onto my elbows and nod emphatically. "Yes. Of course. One of my most profoundest moments."

Manuel doesn't laugh. He tugs up a fistful of grass poking its way into the Fort from beneath the tarp.

"Well?" I ask. "What did you decide?"

"I decided . . ." The grass slips through his fingers. Tumbles into a neat mess on the tarp. "Well . . . what if they're the same?"

"What if what's the same?"

"Your true love and your"—he clears his throat—"your Person. What if your true love and your Person are the same . . . the same . . . person?"

My lungs stop.

Manuel and I stare at each other.

We fall into another silence. This one isn't like the others. It isn't warm and comfortable and familiar. It's weighted. It burns. It's fire in my throat and at the base of my gut.

"Do you . . . ?" Suddenly I'm dying for a different burn—the fire of liquor. I wish the bottle hadn't rolled out of the Fort. I wish it was on my lap. I wish I could twist open its cap and pour another mouthful straight onto my tongue instead of answering. Maybe it would wash away *this* burn, the one at the center of my pelvis. The one I've ignored for so long. "Do you have a . . . specific person in mind?"

He looks down. "Yes."

I become suddenly aware of how hot it is inside the Fort. The liquor and the laughter and the unabashed flailing of bodies—it turned this small space into a makeshift sauna. And the sauna is making me delirious. It's making me want things that I know I can't have. It's even going so far as to make me believe that maybe, just maybe, I *can* have them, and that simply will not do. It won't do at all. I need fresh air. I need out.

"Oh!" I say too loudly. "The brandy! I must have knocked it out!" I duck under the tarp and crawl outside. "Don't worry, just a sec, hold on, I got it!"

Outside, summer is evaporating. Bright moonlight shines on a chilly clearing. I'm not wearing shoes or a jacket. I stoop over to search for the bottle. Cold air, cold moss, cold night. Cold air on my arms, cold moss under my toes, cold night in the sky. I know all that cold is supposed to hurt, but it doesn't. It bounces off, as if my skin were made of rubber. As if every cell were pumped full of novocaine. That's exactly how it feels, actually. Like when the dentist stuck a needle into my face last year. I couldn't feel his drill, not even a bit. My brain *knew* it was supposed to be in pain; it just didn't care. That's what being drunk is like.

A voice laughs behind me. I spin around. Manuel stands outside the Fort, watching me stumble through the weeds. Only then do I realize I said all of that out loud.

I turn hurriedly back and keep searching. "It must be here somewhere. I saw it roll out of the flap earlier, and there's no way it could have . . ."

"Eliot."

I dig one fist into a patch of juniper. My knuckles cry as the needles split them open.

"Eliot."

"Yes?"

"Stop."

I stop.

"Turn around."

I hesitate. Then I rise, slowly, like a gymnast standing on a balance beam. I turn.

Manuel is there. Right there. Right behind me. I have to tilt my head to look him full in the face. My chest seizes. He's so tall. I forget how tall he is. When we lie on the ground, heads on the same level, just as we were in the Fort, just as we always were before puberty dragged us in two different directions—it's easy to forget.

Manuel exhales. His breath makes a little grey cloud in the space between us.

I shiver.

"You cold?"

I nod. I am.

He reaches for the bottom of his sweatshirt. I think he's going to take it off and give it to me. But the sweatshirt is big, big enough for two grown adults to fit inside. Which is exactly what it does; Manuel lifts the bottom and pulls it up and over my head. Then we're both inside a cotton cave, the two of us, and his body is warm and his T-shirt is soft. I giggle. I wrap my arms around his soft T-shirt. I shimmy upward until my head pops out the neck hole. The cold air hits my face, but again I feel it only as I would in a dream. I keep my cheek glued to his chest. Now we're really stuck. Two heads in one hole. I giggle again.

"What are you laughing about?"

"Nothing."

"Nothing?"

I take a deep breath. I clutch him tighter. Nothing is not nothing. Nothing is something. Nothing is the culmination of a decade of friendship. Its logical conclusion. Or maybe its destruction. I don't know. I can't know. But I realize, in this moment, after four years of doing everything in my power to avoid ending up exactly where I am now, that if I don't at least *try* to find out if there's something more between us, I'm eventually going to lose my fucking mind.

I tilt my head back and meet his eyes. He sees it. He sees that nothing is something.

He leans down.

When our lips meet for the first time, the moon is so bright I can almost see my reflection in its surface.

Almost.

I'VE IMAGINED WHAT it would be like to kiss Manuel Garcia Valdecasas many times. By accident, usually. A wayward daydream here and a repressed impulse there. That's the thing about OCD; at any given moment I could simultaneously push down the fear that I wanted to kiss my older brother and the reality that I wanted to kiss my best friend.

But this?

This is real.

You might think it would be weird to make out with your best friend. That it would feel wrong, or there'd be no romantic spark whatsoever. And you know what? You'd be right about one thing: it *is* weird. It's weird to kiss your best friend. It's weird to be wrapped in his arms, the ones you spent your entire life punching like sacks of flour. Your body buzzes with bizarre vertigo, with drunken electricity. You become more and more intoxicated the longer his lips are on you. The farther they travel. It's weird. It's weird how good it feels. It's weird how badly you want him not to stop.

But the weirdest part of all is how quickly the past falls away. How seamlessly he goes from being your best friend to something more. The memories and classifications and limitations that slotted him into the role of Purely Platonic—all of that, gone in an instant. As if you might open your eyes and find an entirely new person above you.

So I do. I crack my eyes open, just a little, just to check. Just to make sure I'm not losing my mind. And I'm not. In fact, just after I open my eyes, Manuel does the same, and we find ourselves in the unfortunate position of locking eyes while so close our pupils cross.

"Freak," I mumble into his mouth. "Stop staring at me."

He laughs.

Let me tell you something about the Fort: it's small. Very small. In fact, you never truly realize how small a space is until you try to make out with someone enormous inside it. When Manuel lifts my body beneath him, to turn over or shift onto our sides, I'm acutely aware of the way his legs scrunch at the knees, the way his spine curls to make itself as compact as possible. We could go back, of course. Back to where there's more space. Back to our cabin, to my bed. Back to a world in which we were just friends.

No, thanks.

He's delicate, but things escalate quickly. Shirts come off. Pants come off. Suddenly we're two bodies in undergarments so thin they might as well not exist. The heat below my stomach rises. The darkness behind my eyelids starts to spin. I understand now that this is what a decade of friendship has driven toward. I'm happy, I'm drunk, I'm terrified, I'm invisible.

And then, from nothing, from nowhere, a face flashes through my mind.

Henry.

Henry's face, as vivid and unmistakable as a shot of brandy.

Jesus, I think. *Near naked, at peak sexual arousal*—that's *what pops into your mind? What are you, an incestuous freak?*

And as soon as I think it . . .

Oh no. Oh shit.

You're in love with your dead brother.

No, don't be an idiot. That's insane.

But you pictured his face while you were aroused. That's all the evidence you need.

That's fake. That's a fake belief. That's false. That's poison.

But as soon as I think it, it can't be unthought. The ticker flashes back to life, scrolling hatred across the backs of my eyelids. DIS-GUST in all caps. I try to argue with it, but I can't.

All of this is happening in my head. Manuel can't hear any of it. I don't pull back from him. I keep kissing, as if nothing is wrong. Because nothing *is* wrong . . . right? My head is just doing what it does. What it's always done. Or at least, what it's done for so long I can't remember what it's like to live any other way.

I try to relax. To focus on the present. I sink out of my head and into my body, the way Dr. Droopy tells me to. What's happening here? What do I feel now? *Here* is the Fort. *Now* is my best friend's mouth on my bare chest.

But they're coming. The unwanted certainties. The intrusive thoughts. Once the ticker starts, it's impossible to stop. You're *here*, I tell myself. I picture Manuel's face, his furrowed brow, his dimpled smile. But it's no use. Henry is back. *His* furrowed brow, *his* dimpled smile. But, no, that's not right, that can't be right. Who is who? I don't know, I can't tell. Their faces blend. Maybe it's the booze. Maybe it's me. I'm here in this Fort, but I'm somewhere else, too. I'm laughing with my best friend. Which best friend? I don't know. *I don't know.*

"Eliot?" Manuel has stopped kissing me. "Shit. Are you okay?"

I open my eyes. I see a blurry outline. I recognize brown skin and a tuft of dark hair. I blink, and it's then that I realize I'm crying.

"Oh my God. Did I hurt you?" Manuel cradles my face in his hands. He retracts them almost immediately, as if afraid he'll hurt me further. "Am I . . . did I do something wrong? Are we . . . do you not want to . . . ?"

"No, no," I say. "No, it's not that. It's . . ." Tears flood my face. I know I'm scaring him. I don't mean to. I try to explain. "It's . . . it's the thoughts. They're just . . ."

Manuel understands. He tucks me into his chest. "Shhh."

I take one heavy, rattling breath, and then I come to pieces against his body. The sobs are as all-consuming as our laughter. I give myself over to them, let them carry me, the same way joy carried me. I ride their momentum. And then they shrink, turning from great waves of sorrow to shallow ripples. I breathe in again. My nose leaves a trail of snot on his skin.

"I'm sorry," I say, though I'm not sure why.

"Don't apologize, Eliot. Don't you ever apologize for something that's not your fault."

We lie there in silence. It's a new kind of silence. A third kind. This one trembles. It feels as delicate as a castle built of sand.

"I love you," I whisper into this third silence. "And not in the way I usually mean it."

Manuel's arms tighten. "I've never meant it any other way."

27

NOW

I DIDN'T BOTHER turning on the lights in my parents' cabin. I didn't want my family peering out the windows of Sunny Sunday and wondering what someone was doing down here. I just wanted a moment of peace and quiet. A moment to recalibrate.

The Wi-Fi in Chelsea Morning was, of course, unbearably slow. I was fairly certain my parents hadn't upgraded the router since they bought it six years ago, caving at last to my siblings' insistence that we needed internet on the island. I clicked on Outlook, and the application bounced slowly up and down for far too long before finally opening my inbox. After another long minute, the inbox refreshed, showing me all the emails I'd missed in the last few days.

There were hundreds. As soon as I saw them, my heart jolted, and I felt a tingle on the back of my neck, as if sweat would soon start to gather there. *So much to do.* So much that I needed to catch up on. I knew that there would be no urgent tasks; my boss promised to handle everything while I was away. Still, now that I could see all the emails piling up atop themselves, unread, I knew that I couldn't just leave them.

I clicked the most recent one, which came from one of our vendors. I read it through twice, then started to type. As soon as I was done, I hit SEND.

Then I did it again.

And again.

I knew how my boss, Cheryl, would respond when she saw me answering. *Why are you on your email? I told you to enjoy your time with your family!* Still, I didn't care. This moment, the simple act of sitting behind my computer and typing up responses, firing them off in quick succession . . . it felt unbelievably good. As if I were lifting a weight from my shoulders that I had tried to ignore all week long.

This was what I loved about work so much. It absorbed all of my attention. Took my mind off Manuel and the Worries and everything else I didn't want to think about. I let the minutes fly past, not keeping track of how much time had passed since I left Sunny Sunday.

Not until the screen door swung open.

I jumped, looking up from my computer. The lights in the cabin were still off, which meant my shocked expression would have been lit up by my screen, like a spotlight.

In the doorway was an outline I instantly recognized. His broad shoulders and runner's legs. His curly brown hair.

"Making a phone call, huh?" Manuel asked, voice flat.

"Um." I drummed my fingers on the computer. "I just thought . . . well, since I was already down here, and my parents have Wi-Fi . . ."

Manuel didn't respond. He stared at me through the darkness. I couldn't see his expression, but I could imagine it: the disappointment, the resignation, perhaps even anger. Slowly, he started toward me. His footsteps creaked on the wooden floor. I shrunk back, waiting for him to lash out with his words.

But when he reached me, all he did was reach down and shut the lid of my laptop. Gently, he picked it up and placed it on the coffee table. Then he held out a hand.

"What are you—"

"Come on," he said, "I'll walk you back to your cabin."

On the walk, Manuel didn't say much, which meant I reverted to Nervous Eliot. The one who can't handle silence. The one who chatters incessantly to fill the empty space. I did an entirely unnecessary summary of the day, of the things that happened, the fights my siblings got into—all of which he witnessed and didn't need to hear again. But I couldn't help it.

When we reached Little Lies, we came to a stop.

"And the *moon* tonight," I said, gesturing dramatically to the brilliant white orb hanging over the lake, casting a glow on the quiet lake. "Wow. Just wow. This reminds me of when we were kids and would sneak out to Sunny Sunday and—"

"Eliot."

I hesitated. "Yes?"

Manuel stepped around to stand in front of me, blocking my view of the lake. "Ask me why I came to New York."

"What?"

"Ask. Me. Why I came to New York."

This was it. The conversation we'd been dancing around since we got here.

The moment I had both dreaded and desired above all others.

It had finally arrived.

I fisted my hand in the hem of my shorts. My heart picked up speed, pulse thudding erratically in my throat. *I shouldn't do this*, I thought. *I shouldn't give in to the temptation, the desire to know what's happening inside his head. I should stay strong—for his sake, if not mine.*

But I couldn't. I needed to know.

The question came out a whisper: "Why did you come to New York?"

He stepped forward, closing the gap until there were bare inches between us. He raised one hand. Grazed my temple with the backs of his fingers. He whispered, "Why do you think?"

I couldn't breathe. I lost the ability to do so around the same time that Manuel's lips came within six inches of my face. "For one-dollar pizza?" I whispered.

He laughed softly, brushing his fingers down my cheek. "No, Eliot. Not for one-dollar pizza."

My heart was seconds from collapsing. "Then what?"

His hand came down to cup my jawline. His thumb strayed upward, gently stroking my cheek. "To win back the love of my life."

I inhaled sharply. *No*, whispered the cruel, familiar voice in my head. *Turn around, Eliot. Run away. You don't deserve him.* I jerked my chin to the side, tore it away from his gentle touch, and stumbled backward. What I didn't realize was that I was standing right at the edge of the boardwalk. My foot missed the wooden planks entirely, flying through open air. I yelped as my body tipped backward, arms swinging wildly as I fell, fell, fell . . .

Two strong arms wrapped around my torso. "Whoa, whoa, whoa," said Manuel, holding me fast as I dangled out over the bramble. He laughed softly, though there was a hard edge to the laugh, an edge of hurt. "There's no need to jump ship, Eliot. You can just tell me that you don't feel the same."

My heart hammered against the arms holding me so tightly. I stared up at his eyes. Did he really think I didn't feel the same way? How could I possibly? How could I, when just inches away from his warm chestnut eyes, like honey, like caramel, like every sweet flavor I'd denied myself for so long . . .

I threw my arms around his shoulders.

I pressed my lips to his.

Manuel stumbled backward, shocked by the sudden embrace. His shock dissolved quickly, however, replaced by a low growl as he scooped up my small frame and nestled me close to his chest. Our bodies started to sway as he carried me up the boardwalk toward Little Lies, all without breaking the kiss. I didn't open my eyes. I trusted him to get me where I needed to go.

The screen door banged open as Manuel carried me into the cabin. Still I kept my eyes shut, determined not to wake up from this wonderful, intoxicating dream into which I'd fallen. One where I never hurt my best friend. Where I wasn't a bad person, where I actually deserved love. I knew it wasn't real, that I would have to face the truth eventually, but for now . . .

For now, I let myself sink into the bed as Manuel laid me down. Let my eyelids flutter open to take in the moonlight glinting off his eyelashes, his jaw, the desire burning in his eyes. It was almost too much, like I could die from how badly I ached for him. A part of me was okay with that. A part of me wouldn't mind if he was the last thing I saw.

Then again, that would mean that I wouldn't get to feel the soft brush of his lips as they kissed down my neck, my collar, the soft skin of my stomach. I wouldn't feel the heat of his palms as they slid down my sides, slipped under the cotton of my T-shirt, grazed the bare skin just above the hem of my shorts.

For the past year, I'd done everything I could to douse my body's ability to become aroused. I ate almost nothing. Exercised religiously. Spent my days staring into the abyss of my work laptop, drowning the little focus I had left in an ocean of words. I didn't want to think about kissing. I didn't want to think about sex. I didn't want to think about anything that could awaken *that* part of my body, the one that terrified me so badly.

But here I was, moaning softly at the feel of my best friend's hands on my body, every touch a flame on the fire building within me. It didn't feel wrong, the way I expected. It didn't feel dirty or evil. I couldn't dwell on my fears; I was too wrapped up in him. I felt safe. I felt *alive*.

"Eliot," he whispered. His fingers toyed with the hem of my shirt.

"Take it off," I said. "Please."

He pulled up the fabric, and I raised my arms to help him get the shirt off my body. He tossed it onto the wooden floor. A light breeze blew in through the open door, raising little goose bumps on my bare skin. Manuel skated his fingers along them, leaving trails of warmth in his wake.

His gaze roved up my torso, my neck, my chin, settling at last on my eyes. Slowly, his fingers danced low, brushing the insides of my thighs. I inhaled sharply. His eyes darkened, and his fingers crawled higher. Up into my shorts. I wasn't wearing underwear, which Manuel quickly discovered. When his fingertips brushed the wet skin around my soft opening, a low groan escaped his lips.

"Eliot."

"Yes?" I asked breathily, trying not to push my pelvis too eagerly against him.

His fingertips brushed over my opening once more. "Try to stay quiet, okay?"

I whimpered.

Then he plunged one finger inside me.

I twisted my neck to the side, moaned into my pillowcase. I knew my family was all over this island. That they could be standing on the boardwalk just outside this cabin, could hear if I let loose. I needed to muffle the pleasure rolling out of me, but it was almost impossible.

"Tell me if it's too much," he whispered.

"Not too much," I practically hiccupped. "N-not enough."

Manuel's teeth glinted in the moonlight as he smiled. His finger moved in small circles inside me, each one eliciting a little thrust of my hips upward. Something was beginning to build within me. Something foreign and warm and wonderful, like a bundle of rope baking in the sun. The rope stretched and stretched, the knot at its center growing tighter and tighter. It was not just in my pelvis. It was every muscle in my body, every vein and artery. They seized up, forming one big, protective knot around the pleasure crackling at my center.

"Condom," I choked. "Tell me you brought a condom."

Manuel's shoulders shook with silent laughter. "Eliot," he said, and my name sounded so beautiful on his tongue I wanted to make him say it over and over again. "When would I have had time to go back to my cabin and get a condom?"

"So, you *do* have one in your suitcase."

"A boy can dare to dream."

I grinned. "What do we do now?"

His fingers were still inside me. They slid slowly out, teasing the bundle of nerves at the very top of my opening. "I have a few ideas."

"Which are?"

He didn't elaborate further. Instead, his head moved down, down, down, and before I knew what was happening, something soft and lush pressed into me, and I gasped, and stars prickled the edges of my vision, and I could say nothing more.

PART III

The Bachelor Parties

28

I WOKE THE morning before the wedding to find my best friend beside me. For a moment, it felt as if the last three years had never happened—the graduation, the goodbye, the move, the mistakes, the distance I drove between us. It was as if I'd been given a second chance.

I pulled the comforter up to my chest and waited for the guilt to arrive. For the cruel voice, the me-but-not-me who pushed me to run away to New York in the first place. Who said, *Cut them off, all of them, for their sakes. To protect them from who you really are.* I waited, and I waited, and I waited, and while the guilt was there, while it still whispered to me that I was lying to Manuel, to myself, to *everyone*—it was oddly quiet. As if someone had turned down a volume knob inside my head.

I must have fallen back asleep, because some time later Manuel woke me with two fresh cups of coffee. I accepted mine and sat up, wiggling until my back rested comfortably against the porch wall. He scooted in next to me. I laid my head on his shoulder and together we watched the sun rise.

WHEN WE GOT to Sunny Sunday for breakfast, we found Mom flitting about the cabin, opening cabinets and talking to herself. "It's fine! It's perfect, actually! We don't *need* electricity. Not really."

"What's going on?" I asked.

"The power is out," she said, opening the bathroom door and slamming it shut.

"That happens," said Clarence from his perch in the circle of couches, "when your private island draws power from a thirty-year-old submarine cable." He, Caleb, and Taz were gluing dried flowers to folded ceremony programs. I grinned openly at the sight of my three adult brothers doing arts and crafts together.

"Yes," said Mom. "But it doesn't usually happen the day before your son's *wedding*, when you're supposed to be getting everything on the island absolutely *perfect*."

"Mom, relax," said Karma, laying a hand on her shoulder to still her frantic search for nothing. "This happens all the time. Remember last year, after the storm? It'll come back on in an hour or two."

"Exactly, exactly, exactly, exactly," she said, two *exactly*s past reasonable.

Manuel and I glanced at each other and suppressed a smile.

"You two seem awfully cheerful," said Karma, raising an eyebrow.

Clarence stood from the couch and walked over. "You really do. Speaking of." He poked Manuel. "We missed you in Tangled Blue last night. It's just not the same without . . ."

I stepped on Clarence's toes as hard as I could.

"Ow."

"What happened?" asked Mom.

Clarence grinned. "Just stubbed my toe, Wendy. That's all."

I cracked open the fridge to grab coffee grounds but jumped when Mom yelled, "Stop!" and I slammed it shut, looking wildly about, afraid I'd just run her foot over with the door. But no. "Keep it *closed*, Eliot. If the power doesn't come back on, we need that cold air to last as long as possible. Every time you open the door, you let more out."

I glanced at Manuel, who widened his eyes dramatically.

"Is everything all right?" asked Pam when she and Tim walked into Sunny Sunday.

At the sight of our future in-laws, some switch controlling both volume and happiness seemed to short-circuit inside my mother's brain. "Oh, yes," she said. "Yes, yes, *yes*! Nothing to worry about! Nothing at all!"

"Would the lovebirds like some breakfast?" asked Karma. She didn't specify which lovebirds she was referring to, but Manuel and I both automatically looked over. We noticed our mistake at the same time, our faces reddening. Karma watched all of this unfold with a grin stretching wider and wider.

Heads down, faces hidden, we accepted scrambled eggs from my sister and paired them with buttered toast. After stuffing the sandwiches into our mouths, we tried to escape out the back door, but Karma stopped us.

"You two skipped out on dishes last night," she said, pointing at the sink full of egg-spattered pots and pans. "Get to work."

At the sink, we worked in silence, hands sunk in the warm, soapy water. To stand next to Manuel and communicate in that wordless way that comes so naturally to us—it was nice. Too nice. I'm ashamed to admit how much I relished it. How much I relished the entire day. How I soaked up his presence, letting it cleanse my body the way bubbles cleanse a plate, washing away the grime crusted to its surface. It wasn't right. A plate is dirtied through no fault of its own, from food and sauces and humanity's sundry backwash. A plate deserves to be cleansed. The same cannot be said of me.

But I gave in, just for a little. Just this once.

———

"AND YOU'RE *SURE* Speedy won't mind us taking it out?" Manuel asked for the fifth time.

"Positive," I said, untying the knot on the MasterCraft's stern. "We both had the same boating lessons growing up, Manny. We learned to drive in this *exact* boat."

"Which is ridiculous, because the ski boat is the fastest on the island."

I shrugged, tossing the rope up onto the dock. "We were thirteen. We weren't exactly at risk of abusing it. We didn't even know what joyriding *was*."

"Speak for yourself."

"Ohhh, that's right." I clapped, sinking into the driver's seat and switching on the ignition. "I forgot about your little *excursions* back in Colombia."

"Shhh." Manuel glanced around frantically. "I told you that in confidence, Beck."

"No one is around to hear us, dummy."

"Che and Juli have ears everywhere."

I switched the boat into REVERSE and backed out of the slip. "You're even more paranoid than I remembered."

"You would be, too, if you used to steal your parents' most expensive car at nine years old and whip it through the streets of Bogotá."

"Who says I didn't?"

"Well, considering you've never even *been* to Colombia—"

I turned around, throwing a pair of ski gloves at his head. "Only because you've never invited me!"

Laughing, Manuel batted the gloves away. I swiveled back around in the chair, easing the boat into FORWARD and guiding us out of the boathouse and into the harbor. This early in the morning, wind was almost nonexistent. We glided atop the glassy water, our boat's wake the only ripple for miles.

"Where are we headed?" Manuel asked.

"Anywhere."

"Excellent. Mind if I drive, then?"

I slid my sunglasses down the bridge of my nose, eyeing him over their top. "You? Mr. Grand Theft Auto?"

He rolled his eyes. "Yes, *me*. The boy who learned how to drive this boat at exactly the same time that you did."

"Fair enough."

I hoisted myself out of the pilot's chair and flopped into the rear-facing spotter's seat, next to Manny. My thigh landed right beside his, grazing his skin on the way down. Both of our eyes darted down to look at the place where our bodies connected, then back up to each other. Manuel grinned. He squeezed my kneecap, then swung himself into the driver's seat.

"*Cuídate, amor*," he said, edging the throttle forward. "This boat is about to fly."

A thrill of nerves shot through my chest. I gripped the glass barrier that shields passengers from the wind. Then Manuel shoved the throttle all the way to the dashboard, and the boat took off at full tilt, bow aimed for the wide channel between the two nearest islands. I craned my neck to look at the speedometer: twenty-five miles per hour, thirty-five, forty, fifty . . .

"Whoa, there, killer," I yelled over the roaring engine. "If you were sick of my family, you could have just told me. No need for the high-speed getaway."

Manuel laughed, a sound I couldn't hear but desperately wished I could. "I could never get sick of your family, Beck."

"Say that again after Clarence and Caleb have had enough whiskey to start fighting over who has the more expansive wine collection."

"It wouldn't be a Beck family event without a few relationship-ending fights, would it?"

I grinned. "No, I suppose it wouldn't."

Manuel smiled. The wind whipped through his hair, pushing his wild curls flat to his head, revealing the full breadth of his handsome face—the tan forehead, the sloped nose, the long sculpted jawline. The sight made it feel as if there weren't enough air in the world to ever fill my lungs all the way to the top.

The ski boat sped across the glassy water, straight down the middle of the channel. There was no land for a hundred feet to either side, no rocks or hidden shoals. We could just fly.

I spun around on the spotter's seat, squatting on my knees. I rested my hands on the console. Then I pushed myself up until my head and shoulders were above the windshield. My hair whipped backward, flapping behind me like a proud flag.

"What are you doing?" Manuel yelled.

"I want to feel the wind!"

Manuel laughed. He didn't ease up on the throttle, just kept speeding forward. I lifted my hands and thrust them out to either side. My fingers spread wide, air rushing past every knuckle and nail, every delicate inch of skin. I was light as a feather. I could take off and fly. I opened my mouth and yelled as loud as I could.

AT THE END of our joyride, we drifted back into the boathouse. We chattered to each other, laughing about things from our past, happy things, things I'd almost forgotten. It had been so long since I'd allowed myself to think about the past at all, but being back here, being with him . . . it was different. It had opened up a door that I forgot existed.

"Do you have any trips to Bogotá planned for this year?" I asked as Manuel tossed me the stern line to tie up.

"I do. This winter." His eyebrows raised as he grabbed the bowline and hopped up onto the dock. "Why? You looking for an invitation?"

"No, no," I said quickly. "Just curious."

"Oh, come on, Beck." He grinned, caramel eyes glinting. "That's the second time you've brought it up this morning. Clearly you want to go."

"I didn't—"

"Besides." He bent over, looping the rope around the silver cleat. "We've been friends for over a decade. I think you're long overdue for a visit to the homeland."

I stayed quiet as I worked on the stern line. This should have been the point at which I deflected or made up an excuse or changed the subject altogether. I waited for the impulse to arrive. To drag me back to reality.

Only—

Only, *was* that the reality? My guilt, my fear, my need to stay away from him—for so long, I thought I was doing the right thing. That I was protecting him from the horrible truth of me. But as I stood there, bent over the cleat, I realized something: I had gone two full hours without any of that. My head was clear. As if being around him was not only okay, it was *right*.

I blinked.

The rope fell limp in my hands.

"The moths," I whispered. "I can't hear their wings."

Manuel finished tying the bowline and looked up. "What was that?"

I lifted my head. "Nothing," I said, smiling. "Nothing at all."

29

SUMMER BEFORE COLLEGE

CHE AND JULI decide to host an end-of-summer party before we head off to college. "Feel free to invite your friends," they say. "But *absolutamente ninguna bebida alcohólica*. Okay?"

We nod vigorously. Then we drive to 7-Eleven and buy three handles of tequila.

In the hours leading up to the party, Manuel and I circle each other like nervous fireflies. We stack Solo cups and spread garbage bags throughout the basement, always sticking close to each other but careful never to touch.

Che and Juli keep a margarita machine in their basement closet. They pull it out whenever important-looking people arrive to stay in their guest room. On hot summer days, they make virgin daiquiris for Manuel and me to sip while we lie on plastic sun chairs out back. We dig out the machine now, while his parents are out buying hors d'oeuvres. We pour in a pound of ice, an entire bottle of premade margarita mix, and two handles of tequila.

Just as the final drop of alcohol falls into the swirling mixture, Valentina walks into the basement carrying a stack of paper plates. Manuel and I freeze. I'm holding the empty bottle. It dangles idiotically over the hole into the machine. We stare at each other, all three of us.

Then Valentina winks and keeps walking.

Tonight is special. Tomorrow, Manny leaves to live in a place I don't belong. I can go see him, but I'll always be a visitor, semi-real, existing in finite chunks of one weekend at a time. Never permanent. Just a friend from home.

For twenty minutes, the party is wonderful. For twenty minutes, Manuel and I guzzle frozen margaritas and dance to ABBA in the backyard. For twenty minutes, I get steadily drunker as we whirl about each other, sometimes grazing palms, sometimes brushing bare feet. Then . . .

Then come the children.

30

DESPITE THE ELECTRICITY being out, Mom was determined to continue with wedding festivities as planned. If anything, her drive to celebrate reached a new level—sheer joy verging on hysteria.

"I don't know what planet everyone else is living on," she said, "but on *this* planet, my son is getting married in twenty-four hours, and his guests will be here in less time than that, which means we need to get to work."

The group dispersed to tend to wedding preparations. The frantic atmosphere reminded me of being back in the office. Of the final few hours before a product launch. As if Taz and Helene were a new brand of gluten-free almond milk, and their marriage was a marketing campaign we'd neglected for far too long. With the bachelor and bachelorette parties that night and the Big Day just twenty-four hours away, it was officially All Hands on Deck. Those of us on the decoration committee were to report to the couches in the corner of Sunny Sunday immediately for alignment on Key Performance Indicators and individual task assignments.

Manuel and I were assigned to different groups. When we waved goodbye for the day, I felt a strange pit in my stomach. As if something terrible were about to happen. As if, were he to leave my side, I might never see him again.

WE WENT ABOUT the day, busying ourselves with the long list of things that needed to be done. Mom assigned Karma, Shelly, and me to the task of braiding flowers into a long chain, a seemingly endless job given the length of chain that was needed to wrap around the patio. Wendy and Pam worked on flower arrangements and place-card settings. Taz and Helene carried folding chairs up from the boathouse to Sunny Sunday. Clarence and Caleb hauled up coolers full of wine and champagne, arguing the whole way about the correct way to hold the coolers' handles.

"No fair," Clarence said after dropping off the first cooler. "How come the girls get to sit around braiding flowers and we have to haul up the heavy drinks? That's sexist."

"Yes, it is," said Karma, "and you can kiss my lesbian ass if you think I give one single fuck."

One hour turned to two, which turned to four. Still the power didn't return. Nobody listened to Mom—who does?—and we opened the fridge whenever we wanted, for soda or lunch meat or leftover fried fish. We all thought the same thing. *Well, if only I do it* . . . But eventually those I's started to add up, and a new smell—subtle but still there—began to drift from the dark shelves.

Every time I opened the door that day, the smell gathered power. No matter how quickly I moved, the stench made it out. I held my breath and opened the door and grabbed what I needed and slammed it shut and drew breath, and there it was, a silent belch, that lingering breath of grey meat and rotting vegetables. And there was no way to know if my mom was right, if it was getting worse because we kept looking or if it would have rotted anyway.

31

SUMMER BEFORE COLLEGE

CHE AND JULI invited them. Well, they invited their *own* friends, many of whom have children, and they brought their kids with them.

At first, I'm excited. As the youngest of a family of adults, I *never* get to hang out with kids. Never get to squeeze their puffy cheeks or hear the sound of their laughter. Caleb is the only one of us with children so far, and he never brings them around.

But tonight . . .

The kids are tiny and adorable. They run about in tiny Converse and tiny baseball caps, or tiny sundresses and bare feet, or with no clothes at all, saggy white-grey diapers shaking joyfully behind. Manuel knows several of them by name. We chase them in circles around the backyard. We scoop them up and twirl them around, falling to the ground and laughing at the grass stains on our knees.

One child takes a special liking to me—a three-year-old named Clara. She has soft blond curls and bright blue eyes. She looks like a cherub, like the winged angel babies I saw flying across enormous paintings when Wendy dragged us to museums in Europe during our Treks of Chaos. Her arms are round and squeezable. Her face eternally curious. She follows me around the party, clinging to my hand like a lifeboat. I love her immediately.

That's when I hear it. When the forgotten whisper stirs at the back of my mind.

Oh, you love her, do you?

No.

I stumble midrun. Let go of Clara's hand.

No. You can't be here right now.

And you can't love a child you just met. That's wrong. That's disgusting.

"No-pants dance party!" Clara squeals, reaching for her sundress.

I try to snatch at her arms. "Clara, n—"

But it's too late.

She rips off her dress. I look away, terrified, before I can see any exposed part of her body. Somewhere on the other side of the party, her parents spy her naked body and laugh.

Please, I try to beg the Worries. Please, don't do it.

It's too late, they whisper. *You think you can escape this? Check your body. Look at the child, then check your body to see the truth.*

Check my body? As in, check for the pulse?

Yes.

Fine, I think. But you're wrong. I'm not going to feel anything. I'm not a pe—

I feel a pulse.

I look at Clara, and I check my body, and I feel a pulse.

Of course I do.

My breath drags heavily in and out of my chest. *Please, no,* I think. *No, no, no.*

But it's too late. Far too late.

I'm already running.

I TEAR OUT of the backyard and sprint up the stairs to the Valde-casases' office. Toggle the mouse to turn on the computer. Type in their password: manuel01. Open the browser. Type, symptoms of pedophilia. Recognize that I'm an eighteen-year-old girl googling whether or not she's a pedophile. Try to stop myself from clicking on any of the results. Click on the first one I see, an article from *Psychology Today*.

Symptoms of Pedophilia

- People have had repeated, intense sexually arousing fantasies, urges, or behaviors involving a child or children (usually aged 13 years or under).
- People feel greatly distressed or become less able to function well (at work, in their family, or in interactions with friends), or they have acted on their urges.
- People are aged 16 years old or older and are 5 or more years older than the child who is the object of the fantasies or behaviors. (An exception is an older adolescent who has an ongoing relationship with a 12- or 13-year-old.)

I scroll frantically through the article. Read every bullet point twice. *Does this one apply to me? Does this one?*

In almost every case, the answer is no. But then I remember that one pulse I felt when looking at Clara, and I lose all certainty that the answer really *is* no, and I circle back around, combing my memories for further evidence in one direction or another. *Sure*, I argue to no one, *I've never acted on pedophilic urges before, but that doesn't mean they aren't there. Right? Right?* I click BACK and move on to the next article. I do this a half dozen times. Maybe more. As I read, light pulses at the edge of my vision. I barely blink. I feel the distinct sensation of falling.

Okay, I reason with myself. *Calm down. Calm down. Let's think this through. Say you* are *a pedophile. What happens then?*

Well, I realize straightaway, I would have no option other than to kill myself. I mean, what's the alternative? Continue living with the knowledge that I secretly want to have sex with a child? Or the opposite—turn myself in to the authorities before I can hurt anyone? Admit to the foulness within me? Become the most hated of all forms of humanity, the cellmate despised even by murderers and thieves?

No. That's not an option. Of course that's not an option. My only choice is to live in limbo. To fear the worst in myself. To hate myself and never tell a soul, not even Dr. Droopy. What could he do, anyway? How could he possibly save me?

I need to get out of here. I'm disgusting. How can I be with Manuel now? How can I even live with *myself*?

And then, I hear the voice again—

Remember when Henry's face popped into your mind while you were kissing Manuel?

Of course I do. One does not simply forget the reawakening of something you thought was gone forever.

You thought we were gone forever.

You thought you were rid of us.

You'll never be rid of us, Eliot.

We're part of you.

We live inside your mind. Everywhere you go, you bring us with you.

Everywhere you go, so do we.

I close out the articles. I sprint out of the office, back down the stairs, out the front door, and into my car. I do not text Manuel goodbye. I do not deserve to text him goodbye. I do not deserve anything.

I drive home. I drive fast, like I'm being chased. I lock myself in my bedroom.

I inhale and exhale. I try to forget what just happened.

I saw a naked child, felt a pulse *down there*, a string of frantic Google searches, a spiral, a spiral, a vicious spiral into a place I never wanted to go.

"Oh fuck," I whisper. "Fuck, fuck, fuck, fuck."

Pedophile.

Disgusting.

Evil.

My phone dings, presumably with a text from Manuel.

Pedophile.

Disgusting.

Evil.

My parents are already asleep. Tomorrow, they'll get up late and go to church. They'll stay all morning. Mom likes to attend the post-service social and soak up the attention of the other pseudo-religious attendees. I imagine for a moment what it would be like to go with them. Mom would be thrilled. I can already imagine the way her face would light up. How her cheeks would balloon, her eyes widen, the same eyes she gave to me, to all of us. To Henry, once. Could I go with them? Absolutely. But I won't. I can't.

And besides—it's not like I believe in God, anyway.

MANUEL CALLS ME thirty times that night. I ignore every one.

32

NOW

"SO." MOM CLAPPED. "What's first on the agenda?"

"First on the agenda is everyone over sixty goes to bed," said Karma.

"Oh, come on." Mom pouted. "I gave birth to Taron. Don't you think I deserve to be at his fiancée's bachelorette party?"

"Did you hear what you just said?"

"I, for one, have less than zero interest in watching my son get shit-faced," said Speedy. "Especially when the only thing I can drink is Cherry Coke. Gentlemen, goodnight."

"Ah, ah, ah!" said Clarence, grabbing the handlebars of Speedy's wheelchair and turning him around. "We need full attendance from the male population tonight."

Speedy sighed lengthily.

"Don't listen to Karma, Mom," I said. "You can stay if you want."

She perked up. "Really?"

"Sure," I said. "It's not like we're going to a strip club."

"Well, we are." Clarence led the men to the back door. Under his arm was a lopsided trash bag filled with God only knows what. "Don't plan on using the back porch tonight, ladies."

Manuel winked at me on his way out. Then the door swung shut, and I found myself standing before five women, all of whom were staring at me, waiting for a good time.

I cleared my throat. "Welcome, everyone," I said, hating myself immediately for doing so. Why was I speaking like a flight attendant? "To Helene's bachelorette party."

"Riveting," said Karma.

Shelly shushed her.

"Obviously, I've . . . never thrown a bachelorette party before, and since we can't do any of the typical activities, I came up with a schedule." I pulled out a wrinkled sheet of paper from my back pocket. On it was a list of activities I'd stolen from Google. From articles titled "Throw the Best Bachelorette Party Ever" or "7 Activities Guaranteed to Wow the Whole Bridal Party!"

I cleared my throat and read them aloud. "First, we'll do a blind wine tasting. Then, we'll do a few rounds of Never Have I Ever. Then . . ."

"Nope." Karma stood up. "Boose, I love you, but where did you get these ideas? Martha Stewart online?"

"No," I lied.

"All right. Well. Not happening. I'm sorry. Helene"—she turned to the bride—"don't worry. We'll show you a good time."

ROCKS AND STRAY roots caught my feet as I hurried to follow Karma through the forest.

"Okay. Here's the plan." She spoke over her shoulder to the rest of us. "The boys are dicking around down on the rocks. My idea is this: First, we pretend that we're going off into the forest. Second, we get rip-roaring drunk. Third"—she halted and dropped her backpack onto the forest floor—"we take these bottles of whipped cream"—she opened the bag's mouth to reveal five aerosol cans and a handle of tequila—"and spray the shit out of the men. Any questions?"

"Just one," said Mom, raising her hand. "Who's in charge of cleanup afterward?"

"As I said before: all women over the age of sixty are welcome to make their exit at any time."

Mom put her hand down and didn't ask anything else.

Karma lifted out the tequila and popped off its lid.

Helene reached for the handle of tequila. "I get dibs on Taz," she said.

Karma grinned. "Obviously."

I WAS DRUNK. Properly drunk. My drunk brain rambled through memories as we ran toward the rocks, as it so often did when drunk.

Did I say drunk four times?

Drunk.

Other than the Fort, the rocks were Henry's favorite place on the island. As kids, we put on plays there for our family, improvised tales of two secret agents or two mountain trolls or two Wheat Sprites battling evil, all lit by the setting sun.

As a teenager, the rocks became a hiding place. Somewhere Manuel and I could secret beers and bottles of rum and talk about the important things in life.

"Ideal woman," I said on one such night. It was the summer before our freshman year of high school. "Go."

"Easy," he said. "Small and sturdy. Nice ass. Ideally Latina."

"Nice," I said. "Glad to know you really value a woman's intellect."

"Hey, hey, hey. I'm being selfless here."

"Are you?"

"Absolutely. I've got more than enough brains for two people. No need to overload."

I shoved him. "King of chivalry over here. You must have slayed the puss back in Colombia. No wonder you were so pissed about leaving."

He didn't laugh when I said that.

"What?" I asked.

"Nothing," he said.

"No, seriously. What did I say?"

He sighed. "It's just . . . I had a life before you, Eliot. I think you forget that sometimes."

"Oh." I pressed the bottle cap into my leg. "No. Of course I don't forget that."

Of course I did. Of course I felt that Manuel had always lived in Chicago, had always split bags of Cool Ranch Doritos with me while we watched *Fresh Prince of Bel-Air* reruns on Saturday night, had always texted me right before he passed my house during cross-country runs just so he could wave hello.

"I lived in Colombia for ten years, Beck. That's longer than my life in America. I had friends and relatives and track and school. My classmates loved me. I didn't get it, back then. My parents' decision. When they said they were taking me to a 'better life' in America . . . you have to understand—I already *had* the best life. A million friends. Promising grades. The world ahead of me. Maybe it's shallow to say, but if I had stayed, I would probably have been the most popular boy at *secundario*. To me, it felt like . . . what the hell could America offer that Colombia couldn't?"

He picked at the label of his Labatt Blue.

"I didn't understand, back then, the strategy behind their decision. I didn't understand economics or education or politics. I couldn't see my country's limitations. Didn't know that there was a ceiling to how far certain systems could go toward supporting a promising young man. Ceilings that didn't exist in America. Or, at least . . . weren't quite so low."

I didn't say anything. How could I? We were sitting on my family's *private island*. What did I know of ceilings?

Manuel paused. After a few moments, the silence stretched long enough for me to know that it was over. Closed. His brief moment of vulnerability. If I tried to push any further, he would shut down.

"So . . ." I cleared my throat. "My main takeaway from this is, no white chicks?"

He burst out laughing. Nudged me with his elbow. "Why? You interested?"

I remember whacking his shoulder hard at that one. "*Cállate*," I said. (Shut up.)

"Kidding, kidding. No. The Latina preference—it's not about that. That's what my mom wants for me, you know? That's what she always tells me. 'White women won't understand,' she says. 'No matter how hard they try. They won't get it.'"

"Won't get what?"

He winked. "Exactly."

AS WE NEARED the rocks, the tinny boom box music we heard through the trees solidified, taking shape as the Rolling Stones. A track Speedy used to play for us in Sunny Sunday.

Helene smiled.

"What?" I whispered.

"This song. It's Taz's favorite."

I didn't know that. I didn't even know Taz listened to classic rock.

I wondered what else we had in common.

"You're so lucky I'm not a groomsman," Shelly whispered to Karma. "If you pulled a prank like this on me, I'd divorce the shit out of you."

"That's fine," Karma whispered back. "I have a better attorney."

We reached the last stretch of forest before the clearing out onto the rocks. Karma drew to a halt, crouching behind a tree. We followed suit. Then, from under the cover of bushy pine, we crept silently out onto the rocks. Mick Jagger was nearing the end of his track. The boys were just above us, moving about at the top of the rocks, near the porch.

I peered up at them. Karma slapped my shoulder, motioning for me to duck down, but not before I got a glimpse of Bachelor Night. Up at the top of the rocks, the boys had scattered the porch furniture: lounge chairs and side tables. Atop them sat various bottles of alcohol—beer, tequila, coconut rum, gin—awaiting the men like stations in a workout class. Up on the porch, Speedy was asleep in his chair.

The track ended. Karma raised one finger to her lips, the other hand a flat stop sign. When the music started back up again, she leapt to her feet, Helene raised her can of whipped cream, Shelly yelled like a bullfighter, and together we charged.

"What the . . . ?!"

They stood no chance. We crested the rocky hill, erupting forth in a grand display of whipped cream and tequila breath. The men were gathered around one of the stations, pulling beers from a side table. And they were sloshed, all of them. Five fish in a barrel.

Manuel stood with his back to us. When he heard Shelly's howl, he spun around, but his long, gangly runner's feet got twisted up in themselves. "*¡Hijueputa!*" He tipped sideways. His neck craned wildly, eyes finding mine just in time to receive a full blast of whipped cream. He grasped blindly about, one hand managing to snag my left elbow and pull me down with him. With my free hand I kept spraying. Covered every inch of his torso in soft, sugary clouds.

A pillow of moss caught our fall. The collapse of its soft surface. In one messy jumble, we rolled sideways. I nearly rolled all the way back down the hill, but Manuel grabbed my shoulders, stopping me just in time.

He looked up. I looked down. I was right on top of him. When he inhaled, I felt his chest press closer to mine. Our breath in unison. Our faces nearly together. His eyes a warm shade of chestnut.

And then, just as the tips of our noses were about to touch, the can of whipped cream vanished from my hand.

"Hey!" I yelled, but it was too late. Fluffy sugar hit my face. Clouded my eyes and ears and nose and lips. Blocked out the moonlight. I squealed and flapped my hands. By sheer luck, one of them whacked the can right out of Manuel's hand, knocking it onto the ground.

I rolled onto my back and wiped the whipped cream from my eyes. Manuel did, too. We started to laugh, our bodies shaking atop the rocks. I blinked away the last bits of billowing white, and finally, my vision cleared.

I turned my head to the side. He was already looking, too, eyes surprisingly heavy and intense. My breath caught in my throat.

"Manny . . ." I whispered.

But just as I was about to say them—just as I thought to voice the words that had bounced around inside my head from the first moment I saw him standing on that dock, which, if I was perfectly honest, had bounced around inside my head since the first day I ever laid eyes on him—I heard it.

The voice.

Don't do it, it said. *Don't tell him. Not when it isn't the truth.*

Not when you know what you really *are.*

Manuel looked back at me. Raised his eyebrows.

And then the porch lights—designed to illuminate the lake during night swims and, therefore, roughly equal in power and wattage to football stadium floodlights—switched on. As did the surround-sound speaker system. Everything reset to the state it had been in when the electricity shut off the night before, which, apparently, was as bright and loud as possible. Clarence and Karma's handiwork, no doubt. Queen exploded from the speakers at a volume loud enough to reach mainland Canada.

"Jesus *criminy*," yelled Speedy up on the porch, jolting out of sleep and covering his ears.

Mom leapt into the air. "The power's back on!" She started to applaud.

You know what you are, Eliot.

Caleb ran over to the system and shut off the music. Speedy, grumbling about already being a cripple and not needing to go deaf, too, turned his chair to face away and cranked it back into a lounge position. He tilted his head back and shut his eyes.

Disgusting.

Immoral.

Evil.

"Eliot?"

My eyes shot back to Manuel. He had pushed himself up onto one elbow and was watching me expectantly. Almost hopefully.

"Were you going to"—he tilted his head to one side—"say something?"

Freak.

Deviant.

I opened my mouth, unsure of what would come out, but a yell cut me off.

"—you just *stop*? For fuck's sake, Clarence!"

I spun around. Across the rocks, Caleb stood, face red, fists clenched, whipped cream all over his cheeks and nose. His glasses were gone, likely on the ground somewhere. He glared at Clarence, who just smiled lazily back.

"Oh, lighten up," said Clarence, rolling his eyes and shaking a stolen can of whipped cream. "It's just a bit of fluffy sugar."

"You know I scratched my cornea two weeks ago. I can't afford to get anything in them." Caleb dropped to his knees, feeling on the rocks for his glasses. "God. You're such a fucking child sometimes. You never know when to let a joke die."

I inhaled, eyes snapping back to Clarence. Though he tried to keep his expression light, I could see the way his spine stiffened, the tightening of his fingers around the can of whipped cream.

"As opposed to you," Clarence said flatly, "a man who is such a mature adult that he can't even admit to the rest of his family that his wife is—"

"That's enough of that!" interrupted Wendy, voice shrill with false positivity. She'd been talking to Speedy up on the patio, but she sprinted down the steps to stand between her two stepsons. "Let's move the party inside and get cleaned up, shall we? Karma, darling, can you—"

"Is this a joke?"

The words were out of my mouth before I even knew I was going to say them.

Everyone turned to face me, stunned. I pushed myself to my feet, wiping whipped cream from my chin. I must have been drunker than I realized, because I didn't even consider stopping myself. Instead, I could only see the vitriol rippling between my older brothers and the ridiculous attempt by my mother to just smooth it over. Could only hear that voice, the one that had fought too hard to reappear and had finally won.

Disgusting, incestuous freak of nature who doesn't deserve to be loved.

I looked around the group. "Am I the only one who sees how messed up this entire family is?"

"Eliot!" Wendy said, shocked to hear such sharp words coming out of my mouth.

"No. Mom, no. You float around these events like the leader of a cult, with your obedient little husband and your five obedient little children. Like we've all grown into these perfect little adults, like we're all best friends, like these events are filled with so much love. But guess what?"

Mom didn't guess. She could only stare, horrified, afraid of what would come next.

"It's bullshit," I snapped. "All of it. You didn't even raise Caleb and Clarence. You were ten years old when Caleb was born. They have their own mother. You try to take credit for the work of a woman you barely know. Meanwhile, you can't even acknowledge the fact that one of your actual sons, one of the kids you actually pushed out of your vagina, is dead. *Dead.*"

Silence.

Then: "She's right."

I turned around. It was Karma who had spoken. We made eye contact, ten years of unspoken fury and grief passing between us. A connection that we'd never been able to acknowledge before that moment.

"Now, let's not get carried aw—"

I rounded on Wendy. "You're an idiot, Mom. We're fucked. Everyone in this family is fucked. When are you going to admit that to yourself?" I moved into the center of the group. The toe of my sneaker caught one of the beer bottles, and it rolled down to the water's edge. "When is anyone going to admit it? Half the people in this family are alcoholics. Caleb and Clarence basically hate each other. I don't think I've ever heard Taz say more than two sentences in a row." I swallowed. "And then there's me. The baby. The one who watches. The *weakest*."

Mom's eyes widened, and Karma gasped, and I knew my words had hit home.

YOU DON'T DESERVE TO BE LOVED.

"That's how you see me, isn't it?" I asked, turning to the rest of the group. "The weak one? The one who needs sheltering and protecting? The one who can't even handle learning that her oldest brother's wife has fucking *cancer*?"

I paused, as if expecting a response, even though the shock on my family's faces told me that I would receive none. I lingered on Caleb's face for a second, half expecting him to drag his wife's illness into my public meltdown. Instead, his face was even. Almost . . . almost *encouraging*.

Could that be right?

"Well, guess what?" I said, turning back to the rest of the group. "None of you have any fucking idea what it's like to live inside my head. *None*. I work so hard . . ."

My voice cracked. To my horror, I realized that I was on the verge of tears. That a lump had built in my throat and I hadn't even noticed, and now it was trying to block my words from coming out.

But I wouldn't let it. Not this time.

"I work so fucking hard to be . . . to be okay." My voice wavered on the word *okay*. "To not be a burden to those around me. To prove that I'm a high-functioning adult who fits in with the rest of the family. But the truth is, it's fucking *hell* up here." I pointed at my head. "I have OCD. I know you can't see it, but I do. And I'm done trying to hide it."

My siblings exchanged wide-eyed looks. Karma took a step forward, as if she wanted to say something, but I held up a hand. I had one more thing to say.

"Sorry to tell you when you're already trapped on this island," I said, turning to Helene and her parents, who were gathered into their own awkward cluster just outside the group. "But you're about to marry into the fucking loony bin. Good luck. We all pretend to be best friends, but we have nothing in common. Nothing. All that ties us together is money and the fact that we're all, each and every one of us, well and truly fucked up."

Speech complete, I let my hand fall to my side.

YOU DO NOT DESERVE TO BE LOVED.

"Eliot?"

It was Manuel's voice. Manuel's beautiful, deep, honey-smooth voice.

The voice to which I knew I could not turn. Not ever. Because the thoughts were back, and I had no doubt that it was my fault. I'd let my guard down. Let myself skimp on work. Let myself have long open days of nothingness. Followed no sort of schedule, ticked no boxes. Of course the thoughts were back. Of course they were. All my routine, all my control—it had gone to shit.

But I shouldn't have been surprised that the thoughts were back. Because where had they gone, really? Not away. Never away. Maybe they hid away for a time, but they were always going to come back. They were always going to return, to whisper the truth to me again.

Because it *was* the truth.

I was disgusting. I couldn't even tell the difference between real attraction and a random pulse in my crotch that told me I might be in love with my dead brother, so how could I ever be sure? How could I ever know if I was a good person, a normal person, or someone royally, disgustingly messed up?

I didn't deserve to be loved. I shouldn't have even *been* there at the wedding, associating with all the people I cared about. Putting them at risk.

I need to get away.

The thought hit me like a runaway ski boat going fifty, mowing me down, drowning me.

I need to get away.

So I did. I turned around and I sprinted straight into the trees.

33

SUMMER BEFORE COLLEGE

I GO THROUGH the day after the party without even a trace of a hangover. Youth is good for that; drink yourself to chaos and wake free of the consequences. Poison yourself within an inch of death—on purpose—and bounce back so quickly you'd think nothing ever happened. Some unknown mechanism lets us skip the pain. Call it genetics. Call it invincibility. Call it the power of a blank slate, of a body not yet punished enough to reveal its cracks. It's an ability of which we aren't even aware, but we miss it when it leaves.

Resilience is wasted on the young. Our ability to push past anything, even embarrassment, even poison. Spring back into life, gait unchanged, suffering nothing more than vertigo and an invisible heap of sorrow amassing in the pit of our stomachs. A growing heap of trauma. Add to the pile with every fake smile, every unacknowledged ordeal. Dig into it only years later. By then, the heap will have grown so large it will be impossible to see all at once. But for now, it lies dormant, growing, collecting misery.

AT FOUR O'CLOCK, a black car shows up outside my house. From my second-floor window, I have a bird's-eye view of anyone who comes and goes. I see the car pull up and know immediately who it is. There are only two cars in the Valdecasases' garage. I duck back into bed and shimmy under the covers.

The doorbell rings. My window is open. Manny's voice drifts through it clear as day. "Eliot?" *Bang, bang, bang.* "Eliot, are you in there?"

If my parents were home, the game would be up. They would answer the door and see Manuel on the front step and insist I come downstairs. They would ask why on Earth I don't want to say goodbye. They would ask lots of questions. Questions I cannot answer.

"Eliot?" He isn't giving up. As soon as the doorbell stops, he pushes the button again. "I know you're in there. I see your light on. What the hell is going on?" *Bang, bang, bang.* "Just come down here. Jesus. I'm leaving, *por el amor de Dios.*"

Yes. Leaving, gone, unreachable. Exactly as it should be.

Pedophile.

Disgusting.

Evil.

I exhale unsteadily.

You don't deserve him.

You never will.

He's better off without you.

The car will drive away. His plane will take off. He'll begin his new life in Boston. From then on, he'll exist only as a number on a touch screen. A number I can ignore. It will pass. He will pass.

And he does. After ten minutes, the doorbell goes silent. I hold my breath. Through my open bedroom window, I hear footsteps trudge down stone steps. A car door slams. An engine roars to life. And finally, gravel flies beneath four tires as my best friend rolls away.

———————

I MOVE THROUGH the week after the party like a body through water. If I kick hard enough, I move forward. But everything above the waterline is a disfigured blur.

I try not to think about the party. When I do, it appears to me with a ghostlike quality, a haze of darkness. So I try not to think about it. About the realization that I could be one of the most vile, disgusting types of human beings on the planet. The type of person who gets bullied by serial killers because even *they* can't look at pedophiles without wanting to hurt them.

I roll onto my side. "Fuck, fuck, fuck, *fuck*."

MY SELF-IMAGE HAS become a mental Jenga. A precarious tower constructed of beliefs I'm only half-certain are real. It's sturdiest in the morning, because overnight I accidentally forget all the bad things I know about myself. I open my eyes with a full, solid tower. But the minute my brain awakens enough to remember its own existence, it begins to look for the things I'm supposed to be anxious about. All day long it searches. Every remembered evil is a block removed.

By the end of the night, I'm a hollow, swaying skeleton of the tower I woke up as. All it takes is a nudge of the pinky, and I fall to pieces.

WEDNESDAY MORNING, MOM pokes her head in the door. "Are you okay, honey?"

"Yeah," I say, eyes on the ceiling.

"Can I bring you some food?"

"I'm not hungry."

She pauses. Then: "Are you sad?"

Beneath the covers, my toes clench. Carefully, I ask, "Why would I be sad?"

"Because of Manuel."

She knows. How does she know?

But then she goes on: "It must be hard being apart."

"Oh." My toes uncurl and my spine relaxes. "Yeah. I'm sad."

"Oh, honey." She reaches out and strokes my hair, which spills over my pillow in a long tangle of dirty blond. "If it's any consolation, I miss him, too."

I almost say, *It's not*, but I bite my tongue. I bite my tongue so hard it bleeds.

EVENTUALLY, I GIVE up. Stop fighting. Let the Worries wash over me.

Lesbian, they say.

Pedophile.

Incestuous freak.

I squeeze my eyes shut and grip the blanket until my knuckles start to hurt. I know I'm not any of those things. I do. Sort of. Sort of not. Whenever I go looking for proof, all I find is more doubt. It's like . . . I don't *think* letting someone's spit stay on my hand counts as cheating on my boyfriend, but what if it does? Who gets to decide, ultimately?

At every moment, I feel the universe watching me. Keeping track of my every move. Every bad, every wrong. But no one else can see it. No one else knows I might be a pedophile. No one knows how awful, how deviant, how disgusting I am.

Dr. Droopy once described self-hate as "addictive." I thought that was ridiculous. How the hell could you crave self-hate just as much as you crave a chocolate cupcake or a drug-induced high?

But I get it now. I do.

I don't know how to turn it off, but what I do know is this: I'm addicted to the Worries. I'm addicted to self-torture and self-hate and any other version of the self that reaffirms my belief that there's a deep, disgusting darkness within me.

And what's the best way to avoid relapse? What did Speedy tell me all those years ago?

Getting clean isn't a question of doing. It's a question of not *doing. Of not going back. Of not getting high again. Of not calling the wrong people.*

Not doing.

I start to research recovery. I read articles on Twelve Steps and relapse. What I find, exactly as my father said in his own story, is that the two highest risks are *people* and *location*:

```
A "high-risk" location or person is one that
brings up memories of time spent engaging in
substance abuse. The best course of action is
to avoid these people and places altogether.
```

The best course of action is to avoid these people and places altogether.

Avoid them altogether.

Avoid them.

AND THEN, A day later, a new voice. Similar to the Worries but not quite the same.

Fat, it says.

Lazy.

Get up, you sad piece of shit. You've been lying in bed for days. Go for a run.

I nod to no one. Exercise. Yes. Exercise is good. Running is good. Running helps sweep the Worries away.

I get up. I tie my shoes, numbly. I look up, right into the full-length mirror on my closet. Right into an eyeful of the rolls and wrinkles folding my stomach. I see those rolls, and I think about the pelvis they protect, the same pelvis that pulsed when it saw a child.

And then, from some ugly pit of my mind—that same place that cracks open in the seconds just before you slip into the safety of sleep, that brief glimpse of the black unconscious shielded from you by your waking mind—a thought creeps to the surface. *I hate this body*, the thought says. *I hate it. I would burn this body alive.*

I RUN EVERY day for the rest of the week. And as I run, I make a plan. Just a shell of an idea, really. One that will infuriate my parents and push away my best friend and drive me far into the jungle, far from any of the "acceptable" paths my siblings have already worn down for me. But it would do something else, too. It would protect. It would allow me total control over my diet, my exercise, my routine, and by proxy, the inside of my head.

On Friday, my phone buzzes. The device vibrates loudly atop the glass surface of my bedside table. I lift it up. There, on the screen, is a name and face I know all too well.

This time, I pick up.

"Jesus, *finally*," comes Manuel's voice through the speaker. "Are you okay? *Jesus*. I've been worried sick. I just finished Freshman Week. I didn't know if you'd pick up since you didn't answer any of my other—"

"Manuel," I say. "Stop calling."

"Stop . . ." His voice goes dead. He whispers, "What?"

"I'm sorry." I wait for tears, but they don't come. Already, my body knows that this is the correct decision. That it doesn't deserve to hear his voice. Not even over the phone. He was my Person all

these years. My primary connection to a life spent in Worry. If anyone would bring about a relapse, it would be him.

"Eliot, what the hell?"

"Don't call me."

I hang up.

I log in to the University of Michigan's online platform for accepted students. I click RESCIND. Then I bend over the carpet and
dry-heave until it feels like my throat might pop from my mouth
like a paper snake from a can of peanuts.

I CHOOSE NEW York. It's a city to which my family has no known
ties, and I vow to make it my own. I'm going to start fresh—*truly*
fresh, for the first time in my life. No Beck family privileges. No
siblings who came before me. No contact with anything that could
trigger the return of my OCD.

Mom and Speedy are, naturally, furious. "You're making a huge
mistake," Mom says in one of our frequent, low-intensity argu-
ments. "College degrees do nothing but help you. By not getting
one, you're closing hundreds of doors and opening none."

"You're wrong, Mom," I say. "I'm opening the only door that
matters."

"You realize that we won't give you a penny if you do this?"
Speedy asks.

"Yes."

"And you realize that if you went to college, we would pay for
your entire life for four years straight?"

"Yes."

"And you still want to do this?"

"Yes."

Mom's eyes roll up to the ceiling, as if she's searching for God.

"Guys. Relax. I'll get a job. I'll get a roommate. I'll support myself. I'm a hard worker. You know this. And it's always been my dream to live in New York."

"It has?" asks Speedy.

"Yes."

This is semi-true. I did indeed decide that it had always been my dream to move to New York—three days ago.

My parents look at each other. I know that look. It's a look I've seen hundreds of times. It's the look that says, *This is a bad idea.* It says, *This is a bad idea, and if she were our first kid and if we were twenty years younger and not so damn tired, we would stuff her into the back of the car and drive her to college ourselves.* It's the same look they always share immediately before I get away with something my older siblings would never have gotten away with.

There will be more low-grade fights after this one. More cajoling, more forehead grabs and eye rolls, but it doesn't matter. With that look, I know I've won.

34

NOW

UP THE BOARDWALK. Far from the rocks. Far enough to guarantee no one could see me. Veering left, deeper into the woods, holding nothing more than a flashlight and the heavy weight of regret. Dinner roiling about in my stomach.

No more than ten feet from the boardwalk, I tripped and fell. Hands and knees. I started to retch. The tequila and whipped cream . . . it was sloshing about inside me, sickening me, like a sailor being tossed back and forth on a wavy sea.

"Fuck," I groaned. I retched again.

I don't want to be here, I thought. *I should never have come. Should never have left the safety of New York. I knew this would happen. I knew it would happen, but I went against my better judgment. Now look at me.*

I gave up. Collapsed into the mud. Rolled over. Faced the sky. The moon glowed high and bright, a mockery of my crumpled form.

I knew Henry was coming long before I felt him. He settled over me—a chill and a shiver, a cold blanket trying and failing to protect me from the night air. Normally, I would have run. Hopped to my feet and sprinted from the trees as fast as I could. Not this time. This time, I stayed. Blinked up at the moon.

Tears pooled at the edges of my eyes and dripped down my cheeks.

"I know you're there," I whispered, but nobody replied.

"ELIOT?" THE VOICE came from far away. I knew it was Manuel from the way he said the first vowel of my name. "Jesus, Eliot, are you okay?"

Heavy clunks as his flipper-like feet pounded through the trees. Dirt puffing as he landed on the ground. His face above me, silhouetted by the night.

"Are you . . . wait. Are you crying?"

I didn't respond.

"What happened?"

I shook my head.

"What *happened*?"

I didn't say. I couldn't.

I'm not who you think I am.

My lungs caught a sob as it rolled up my stomach.

Manuel hesitated. Then he leaned over and gathered me into his arms. I went limp. He untangled my heavy limbs and folded them to his chest like a blanket. All of them, all of me. Legs bound by the curve of his elbow. Head cradled in the soft hollow of his palm. Eyes shielded from the moonlight. He started to walk.

Don't let him do this, the voice said, but I was too tired to fight.

"Where are we going?" I mumbled into his shoulder.

"To bed."

MY BODY BOUNCED gently against Manuel's chest. When we reached Little Lies, he said, "We're here."

I didn't move.

"Eliot?"

Into his shirt, I whispered, "I can't do this."

"What?"

"I can't do this."

He gently set my feet back on the boardwalk. He peeled my head back from his chest and cradled it in his hand. His eyes searched mine. "What do you mean?"

I opened my mouth. Nothing came out.

"Are you talking about you and me?"

I didn't know how to respond. I looked at my best friend's face, but all I saw were the words inside my head.

Vile.

Disgusting.

"No," I said.

"No what?"

"No." I shuffled backward. "I mean . . . yes. I'm talking about us."

His hands quivered in the space between us, like birds lost midflight. "I don't understand."

My chest twinged. I pretended not to feel it. "I didn't talk to you for three years, Manuel. *Three years.* What does that tell you?"

"You were hiding."

"No. *We aren't family.* That's what it tells you. Maybe it feels like we are because my sister fawns over you and Wendy gets all Mother Hen when you're around, but guess what? It *doesn't mean anything.* My mom tells *everyone* they're part of our family after she's had enough to drink."

I knew that the hurt he wore was a hole filled for the last decade by my family.

I also knew that I couldn't tell him so, because to draw him closer would be far crueler than to push him away.

"All that stuff when we were kids?" I said. "Her inviting you over all the time, taking you on all our vacations, basically adopting you? That had nothing to do with you. Nothing. That had to do with grieving her son."

Manuel took a step back.

"All of that—it was about Henry."

Another step back.

"There was a hole in her life, and you filled it. Not because you were special—because you were there. You could've been anyone. You could've been a girl or a dog or a sad little homeless kid or even a fucking houseplant. Okay? That's the truth."

"Wh-why are you doing this?"

"I . . ." Taco started to inch back up my throat. "I just . . ."

Let it sit.

Let it hurt.

This is your fate.

"You know what?" He leaned his massive frame over my head and pushed open the screen door. "Don't answer that. I don't care." He held it open, and I stumbled inside. "We're done here."

He let go of the door. It swung shut.

Something sharp stabbed my calf. The corner of my porch bed. I closed my eyes and leaned backward. The corner pressed harder. I felt the shallow crater it made in my flesh. When I opened my eyes and looked down, I didn't recognize my feet as being attached to my body.

We're done here.

I crawled into bed and pulled the comforter up until it covered my entire body, like a morgue sheet. Like a dead body finally giving in to its fate.

PART IV

The Wedding

35

NOW

TODAY'S THE BIG day. Hooray. Think I'll celebrate by staying in bed all morning.

36

NOW

I'M AN ADDICT.

I admit it, okay?

My name is Eliot Beck and I'm an a-d-d-i-c-t.

DID YOU KNOW you can be addicted to nothing? To the *sensation* of nothing? You can crave the ability to look inside yourself and find nothing, no guilt, no sadness. No anxiety or terror or unfounded doom. No memories threatening to eat you alive from the inside out.

That's what obsessive work gave me. That was its blissful result. It cleared everything out, leaving only space for the next task and the next and the next.

As soon as you first achieve that feeling, it's over. You're toast. To look inside yourself and find nothing, nothing at all, just silence, just emptiness—it feels good. Fuck, it feels *so* good. Better than sex. Better than any pill or bottle or puff of smoke pulled into your lungs and pushed out, way out, gathering into a delicate cloud before disappearing altogether.

37

THE WEDDING WAS in three hours. Doubtless they were all gathered around the massive mirror in my parents' bedroom, the whole bridal party, drinking champagne and smearing lipstick onto each other's faces. The boys were to get ready in Chelsea Morning, but really they were goofing off on the water trampoline. I could hear their happy hollering from the screened-in porch of Little Lies. They probably wouldn't even change out of their swimsuits until the very last minute.

Helene stuck her head into my cabin to invite me to come get ready with the rest of the bridal party. I told her I wasn't feeling well. That I should just get ready alone. That I didn't want to risk getting her sick. She walked over and gave me a willowy hug. Then she looked me in the eyes and said, "Don't worry about the wedding. You just focus on feeling better. Okay?"

Well. I definitely felt worse after that.

All addicts are liars.

My father told me that when I was fifteen. By then, I knew all about his past: the cocaine, the alcohol, the ultimatum from my mom. Everything.

I know what you're thinking. *If you're an addict*, you're thinking, *that means you're a liar. How can I believe what you say?*

It's a valid question. And I've got the answer for you.

We addicts don't just lie; we believe, too. If you aim to deceive others, the first person you convince is yourself.

AT THREE P.M., I spotted another figure coming up the boardwalk. Manuel.

"Shit." I scrambled into bed and pulled the comforter. Just in time—I heard footsteps turn onto the last hill before the front door. The door swung open. More footsteps. The door swung shut. I exaggerated my breath into the long, throaty exhales that sleeping people make. A pause. Then more footsteps, this time walking away.

FOR SO LONG, I thought my obsession with work cured me of my OCD. I thought that because the scariest thoughts—the ones that damned not my ambition but my moral character—were gone, I was saved. Research every copywriting technique known to man? Build templates over and over in your mind until they're as close to perfect as possible? Refuse to take a single day off? Panic spiral on the weekend, when you have too many free hours? Absolutely. Hand it on over. Progress, as my old shrink called it.

It wasn't so much a question of the thoughts coming back. I saw that now. They'd been quiet for a long time, the crazy thoughts, the ones most disconnected from reality: that I was a sociopath or a cheater or in love with one of my siblings, or any number of the terrible, outrageous things that I, at one point or another, genuinely believed to be true of myself. So quiet, in fact, that I believed them to be gone. Forced off the island. Drowned in the water of my mind.

I was wrong.

THERE ARE MANY different ways you can use the word *excess*. You can attach it to a noun to indicate that the object in question exceeds the necessary amount. For example: *Karma's bakery shares their excess cupcakes with the homeless population of Chicago.* (They do, in fact.) Or: *The parents were glad to be rid of their excess child.*

In copywriting, we speak of *wringing excess words from the page.* This idea refers to the overflow, the words that do nothing more than distract from your core message. Look—people don't like to read. They might claim they do, but they're lying. The human brain does whatever it can to cut the excess, to skip words or phrases unnecessary to grasping the overall message of the piece. Nobody looks at an instruction manual with the intent to read every single bloody goddamn microscopic word in its overstuffed pages. Absolutely not. You read enough to understand that screw A goes into hole B, then you throw six hours of some poor copywriter's life straight into the recycling bin. Goodbye and good riddance.

Of course, *excess* need not modify a noun; it can also *be* a noun. One way to use it mirrors the word's function as an adjective: *an excess of something.* An excess of cupcakes. An excess of children. *Any more than four can be considered an excess of children.*

And finally: *excess* itself. A standalone concept. No modifiers, no qualifiers. *Living in excess. A display of excess.* This usage can be applied to a wide range of scenarios; the only requirement is that the situation in question be so over the top it seems disconnected from reality.

This place, these summers, this family . . . it's one *enormous* display of excess. Isn't it? I mean, for God's sake, who needs an entire island? Who needs ten boats? Who needs six children? Just stop at 2.5, like everyone else. Biology can only handle so many variations on the same pair of chromosomes. Eventually it runs out of useful combinations. That's why the youngest kids turn out so messed up, why we drop out of college or get arrested for stealing cigarettes or suffer silently beneath the weight of debilitating mental illness. We're made of leftovers.

IN A FAMILY of eight, if you want to be heard, you yell.

But there's more than one way to yell, isn't there? There are thousands of ways. Infinite. As many ways as there are children in a family. Addiction, isolation, starvation, workaholism, excess—

In some ways, these methods are even more effective than yelling.

In some ways, the loudest screams are silent.

From: Memory & Other Executive Functions <memory@eliot-beck.org>
To: Conscious Mind <consciousness@eliot-beck.org>
Subject: Press Release on Obsessive-Compulsive Disorder

···

Below is a brief press release detailing some Hard Truths® with regard to Obsessive-Compulsive Disorder. Read & syndicate as necessary.

When you say you have OCD, most people think it means you wash your hands a lot and keep your room hyper tidy. They picture Jack Nicholson in *As Good as It Gets*, stepping over sidewalk cracks and eating breakfast at the same table in the same restaurant every single day. We're the quirky misfits of psychological disorders. Harmless. Neurotic. Adorable, even.

That depiction? Bullshit.

OCD isn't about washing your hands. It's about living in constant fear of the outside world or, in many cases, of yourself. It's a mind that attaches itself to whatever obsession it can find. One stuck in permanent fight-or-flight. One that can't stop looking for tigers, even though it left the jungle millennia ago.

But when you get good at refocusing that obsession on something else—I mean, *really* good, incapable of thinking about *anything* but work or food or drugs or whatever it is that you choose—you look inside and find nothing. No fear. No sadness. No guilt or terror or memories threatening to eat you alive from the inside out. Nothing. Only stillness.

And sure, you might not have a social life. You might ignore your family's calls. You might not see your best friend or the love of your life or maybe both of those things in one. But it's worth it.

If running away from your Worries means running away from *everything*, that includes your heart. That includes all those most unbearable of emotions, the kind that make you want to crawl into a hole. The kind that make you want to disappear.

So you do.

You disappear yourself.

38

NOW

JUST BEFORE THE ceremony, the bridal party assembled inside Sunny Sunday. I had finally pried myself out of bed and slipped on my bridesmaid dress, a delicate thing, light lavender, all lace and satin. It probably would have made me feel beautiful if I didn't hate myself so much.

This was it, I decided. My last event with my family. I would get Taz married, get through the reception, go right to bed, take the first boat to town in the morning, drive back to Brooklyn, and never return. It wasn't fair to my family. It wasn't right, that they should have to associate with someone as disgusting as me.

When I walked into Sunny Sunday, the guests were already out on the deck. Clarence was yelling at his phone, which had chosen now to disconnect from the Bluetooth speaker system. The bride and her father had yet to arrive. Everyone else—including Taz— was ripping shots of champagne in the kitchen. I drifted around them and made my way toward the back of the cabin. Bedsheets dangled over the all-glass doors, hiding us from the guests. A makeshift curtain. I nudged the sheets aside and poked my head out to see how the decorations ended up.

Outside, the deck as I knew it was gone. Unrecognizable. No more tacky green lounge chairs or spindly plastic tables. In their place—a North Woods wonderland. Long chains of flowers, an aisle laden with blue-green satin, a massive arch made from oak branches that had been painstakingly braided and bent into an upside-down smile. I picked out the back of Mom's head in the front row, with Dad's chair parked to her left. The other guests—friends, cousins, ballerinas, acquaintances—milled about the remaining rows. The newcomers had only just arrived; their voices had floated into my cabin as I'd finished getting ready.

I gazed around. It was truly amazing; in just four hours, my family transformed a drab sundeck into a veritable paradise. All I did in that time was lie in bed and achieve a full-scale meltdown.

Manuel was seated in the second row. As if alerted to my gaze, he turned around in his seat. We locked eyes. I dropped the curtain and hastily backed away.

I bumped into Taz.

"Whoa, there," he said, catching my shoulders. "You running from someone?"

I laughed idiotically.

He smiled and turned to walk outside. But before pushing open the curtain, he looked back. "Hey. Everything okay with you? I heard you weren't feeling well earlier."

"Yeah," I said.

He seemed to be waiting for more. When I didn't offer it up, he hesitated, then said, "Well, okay then," and turned to leave again. I watched his shoulders slide through the flap in the curtain. Then, just before they disappeared, just before I could stop myself, I blurted, "No, actually."

Taz turned back. He tilted his head and looked at me. "No? Everything isn't okay?"

"No."

"Is it . . . Manuel?"

"How'd you guess?"

He shrugged, smiled. "I might not say much, but I do pay attention."

"Yeah, well." I looked down. My eyes fell immediately on a wrinkle at the hem of my skirt that I hadn't noticed before. Great. Now I could look forward to everyone staring at it during the ceremony.

"Do you want to talk about it?"

I looked back up. Taz's eyes—green, same as mine—squinted. Studied me. I was being watched by my own eyes.

"No. Well, maybe. Well . . . I don't know."

His cheeks were flushed a happy pink that didn't match the concern in his eyes. Rose pink. *The color of love*, I thought. *Love and alcohol.* Immediately I felt selfish for saying anything to him at all. "Listen. Ignore me. This is your wedding day. I don't even know what I'm talking about. Go out there and get married."

I turned to leave, but Taz grabbed my wrist.

"Eliot, stop."

I glanced back up at him. I could see he wasn't going to let me leave. When did my brother get so strong? "I just . . ." I swallowed. Speech had taken on that slippery quality, the one that accompanies lack of food. Words slid from me without my consent. "How did you do it?"

He cocked his head. "Do what?"

"The soulmate thing. You and Helene. No fighting. No drama. Perfect relationship. How did you do it?"

To my surprise, Taz started to laugh. His grip slackened. "Jesus, Gup." His eyes sparkled. "And here I always thought you were the smart one in the family."

"What?"

He looked at me incredulously. "You think we have a perfect relationship? Christ. Nobody has that. I mean . . . we got in the biggest

fight ever just a week before coming out here. We almost called off
the whole wedding. Seriously."

My mouth opened.

"Hardest day of my life. If you want to talk about fighting and
drama—"

"But." My lips dangled open in that idiotic shape they make
whenever I'm wrong. "But."

"But what?"

"But then . . . if things were so bad, why did you stay with her?"

"Oh, well, that's easy." Taz shrugged. "She's my Person. When
you find your Person, you don't let them get away."

He squeezed my shoulder, winked, and exited through the curtain, leaving me standing alone before it. Breath dragged itself in
and out of my mouth. In, out, in, out. The sheet puffed in and out
along with me, like an extra set of lungs. I spun around. Power walked
to the bathroom. Shut the door behind me and started to cry.

BY THE TIME I wiped my nose and walked out of the bathroom,
Clarence had sorted out the sound system. The bridesmaids and
groomsmen were now assembled into two lines behind the curtain.
A new champagne bottle was making its way down the line. Every-
one was nice and lubed up. Jazzed. Excited to marry the shit out of
Taz and Helene.

The procession was led by a pair of high school groomsmen I
recognized, part of the boatloads of people who had arrived while I
hid in my cabin. After them came two pairs of friends I'd never
seen before. Then Clarence and a long-limbed beauty, clearly a ballerina. Then Karma and Shelly. Shelly held her wife's hand with
three loose fingers, letting it dangle to the side. She stood at a slight
remove, head turned, gaze out the window.

And me. Just me, no escort. Might as well be a flower girl.

The windows were open. Outside, I heard a chorus of birds. White-throated sparrows. Lots of them from the sound of it. The same call I heard that day in the woods multiplied half a dozen times. I smiled.

"What are you grinning about?" asked Karma.

I pointed to the window. "Do you hear the birds?"

She tilted her head. "Are those . . . ? Those are the birds that Speedy likes, right?"

"Yeah." I nodded.

Clarence passed the bottle of champagne back to Karma, who accepted it with a wink.

"So." My sister took another swig of champagne. "You a bird freak now, or what?"

"What?" I asked. "Oh. No, no. No, not at all."

She wiped her mouth and offered the bottle to me.

I waved it away. "Theirs is the only call I know. Manuel and I used to sit inside this hollowed-out old tree trunk and listen to them."

"You mean the Fort?"

"What?" I stared at Karma. "How do you know about the Fort?"

She shared that look with my siblings—the Youngest Child look, the one that said, *Must be nice to be so young and stupid.*

"How could I *not* know, Boose? You talked about it all the time. Literally *all* the time. Nonstop monologue on the *castle* you were building for yourself. I finally asked to go see it just because I thought it would shut you up, but you wouldn't take me. You wouldn't take anyone. You called its location 'cassified.' I think you meant *classified.* It was cute. Annoying as hell, but still cute." She ruffled my hair. "Guess some things don't change."

My brain tried to tick forward. "That doesn't make any sense.

Why would Henry and I build a place we didn't want to take anyone?"

"Henry?"

"Yes. Henry. Our dead brother." I sighed. "Or have you caught the same strain of amnesia that Mom has?"

"No, that's not what I . . ."

At the stereo, Clarence pressed PLAY on the wedding CD. The first notes of "Come On Eileen" echoed through the cabin.

He jogged back over. "Bit of an odd song choice for a wedding, no?"

"Taz is nothing if not odd," Karma said without looking at Clarence. She was still staring at me. "Eliot, you didn't build the Fort with Henry."

"Yes, I did," I said.

"No, you didn't."

"Yes, I did. We built it together. It took all summer."

Her voice, when she spoke, was softer than usual. "Eliot, that's impossible."

What the hell was she talking about? She didn't even *know* about the Fort back when I—when *we*—were building it. It was just Henry and me. Just us. Our little secret.

Right?

Taz poked his head inside. "Everyone ready to go?"

I should've been readying myself to walk, but I couldn't. I was somewhere else. Stuck eleven years in the past. "No, it isn't impossible," I said, as much to myself as to Karma. "I remember. I remember yelling at him to slow down every time we ran out there. I remember digging chunks of dirt out of the ground with our bare hands and pinning up the tarp and . . ." The room blurred. The cabin was already pretty fuzzy, probably due to the fact that I had skipped both breakfast and lunch, but now it started to spin. A ring of light gathered at the edge of my vision. "And . . . and . . ." I put my head into my hands, forgetting they held a bouquet. Rose petals gagged the inside of my nostrils.

"Eliot."

"I built the Fort with Henry," I said into the bouquet. "I know I did. We built the Fort and then we sat inside it and listened to white-throated sparrows. We did."

"Eliot."

I lowered the bouquet slowly. Karma's face emerged from behind its petals: first the blunt bangs, then the shiny forehead, then the eyes. Sad, drooping eyes.

"You built the Fort alone," she said, "the summer Henry passed." Silence.

I breathed out. "No, I didn't."

"Yes, you did."

"No, I *didn't*. That's not possible."

"Come On Eileen" ended. "Mrs. Robinson" began—the official cue to begin the procession. At the front of the line, Taz's high school friends pushed back the curtain. Clarence tucked a flask into his jacket and straightened his lapel. "Another odd song choice. What kind of marriage are they expecting here, exactly?"

Karma ignored him. "It is possible. You worked on it all summer. Said it was a matter of 'life and death.' You used that exact phrase." She laughed. "Little Eliot. So serious, right from the start. I tried to correct your grammar, to tell you it's life *or* death, but you looked at me like I was insane. 'No, Karma,' you said. 'You can't have one without the other.'"

The patch of forehead above my eye started to throb.

"God only knows where you heard *that* phrase. You were only— nine? Ten? I asked Mom and Dad if they thought I should go out there and check on you, make sure you weren't building a bomb or something. They told me not to worry. 'Everyone grieves differently,' they said, 'if this is what she needs to do, let her do it.'"

"That's not true."

"It is."

"That's *not true.*"

But the more I thought about it, the less certain I became. I'd never been able to trust my own eyes. Eyes filter through the mind, and my mind shows me only what it wants to see. And what it wants is almost never the truth. A noise somewhere between a gasp and a groan bubbled up my throat. I muffled it with the thorny pillowcase of roses.

"Eliot?"

I didn't lower the bouquet.

"Are you okay?"

I felt a set of fingers wrap around my forearm. Karma's voice whispered, "I gotta go, kid. Love you." The fingers squeezed once. Then they disappeared.

When I looked up, she was gone. Everyone was gone. I stood alone behind the makeshift curtain. Just me and a lavender dress and a mangled fistful of flowers. Outside, the tempo picked up, as if Simon & Garfunkel knew I was lagging behind.

"Eliot?" said a voice behind me.

I jumped and spun around.

There stood Helene, stunningly beautiful in bare feet and a simple white dress, loose and embroidered, almost like a nightgown. The kind of dress you can actually dance in. On her elbow was her father. "Are you trying to keep me from marrying your brother, or do you just like a big entrance?"

"I . . ."

"Well, let's get on with it," said Tim. "Some of us are eager to get rid of their only child."

Helene beamed. When she looked at her father, her eyes sparkled with more love in one glance than mine have emitted in the course of their entire existence. I didn't know how to respond—whether I should laugh or cry or apologize—so I turned around and tripped over the flimsy curtain as I pushed out into the afternoon sun.

The first thing I saw after my eyes adjusted to the bright light was Manuel. Every face in the crowd had turned around to watch the procession, but my eyes fell on him immediately. As if I was already looking for him. For his wild curls and dark lips. We locked eyes. I looked away. Trained my gaze on the hem of Karma's dress, which dragged along the patio's mismatched slats of wood. The cloth dipped in and out of each crack.

I didn't build the Fort with Henry.

I tried to remember. Tried to dig up memories of my brother in a way I hadn't in a long time. I placed myself back in the center of the island. I flexed my fists. I tried to remember exactly what they felt like as we built the Fort. When I plunged them into the wet earth, fingers breaking soft dirt, arms ripped apart by juniper needles.

My hands plunge into the wet earth. Dirt squeezes into the cracks of my fingernails. Juniper needles rip at my skin.

Karma's dress drifted left and Clarence's shoes turned right.

A stack of bracelets jangle on my wrist, a rainbow assortment of little plastic circles. This year's fashion trend. Everyone has them. I begged my parents to buy them for me. By the end of the school year, I had over thirty. By the start of next year, all will be in a trash bag.

I made it to the end of the aisle. I looked up and took my place at the very end of the bridal party, farthest from the altar. The music changed. Simon & Garfunkel were gone. The wedding march began. From the center of the curtain, Helene emerged with her father. All eyes followed as she approached. In the crowd, my mother beamed. Helene reached the front. The music ended and Caleb began to speak.

I look up from the bracelets on my wrist and see Henry's smiling face. He laughs as he throws tufts of grass over his shoulder.

I glanced at Speedy, who was parked right before me in the first row. His knees jiggled. Was that possible? Could unmoving legs move of their own free will? His face smiled up at the ceremony with the kind of peaceful contentment only accessible to those who have seen death.

Caleb was saying something about everlasting love. Love and the work that goes into maintaining it. I tried to listen, but my mind kept spiraling through distant memories. I blinked.

I blink. Henry's face disappears. In its place is an empty clearing.

At that moment, somewhere in the trees that hang over the roof of Sunny Sunday, a white-throated sparrow let out its call. I shivered. There it was again, that ghoulish feeling, the sense that I was standing directly atop my brother's ashes.

I look down. I'm still digging. My bracelets still rattle. When I look back up, the clearing is still empty. Henry is still gone. White-throated sparrows cry in the trees above.

How idiotic. How impossible. Henry's remains couldn't be on that porch, with its many slats and holes to slip through. I tried to ignore it, to focus instead on Caleb's speech. But my focus didn't want to go there.

I'm a little girl afraid of death. I'm a little girl who does not understand the idea of souls, the idea of rest. Who needs a place to mourn her brother. Who needs to believe that he is safe underground, that his ashes will stay warm. That she'll always know where to find him.

My knees buckled.

"Whoa, whoa." Karma grabbed me by the elbows. The service stopped. Thirty pairs of eyes turned to me. Karma squinted into my face, which I can only imagine was the color of a young corpse. "You good, dude?"

I am a little girl who sees the consequences of her actions. I see them in the shape of a father curled up in the middle of a bedroom torn to pieces. I hear them in the mangled sounds spewing from within him.

I twisted my mouth into a smile. Shallow breaths dragged in through my lips. "I'm fine," I heard my voice say.

The service resumed. Manuel's eyes remained on me.

I'm not fine.

My hands plunge into the wet earth. Dirt squeezes into the cracks of my fingernails. Juniper needles rip at the skin of my arms. White-throated sparrows cry in the trees above.

When at last the hole is deep enough, I lift the heavy plastic bag at my feet, the one I pulled out of the errrn that morning—the one stuffed with the lifeless grey powder I'm told is my brother. My arms quiver as I lower him into the hole.

I find my father on the floor of his bedroom, crippled by the weight of something he believes to be his fault. I understand that I can never tell him. I understand that telling him means digging Henry back up. I cannot allow that to happen. I let my father carry a burden he should never have had to bear. I let him carry it for more than a decade.

I build a fortress atop the ashes of my brother.

The crowd erupted, jerking me out of my trance. At the altar, Taz draped Helene over his arm and planted a spectacular wedding kiss onto her lips. Speedy whistled through two fingers. The porch shook with joyous shouts. I clapped feebly. Clarence produced a champagne bottle from nowhere and popped the cork. It flew over the porch railing, into the waves below. The happy couple clung to each other and sprinted down the aisle. The audience unleashed a shower of snow-white rice, the grains of which would surely slip through the cracks in the porch and plunge straight into the water. It was over. They were married.

In the trees above, white-throated sparrows cried.

39

THE FEAST THAT followed was one for the books.

After Taz and Helene made their exit, Mom stood and clapped twice, like the queen she knew herself to be. The guests rose as one and hoisted their chairs high above their heads. They rearranged them into a circle stretching from one end of the porch to the other. While they worked, the bridal party—myself included, Karma dragging me along like a disoriented puppy—went around the side to the screened-in dining porch to fetch the table. We each cupped a hand under the heavy wood and lifted. Caleb and Clarence and the other men raised the table so high that none of the girls could reach. Karma jumped up and down.

"Absolutely useless," said Clarence with a grin.

They carried the table out to the patio and settled it at the center of the circle of chairs. We set it with remarkable speed, probably because there were no frilly napkins or extra soup spoons involved. Just plates and glasses and candles and place mats.

And food. So much food.

I dragged the deepest breath I could manage into my chest. Drifted back to the patio railing.

I know where Henry is.

The rest of the group milled about. They didn't know where to place their bodies; no name tags sat on the place mats. "Sit wherever," said Wendy in a tone so cheerful it sounded prerecorded. "Taz and Helene want everyone to choose for themselves."

Arms trembling, I flipped my body around to face the water. The wind that stirred the trees in the morning had completely dissipated. Not a ripple cracked the lake's surface. I tried to take another deep breath. My lungs filled only halfway.

"Eliot?"

I turned around. Everyone at the table was staring at me. A pair of warm chestnut eyes bludgeoned my chest. Karma gestured to the spread and said, "Waiting on you."

"Right."

I walked over to the last open chair, between the two groomsmen I didn't know. Manuel was right across the table. I tried not to make eye contact as I sat down.

Moments later, the door to Sunny Sunday burst open. Taz and Helene emerged, yanking the curtain from the wall as they did. Helene had changed into a short, flowery dress. Taz's jacket was gone. They ran out onto the porch, holding the curtain, letting it flap behind them like an enormous cape. The table burst into applause.

After the newlyweds took their chairs, everyone dug in.

It was the most delicious-looking table I'd ever seen. Every bit was covered by the different dishes we'd listed in our group chat. Fettuccini alfredo. Pulled pork with an extra bottle of Sweet Baby Ray's sauce. Deep dish pizza that looked suspiciously like Lou Malnati's. Ceramic basins filled with salsa and guacamole and hummus ringed by a mountain of tortilla chips. And more. Not an empty inch of wood remained.

Of course. Leave it to Taz to choose everyone else's favorite foods for his wedding.

And leave it to Karma and Shelly to make it all perfectly.

Any unoccupied table space held an uncorked bottle of wine. Along the perimeter, champagne waited in ice buckets. The whole thing looked downright medieval.

I couldn't have been less hungry if I tried.

Oddly enough, even though I've been nothing short of an anxious mess for more than a decade, I've never had a panic attack. Never. But I suspected that I was slowly descending into one at that moment.

Karma eyed my empty plate. Trying to act normal, I dug into the nearest dishes at random, slopping a bit of each onto my plate. I even took hummus, which I've never actually liked.

When I looked back up, Manuel was staring at me. His eyes dropped to my plate, then raised slowly back up to my face. They narrowed.

I looked away.

The toasts began. Karma and Clarence went first, of course, giving a rowdy speech I couldn't pay attention to but surely set a high bar. They concluded by saluting the evening sky with their champagne flutes and insisting that the new couple join them in a celebratory chug. Helene giggled and obliged.

As the toasts continued, I started cycling through the memories again. I couldn't stop. That's the thing about OCD. You examine yourself from every possible angle—how do I look as a lesbian? A cheater? A heartless bitch? You never thought that you were a lesbian before, but now that the possibility has arrived in your mind, you must examine it from every angle possible. Where logic talks, OCD screams. And by then, you've bought so fully into its hollering that you can't tell which one was the truth and which one was the worry. And you think in circles, and the circles are endless, and they consume you, and you forget that you used to have a personality outside those circles.

Most of the time, the things I worried about were cruel illusions. Not this time. This time, I'd uncovered something truly horrendous. Truly unforgivable. I'd stolen something that didn't belong to me, and I'd taken my father's legs with it.

I did my best to eat—a bite of fettuccini here, a mouthful of pulled pork there—but I truly had no appetite. None at all. My body was shaking. My fists were balling into little claw shapes of their own accord, as if I were playing at being a wolf. My heart was hammering in my chest. I felt so oddly aware of my own breathing. *Too* aware. I feared, for a moment, that I would forget how to breathe at all.

I couldn't help it; I glanced up at Manuel.

And immediately wished I hadn't.

He was watching me shake. Watching my little clawed fists. For all I knew, he'd never *stopped* watching me. By then, his eyes had narrowed to previously unforeseen levels of suspicion. When my gaze landed on him, his eyes flicked up to meet mine. They narrowed even further. He pushed back his chair—clearly with the intention of coming over to speak with me.

I jerked my chair back and blurted out the word "Bathroom" to anyone who was listening. As I stood, the patio tipped onto its side. I caught myself on the back of Groomsman A's chair.

"Are you all right?" asked Groomsman B. He grabbed my elbow in an awkward attempt to keep me upright.

"Yes." I gripped the back of the chair and squeezed my eyes shut. When I opened them again, the patio stood upright. I blinked. The men were staring at me. Manuel was staring at me. I smiled feebly at the groomsmen and turned to run away. As I darted around the table and into Sunny Sunday, I felt Manuel's eyes follow.

I burst through the bathroom door and teetered to the sink, catching myself with one hand on either side of the basin. My legs wobbled. I let go and sunk to the bathroom floor.

The door swung open and knocked into my shoulder.

"Shit," rasped a familiar voice.

I cringed. The only door on the island with an actual lock, and I forgot to use it.

Dad's chair bumped into the doorknob. His head peeked around the frame. There they were again—those eyes, both piercing and wrinkled. Careless but wise. Eyes that had seen fifty more years of life than I could even begin to imagine.

"Whoops," he said. "My bad."

He wheeled backward, attempting retreat.

"Dad." I scrambled to my feet. "Dad."

"What? What, what?" He pulled the door back open, hair flapping wildly.

Vertigo pulsed at the edges of my vision. I steadied myself on the bathroom sink.

"What's wrong?" he asked.

I blinked several times to bring his face into focus.

"*What*, for God's sake?"

The words bubbled out of my mouth all at once. "Can you fix me?"

"Fix you?" He shook his head, bewildered. "Are you broken?"

You have no idea.

"Yes."

"How are you broken?"

I looked down. The tiles swirled. Then, quiet as a whisper: "They aren't gone."

"What aren't gone?"

I shook my head.

"What the hell are you talking about, Eliot?"

"The thoughts. My *things*, as you call them."

Pause.

"They aren't gone."

"They came back?"

"No."

"Then what?"

I couldn't respond. I just kept shaking my head, eyes on the tiles.

"Eliot."

Shake.

"Eliot, look at me."

I did. I looked up into the aging eyes of my father.

"You can tell me. You can tell me if they came back," he said.

I swallowed. "Does it count as coming back if they never left in the first place?"

We stared at each other. He looked so *old* then, with his wheel-chair and his wisps of blond hair.

"So, can you fix me?" I asked. I could hear the plea in my voice. It sounded pathetic. "Can you? The way you fixed yourself, your addiction? I mean, you did it all yourself, right? No rehab, no nothing. Can you show me how?"

"Eliot, I . . ."

What the hell am I doing?

"I . . ." He fiddled with his wheels, pushing them nervously back and forth. "I don't . . ."

That man. That poor man. A lifetime flattened beneath the weight of a secret he should never have had to bear. Who, at almost seventy years old, had survived addiction and lost his legs and married three women and fathered six children and escaped death twice. Who probably never wanted me—the last-minute addition to our family, tacked on with fertility's last breath. It was time to relieve him. It was time.

"No. Dad. Stop."

"Stop what?"

And then, before I could stop myself: "I know what happened to Henry's ashes."

"You . . ." His face paled. "What?"

"His ashes. You told everyone you scattered them somewhere in the middle of the island. I know that's not true."

"You . . ."

"I know you lost them."

He wheeled backward, away from my words.

"Or at least, you *think* you lost them. But that's not true, Dad. That's not what happened."

"Eliot. You don't know what you're saying."

"Yes, I do." I stepped forward.

"No, you don't. What are you doing, Eliot? Why would you say something so cruel?"

"Because it's true, Dad." I took another step forward. Another. "You didn't lose Henry's ashes. They weren't lost."

Dad rolled farther away. I chased him out into the main cabin.

"They weren't lost. They were hidden." I paused. "And I know where they are."

His eyes shrunk, hardening to marbles.

"You remember the Fort? The one I built, way out in the woods?"

He nodded. His face was pale as lace.

"It's not a fort," I said. "It's a tomb."

His mouth dropped open. We stared at each other. The air brightened and darkened, lightened and ladened, released my lungs and squeezed my chest so tightly I could no longer breathe. It happened all together, all at once. And it felt to me then, as we stood across from each other—Eliot and Speedy, youngest and oldest, separated by a distance of almost three full generations—that my father and I were truly seeing each other for the very first time.

"I'm sorry, Dad." My eyes started to well up. "I . . . I didn't know back then. What I was doing. I thought I was doing something kind. For Henry. I didn't . . . I didn't know . . ." I inhaled raggedly. "I'm so sorry."

I had no idea what he would say to me. To this one final confession. I felt just the way I had as a child, back when I first threw myself before him, begging for his forgiveness. I felt raw and naked and terrified. I braced myself for his response.

But then, "*There* you are."

I looked up. Manuel stood before the makeshift curtain. He paced forward. "I've been waiting for you to come back. You and I need to . . ." When he saw the look on my face, he stopped. "Oh." Glanced down at my father. "Is everything all right?"

Speedy wheeled backward. Tires on sticky floorboard.

"Manny," I croaked.

"What happened?"

"I lied to you."

"What?"

A strange throb echoed at the base of my skull. "I'm sorry."

"Eliot, what the hell are you talking about?"

"I'm sorry." Tears started to drip down my face. "I'm so sorry, Manuel. I hate myself. I hate what I did to you."

"Don't . . ."

"I'm a bad person. I'm fucked up." I was crying in earnest now. "I left you. I disappeared. And I didn't even tell you why. You deserve to know why."

"Eliot—"

"The thoughts I have . . . They're disgusting. They're awful. I can't even say them out loud. I can't . . ."

"Eliot."

"No. *Stop.* You don't know. You think you do, but . . . I'm sorry. I h-hate myself. I do." I stumbled forward. Manuel caught me. I sunk into the depths of his arms. "I don't understand . . . why my brain won't just l-leave . . . leave me alone."

I felt the tears try to disappear, like they always did, but I didn't let them. I forced them out, wringing the sadness from my gut like the last drops of dirty dish soap. It was loud. That strange hiccupping noise, the one that sounds like laughter. Gulps and gasps, the constant search for oxygen.

When the tears finally started to subside, all was quiet. Speedy had vanished. Manuel's chest rose and fell.

"Eliot."

I didn't look up at him. I was too afraid of what I might see.

"*Eliot.*"

I clung tighter to his body.

After a moment, two fingers landed lightly on the bottom of my chin. My neck crinkled as Manuel tipped my face up to look up at him. His eyes searched mine.

"What?" I asked.

"I wish . . ." he started, then trailed off. He glanced away, then back to me. "I wish you could see yourself the way that I do. The way that . . . that everyone does."

I started to shake my head, but he stopped me. He laid one hand on either side of my face, stilling the motion before it could even begin.

"Eliot," he said. "You are not a bad person."

I tried to shake my head again. "You don't—"

"Yes, I do. I know you. In fact, I know you better than I know anyone else on this entire planet. You're . . . stubborn and impulsive and moody, and it's next to impossible to get you to shut up once you get going."

I coughed out a laugh.

"But you're also my best friend. You're the girl who defended me from bullies twice her size. Who made me sit through terrible dramatic readings in Spanish. Who took me into her family, who forced me to dance, who radiated sunshine so bright it was sometimes hard for me to look at. And losing you"—he choked—"losing you hurt more than anything I've felt in my entire life."

Tears started to run down my face again.

"You are a daughter beloved by her parents, a sister adored by her siblings, and my best friend in the whole fucking universe." He paused. "But you are *not* the thoughts in your head. Do you hear me?"

I tried to hear him. I did.

"Those thoughts—the ones that scare you so much? They don't scare me, Eliot. They don't scare me one bit. And you don't . . . you don't have to hold them all by yourself." His hands gripped my cheeks tighter. "You never have. I'm here. I'm here, Eliot. Let me carry them with you."

I choked on nothing, on air. I was falling. I was falling so fast.

"I have to tell you something else."

My eyes flicked up to his. "What?"

"It's about that night. The one right before I left for college."

My chest constricted. My eyes fell.

This is it, I thought. *I have to tell him. After what he just said . . . This is the moment where I come clean. When he finally hates me, once and for all.*

But then—

"I already know what happened."

"You . . ." My eyes darted back up. "What?"

"I know, Eliot. It . . . it took me a while, but eventually, I put it together."

"But how—"

"You. The little kids. And the way your thoughts work, telling you you're a lesbian when you aren't or cheating when you aren't or essentially *anything* you aren't . . . I know how your mind works, Beck. I might even know it better than I know my own." He paused, stooping to catch my eyes with his. "It wasn't hard for me to put two and two together. A simple look at the history on my family's computer just confirmed it. I knew, Eliot. I knew, and I tried to tell you the next day. I tried to tell you the next month. I've tried to tell you for three years straight, goddammit, but you won't listen."

"But . . ." I swallowed, unable to tear my eyes away from the pools of liquid chestnut staring so intensely at me. "But . . . if that's true . . . then, why are you here? Why did you . . . You . . . You let me kiss you . . ." I shook my head. "I don't *understand*."

"I let you kiss me because I *wanted* you to kiss me, Beck. I already told you: you aren't the thoughts in your head. And you certainly, without question, are *not* a pedophile. Or a cheater. Or a murderer. Or *any* of the things your brain so wrongly tries to convince you that you are. You are a *good person*, Eliot Beck. One of the best that I've ever known."

I felt as if I could collapse. As if my legs would finally, after three years of carrying this secret, just collapse.

OCD made me want to give up. It made me think that it would be easier just to be alone. To cordon myself off from everyone who loves me, to protect them from me. It told me this story over and over again. It made this life sound so easy, so compelling.

But that story wasn't true, was it? It was just a story. Because being alone was miserable. I hated life without my family. Without Manuel. I hated the loneliness, the constant crying. OCD wanted me to think that I needed to be alone. It wanted to isolate me. To tear me down. To make me think that all I need is *it*.

But now I see the truth.

My mouth opened. "Manny, I—"

"Eliot."

When I looked over, I found Karma standing in the doorway to the patio beside Speedy. Speedy's face was slathered in shock, pale white, as if he were still processing what I had said to him earlier. But when I looked at Karma . . .

Freezing cold water washed over me.

Her body was hunched over, her fists tight at her sides. Her face was screwed up, as if she were fighting a wave of fury. Breath dragged in and out of her nostrils, her chest rising and falling beneath her purple dress.

Speedy told her.

She knows, and now she hates me.

Beside me, Manuel looked between the two of us. "Eliot?" he asked. "What's going on?"

I couldn't look away from Karma. Her gaze was drill sharp and terrifying. Behind her, my siblings were starting to take note of the scene unfolding just inside the doorway. I saw Taz stand from his chair, saw Caleb crane his neck to try and get a better view. Everyone looked confused, even concerned. I opened my mouth—to say what, I'm still not sure—but snapped it back shut when Karma began to storm forward. Her eyes beat into mine like two bullets trained on twin targets. Her small legs swished back and forth inside the purple fabric, heels pounding the wooden floor. It took everything within me to not recoil. To not turn around and run. What was she going to do? Ream me out in front of everyone? Yell at me for stealing the remains of our dead brother? Hit me?

Instead, to my great surprise, she did none of those things.

She hugged me.

Her strong little arms wrapped around me, pulling me tight to her body. I went stiff beneath them, shocked at her embrace. She only hugged me tighter.

"You were so young," she whispered against my skin. "You didn't know what you were doing. It's okay, Boose. You were just a kid. You don't have to carry it alone anymore."

I nearly choked on the air in my throat.

Over her shoulder, one by one, my siblings stood from the table and filed into Sunny Sunday, pulled inside by curiosity about what was going on with their sisters. I watched the scene register on their faces—Karma's arms around me, my rigid body, Manuel confused beside us. And I watched as they all made the same decision: to walk right up to us and join in. First Taz, then Caleb, then Clarence, even Shelly and Helene. They walked around the side of us, or behind, and added their arms into the throng. They surrounded me, my family, one big mass of bodies enveloping me, pulling me close, acknowledging me in the way I had always so desired.

"You don't have to carry *any* of it alone," Karma whispered, and I knew she didn't just mean Henry's ghost.

And that's when I started to cry.

40

THEN

"YOU'RE SCARED OF spiders?" Manuel asks. It's our first summer together on Cradle Island. "That's stupid. Spiders are completely harmless."

"That's not the point," I say.

"Yes, it is." He palms a tree spider crawling up the wall and drops it into his mouth.

I squeal. "Did you just *eat that*?"

He doesn't flinch, just spreads his lips in a cheeky grin. When he does, the spider crawls out the corner of his mouth and down his chin.

"Ewwww!" I whack his arm. "That's gross! That's disgusting! I can't believe you just did that! You're such a weirdo!"

At the time, I don't understand why this boy put a spider in his mouth. I don't yet know that, sometimes, people do things that don't make sense. Sometimes it's for the wrong reasons, and sometimes it's for the right reasons. Sometimes it's just to make the other person feel safe. To show them they have nothing to fear or, if that's not possible, to cling to them while you both cry together.

41

NOW

SOFT EARTH CHURNED beneath our shoes as we trekked through the forest at sunset. I walked with Manuel's hand wrapped around mine, pausing whenever he held up a branch for me to duck beneath. Pine needles fell into updos. Dirt clung to the hems of our dresses. The Nurses carried my father over moss-peppered rocks and tangled roots of trees. We were headed toward the Fort, a shovel in Caleb's hands.

The wedding had become a funeral.

Taz and Helene didn't seem to mind. Everyone had taken the news of what I did as a child slightly differently, some with shock, others with dawning realization. Helene had only nodded, as if she'd suspected it all along. I wondered if she truly had felt his presence. His spirit's unrest. I wouldn't be surprised if she had. But none—not a single one of my family members—had been upset with me. They had handled the news with gentle acceptance, even with love.

When we reached the Fort, the first thing we did was to take it apart. To pull down the tarp, untangle the lights, pick up the blankets softened and gone grey with the passing winters. We removed everything until, for the first time in over a decade, the Fort was a fort no longer. It was just a patch of earth partially protected by a fallen tree.

Then Caleb started to dig.

It didn't take long. How deep could a ten-year-old go on her own? The bag containing Henry's ashes was only a foot down. I couldn't believe they had survived this long, but then, that was Henry, wasn't it? Always exceptional. Always resilient.

With tender hands, Caleb lifted the ashes from the ground. He stood—holding the bag so carefully, as if he feared it might explode—and passed it to Speedy, who had been placed back into his chair by the Nurses. Now our father would finally get to do what he had always promised. He would scatter his son on Cradle Island, and he would do so alone, with only the Nurses carrying him along, so that we would not know where Henry was laid to rest. So that he would be the entire island, not just one spot. And so that my father could finally say goodbye.

The family gathered around. I held Manuel's arm. Karma held Shelly's, Helene Taz's. Caleb and Clarence stood beside each other, backs ramrod straight, just how I remembered them from the last time we did this.

Speedy adjusted himself on his chair, shifting the bag of ashes in his lap. He looked out over all of us. Gone was his usual sleepy in-difference, gone was the pale shock of earlier that night. This was the father I remembered—so sturdy, so strong. My mother walked over and took her place beside her husband, settling a hand on his shoulder.

"At Henry's last funeral," Speedy said finally, "I did all the talk-ing." He looked at each of his children in turn. "I thought that maybe one of you would like to speak tonight."

We all glanced expectantly at Caleb. Our patriarch. We all as-sumed it would be him.

Instead, the one to step forward was Taz.

Quiet Taz, the wallflower, whose wedding we had interrupted for this makeshift ceremony. He walked over to stand beside the hole that Caleb had just dug, then nodded at our dad, who nodded back. Then he turned to face the rest of us.

He cleared his throat. "It means more than I can say that Henry could be here with us tonight," he said somberly, gesturing toward the dilapidated bag of ashes on Speedy's lap.

In the pause that followed, a sort of half-choking sound could be heard. We all glanced around, searching for its source—which we quickly discovered to be my half brother. Clarence had covered his mouth with one hand. He seemed to be holding in hysterical laughter.

"Clare," Caleb said warningly.

"He said—" Clarence started, then seemed to take a few steadying breaths.

Taz blinked in confusion. "What?"

"You said . . ." Clarence choked out. "You said . . ."

And then Karma started to laugh, too. It wasn't much, just a snort that she tried to cover with her fist. Shelly shot her a look, but it was no use: Karma collapsed into Clarence, giggles getting the best of her. Shelly's lips twitched, even as she tried to appear serious. Over by the hole in the ground, Taz seemed to recognize the absurdity of his own words, and laughter washed over him, then over Helene, rippling out to hit Manuel and me, too. Even Speedy started to laugh, low chuckles that rattled through my chest. Only Wendy was left looking around, clearly confused about what was so funny—which only made us all laugh harder.

Caleb was the last to lose it. Caleb—so serious, so stately—crumpled over with barely contained gasps of laughter. Clarence smacked his shoulder. Caleb straightened up and threw his arm around his brother's shoulder, letting his laughter soar high into the trees, free, joyous. For the first time in over a decade, I saw my half brothers as I remembered them from my childhood: best friends, inseparable, carefree. And so our laughter grew together, ruffling the treetops, echoing up toward sunset.

And Henry—

Henry would have loved it.

ON THE WALK back to Sunny Sunday—we *did* have a wedding reception to throw, after all, along with several dozen confused guests awaiting our arrival—I turned the words over in my head several times before I actually spoke them aloud.

Manuel and I brought up the rear of the procession. We followed my family through the forest, walking in silence until we reached the boardwalk again. Everyone ran ahead, eager to get back to the festivities, but we walked slowly. Put some distance between ourselves and the rest. When we reached the top of the boardwalk, the peak, before it sloped back down toward Sunny Sunday, I stopped.

Manuel turned around. Behind his head, the sun had finally set. Reds and pinks danced around his wild curls. "Everything okay?" he asked.

"Why did you let me kiss you?"

"What?"

"That night in Little Lies. Why did you let me kiss you, Manuel?"

He shook his head. "I already told you: I wanted you to."

"You . . ." I looked down at our hands, which were twined together like a pair of matching socks. Even now, the closest to happiness I had come in a long time—even now, I felt the Worries knocking at the back door. Waiting. Waiting their turn to spring back to life. They would always be there, I knew that now. They would never go away altogether.

I would just have to learn how to cope with them as best I could.

"But why would you want me to?" I looked back up at him. "After everything I did, everything you know about me . . . why would you want me to kiss you?"

Laughter played in his eyes. "Of course I wanted you to kiss me." He stepped forward, taking my other hand. "I love you, you idiot."

For the third time that night, I started to cry.

"I've loved you since that first moment on the playground, when you threw wood chips in those bullies' faces." His eyes shimmered. "I love you when you're angry, I love you when you're sad, and I love you when your head is filled with thoughts so terrifying you don't think you can share them with me. In fact"—he squeezed my hand—"that's when I love you most."

"But wh-why? I don't understand. Why would you love something so horrible?"

"Listen to me." His hands came up to hold either side of my face. "I know your brain scares you. I know it tells you things that aren't real. But you must know that, to the rest of the world . . . it's something wonderful. Something enviable. Something creative, and powerful, and brilliant to a fault."

"I'm not the brilliant one, Manuel. That's you."

He stared at me for a long moment. "You really can't see it, can you?"

"See what?"

Manuel lifted one hand and fluttered his fingers over my temple, then cupped my forehead with his palm and smoothed my hair back. He whispered, "Your brain is the most beautiful thing I've ever seen."

Behind him, the sunset was fading fast. Soon the light would be gone, and darkness would claim us once more.

"I love you, too," I whispered. "I love you so much. And I'm sorry. I'm more sorry than I can ever say, Manuel."

Manuel wrapped his hands around my torso and lifted me up,

pressing me to his chest. I inhaled. He smelled big and familiar, like an entire house. Like an entire life.

"I've told you once, and I'll tell you again." His words were the last thing I heard before the sunlight disappeared for good. "Don't apologize, Eliot Beck. Don't you ever apologize for being who you are."

Acknowledgments

THE FIRST PEOPLE I ever told about my Worries were my mom and my older sister, Skatie. I remember the moment clearly. We were sitting at the back of a Thai restaurant in London. I was staring into a bowl of fried rice. The rice was greasy—just how I liked it—and the individual grains shone like little oiled stars.

I didn't go into lunch planning to tell them. A full year had passed since the Worries began, and I had sworn that no one would ever find out about their existence. But as I stared into that bowl of shiny fried rice, something strange happened. It was like I left my body and someone else slid inside. Someone far braver. Someone who wasn't afraid to ask for help.

"I've been having these thoughts," I said suddenly, interrupting whatever my mom and sister were talking about. They stopped talking and turned to face me. I felt suddenly shy, like the brave person who took over my body a split second before had already departed. I am the youngest child, and, like Eliot, I wasn't used to having my family's undivided attention. "These . . . worries. And I can't make them go away."

I don't remember the conversation that followed, just that by the time we were back in the US, my mom had set up an appointment with a psychologist.

I had to see several therapists before I found the right one for me. Her name was Debbie, and she's the one I want to start by thanking.

She was the first person to whom I ever admitted the true contents of my thoughts. The first person to take my hand, look me in the eye, and say: *You aren't the monster you think you are.*

Debbie—thank you. Thank you for being the friend I needed at fifteen. Thank you for letting me ugly-cry on your couch, and your armchair, and, occasionally, your carpet. Thank you for listening when I brought in my journal and read aloud its crazy, tearstained entries. Thank you for nodding resolutely when I was done and telling me I was going to be a writer. I know it's against the rules to say so, but I love you anyway.

To my mom and dad—thank you for the hugs. Thank you for the popcorn. Thank you for paying all of those therapy bills (there were, unsurprisingly, a lot of them). Thank you for listening, even when you didn't understand. I am so, *so* lucky to have you for parents.

To Skatie—thank you for always saying the things I don't want to hear. Thank you for movie nights and Thai food and long Face-Times and generally being everything I could ever want in an older sister. I forgive you for trying to steal my clothes every time you came home.

To my agent, Kim Whalen—I don't know what I would do without you. Thank you for helping me navigate the confusing world of publishing, for never being fazed by my crazy emails, and for generally always being in my corner. You fight so fiercely for my books. I appreciate you more than I can put into words.

To my editor, Kristine Swartz—I was so nervous when you read the first draft of this book. Thank you for instantly understanding Eliot. Thank you for helping me bring her story to the people who need it. You're a rock star.

To the entire team at Berkley, but especially to Mary Baker, Yazmine Hassan, Chelsea Pascoe, Christine Legon, Lindsey Tulloch, Will Tyler, Colleen Reinhart, and Jacob Jordan. This book would not be on shelves without you. Thank you, thank you, thank you!

To the Punta Mita crew—you know who you are. You are my best friends in the world, and I don't know what I'd do without you. You keep me sane. I love you all with my whole heart.

To Pontus—my real-life Manuel. We may not have met as kids, but you're still my best friend in the whole world. You get me better than I get myself. By the time you read these words, you'll be my husband. I'm so grateful that I get to spend the rest of my life with you. Thank you for the endless support you give to my writing. For reading drafts and acting as a sounding board and giving the best hugs when I'm struggling with getting the words onto paper. I love you.

And finally, to every person who sees themself in the pages of this book—you aren't the monster you think you are. In fact, OCD attacks the things we care about most. If you worry you're a murderer, it's probably because you hate violence in all of its forms, and so on. The brain is a confusing place, but you can take comfort in the fact that thoughts are just that: thoughts. It's your actions that define you. Speak up. Ask for help. You deserve love and support—and I'm sending all of mine out to you.

How to Hide
in Plain Sight

———

Emma Noyes

Discussion Questions

1. The book's title, *How to Hide in Plain Sight*, is a reference to how mental health struggles can be invisible to others. What are the hidden battles the characters in this book fight? Do you also have burdens that aren't visible to outsiders?

2. Eliot's family comes across as both very close and isolated from one another at the same time. Discuss the elements that unite them and separate them as a family.

3. Eliot and Manuel's friendship started from a one-sided effort, but eventually became a crucial connection for both of them. Do you have important relationships that started off similarly?

4. Why do you think Eliot was so drawn to Manny as a child?

5. Eliot's father, Speedy, has no discernable medical cause for his paralysis. In contrast, Eliot has no physical manifestation of her medical diagnosis. Discuss the contrast of their situations and what that could mean for the characters.

6. Cradle Island is a touchstone point for Eliot's family. Do you also have a place that has a lot of emotional importance to your family? Where is it?

7. The end of the novel has a big revelation regarding the ashes of Eliot's late brother. What do you think the significance is behind her actions as a child?

8. Eliot is able to finally be honest about her struggles with her family and Manny by the end of the novel. How do you think this will impact her relationships with them, and how do you picture her life after the book ends?

Turn the page for a preview of

GUY'S GIRL

by Emma Noyes, available now!

GINNY ISN'T SURE which came first—the bad habit or the boy.

They showed up at almost exactly the same time, like two trains pulling into one station from opposite directions. And when they left, it took much longer for one to go than the other.

On the surface, the two seem completely disconnected—one a human being, the other a human defect—but at their core, they're both powered by the same thing: false versions of love. One, the wrong way to love another; the other, the wrong way to love yourself.

She didn't mean to become bulimic. Does anyone? Does anyone go out looking for mental illness? Well, she didn't, in any case. It just kind of happened. Just the way things did with Finch—piece by piece, she fell into something intoxicating, something dangerous; and by the time she realized what was happening, it was already too late.

ADRIAN REMEMBERS THE exact moment he decided not to fall in love.

He was eleven. His mother hadn't stopped crying in a week. He didn't quite understand what had happened with her and Scott. In fact, it would be years before he grasped the full breadth of his stepfather's betrayal.

He climbed the rickety stairs of their new home in Indianapolis, one half of a duplex they shared with a cloudy-eyed couple who had strange pockmarks all over their faces. A bowl of porridge balanced in one hand, a mug of coffee in the other. His mother wouldn't eat, but he still had to try.

He nudged open her bedroom door. Inside, she was curled up with her head on the pillow. Even half-conscious, she looked miserable. Wrinkled forehead. Puffy eyelids. Lips moving silently, as if in prayer.

He set the bowl and mug down on the bedside table.

I don't want it, he thought. *I don't want it, and I never will.*

PART I

GINNY MURPHY IS wasting away again.

She can feel it as she drags her suitcase up the fifth and final staircase of her friends' walk-up in SoHo. The tremble in her limbs. The pop of stars at the edge of her vision. It's six p.m. and she hasn't eaten a thing all day.

If Heather were here, she wouldn't let Ginny get away with starving herself. She would pull out her phone and find a list of every muscle, every neuron, every organ that needs energy to survive. Then she would force-feed Ginny a donut.

When she reaches apartment 5E, Ginny pauses to straighten her skirt and blink away the lights clogging her vision. She hesitates. Alone in Minnesota, where she lives, hiding her habits is easy. But here, visiting a group of boys who have known her since their freshman year of college?

Not so easy.

She raises one fist and knocks twice.

"*There she is!*" comes a voice from inside. She hears footsteps, then the door swings inward, revealing a bushel of red hair and a grin so wide it seems to take up the whole doorway. "Ginny fucking Murphy," says her best friend, Clay. Then she's swept up in a frenzy of freckled arms and spun around the hallway. Ginny laughs. She can't remember the last time she heard that sound come out of her mouth.

Clay sets her down and grabs her suitcase. "Welcome to Manhattan."

ADRIAN SILVAS IS on his six p.m. break. Fifteen minutes to leave Goldman and pick up a coffee from the Gregory's on East 52nd: cold brew, no sugar, a splash of almond milk. A pick-me-up for what's sure to be another long night. It doesn't matter that it's Friday. It doesn't matter that the managing directors left already. Analysts are to stay at their desks until their eyeballs bleed.

Adrian went into investment banking because that's what everyone said he should do. Just like he applied for the scholarship to Harvard because that's what everyone said he should do. Just like he became the vice president of his Final Club because that's what everyone said he should do.

When he signed with Goldman Sachs, he had no idea what he was in for. How long his hours would be. How mind-numbing the work was. How truly and utterly it would suck the soul out of his body. Now he's a man with more money than he knows what to do with and no time to spend it.

"*Eső után köpönyeg,*" his grandfather would say. *After the rain comes the raincoat.*

CLAY LEADS GINNY down the short hallway toward the living room. They don't make it more than three feet before she's accosted by a flurry of curly light brown hair and grey cotton.

"Gin-a-vieve!" yells the flurry, crashing into Ginny and squeezing her tight. "You made it!"

"Tristan," Ginny says into her friend's shoulder. "How many times do I have to tell you? My real name is—"

"'*West Virginia*,'" Tristan sings, releasing Ginny's shoulders and throwing one hand into the air. Clay leans up against his roommate, and together they sing: "'*Mountain mama, take me hooome, country roads.*'"

When they're done, Clay grins down at Ginny. "Bet you missed us."

"I saw you came in on a seven fifty-seven," Tristan says, suddenly serious. "Was it wide-bodied? God, I would give my left arm to be on a sweet, sweet wide-body right now. Did you know it's been over a month since I've been on an airplane? I think I'm going through withdrawal. But I downloaded this app, look at this, and—"

And he was off.

When they met freshman year, Ginny didn't think she would like Tristan; he talks enough to fill three conversations at once, and his favorite topics are finance, finance, and finance. He is obsessed with shorting stocks and would love nothing more than to ruin a small country's economy.

However, he will also say yes to anything, laugh at anyone's jokes, and try any food you put in front of him. He is insatiably curious—and strangely childlike in his obsession with airplanes.

She adores him.

Ginny loves boys. Not in a sexual way; frankly, she hasn't felt attracted to anyone in years. No—what she loves about boys is their company. Male friendships aren't like female friendships, she thinks. They're easier. Free from the drama.

She loves male bodies, too. Their sloppy haircuts and predictable clothing. The strange shape of their calves—thin at the ankle and round in the middle, like telephone poles swollen with last night's rain. The stupid, honest way they make themselves laugh.

But she loves *her* boys most of all.

Now Tristan chatters eagerly about the flight-tracking app on his phone as he leads Ginny and Clay into the living room.

The boys' SoHo apartment is the quintessential postgrad shithole: creaky floor planks, white wall paint, and a shower that looks like it was built before the fall of the Berlin Wall. Every boy living in this apartment is over six feet tall; Ginny isn't sure how they fold their legs up tight enough to shit on the pint-sized toilet.

"Tristan," says a low, raspy voice from inside the living room, "if I have to hear one more fact about domestic flight patterns, I'm going to throw myself off the fire escape."

Ginny inhales. He's here.

Finch.

She steps into the dim light of the living room, and there he is: Alex Finch, the fourth and final corner of their friend group. Sitting in a low armchair, aux cord plugged into his phone, guitar balanced on his lap. Finch is studying to become an orthopedic surgeon at NYU. He has close-cropped blond hair and a crooked smile. He's completely brilliant and also stupid, in the way that all brilliant men are also stupid.

When Ginny thinks about freshman year, she thinks about Finch. About his hands on her waist, on the hem of her shirt. The feel of the fabric as it peeled over her head. His eyes as he took her in for the first time. She thinks about kissing until her cheeks are red with the burn of his stubble.

Stop, she thinks. *Turn it off.*

She forces a smile onto her face and steps forward. "Finch. Hi."

"Gin." He sets aside the guitar and stands. In two long strides he's before her. "It's great to see you." He wraps both arms around her and pulls her in for a hug.

Ginny tries not to inhale for fear that his scent will be too familiar.

After untangling herself from Finch's hug—which lasts just a second longer than is appropriate—Ginny walks over to the worn grey couch and sits. Now that all four of them are standing in the small living room, there isn't much space to breathe.

"So." Clay sets her suitcase on the floor beside the television and crosses the two steps that take him into their tiny kitchenette. "Tonight, we're thinking poker and pregame until Adrian gets back, then hit the bars."

Clay is their ringleader. He may not talk the most—that award rests firmly with Tristan—but he holds the most power. He makes plans and leads the charge. Right now, he works for a government consulting firm, but will probably one day be president of the United States. The man could make friends with a houseplant.

"I bet I can get us a table at Tao," Tristan says. "The owner is a personal friend of my father's. Just last year, we visited his house in the Hamptons, and—"

"Shut up, Tristan," say Ginny and Clay in unison. It rolls off the tongue—their old mantra, words they spoke whenever their friend

started going on about his father's connections or late-stage capital-
ism. They flash surprised grins at each other. Clay's teeth are brilliant white beneath his red hair, and the sight is so familiar it nearly
cracks Ginny in half.

"So." Clay winks and turns around, opening the small refrigera-
tor in the corner. "How's work, Gin?"

"Oh, you know," she says, shifting on the couch. "It's work."

"But you work for a *beer* company," Clay says over his shoulder
as he rummages around, looking for cold alcohol. "That's epic."

"Right," Ginny says. "But I live in Minnesota."

During the fall of her senior year, Ginny signed with Sofra-
Moreno, a global beer conglomerate. When SM started recruiting
her, she was a senior in college studying history and literature—
proof that your degree means absolutely nothing and you can do
whatever the fuck you want after college, provided you're a good
enough liar. What? She was going to get paid almost six figures a
year to study the history of beer? Absolutely not. She has to at least
pretend to contribute to the company's bottom line.

When she signed her contract with Sofra, Ginny was ready for
an exciting global career. She imagined visiting breweries around
the world. Rubbing elbows with executives. Climbing the ladder.
Maybe even getting her Cicerone Certification, becoming a som-
melier of beer.

Right up until they placed her in Minnesota.

She was going to say no. She was going to look for another job.
But then her classes picked up in earnest, and all Ginny's free time
disappeared, and she just sort of fell numbly into her future. Into
the path assigned.

"The Twin Cities!" Tristan claps. "You're lucky to live there. Did
you know you can fly to a hundred and sixty-three different cities
out of MSP? It's one of Delta's primary hubs, and Delta is the best
airline in—"

"*Tristan.*" Finch cuts him off before he can really get going.

Tristan and Finch don't get along. It's not that they don't like each other; it's more that they are two sides of the same coin. Both are stocky, both have lopsided grins and curly hair—Finch's short and blond, Tristan's long and light brown—both come from money and attended East Coast private schools where they rowed stroke on the varsity crew team. During freshman year at Harvard, they were often mistaken for brothers. As college wore on, however, the two split, as if in direct reaction to this unwanted comparison. They leaned as far into their differences as they could. It's the same logic behind why neighboring countries are always at war with each other: we despise those who are too similar to us.

For his part, Tristan became the quintessential finance kid: majored in economics, joined Harvard's consulting club, interned at a bank, dressed in button-downs and Sperry's. Kept a close shave and an even closer eye on his portfolio.

Finch, on the other hand, shed as much of his upbringing as he could. He grew out his hair, traded slacks for joggers, and spent all his free time either with his guitar on his lap or in the physics lab with a bag of weed in his backpack.

Ginny looks away from Finch, forcing her mind in a different direction. To the final occupant of Sullivan Street. The absent party: Adrian.

Of all the boys living in apartment 5E, Ginny knows Adrian the least. He was a last-minute addition to the boys' apartment. An outlier. Back in college, in the limited interactions Ginny had with him, he was roughly as friendly as a potted cactus. But if she wants a place to sleep during her visit to New York, she has to put up with him.

Finishing his search in the fridge, Clay pulls out the ingredients for mixed drinks—exactly what Ginny feared he would do. *One shot of tequila is 100 calories; 8 ounces of lemonade is 100 more . . .*

She stands, crossing the tiny room to crack open a window. Cool air filters into the room. She inhales deeply before walking back to the couch and sitting down.

Clay pours four cups of tequila and lemonade. Finch lights a cigarette and fiddles with the Bluetooth speaker, setting up a playlist of songs for their pregame. Tristan tries unsuccessfully to steal the aux cord from Finch. All the while, they chatter—about work, about sports, about the girls they're seeing. Every time Tristan mentions wide-bodied airplanes, Ginny and Finch throw napkins at him.

Their voices wash over her, and she finds that, for just a brief moment, her anxiety dissipates. It feels good not to be *the girl* anymore. To just be one of the group. One of the guys.

She inhales, filling her body with cool air and secondhand smoke.

© Magdalena Iskra

EMMA NOYES is the author of *Guy's Girl, How to Hide in Plain Sight*, and the Sunken City trilogy. She grew up in a suburb outside Chicago and attended Harvard University, where she studied history and literature. She started her career at a beer company but left because she wanted to write about mermaids and witches—eventually publishing her first YA fantasy series. She now lives in Chicago with her Swedish husband and accident-prone Pomeranian.

VISIT EMMA NOYES ONLINE

EmmaVRNoyes.com
🅞 EmmaNoyesMaybe
♪ EmmaNoyesMaybe

Ready to find
your next great read?

Let us help.

Visit prh.com/nextread